CW01655613

PILLARS OF EVIL

A Charlie Glass Thriller

J.J. CARSON

DEDICATION

For Janette …

"The fringes of their deserts were strewn with broken faiths."

- T.E. Lawrence

FOREWORD

In 2020, the American oversight authority, SIGAR (Special Inspector General for Afghanistan Reconstruction) reported that the United States lost $19 billion in Afghanistan since 2002, due to "waste, fraud and abuse."

Source: www.voanews.com

CHAPTER 1

Rural Virginia, 2006

Darkness reluctantly turned to dawn. A pine-scented mist clung to the neglected and isolated gas station. An old sign from the long defunct *Standard Oil* swung precariously, despite the absence of wind. The station sat at the junction of three roads, each one led to, and from, nowhere in particular.

A solitary pump that no one had ever queued to use rusted patiently out front. The county's least convenient convenience store remained closed. The wooden building needed renovation.

A long-abandoned garage and mismatched workshop leaned on its side and looked in desperate need of a bulldozer. Across in the shadows of the unpaved lot lay a battered 1960s rust-red Bronco. With tousled blonde hair, crumpled clothes, and precious little sleep, Special Agent Charlie Glass sat at the wheel.

One at a time, she watched the station's lights come on, in sleepy sequence.

The tarnished old bell announced the opening of the front door. An elderly man ambled out, pulling oily denim dungarees over his rounded shoulders. The man and his overalls had grayed overtime. He unchained the padlock around the gas pump, then safely negotiated the rain-filled potholes on his way to the overgrown grass verge. With creaky deliberation, he flipped the old sign over to reveal to the world that the station was now *OPEN*. He doddered back to the store in anticipation of the morning rush. As he eased back inside, Charlie jumped across from the jeep, hastened on by the sudden squally shower.

Through the faded stickers plastered over the glass door, she noticed the old man prepping for the day ahead. He jumped at the clanging of the doorbell. "Gracious, Charlotte. You scared me. Up early this fine morning?"

"Hi, Ike, not too fine from where I am standing." She turned away, flicked the rain from her bobbed hair, and awaited the customary friendly interrogation.

"So, how are you settling in? How's that dog? He looks a fearsome creature. You brought him back from Iraq, didn't you?"

Charlie always waited for the ending of the first salvo of questions before offering any responses. "We're all good. Yes, his name's Rostam. Don't worry, he's a gentle giant. He wouldn't hurt a fly." Only the last sentence was a lie.

"Your dad is so happy to be hosting you. It's been too long. So, how long are you up here for?"

Never rude, but never one to waste words. She got down to early business. "Not here for long. I need some quarters."

"You still have no phone up in that cabin?"

"You know how it is, Ike. Pop is Pop. Like the cabin, he's set on a single track."

"And you're following him down that path?"

"Well, you never know." *Never have and ever will.*

"There is a lot to be said for sticking to what you know."

Charlie wondered if Ike was trying to convince her or himself. "It's his retreat from the world. He says the telecoms companies will bring cell coverage before he needs to spend the money on a landline."

Ike scoffed. "Good luck with that."

Charlie exhaled. "Could I get that change for the phone, please?"

Ike smirked, accustomed to her directness. "Bit of a rush this morning, Special Agent?"

"Something like that." She pushed over a twenty-dollar bill. Ike's eyebrows lifted, unsure if he had just made a sale or not. Charlie took the hint. "I'll snag some morning rolls, cheese, and milk." Ike carefully rang up the charges as his valued customer quickly selected the goods from a stand that also housed cheap children's toys and cleaning materials. With the transaction complete, she raced to the phone, weighed down with quarters and unnecessary purchases.

After dumping the thin plastic bag on the faded linoleum flooring, she produced a small black address book from inside her red-checkered lumberjack jacket. When the book fell open, some old, folded papers and a couple of tattered business cards made a break for freedom. They were rounded up, then superficially blow-dried. She flipped a coin into the slot of the old chrome phone box.

The Regan-for-President sticker on the side had lost its luster.

With the book in one hand and the receiver jammed under her chin, she jabbed the number into the keypad. In the intervening seconds it took for the phone to be answered, she drummed the phone box. When the voice came, it was as professional as it was helpful. "Good morning, thank you for calling Operator Services. How may I assist you?"

In the background, Ike waltzed around aimlessly with a dirty mop for a dance partner. Charlie lifted the handset closer and dropped the volume.

"Agent check-in. Special Agent Charlotte Glass. Access Code: 4566BB."

As she spoke, papers and cards escaped from the book when the receiver slipped from under her chin. "Damn it." A repeat of the number was requested and confirmed back to the operator before composure and errant paperwork were both regained. "Thank you, Special Agent Glass. How may I direct your call?"

"Direct line access, please. Associate Executive Assistant Director, Joey Sizemore."

With mutual thanks exchanged, the call was politely passed through. Ike was intrigued; his phone had never seen so much action. "Everything okay back there?"

"Just fine. Thanks."

She turned her back on Ike's amateur surveillance. The phone gave two further rings before a bubbly voice answered. "Federal Bureau of Investigation. Associate Executive Assistant Director Sizemore's Office."

"Sorry, I was told this was his direct line. I'd like to speak to Joey."

"It's as direct as you can get, ma'am. This is his personal assistant. What does your call relate to?"

Charlie pressed on, irked that she was being screened on a direct line, and even more annoyed she had been called ma'am. With Ike hovering, she didn't want to elaborate. "This call has been security cleared. I have security access and need to speak to him immediately."

"I am afraid Associate Executive Assistant Director Sizemore is unavailable at the moment. Do you wish to be connected to his voicemail?"

She rolled her eyes. Her frequently unavailable boss was trying to make this permanent. Charlie did everything to stay grounded. "No. It's Charlie Glass, put me through."

"One moment, please." Charlie waited in hope rather than expectation. The wait quickly turned into a stew. Charlie couldn't stand the man. With such a weak-willed boss rising through the ranks, she suspected nepotism was alive and well in the Bureau. Ike loitered nearby, sight unseen. Eventually, the connection clicked open. "Special Agent Glass, glad to hear from you." The voice dripped with officialdom. The condescending undertones were hard for her to take so early in the day. "Morning, boss. Just calling to confirm arrangements."

"You've had the briefings, read the mission files and done your research, I am sure."

Charlie confirmed. "I have. Any last-minute changes of plan, reroutes, or changes to the contacts? I am good to go, otherwise."

She fumbled some coins into the phone to buy some time. "Are you using a payphone?"

"Yeah, up in the mountains in Virginia. Catching up with family before I head out."

"Pop. Isn't it?" Sizemore sprang at the chance to display his limited knowledge and non-existent empathy.

"It is." She hardly cared.

"And how is he doing?"

"Just fine." She cared even less.

"So, this couldn't have been done by email?"

"Sorry, boss. No internet for a few miles. So, the mission?"

"Yes, quite right. You're all set. Your flight to Afghanistan leaves in four days. How are you? All set?"

"I am. I'm up for the challenge." She chided herself for sounding like a keen recruit at her first interview, eager to impress.

"Very well. Any last-minute changes will be emailed to you. They will hit your BlackBerry when you return to civilization. You're all set. Go find that money!"

Ike's shadow darkened a section of checkered linoleum. "Yes, sir. I'll drop you an update when I land in theater."

"Good luck. You'll do us proud." The phone clicked dead before Charlie could respond. Ike emerged from behind the shelving, feigning the fine-tuning of his lackluster retail space. "That you done, Charlotte? Everything okay?"

Playfully, Charlie treated the old eavesdropper to a lesson on manners. "It's bad business. For your safety and mine, say nothing to anyone."

"For my safety? What the hell does that mean?" For once in his life, Ike had heard too much. Charlie laid it on thick. "It's just what it sounds like. FBI business. Say nothing to anyone, especially your wife. Things will be fine. Trust me. This call never happened; you never saw me. Understood?"

The old man put on a brave face. "I don't scare. I did two tours in Nam. PBRs. Don't you worry. I can handle myself. He lifted his arm to show a faded, withered tattoo of what may have started out looking like a gunboat. The image looked to have sank a little over time.

The old garage owner nodded defiantly. Charlie bowed her head with respect. At some stage in his life, she knew Ike may have been bad to the bone, but now those bones were brittle. With a supportive wink and a tap on the old store owner's arm, Charlie exited the store, provisions in hand. Outside, the squall had intensified.

Head down, she skipped out between the craters, then climbed up into her jeep. Behind in the store, she noticed an anxious Ike flipping the sign on the door to *CLOSED* and shuffling off behind the scenes. He seemed to be forgoing the morning's takings in favor of a lie-down.

With a wry grin, Charlie kicked the Bronco through the rain, up the narrowest of the mountain tracks.

Next stop Afghanistan.

CHAPTER 2

Kandahar airfield, Afghanistan,

Standing at attention on the ramp of the C-130 transport plane, Charlie lifted the heels of her combat boots to stretch her calf muscles and gain a view. The gigantic rear ramp lowered too slowly for her liking. A clear sky revealed itself just before the incredible snow-capped mountains fell into view. A chilled wind, laced with anticipation, swirled in from the back draft from the four T56-A turboprop engines. As the door lowered, her pulse rose. When the ramp finally deployed, the green lights flashed. The bronzed, flight-hardened loadmaster barked his disembarkation orders, ordering off his pensive payload. The International Security Assistance Force flight was on a quick turnaround.

A line of five newbie analysts disembarked at a pace. Standard issue RayBans, creased white shirts, and graphite pants, were the uniform of choice for these pencil pushers. Scurrying across the tarmac, they crouched and swiveled like sparrows waiting for a hawk. Beside them marched four private security guards, clad in black, reinforced with Kevlar and ready for action. Twenty camouflaged uniforms followed on in a rag-tag column. Kit bag slung over her shoulders, Charlie moved up to the procession, keen to move on. The other soldiers followed behind with strained gaits and gawping eyes. Hunched and bunched, the first timers took up the rear, fearful of everything in and out of sight.

An icy wind cut the low, cloudless sunlight to shreds. With no gloves and thermals, Charlie was ruing her lack of protection from the elements. She hoped that would be her only regret, during her brief tour of duty in Helmand province. The long-haul journeys that led to the short-hop flight across from Kabul had taken its toll on the passengers.

Wearily they trudged the tarmac, dodging the trucks and forklifts transferring supplies to and from the various planes. A military bus idled nearby. Once on board, the crew was whisked across the dusty runway toward the relative safety of the airfield terminal. Through the gritty side window, Charlie gazed in awe at the mountains climbing high above. The heavenly hues hung in contrast to the drab airfield and its khaki coated surroundings. A gray air traffic control stood like an aged sentinel, watching over the corrugated roofing of the ageing complex.

The faded green concrete archways looked jaded, despite the frantic levels of activity on the base.

First off the bus, Charlie scampered down through the dust-clogged, air-locked entrance. Inside, she discovered a surreal world filled with wary arrivals and weary departures. The building's archway ceilings crouched low overhead. Battered plasterwork and subdued lighting fell on oversized sofas upholstered in filthy velour and ripped braiding. Everything and everyone seemed a little frayed at the edges. Heading in an entirely different direction, a collection of squaddies lay in wait for their flight home. They looked duty-free yet fatigued. *Australians. Quiet for once.*

With the formalities of customs registration behind her, Charlie bolted for the exit, eager to face new destinies. On the other side of security, the arrivals hall seemed more downcast than anything she had encountered in Iraq. High on scrutiny, yet low on energy, the crowd milled with mistrust and mystery. She could have stayed there all day, marveling at the masses, but there was work to do. At the edge of her eye line, closest to the exit, stood a young Caucasian man waving a sign in her general direction. The sign read 'Gladstone', the name she had been told to look out for. On approach, observations were made. Pale and badly drawn, the sign and its holder made the perfect match. Fully loaded with ID badges and sunblock, the man seemed keen to meet, greet, and then beat a retreat. Charlie had seen the look before; keen for it all to be over.

"Special Agent Charlotte Glass, a.k.a. Mister Gladstone, reporting for duty."

The spindly creature twitched, swiveled, and muttered. "Ross, Central Intelligence Agency." His limp, wet handshake tainted Charlie's initial assessment. She smiled, all the same, and tried to close the gap between them.

"Do you have a first name, Ross?"

"It's John, but Ross will be fine."

"Well, it's a pleasure to meet you, Ross." He pulled an over-the-top side-step and ushered her on past him. "So, I'm set as your liaison, but don't worry, I won't get in the way. I am based out of Kabul. *Where evil emanates.* I'll be heading back there shortly once you're settled in." The tips of his mouse brown hair had tinted in the sun.

With the complexion of a sweaty geisha, Ross looked as if he had never spent a day of his life outdoors. Thin hair and thinner lips made him difficult to age. His fragile jawline screamed analyst, not anarchist. The whites of his eyes were stained and strained. *Tainted by substance abuse or sleep deprivation?* Charlie was unsure. Investigations continued. "Have you been out here long?"

"Long enough to hate the place. Mind you, that only took a day." He pushed on through the crowd toward the cordoned exits, careful not to get his blue suit tarnished by the locals. Exchanges over the flight, the weather, and inquiries regarding the local news lightly peppered the transit into the segregated area within the airport perimeter. Unlike the crowds, the conversation seemed one-way traffic. Faced with the returning vague disinterest, Charlie closed her lines of polite inquiry, pulled on her wraparound shades, and stepped out into the glare of the lowering sun.

Twenty feet away under the towering concrete blast wall idled a jet black, freshly washed Chevy suburban. High axles and blacked-out windows completed the CIA makeover. A hulky, dark-skinned local with a darker suit, jumped out from the air conditioning to handle the baggage. Introductions were offered, as the kitbag was stowed in the back.

"Hi, I am Charlie."

The driver's blank response was cordial, yet uninformative. "Welcome to Afghanistan."

"Are these things not RPG magnets?"

A solitary bead of sweat lingered on the brow of the pensive driver. "Don't worry, ma'am."

"Ma'am? I'm not the Queen. Charlie will do fine."

The driver was well-trained. "Yes, ma'am." No facials expression was offered.

"Okay, let's go." Ross had heard enough. The driver raised his eyebrows, rucking the furrows on his prominent forehead. "Yessir!" Charlie sensed irony in the driver's baritone voice.

Before clambering in the back, Ross opened the front passenger door and offered it to Charlie. *Chivalry or cowardice?* Charlie couldn't pinpoint the reasoning. When Ross cowered low in the back, her answer formed. She was unsurprised when he pulled on his seatbelt and hunkered down low. She was surprised when he threw her a headscarf and a long, gray robe. "What's this?"

"It's a chapan. Throw it on. You're quite the sight."

The long, flowing robe fitted loosely, giving her a bedraggled look. The lanky sleeves didn't help. "Is all this necessary?"

"Maybe, maybe not." As the driver moved the SUV, Charlie donned the garb. She then turned to the driver. "So, you're a local, then?" She left the question open-ended, hoping the driver would introduce himself. Ross piped the answer in from the back seat. "If you want something done, hire a local."

As if spurred on by the compliment, the silent driver took charge of negotiations through the security checkpoints. Battle-weary US troops took the lead as life-weary Afghan troops tried to appear to care about proceedings. Progress was slow on all fronts.

Ross fidgeted in the back, all the way through the infuriating process. "The airport is like the country; easy to get into, difficult to leave." With the last check complete, the final barriers were lifted. The driver slammed the accelerator, keen to get all the faux security in his rear mirrors. Barging his way out into the traffic, the SUV sped ahead. Weaving in and out of the lanes with equal quantities of aggression and arrogance, the driver pushed on.

"You drive like you own the place."

Again, the response came from the back seat. "Well, we built the damn thing, so I guess we own it."

After yet another near miss with an oncoming car, Charlie gripped the door handle, more than a little concerned. "If you drove like this in Iraq, you'd be mistaken for a suicide bomber."

"This isn't Iraq, Agent Glass. You will find that to your peril."

Charlie craned her neck to face down Ross' veiled threat. He couldn't face her. Instead, he stared out the side window, avoiding eye contact. Charlie let the moment pass. There would be time enough for interrogation. *Just play nice.* She told herself.

Across in the distance, the lowering sun tinted the stunning backdrop. Two peaks clung to the mountain range in the distance. Above, high arching stainless steel streetlights flickered on to light the wide boulevards. All manner of transport peppered the roadways.

"I can't believe how many Afghan flags there are. They must really love their country."

"They don't. We put them up. We spend more on flags than we do on sanitation. It's all about the optics."

"The optics look pretty dirty from where I'm sitting."

"Welcome to Afghanistan. We throw money at everything. I guess that's why you're here."

"It is. What can you tell me?"

Ross ploughed on; oblivious he was telling tales in front of the locally hired staff. "Most of the thefts grew out of shortcomings in the management of the deployments. There was a heavy dependence on cash transactions. The award of local high value contracts was too hasty and way too shady. Slack oversight within the ranks and a culture of corruption seduced some troops."

"So, they give it all away, then drag us in to find out where it's gone?"

"Something like that, but they don't really want an answer."

Charlie twisted her view into the back seat. "Why?"

"The truth hurts. Poorly trained operatives forced to handle large cash transactions in a region where bribes, kickbacks, and petty theft are the norm. It was all a little too tempting."

"And too easy?"

"It's easy to come late to the party and complain about the leftovers."

Facing Ross' well-made counter, Charlie eased off. "So, price fixing and financial corruption are rampant in Afghanistan?"

"Not rampant. No worse than you've experienced in Iraq."

"Then that would be rampant."

"And so, you're here to clean house?"

Despite Ross' mocking tone, Charlie grinned. She ran a mental profile on her new liaison. He seemed timorous, like an analyst who ticked the wrong box and wound up in hell. She dug in. "We don't really know. It could be from thefts on the inside, gross negligence, poorly trained operatives, or overly keen giveaways. I'm here to find out."

"And what does your gut tell you?"

"Lay off the local food and don't jump to conclusions."

Ross mopped his brow and stared out into the traffic. "Wise words." He guzzled an entire bottle of water in one nervous sitting. Charlie was left up front, high, and dry.

She broke the silence that followed. "This is quite the welcoming committee. I am grateful for the support."

"Standard procedure, besides I had business to attend to at the airfield."

"So, I'm not that important after all?" she joked.

Ross's response held no humor. "None of us are."

"Anything interesting?"

"Where?"

"Your business at the airport. Anything interesting?"

"Not to you." The view out the side window was again preferred by Ross. He kept things professional and distant. Charlie followed his gaze. Outside, the roads narrowed and filled as they moved on toward the compound. Crowds swarmed. Innumerable telephone cables blotted the skyline, as they jumped across poles and buildings.

Water towers stood tall amongst the various designs of minarets. Carefully designed and lovingly maintained mosques stood out from the drab and weary buildings that made up most of the town. An occasional dash of color clung to the most optimistic buildings. A car alarm bleated noisily as the traditionally dressed crowd simply walked past in a trance. Heads were lowered, businesses were minded. Kandahar seemed a world away from the vibrant excitement of Baghdad. Ross brought her back from reality.

"So, you've read your briefing notes?"

"Just as you've read my case file."

"So, finding money is your specialty?

"I stumbled on it."

"False modesty. You're gaining a reputation for getting results. You're quite the princess warrior."

"I like the warrior part. Just go easy on the princess." Charlie was puzzled at where Ross could have been receiving his intel. Reports of her activities remained subdued through official sources.

Ross bobbled his head. A trace of a leer lingered at the corner of his mouth. "One thing confuses me. Why bring the FBI into the area? We've got this handled."

Charlie bit. "According to our sources, you don't."

"Shouldn't you sugar coat that with a 'with all due respect'?"

"Yeah sorry. With all due respect. The Army Criminal Investigative Division isn't getting the results. Money is going missing, and suspects and answers are few." No retort came. "So, how did you end up here, John Ross?"

"Long story."

"I've got the time. Besides, I need to take my mind off this driving." The driver didn't appear to be taking hints.

"I grew up in the middle east. My father was a missionary in Lebanon and Jordan before it became too dangerous to be a Christian. After moving back to the States, I graduated top of my class at Georgetown, reading middle eastern history. After 9/11 like so many, I answered the call. I joined the CIA as an analyst. Because of my background, I was fast tracked into the field. I have been here behind a desk, tapping keyboards, ever since."

"Never want to strike out into field operations?"

"I will leave the heroics to the heroes like you. I want to lie forever in the shade, till I become a shade myself."

That would explain the skin tone, mused Charlie, inwardly.

Out on its own, the mountain range in the distance watched over proceedings. A tonal recession of gunmetal blue tainted the sunset. The night was closing in. Suddenly, the SUV lurched to a safe pace. The speed reduced further as they approached a security post. Guards, razor wire, barricades, and blast walls crept into view. Outside the walls of reinforced mesh filled with stones and sand sat a young family. The head of the house sat on his haunches, head in his hands. His tattered clothes hid everything but his anguish. Beside him sat a woman, covered head to sandals in a blue burka. In her hands she held a crumpled piece of paper. Rocking by her side sat their infant young son, chewing on the sleeve of his filthy tunic. Charlie couldn't break eye contact with the distraught family unit. "What's their story?"

Ross had little clue and less interest. "Probably a collaborator that we've left high and dry. Happens all the time."

At the security points, the local police were being trained by ISAF forces. Gesticulations were animated and exaggerated, yet the comprehension levels seemed stymied by a lack of interest. Neither party seemed on the same page of the instruction manual. Passing through the barricades, interactions minimal. Papers were checked and badges were flashed.

Much to Ross' annoyance, their passage was halted by a short and sorrowful convoy. A troop carrier, missing a wheel, was being towed in by a Bradley fighting vehicle. Behind the conjoined siblings rumbled a truck with a hoist, carrying the remains of another burned-out troop carrier.

Charlie crinkled her forehead. "This happen a lot?"

"Like I say, welcome to Afghanistan." Ross held no expression as the SUV followed the battered vehicles towards the security compound. "This is the reality of Operation Enduring Freedom. We're enduring and they're far from free. Our lofty ideas of good over evil are all bullshit. They have sent thousands of troops over under the ISAF banner. Canadians, Australians, Danes, Germans. Did you notice the guards back there? They were Canadian policemen. A coalition of the gullible." He reached through into the front and handed Charlie a file and a key on a short rope.

"Here you go. You've been allocated unit 15 of the housing unit. Upstairs level on the containers. Your local notes are in the file and your ISAF uniform is on the bed. You need to show the ISAF green disk logo when on base."

"And when I am off base?" quipped Charlie.

"That won't be a thing."

We'll see about that.

"You'll find out soon enough that no one wants you here. Least of all anyone on our side. This bunch invented the term, *closed ranks*. They won't be inviting you on any sightseeing missions. If they invite you for a water cooler gathering, I'd get them to taste the water first."

Charlie wasn't one for hyperbole. "It won't be that bad."

Ross wasn't so sure. "You'll see two sets of walls. The walls of the camp and the walls they will build to stop you from finding anything."

"I can be quite convincing."

"Well, they will remain to be convinced."

Charlie reserved judgment. Ross pointed ahead. "Okay, we're about a mile out. Your local briefing notes are up in your unit. Directions, layouts, office details are all covered. The central office staff has been informed of your coming."

"Great, so they're probably in there now shredding documents?"

Ross shrugged. He made it obvious; things would not be easy. "There will be no helping hands, no lines of support. Amongst all these so-called allies, you'll make no alliances and get no assistance. You've got to expect that. You're going after your own."

Suddenly, the traffic snarled, forcing the driver to slam on the brakes. Ross slid forward off his seat. Charlie held the dash and her composure. Ross didn't. "Jesus Christ, what is this?"

No answer or apology came. Before Charlie could process the insights, Ross tapped the driver on the shoulder. "Next left."

Charlie thought the deviation strange. "Why are we moving off the highway? Is the base close?"

"No, but the traffic ahead is terrible. If we get caught, we'll be hours. This is a shortcut."

Charlie noted the immediate drop in social standing within the neighborhood. The street energy darkened with every change in direction. Onward and downward, they drove into ever narrowing streets. "Is this safe?" she asked.

Ross scoffed condescendingly. "Of course not. This is Afghanistan."

As they drove forward into more encroaching crowds, the subtle glances from outside descended into hate filled glares. Charlie was set on edge. "We shouldn't hang around here?"

"Relax, we do this all the time."

"In a blacked-out wagon that screams CIA?"

"It's been done before. Don't worry, we're nearly at our cross street. We'll be through this soon enough."

On a side street, real world Afghanistan swung into view. The level of wheeled and pedestrian traffic increased. The sights and sounds intensified, their pace slowed. Charlie shuffled in her seat, a little discomforted by the immediacy and depth of the immersion into local culture. Everyday life buzzed and bustled outside. Wooden racks made from planks of various sizes and quality displayed fresh vegetables of various sizes and perfect quality. Charlie bristled as the crowd spilled off the sidewalks to within touching distance. Worryingly, the SUV slowed to touching speed. "Why even take the risk?"

"Relax. This is the quickest way. I have things to do, over in Kabul, after we drop you off. This will get me there on time."

"Kabul? You get about for an analyst."

"And you get about for an archeologist."

At a crosswalk, an underage cigarette seller was doing a rip-roaring trade out of a small set of drawers. Next door a narrow-framed aluminum greenhouse had been cut down and welded up to the side of a garage. Freshly baked breads hung in rows. The hefty baker chomped down gratefully on his homemade delights, as he swiped his floury hand at a horde of angry houseflies. Beside him, a young girl in a striped jumper and black shroud rasped her voice to rustle up the custom for her dad. Humanity milled all around, yet the sinister undertones unpleasantly surprised Charlie. Suddenly, a rock thumped off the SUV. Everyone on board flinched. Another stone hit the window beside Ross, causing him to flinch. "What the hell?"

The next stone cracked a window. Charlie swiveled her gaze; the world had woken up to their presence. Ross pivoted in panic. "Get us out of here!"

With the yelp of encouragement from his boss, the driver barged through the narrowest of holes in the traffic. Day one and she was already fearing the world she had just entered. "Why did you bring us this way?"

Ross ignored her. He was too busy losing his cool. "There! There!"

Charlie scolded herself for being afraid. She wasn't helping.

The driver spun the SUV across and into a narrow channel at traffic's edge. Pedestrians were pushed to the side. Push came to shove as the SUV was bundled up onto the sidewalk to make its break. Shouts and complaints grew, as did their profile. Things were spiraling. After turning left into a narrower alley, the local wildlife crowded in further.

Up ahead, a roadblock slowed their progress. Chaos reigned as the vehicles leading up to the tributaries of a circular square became blocked from all directions. Corners were cut, and lanes were jumped as they barged their way across medians and sidewalks. Tensions were building inside and outside the SUV. The driver squirmed when the displaced pedestrians steadied themselves using the hood of the vehicle. It was edge-of-the-seat stuff for Ross, too. "Get through this. Damn it, we've got an SUV for that very purpose. Push on."

As the driver obeyed, the shouts increased, and the glares intensified. Slaps bumped and banged on the door skins, and the locals made their presence and annoyances felt. "Drive on. There!" Ross pointed to the source of the issues, a police patrol misdirecting traffic. When they eventually noticed the SUV, two outrider policemen moved forward and ushered them through. The driver and Charlie breathed. Ross berated those responsible. "About time. What do you think you're playing at?" The lead patrol officer flashed his white-gloved hands toward a side street. Charlie was unsure. "Do we like this?"

"It's better than being stuck here with these peasants. Drive!"

It felt to Charlie that Ross was losing his way and losing the plot. The police held up the last pair of offending pickups, freeing up a small space in the mayhem for the SUV to pass. They bullied through and parted ways with the chaos behind. "Where does this go?"

"Who cares? We're free on a roll now." Ross rapped the driver. "Put the base into the Sat-Nav and get us home, pronto." Charlie found it unsurprising that either Ross hadn't remembered the driver's name or had deliberately chosen not to use it. With one eye on the Sat-Nav and one on the road, progress was jittery. When a young boy ran out in front to retrieve his football made from rolled up duct-tape, the driver jammed the brakes and slammed the horn.

"Stop that. We don't want to bring any attention. Just drive!" Ross was sweating, despite the air conditioning. As the roadway narrowed further, the sense of being funneled into a trap grew more palpable. An enforced left-hand turn added to the drama. "Agent Glass, get in the back."

Charlie looked around, perplexed. Ross had pulled the split back seat down. "I don't like this. Get in the back."

"I can handle myself."

"It's not for your protection, it's for ours. If they see you, it could spell trouble.

Charlie faltered as the crowd swarmed. "Is all this necessary?"

Ross's voice crumbled at the edges. "We don't have time for this. Get in the back!"

The change in tone sent Charlie backward. When she slipped back between the seats, the driver prayed. The beads dangling from the rearview mirror were yanked around his fist. Charlie thought the move strange, as the beads seemed to impede his grip, just when a high-speed getaway driving could be needed. "Where are the guns?" she asked expectantly.

"We have none."

"What?"

"It's not standard protocol."

"Jesus! Then get this thing out of here. We're sitting ducks."

As she clambered into the back seat, the crowd maddened. As the interest in their SUV grew, so did the crowd and their ire. Calls turned to yells. Screams became shrieks. Angry faces closed in like wolves circling a lame beast. Suspicion led to mistrust. Mistrust morphed into resentment.

Resentment descended into anger.

The team cowered.

A new salvo of rocks peppered the SUV. Pummeling fists followed quickly. The crowd locked the road, preventing progress. Angry bearded faces spat bile. A door mirror was yanked off. The baying mob rocked the SUV from side to side. A collective, pathological hatred for Westerners seemed to drive them on. The driver yelped in panic as the SUV took a battering.

Through the gap in the seats, Charlie caught sight of two masked men brandishing AK47s. The gun barrels banged the sides of the SUV as the gunmen yelled incoherent obscenities. Ross pushed her on through the back. "Get down!"

When they fired into the air, the crowd crumpled and cowered. With an AK47 pointing directly at his face, the driver didn't trust the bulletproof glass. The door was opened.

Desperate at the desertion, Charlie fought the urge to yell.

Coward!

Pulling the driver from the vehicle, the bearded banshees outside screeching in rabid rage. His fate seemed sealed when a single gunshot rang out. The blood lust from the locals seemed unquenched. Murder had come early to Afghanistan. Charlie shook in rage and fear at the murderous consequences of Ross' naive choices. Petrified, Charlie closed up the back seat, leaving only a small gap to stare through.

Ross was on the floor of the SUV, in a ball, yelping like a child. Grappling with the door handles and locks, the hijackers made their next breakthrough. In a flash, the back door was released, and two more attackers piled into the vehicle. An imploding Ross was dragged kicking and screaming from the SUV. Charlie fought the urge to weigh in.

The cries and yelling moved back out into the street, giving her the time to prepare. If they opened the trunk of the SUV, she was ready to pounce. Two bullets blasted the SUV, shattering the windows and her confidence. She cowered under fire. Outside, it sounded like Ross was savagely beaten, then hauled away.

The SUV stopped rocking. Encouragingly, it felt like the SUV was no longer the ground zero for hatred.

Only when it sounded as if the voices of rage were moving off did Charlie raise her head from the floor of the SUV. Slowly, she opened the rear seat. Ready to dart back in at any split-second, she peered out from the rear compartment. She lifted her head gingerly.

All around the crowd milled and spilled. She counted five AK47s raised high above a small crowd moving in unison with the kidnappers. Ross' blue suit was barely visible. He was being dragged away with a bag around his head. The locals were already joining in on the act. Punches were thrown. Kicks found their mark and spit rained down. She had witnessed violence before, but the evil spewing from the barbaric, baying mob shook her to the core.

Juddering, she pulled out her phone. *Who do I call?*

She didn't know the emergency services numbers. *They likely wouldn't help.*

No number on the phone could send reinforcements in the time available. She decided to lock the SUV doors, set in motion calls for a rescue, and wait.

The problem was, she didn't know her location. Worse still, she had a colleague in distress.

Helpless, she barged through into the SUV cabin and contemplated a ram raid on the crowd, but she knew that would be a suicide mission. When the mob headed toward what looked like a river, Charlie seized her chance. Clambering over and into the driver's seat, keeping her head well below the line of the windows. Once in place, with the key between thumb and forefinger, she stalled. "Argh!" She couldn't desert Ross.

Despite the odds, she needed to do her part. Her headscarf was pulled fast and firm across her face. This was no time for slip-ups. A flash in front of the mirror told Charlie it was all she could do. She pulled the keys from the ignition, pulled a deep breath, yanked open the driver's door and leapt from the SUV, locked it, and joined the maddening crowd. The crowd had already gathered on the edge of a wooden bridge.

Waves of curiosity two streets back had twisted into a sea of hatred. An interested crowd had descended into a baying mob in a matter of minutes. The view was desperate. Any attempted escape seemed impossible. When the beatings escalated into a pummeling from the AK47s, Charlie knew the cause was lost. The crowd cheered with every blow the infidel took. Whether they wanted this, they were forced to cheer and jeer. Charlie bit her lip, at the sight of a gasoline can being lifted overhead like a prized trophy. The sight of a rope flapping like a lasso threw yet more horror into Charlie's steps.

She stalled. *Move forward or backward?*

Whatever was going to happen was going to happen, with or without her intervention. In a scene resembling a biblical stoning, the crown piled in and around the body, desperate to view proceedings, desperate to vent their spleens. At any split-second glance of eye contact, she could join the head of the funeral procession. Four bearded men with headscarves around their faces led the mob. Shaking with rage, she leered at the wanna-be terrorists. *The worst kind of cowards.*

Much to Charlie's horror, a roar went up as they poured gasoline over the crumpled body.

When the noose went over Ross' hood, Charlie gasped and looked away. The four leaders hauled the body across and over to the steel bridge spanning the river. The crowd parted and cheered at the prospect of the lynching of an invading infidel. Word had traveled, yet more crowds gathered.

Even the crowd gasped when his body propped up high in the middle of the bridge. The emergency alarms in the distance fell on ears deafened by hatred. Charlie looked at Ross' beaten and broken body and hoped that he was already dead. When a lighter kindled the gasoline infused body, the crowd ignited. Bullets from the AK47s filled the sky. Charlie told herself she could hear no cries. She convinced herself Ross was already dead. When the body fell off the bridge, the rope went tight, and the neck snapped. Charlie forced herself to look back to see him swinging violently from the bridge. His body lurched and swayed under the momentum of the abrupt fall. The flames engulfed the body, temporarily silencing the crowd. A shocked silence flattened the mob.

Gunfire lit the sky.

The crowd regained their voices.

Charlie needed no more evidence. As the only white face in a rabid crowd of Western haters, she fled in fear for her life. *Time to go.*

Jostling her way through the cocktail of vitriol and celebration proved difficult to stomach. She surged forward with all hopes of saving Ross long gone; the mission had turned to self-preservation. She clung for dear life to the headscarf and kept her gaze low on the ground. The buffeting threatened to dislodge her headgear. The narrow street only exaggerated the intensity and channeled the hatred.

At the corner she turned to see the body cut from the bridge, sending it plunging into the river below. Another salvo of shots celebrated the dark event. Charlie charged back to the SUV, head down, grateful for the concealment given by the headgear and the chapan. She bibbed the alarm, unwilling to check if she had been noticed or not. Thankfully, the crowd had moved to the murder scene and were not swarming the SUV.

Back inside the vehicle, she gently lit the engine, slipped the gearbox into reverse, and withdrew from the hijack site without looking up. As soon as the vehicle moved, the alarm was raised. A snarling horde quickly encircled her, baying for more blood. When they saw a Western woman was driving, every panel on the SUV came under attack. Fists and feet made their mark. An arm jammed its way in through the broken passenger window and grappled the door handle open. Another local pulled at her hair through the busted driver's window. Charlie panicked and hit out.

In an all-or-nothing panic, she floored the SUV, scattering everything in her wake. The SUV jumped and bumped over curbs and debris as the crowd's yelling intensified. Eyes to the rear, she threw caution and bystanders to the wind. A market stall was demolished, a hand cart smashed, a tea stand was flattened. Charlie knew she must have hit half a dozen people, and some of those tire bumps could have been bodies, but she didn't care. *If you stop, you die.* When yanking the SUV around a ninety-degree bend in reverse, she side-swiped three Tuk-Tuks, and sent a moped rider into an open shop front.

The SUV screeched onwards, wheels spinning in the dirt. Almost immediately, a screeching Charlie jumped on the brakes. To her horror, she had barreled into a dead end. The angry mob gathered around.

As the bravest of the crowd closed in, Charlie yelled in panic. The escape route was now blocked by revolt. The mob had their sights on a new victim. Sentenced to death for crimes unknown. All around the walls of angry people closed in. Straight ahead lay a high dirt wall with a busted wooden gate sitting under a cracked stone archway. In a split second, she charged for the would-be exit. Uncertain if the doorway was even wide enough, she gunned the engine. Tires gripped. Grit flew. Careering headlong through the human turmoil, she burst a hole in the circling crowd.

Body parts hit car parts.

"Argh!" Charlie pushed on.

Under a barrage of yells, the SUV tore toward the doorway. Charlie closed her eyes and threw her torso horizontally across the front seats. The SUV crashed through the wooden doorway. Timber, dust, and debris splintered the SUV, smashing the windshield and buckling the roof. The impact from the steering wheel dislocated her left thumb. She clung on regardless.

Once through the doorway, she lifted her shoulder to gain a view. Terrified, she kept the pedal down and braced for further impact. The sandstorm passed rapidly. She had driven into a compound. A true dead end. As the revs on the engine dropped, the descending crowd rose in volume and intensity. Across the compound, she spied another large door. Without delay, she slewed the SUV towards the new target. Accelerating towards the enormous doors, she held firm. With every yard gained, she feared the bigger, more substantial gates could not be breached.

She held on for dear life, crying out in defiance. Crashing through the gates, sent timbers flying through the already busted windshield. The seatbelt crushed her ribcage, but the SUV held firm. Out the other side, she hurtled into a busy roadway. A passing bus side swiped her pushing the SUV round into the direction of traffic. Never lifting her pedal or her eyes, she pushed the SUV forward at a pace. Horns blazed as she thundered across then up the busy road. It was impossible to see through the busted shield, so she leaned out the window to gain a view. With more space to maneuver, her pace increased.

No looking back.

Gradually the crowd thinned, but the traffic intensified. She slammed the SUV into a ninety-degree turn and floored the gas pedal. Smoldering rubber from a punctured tire splattered as it was ripped from the treads. She slowed for nothing and stopped for no one.

At a speed that sent fear into those around, she completed a crash course through the traffic. Only when she was at least a mile from the terror did she dare to breathe. Five hard driven minutes later, she checked her mirrors. She charted her course at speed. At a quiet section of traffic, she pulled over and kicked the windshield from its housing. Her left thumb was rehoused. It took some time before the fog of fear lifted and she had a mind to view the Sat-Nav. Eventually, she worked out her position compared to the location of the camp. She was now miles away from danger, but further away from home.

The next moves took her out onto the edges of the neighborhood. A circuitous route was then followed at a pace designed to avoid attention. The SUV struggled on with only three wheels on the wagon. The biggest threat was that the curiosity of an SUV with a busted rear tire could attract unwanted attention. For that reason, the headscarf was tightened at every twist and turn in the road. Driving an SUV with its windows shot out made the task a deal more difficult. Thoughts of dumping the car were blocked out over fears of getting lost without her Sat-Nav. Head down and foot down, she sped on, not stopping for red lights, not heeding the pedestrian signals. As night closed in, she welcomed the cover it gave. Shaking from the cold blasting in through the windows and the terror coursing through her veins, she rode on street after street.

When she eventually rounded the corner that led to the compound, both her pace and her heart slowed. She had come too far to be misidentified as a suicide bomber. She slowed further, dipped her lights, and coasted in under the searchlights. The first lines of control were four Afghan policemen, in full regalia, armed to the teeth, dressed to suppress. Charlie removed her headscarf and stuck her head and one arm out the window.

When the first policeman saw her, he lowered his weapon and stared. His colleague followed suit. Screams of excitement rang out, causing the guard house door to open. Out stumbled a rotund officer in a camouflaged uniform. The broad beam that he threw in her direction could not have been more welcoming. Charlie slowed to a halt; head lowered. She looked up and spotted the maple leaf badge of a Canadian policeman. His ruddy face peered in warmly. "Howdy, miss. My, but you're a long way from home."

Against all her beliefs, she dropped her head onto the steering wheel and wept, like she had never wept before.

CHAPTER 3

Two sleepless days later, Charlie sat on a wooden chair, way beyond repair. Every time she leaned forward, the table tipped because of a buckled metal leg. The orange lightbulb hurt her tired dry eyes. *Bleak* was the only word that fell into her weary mind. Her first day on Afghan soil had been ripped from the pages of a horror story. Hoping the worst was behind her, she told herself to power through. But right here and then, telling and doing seemed two different ideals.

An old wall clock marked time with a tick that resembled Chinese water torture. She was giving it one more minute before the damn thing was going to be smashed. The self-contained office studio she had been allocated, for her own safety, was one part bedsit, two parts jail cell. She hated it. So far, all efforts to gain an early release had fallen on sympathetic, yet ineffectual ears.

A knock at her door broke the moment. Charlie pulled the door to find a loitering white man. She processed the visuals. *Khaki combat shirt, epaulets, and short sleeves. Designer stubble. Buzz cut, hiding his premature balding. Thirty going on fifty. Bulky stature. A chiseled jaw blunted by too many years away from the gym. Thinning lips. Rimless sunglasses indoors?*

Annoyed at having been kept under virtual house arrest since Ross' death, Charlie was ready to do battle. She liked her opening line. "What, are you blind or auditioning for a *Risky Business* remake?"

"Sorry?"

Charlie had to explain. "The indoor shades."

The man seemed lost, disinterested or both. "I'm O'Hara."

"CIA?" Charlie guessed.

"What makes you say that?"

"It was that or you're Mormon. And there aren't too many of them around here."

The grin she received was far from genuine and not borne of amusement. As if discomfited by Charlie's observation, the agent stuffed his sunglasses half inside his breast pocket. Pleased with the early win, Charlie went on the offensive. "Are you not recording this interview? Where's my lawyer?"

O'Hara lifted his hands. "That's unnecessary. You're not being detailed or interviewed."

"So, I'm free to go?"

"When things are safe for you. How are you feeling?"

"Like I saw someone beaten, hung, and burned to death, and I've been left to think about it for two days."

"Do you need a counselor or a chaplain?"

"No. I need a debriefing and a chance to get out there. What's going on? I need to make calls. I have people back home who depend on me."

"Really? Who? I've read your file."

"Screw you. Get me out of this, now!"

"It's not as easy as that."

Charlie flailed. "Nothing's ever easy with you guys. Why not?"

"The situation is too kinetic."

"But you recovered the body, right? I gave the guardhouse directions and a location."

"It's complicated."

Charlie was incredulous. "In what way? They threw him off a bridge, goddammit. What's wrong with you people?"

O'Hara got defensive. "We did all we could. We sent out search parties."

"And?"

"Nothing. He'd been cut down into the river."

"What about dredging with grappling hooks or setting up search teams?"

"As I said earlier. The situation is too kinetic. We couldn't send more people into that pit. And anyway, the last thing we want to do is have to explain a dead body."

"So, to avoid the fuss, you-"

"We sent a search party but didn't find him."

"How long did you look?"

"Long enough to attract some unwanted attention."

"What if the body turns up in the wrong hands?"

"Your initial report states he was burned to a crisp."

"I didn't say that. I said unrecognizable."

"Well then, we won't have a dead Westerner's body showing up on CNN."

Charlie nearly exploded. "So that's a positive?"

"Apologies. A poor choice of words."

"Don't apologize to me. Apologize to his family."

O'Hara almost smirked. "Don't need to. We have bereavement services that handle that."

"You are quite the callous asshole, aren't you?"

The agent shrugged. "I've been called worse. Look, it's standard protocol. We'll say he is MIA on a mission. Big brave soldier, patriot, and all that. Give him a star on the wall at Langley and a full military funeral."

"Seriously?"

"Would you prefer his family knows the truth? He made a blunder and was burned to death by an angry mob?"

"So that's it?"

"No, but it's making the best of a terrible situation. Christ, why was he even down there? He was an analyst. Not very analytical for an analyst."

Charlie barked back. "He was based in Kabul, not Kandahar. He couldn't know everything."

"Then why was he here?"

"To meet me."

"Why are you so special? Perhaps he saw your profile pic and wanted to meet and impress a pretty woman."

All the while, Charlie had been scanning her interviewer. She'd been forming opinions. So far, she wasn't liking what she saw or heard. She kicked on. "So, you're one of them?"

"One of what?"

"A boorish, misogamist."

O'Hara snapped back, clearly annoyed. "I'm the one asking the questions."

"I thought this wasn't an interview. Get your story straight, Agent O'Hara. Isn't that what you CIA types do?"

O'Hara simmered. "You don't know me."

"I know you well enough."

The sneer on O'Hara's face was more than enough to kick Charlie into gear.

"You're a nervous man who drinks and smokes too much. Likely, you have no wife. You're a proud Irishman. Probably never been to Ireland in your life. Bet you sit in the corner of a fake Irish bar in Georgetown and talk bullshit about the old country over a glass of the black stuff. I bet you even have a tattoo. I'm going with a map of Ireland or something obscure to support the Irish Republican Army."

O'Hara boiled. "If you're trying to talk your way out of here, you're going about this the wrong way."

Charlie ignored the threats. "So how did I do?"

O'Hara's expression gave her the encouragement needed to explain her reasoning. "Your pinky ring's silver, with two hands clasping a heart with a crown resting on top. That's an Irish Claddagh ring. Hence the proud Irishman. But I bet you don't even know what it stands for. You just wear it to look cool. Like these geeks that wear Nirvana t-shirts but couldn't name a single one of their songs."

O'Hara fidgeted with his ring, clearly angered that she wasn't far out.

"It's a traditional Irish ring that represents love, friendship, and loyalty. The heart represents love, the hands represent friendship, and the crown represents loyalty. You don't know that?" She didn't wait for the response. "Of course, you don't. Well then, you won't know that it's not an Irish original. The ring's heritage predates anything similar in Irish history. It originated in Galway around seventeen hundred, but its origins stretch back to Roman times.

The band saying, *No tengo mas que dar te.* In case you don't speak Spanish, and I suspect you don't, it means *I have nothing more to give you.*" She piled it on. "Oh, and you probably don't know this either, but Antrim is a county in Northern Ireland."

"Screw you."

Charlie was almost enjoying this. "Oh, and you're left-handed."

"How do you know all that crap?"

"Because I'm an investigator. That's what we do at the FBI, we investigate. We don't interfere. We don't meddle in other people's lives. What we definitely don't do is reduce rich histories into four-letter words, like crap."

Charlie loved watching the bully boy squirm. "Your eyes are bloodshot early in the day. Your pristine uniform and stubble say you haven't been traveling. You don't strike me as a light sleeper, so substance abuse is the most probable cause. If you're smart enough to get into the CIA, you're smart enough to see the damage hard drugs can do. Pills are scarce across here, so I'm guessing it's drink. Don't tell me, Irish whisky? How did I do?"

O'Hara's look of disdain told Charlie she had done fine. "You have no wife, otherwise you wouldn't be spending so long out here. This isn't your first gig; those boots are well worn. My guess is she left you after one too many drinks, arguments, or tours of duty. Tell me I'm not wrong."

O'Hara's inner anger blistered to the surface, but he couldn't seem to argue. "And I'm left-handed, how?"

"That relates to the smoking that I mentioned. Your left-hand fidgets with your shirt button when you're annoyed. Look at your fingers. The nicotine stains are subtle, but they are there. That's the hand you hold your cigarette with, your left hand. Speaking of hands, you bite your fingernails, a sure sign you get nervous."

O'Hara couldn't hide his annoyance or his admiration. "It's a harp."

Charlie leaned in. "Sorry?"

"My tattoo? It's a harp."

Charlie slapped the desk at the breakthrough. "Aha, I knew it."

O'Hara turned the tables. "If you're so smart, how come you know nothing about what's going on?"

"I just got here."

The side of O'Hara's mouth lifted sardonically. "You only just met me, yet you know everything."

"That's different."

"Why?"

"That was just profiling."

"Educated guesses?"

Charlie wasn't arguing. "Maybe."

"Well, take some educated guesses at what the hell's going on."

"Look, I wish I could help you, but, like it said on that old ring, *No tengo más que dar te.*"

"*I have nothing more to give you.* I get it."

Charlie's tone took a step back. "Look, I am here to investigate the theft of government funds. Stealing from the US treasury is a federal crime. It's as simple as that."

"All on your lonesome? What are you, Supergirl? I thought you lot hunted in packs?"

"I'm the advance party. There are four of us. Each one gets an office to investigate."

"That's what you're doing? Investigating?"

"What is it Regan said? *Trust but verify.*"

"So, you're verifying."

"Yeah, I guess I am. Poor choice of words from my side. I'm verifying, and if we find anything, we call in the cavalry."

"But why you guys?"

"Ask your bosses. They helped set this up. No one in Kandahar could be trusted. Like I said, stealing from the treasury is a federal crime. That's what we do." She took a guess. "That's why you're here, a full two days after the killing. They flew you in to investigate. Am I right?"

"Nearly. We've been flown in from Kabul, true, but we're here to clean up, not investigate."

"So, no verifying?"

"More like, sterilizing."

"So, he dies at the hands of insurgents, and you cover it up?"

"It's the best we can do."

"For your reputation?"

"For his legacy. He screwed up. The first thing you learn in Kandahar is the no-go areas. We never go into that part of town. Everybody knows that. Come on. It's as if he wanted to die."

Charlie shot him a look of puzzlement. "That's the dumbest thing I've heard from any CIA agent, and I've heard a lot of dumb statements from you guys."

O'Hara stepped back in. "This is getting us nowhere. Save your scruples for someone who cares. You do your job and I'll do mine."

If she had just a little more energy, Charlie would likely have smacked him in the mouth. Hard. Twice. O'Hara moved to avoid opening new wounds further. "Look. We all have a job to do. We left you for a day to recover from your ordeal–"

"Yeah, and let the trail go cold."

"Please. We need to find out as much as we can from you for our records."

"If it's for your records, why aren't you recording this?"

"You're not a suspect, Agent Glass. We're merely gathering information. We read the report you made to the Canadian police. It sounds like a straightforward case of mob justice."

"So why aren't the Canadians leading the investigation? It's their jurisdiction."

"We want to keep this behind closed doors. Look after our own. Keep it off the streets and the broadsheets."

"Makes sense, I guess."

"So, what can you tell me about Ross?"

Charlie shrugged. "Nothing, I just met the guy. He seemed a loner. Not very pleasant. Out of his depth. It would seem out of character for him to take risks."

"Considering you just met, you formed a pretty damning opinion of him."

"You should hear what I've got to say about you."

"I just did!"

Their stares lasted long into the uncomfortable range until O'Hara broke the ice. "Listen, we're on the same side here. This one stinks. He broke protocols and paid for it with his life. We've seen no such mob-based anarchy in months. It escalated way too quickly. It's as if they knew he was coming."

Charlie sneered. "So, the blacked-out SUV wasn't a clue?"

"You mentioned police outriders in the report?"

Charlie lowered her chin briefly in acknowledgment, so O'Hara continued. "We've found no trace of any police patrols in the area."

"Oh, and don't tell me, the local police can't help."

O'Hara sneered. "Missing files."

"It could be genuine incompetence. By now, you'll have met them."

O'Hara had another angle. "Possibly the driver was in on it?"

Charlie gave the suggestion some consideration. "No, Ross was giving him directions. Besides, didn't you read my report? They shot him."

"Did you see anybody?"

Charlie felt the need to defend herself. "No, I was a little distracted, escaping a lynch mob. I saw him dragged away and heard the shot. I know what I saw."

"Was there anything he said that made you suspicious? Think."

Charlie did what was asked of her but couldn't muster any response other than a shake of the head.

"Okay. Well, we have your report–"

"So, what next?"

"We do our job and you do yours. We change protocols, confirm travel routes, and make sure Ross gets the funeral he doesn't deserve."

"And me?"

"You make sure this stupidity isn't repeated. We'll drop you off at your housing unit. Your mission remains on track. Go find the stolen money. Report back through standard channels to the

US. No one here is to be trusted. But you already know that. We just chalk this down as an unfortunate incident."

Charlie shook her head at the terminology, rose, and moved for the door. "I need some air."

O'Hara closed down the interview. "Please remain seated. We have arranged for your transfer to arrive within the hour. Remember. None of this gets out. Talk of this to no one. There's no need to add to the official report you've submitted."

"Unless I remember something?"

"Of course."

Charlie kept her seat. When O'Hara reached the door, he turned and pushed out a smile. This time, it almost looked genuine. "It was good to put a face to the name, Agent Glass. You're quite the article. Don't take this the wrong way, but I hope we won't be seeing each other any time soon."

"Likewise."

O'Hara stalled halfway through the exit. "How did you know I've never been to Ireland?"

It was Charlie's turn to smile. "I didn't. I was on a roll and took a guess."

O'Hara pointed a playful finger in her general direction and considered his response. None came.

A wry shake of the head was his parting gesture as the door clunked closed behind him.

Once alone, she set her thumping head down on the table. She felt sickened. Sickened by a mob, so ready to murder innocents. Sickened by the callous nonchalance of her own people. She hadn't known Ross long enough to understand if he was a good man, but he was a man all the same. A fellow human, a mere mortal. No one should ever have to die such a death. No one's legacy should ever have been so heartlessly dismissed. She had witnessed terror before, but that failed to lessen the impact of the day's events. Far from immune to threat, her senses jangled at the dangers inherent in her surroundings. The scenery and the costumes may have changed, but Afghanistan threatened just like Iraq.

The same old terrors on a new background.

CHAPTER 4

Another day, another untraceable, crooked dollar.

Charlie sat alone again, in the back of a prefabricated trailer. The tiny room was dim and minimalist; one metal table, one swivel chair with a busted caster, a lamp with no bulb, and no window. The gloom matched her mood.

She hoped week three of her twenty-week deployment would pass without the reappearance of another deadly lynch mob. She would have counted the days on the calendar on the wall, but it was a year out of date. The terrors of the first week had brought to mind the nightmares from her time in Iraq. Thankfully, she had slept through the previous night; a first since her arrival into theater. When she lifted her hand to check for tremors, the shaking had reduced to a barely perceptible quiver.

That's where her progress ended.

All efforts to uncover the corruption within the sector had proven fruitless. Indeed, she had found no irregularities in any of the paperwork.

The only sign of guilt came from the attitudes of the staff. A mixture of US Army grunts and administrators seemed to work feverishly with the local hires to erect a veil of secrecy around their activities. Deflection and obstinacy were the favored tactics.

But she had held her ground and kept digging. She told herself. *Only the guilty have something to hide.*

Walls of silence, built around mountains of paperwork, impeded all forms of progress. The leaking loud aircon unit rattled her senses. A requisition for the attendance of a maintenance engineer had been filled out in triplicate, twice. It seemed even he had gotten lost in the system. With the system on a manual shutdown, the stifling midday heat was being endured in a vain effort to sharpen her focus. As she suspected, no support had been made available to help her investigations.

When food was sent out for, she wasn't asked. When she joined her colleagues in the DEFAC dining facility, conversations stopped.

Her questions were left unanswered, their food was left unfinished.

Her solo investigations were neither supported nor welcomed. Nothing matched. Nothing added up. Courteous interactions were minimal. Offers of support from the other soldiers in the unit were few, far between, and prone to retraction. All meetings were held without her attendance, well out of earshot. Water cooler discussions dried up when Charlie showed up.

It was obvious that she was unwelcome. Everyone was a suspect, and all ranks were closed. If files were requested, they could not be found, forcing her to track down her own information. Lugging box after box of vague and complicated paperwork between buildings was backbreaking and soul-destroying.

When she called back to the States to complain about the lack of co-operation, her boss never picked up. The two messages left on his answering service were never returned. Texting had also proven to be a pointless exercise. When her mind emptied, thoughts of the horrors of Ross' death and her narrow escape leached into her psyche. She forced herself to stay busy, despite the futility of the work.

With the night closing in, and with nothing to shed light on proceedings, she lifted her combat jacket and headed for the door. At least one person stayed behind each night to act as guard, preventing any off-piste inquiries.

Tonight, there were multiple night watchmen. Walking back through the office, the sneering and leering from the posse of administrators burned holes in her skull. Being unpopular did not bother her in the slightest, but the monotony of the work at hand and the lack of success rattled as much as the old cooler in her room. Bereft of success, she called it a night.

On the way out, she hovered at the water cooler and loaded ice-cold water into a paper funnel. "Anyone need some water?" She threw the offer around the room, but no one caught it. No one even looked up. With a shrug, she swigged the water and repeated the process. After unlocking and opening the office window, she took in the view of the mountains in the distance. Fresh air filled her lungs.

A gruff order rattled across the office. "Shut that window! You'll get dust everywhere!"

"Sorry!" she replied timidly.

Suitably chastised, Charlie slid the window closed, and heading out the door. Head lowered, she competed her walk of shame, to the soundtrack of the office members mutterings and poorly concealed sighs. Although mumbled, the messages were clear.

She was not trusted.

She was not liked.

She was not welcome.

As Charlie eased outside a poorly concealed grim slipped into view.

She couldn't give a crap.

She liked it that way.

CHAPTER 5

Later that night, Charlie sat alone at a corner table in the dimly lit mess hall, her fork idly rearranging the food on her plate into meaningless patterns.

The meal was barely worth eating, dry meatloaf drowning in watery gravy, limp green beans that looked like they'd given up on life, and mashed potatoes that had the texture of paste. The tang of processed food hung in the air, mixing with the faint scent of overcooked vegetables.

She set her fork down, wrinkling her nose. When she was back home in Paris reminiscing about life in the field, the cuisine never entered her mind. Now she knew why.

Around her, the mess hall was winding down. Two orderlies pushed mops in slow, lazy arcs across the floor. Their circles and their work rates seemed to be decreasing by the minute.

They were clearly waiting for the clock to release them from duty.

Behind the counter, a handful of staff muttered in hushed tones, glancing in her direction with looks that weren't exactly welcoming. Their sideways stares crawled under her skin, but Charlie kept her expression calm, her posture rigid. She knew why they were watching.

They hate me. Every single one of them. The thought wasn't new, nor did it carry any sting of surprise. She had come to terms with the realization, investigating your allies was a surefire way to turn them into enemies.

The days spent so far had been a dirge. She'd arrived in a world filled with deaf ears, cold shoulders, blind alleys, and brick walls. No one had lifted a finger to help. In fact, the only finger they'd lifted had been a collective metaphorical middle finger.

Investigations were not going well.

Just as her one woman pity-party was just about to get into full swing, the heavy airlock doors at the far end of the room suddenly creaked open, breaking her chain of thought. Charlie looked up just as a stocky man entered, his fatigues clinging to his damp frame. His round face glistened under the flickering lights,

Up close the soldier's patchy moustache did it's best to make contact with the sparse goatee framing his chubby cheeks, giving him a strangely affable appearance.

The staff behind the counter perked up at his arrival, their previously dour faces lighting up. One of them ladled extra helpings of food onto his tray, smiling like he'd just walked in carrying good news. Charlie noted the easy way he interacted with them, quick jokes, a nod of thanks.

Popular man. Wonder why.

His gaze swept the room.

When his dark eyes landed on her, his lips curled into a half-smile. He strode toward her with the kind of confidence that made it clear he was used to being welcomed wherever he went.

"Mind if I join you?" he asked in a friendly tone. He didn't wait for a reply, sliding into the chair across from her and setting his tray down with a thud. "Place is a ghost town tonight."

Charlie instinctively tensed, but she gave things her best shot. "Sure."

"Sergeant Emilio Sanchez," he said, offering a broad smile that revealed a slightly crooked front tooth. "People around here call me Emilio."

Charlie tilted her head slightly, studying him.

She knew who he was.

Sanchez was a name that had popped up repeatedly in the files she'd spent hours poring over. He was a key figure in the administration she'd been sent to investigate. He looked heavier in person than he did in his file photo, and decidedly more... approachable.

"Charlie," she replied, her voice carefully neutral. No hand was offered.

Sanchez grinned as though her brusque tone didn't bother him. "Yeah, I know who you are. You've been the talk of the base since you got here." He picked up his fork and jabbed it into the pile of enchiladas on his tray, cheese stretching as he lifted a bite.

Charlie's lips tightened. "I'd imagine so."

Sanchez didn't miss a beat. "You've got people buzzing. It's not every day the bigwigs send an FBI agent to poke around our little operation." He chumped down the grub with the enthusiasm of someone who hadn't eaten all week. "You find what you're looking for yet?"

Charlie arched an eyebrow. "I wasn't aware you were keeping tabs on me, Sergeant."

"Not just me," Sanchez said, laughing softly. He waved his fork toward the counter staff without turning. "People talk. Small base like this, it's hard not to notice the newcomer. Especially one who keeps asking questions. And one as pretty as you."

Charlie leaned back slightly, her gaze steady on him. "I'm just doing my job."

"Of course," Sanchez said, raising his hands in mock surrender. "I get it. You're here to shine a light on the dark corners, figure out who's been stealing the hub caps, right?" He winked, as if they were co-conspirators.

Charlie didn't respond immediately. He was eating like a man who didn't have a care, or a table manner, in the world, but there was something in his demeanor. She couldn't tell if he was trying to charm her, disarm her, or both.

"Food's not great," Sanchez said, breaking the silence. "But it beats starving. You want the real tip? If you bribe the cook with a pack of smokes, you'll get tamales on Sundays. They're almost edible." He grinned.

Charlie allowed herself a small smirk, though her guard remained firmly in place. "I'll keep that in mind." She guessed she would like him if he wasn't on her suspects list.

Sanchez leaned back, fork still in hand. "So, Charlie, can I call you Charlie? How are you liking it here so far?"

"It's fine," she said curtly. "I'm not here for the scenery."

He chuckled, the sound rich and genuine. "I figured as much. You strike me as the no-nonsense type. Straight to business."

"And you're not?" Charlie asked, tilting her head.

"Me?" Sanchez spread his arms wide, the picture of innocence. "I'm just a guy trying to make it through the day without stepping on any landmines, literal or otherwise."

Charlie's lips twitched, but she didn't let her amusement fully surface.

Sanchez noshed away before speaking again, this time with his mouth full. "Look, I get it. You're here to do your job, and that job's probably not making you a lot of friends. But I've been around long enough to know that you catch more flies with honey."

Charlie's eyes narrowed. "Meaning"

"I can help," Sanchez said quickly. "Just saying, it doesn't hurt to have someone watching your six."

"What are you saying?"

Sanchez's smile widened, his dark eyes gleaming with something unreadable. "Hey, I'm a team player. You won't find many around here. You need anything, you let me know."

Charlie stared at him for a moment, trying to read between the lines. Was he genuinely offering to help, or was he trying to get close enough to learn what she knew?

"Appreciate it," she said finally, her tone clipped.

Sanchez leaned back in his chair, wiping his mouth with a napkin, and setting his fork down against the sloppy tray. He gestured toward Charlie with an easy smile. "So, Charlie, what's your story?"

Charlie raised an eyebrow. "My story?"

"Yeah. Where're you from? What got you into this whole FBI gig?" Sanchez said, leaning forward like he was genuinely interested. His dark eyes twinkled with an openness that was hard to fake.

Charlie shrugged, keeping her expression neutral. "Not much to tell. I grew up in the mountains of Virginia. Majored in Arabic in at university. Figured this was the logical next step."

Sanchez gave her a knowing look, his lips lifting into a smirk. "I bet there's a whole other back story to that. You come with a strong reputation." He grinned.

"I'd check your sources. There's not much to me." She allowed a small, polite smile to form. "What about you? What's your story, Sergeant?"

Sanchez said, chuckling. "Not much to me either, I guess, apart from my family." He straightened up, tapping the edge of his tray thoughtfully. "I'm from Texas, born and raised. Joined the military straight out of high school. Figured it was either that or get stuck working on cars in my uncle's garage for the rest of my life. Not that there's anything wrong with that, but... I wanted more."

Charlie nodded faintly. "And you found it?"

"Oh yeah," Sanchez said, nodding emphatically. "Twenty years later, I've seen more of the world than I ever thought I would. Done my share of good, done my share of dumb, survived and now I'm ready to hang it up. This is my last tour."

"Last tour?" Charlie repeated, her tone optimistic.

"Yep. Next month, I'm out of here for good." His face softened as he reached into his pocket and pulled out a worn leather wallet. He flipped it open, retrieving a photo and sliding it across the table toward Charlie. "That's my wife, Maria. And those two troublemakers are my girls, Sofia, and Elena."

Charlie glanced at the photo. A dark-haired woman with a warm smile held two young girls, one grinning toothily and the other mid-laugh. The girls had the same mischievous sparkle in their eyes as Sanchez. She smiled faintly, though her expression remained guarded.

"They're beautiful," she said.

"They're my world," Sanchez said, his voice thick with pride. "I can't tell you how much I miss them. Sofia's turning eight next month, and I've missed three of her birthdays already. Elena's five, and half the time I feel like I barely know her. Maria... God bless her, she holds it all together. I don't know how she does it." His voice cracked just a little, but he covered it quickly by clearing his throat.

Charlie nodded again, her gaze flicking back to the photo. "Must be nice, knowing you'll be home soon."

"It's better than nice," Sanchez said, his grin returning full force. "It's everything. No more deployments, no more mess halls, no more eighteen-hour days. I'm going to retire back to San Antonio, buy a little spot, and open up a Tex-Mex restaurant. Real food. None of this slop."

Charlie glanced at his tray, where an enchilada half-covered in cheese sat as he scooped another bite into his mouth with gusto. Her lips twitched, but she kept her voice steady. "Doesn't seem like you hate it that much."

Sanchez paused mid-chew, then burst out laughing. "Fair point. But when you've eaten this junk for as long as I have, you find ways to convince yourself it's not that bad."

Carlie laughed. "You gotta do what you can to survive."

Sanchez noticed her smile and leaned forward, pointing his fork at her. "There it is! I knew you had it in you. A smile suits you better than that scowl you've been wearing since I sat down."

"I don't scowl," Charlie said, the laughter fading into her usual neutral expression.

"Sure you don't," Sanchez said, shaking his head with mock seriousness. "But hey, I get it. You've got walls. I just hope you know you don't have to keep 'em up with me. I'm not your enemy, Charlie."

Charlie looked at him for a long moment, searching his face for any cracks in the friendly façade. If there were any, they weren't visible. Sanchez's grin stayed steady, his dark eyes soft and warm.

"Noted," she said finally, her tone giving nothing away.

Sanchez chuckled, leaning back in his chair. "You're a tough nut to crack, you know that? But I like you. You're sharp. You remind me of my eldest, Sofia. She's got that same 'don't mess with me' look about her. I'm telling you, she's going to run the world one day."

Charlie couldn't help the small grin that crept back onto her face. "She sounds like a handful."

"She is."

Sanchez finished his food and stood, brushing a string of cheese off his uniform. "Just remember, not everyone's as friendly as me." He paused, his gaze lingering on her. "Be careful, Charlie. People here don't like being poked."

"Understood."

"I mean it."

"I understand, honestly I do."

"Oh, now remember, when I get that restaurant open, you're going to want to stop by. I'll save you a table."

Charlie smirked. "I'll hold you to that."

"Deal," Sanchez said, standing and brushing cheesy crumbs from his fatigues. He looked down at her, his expression still warm and open. "Anyway, I'll stop bugging you. I've got to hit the sack."

Charlie nodded. "Goodnight, Sergeant."

"Goodnight, Charlie," Sanchez said, his voice lighter than it had been earlier. "And hey, next time we talk, I expect more than three-word answers, okay?"

"We'll see," Charlie said, her tone dry but not unkind.

Sanchez chuckled and gave her a two-finger salute before turning and heading for the door.

As he walked away, waving, and thanking the staff for their time and fayre. Charlie's eyes followed him until he disappeared out through the double doors.

Whatever his angle was, she wasn't about to let her guard down. Friendly faces often hid the sharpest knives.

Unable to finish her supper, she stood, gathering her own tray.

She didn't know what Sanchez's game was, but she knew one thing for sure: she couldn't trust him.

He never put his tray away.

CHAPTER 6

Lying on her bunk, back in the housing unit, Charlie stared at the paneled ceiling.

Her mind was as blank as the walls of her unlocked cell. Tonight, as with most nights, she turned to her best friend in Afghanistan, her short-wave radio scanner. On her tours of the camp, she had become acquainted with a gossiping quartermaster, over at the central storage facility. Charlie had used his obvious attraction toward her to secure the use of the radio. Playing down her knowledge, she convinced the quartermaster to loan out the scanner to help her learn the local lingo.

Night after night, she would flick the device across all available frequencies to pass the night away. Tonight, was no exception. The scanner was flicked on, and the dial slowly twisted across the frequencies. Hitting her favored frequency, she listened in to an army night patrol, running raids on reported terrorist enclaves. Gang activity seemed on the up, in line with emerging sectarian violence. So far, all the spot searches had delivered no suspects and a great deal of ill will. Frustrations were high and growing between the factions. All random phrases and codes had been jotted down, yet the notebook entries were sparse and made no sense. Still, the radio helped pass the time of night.

She checked her watch. 0200 hours.

The time had come. *Time to move.*

Leaping from her bed, she pulled her lucky talisman and tumbled the artifact between thumb and forefinger. Every other trinket from her growing list of adventures lay safe and sound in her keep-safe box back home. This felt like her amulet against evil.

It gave her strength.

Together, they were invincible. It was an illusion that had served her well so far, a superstition that could not be broken, even at gunpoint.

With a kiss for luck, she pulled the talisman over her head and threw on her combat jacket. Her boots were tied around her neck; a utility knife and torch were pocketed before the room light was killed.

Slipping out of the darkness, she moved out onto the poorly lit gantry. Quiet bootless steps made their way down the steel staircase and across the first section of gravel.

Once past the main accommodation, her socks were dusted down, and her boots pulled on. She checked to confirm none of her colleagues sleeping in the housing units had been disturbed.

So far, so good.

In the foreground, the soldiers' tents stood to attention. Row upon row of canvas shrouds lay before her, each possessing a camouflaged air conditioning unit. Given the time of night and the plummeting temperature, nothing stirred. The camp lighting was minimal to obfuscate the actions of any would-be snipers and mortar bomb slingers. The walk between shadows aided her concealment.

She lengthened her confident strides.

The timings of the sentries patrolling the compound had been checked over the last two nights. Once to track the movements, the second time to confirm them. Her planned schedule was tight, but doable. It seemed perverse to Charlie that military precision in guard duties made it easier to navigate. She hoped tonight some slack-jawed loser wouldn't be ten minutes late, or heaven forbid, one minute early.

She checked her watch. *Action stations.*

Stepping on to meet her destiny, she hoped Uncle Sam's training would keep the well-oiled surveillance team bang on time.

No challenges were met on her march back to the office complex. Without a glance in any direction, she tramped confidently down and through into the building.

Only when she found the safety of the darkness did she crouch and check her sightlines. She took in the view and took on air. They were both clear. She matched her watch check with the memorized sentry schedule. *Ten minutes. Go!*

After finding, then climbing under the office window she had opened earlier, she pushed her knife into the bottom of the lower sash. Her ruse had worked. The unlocked aluminum frame slid open without a sound or a struggle.

No damage done.

After one last check of her surroundings, Charlie pulled herself up and into the opening, kicking the sides of the building for purchase. Her entry could have been more dignified, but nothing broke on her landing. The window was slammed and actually locked this time around.

With no prying eyes, the torch was pulled. Late night investigations were set in motion. First off was a run between the eight desks. The first two opened freely. They were ignored.

Desks three, seven, and eight were all locked. The remaining desks opened freely. That gave her three suspects. If you have something to hide, you wouldn't leave it in an unlocked desk. *Seven Minutes.*

The list shortened. Cartwright, a sniffling clerk with meticulous attention to details, usually occupied desk five. His workstation was immaculate, well-ordered, and laid out in line with regulations. He was a follower of protocols. Charlie deduced his desk was locked because that's what it says you do in the manual. His desk sat in the middle of the room, in full view of everyone. That made it highly unlikely that he would commit major fraud in the center of an open office.

Still his desk was locked. So, he made the list.

Five Minutes.

That left locked desks, seven and eight. They sat apart from the rest, in a corner, facing the room. Charlie recalled their occupants. Barrie and her dining companion, Sanchez.

Both sergeants, were lifers in the army.

Sanchez, she had at least chatted to her. But since that meeting, he had been high on rhetoric but low on visibility. He hadn't really helped, but then again, she hadn't really asked.

Sometimes she was her own worst enemy.

Barrie complained all the time on every subject yet never seemed to care about anything.

They did not strike Charlie as soldiers who would rigidly follow protocols. She deduced their desks must have been locked, for other reasons. The frantic scanning continued under the flashlight. The notice boards were studied next. She was never allowed near enough for long enough to make any detailed examination possible during office hours.

Tonight, was the night.

Little of note came to the fore until one curiosity flashed into view. The team's timetable seemed skewed. Every Friday, Sanchez, was slated for some time off. No one else had that luxury of that uniformity in their schedule. On its own, the timetable would have held no clues, but the curiosities surrounding Sanchez were mounting.

It wasn't much to go on, but it was a start.

One Minute. Time to fly.

She mentally noted the lock numbers on the three suspicious desks, retraced her steps, and exited the building by the front door, resetting the night latch behind her. She had her first lead, and two suspects in her sights.

That she had crossed the line into borderline criminality did not bother her. She had a job to do.

She was playing by the rules, her rules.

CHAPTER 7

The following day had been spent preparing her next moves. The die was rolled.

After surviving the culinary gauntlet that was breakfast at the camp's dining facility, Charlie worked her way back across camp.

Unlike her original Iraqi station, the Afghan camp was tiny and less organized. Dust, traffic, and people flew in all directions. She found her voice and lost her temper when a Humvee thundered past in full flight.

Skidding gravel cast a veil of gritty dust, forcing her to turn away from the vehicle's wake. For a host of reasons, she closed her eyes and counted to ten. By the time she had reached the quartermaster's station, the dust had almost settled. Her nerves were a different matter altogether.

The two-level assembly of shipping containers were makeshift, although they looked to have been there for years. The air conditioning units clamped to the side of each unit lay silent. Unsurprisingly, in the biting air, nothing whirred.

She stalled at the foot of the steel stair framework, holding the containers together. She waited for a lull in the pedestrian traffic, plonking down the steelwork. The four descending grunts did not look enthralled with the prospects of the day ahead. It also sounded as if they had just left the quartermaster's office empty-handed, an outcome they seemed unimpressed by.

Charlie climbed the steps, intent on singing a different tune.

The old-fashioned bell above the door on the quartermaster's office clanged to announce her arrival.

As Charlie stepped into the quartermaster's store, the scent of oil and faintly metallic air filled her nostrils. It was distinct, utilitarian, and entirely military.

Old-school war-mongery, she thought dryly.

She liked it.

The store stretched out through the back, a maze of shelves stacked high with neatly arranged boxed, folded uniforms, crates, ammunition, tools and so much more. The activity levels matched the lighting, toned down and quiet.

Perfect timing.

This was no random drop-in. Charlie knew the quartermasters worked on a shift rotation. She had her favorite, Harry Benning. She'd tracked his schedule for days, waiting for the right moment.

And now here she was.

And now there he was.

From behind a stack of crates, Harry appeared, shuffling into view. His gait was slow, deliberate, and unhurried, the years weighing heavily on his frame. His hair was sun-bleached to a coppery tone on the sides. He looked and acted like he'd long since retired on the job. Overweight, under-stressed, and far too chatty for a soldier. He seemed an oddball to Charlie, someone still clinging to their youth, long after they had let themselves go.

Charlie though the only thing Harry would be able to fight would be sleep.

And even then, that would be a losing battle.

"Charlie!" Harry's face split into a grin, his lined features lighting up like an old lantern. How's my favorite agent?" His voice carried a warmth she hadn't heard in days.

"I'm the only agent you know."

"Doesn't stop you from being my favorite."

Charlie returned his smile, leaning casually against a nearby shelf. "You're the only friendly face around here, Harry. It's nice to talk to someone who doesn't look like they want to stab me in the back."

Harry chuckled, waving her words away like they were nonsense. "Ah, they just don't know what to make of you yet. Give it time."

Charlie allowed the faintest smirk and went on her charm offensive. "Oh, I think they know me well enough."

After brightening his day through her reappearance, she set to work buttering up the store man, enquiring after his health, and filling him in with the newly selected briefings from the radio scanner.

Harry responded in kind with warm conversation, until Charlie decided it was time to strike. "So, do you want a fight?"

Harry's belly laugh echoed through the store. "Come on then, let's see what you've got." He flipped the "Closed" sign on the door and motioned for her to follow.

Harry led her deeper into the store. The shelves grew taller and more densely packed, the rows narrowing into a labyrinth of equipment and supplies. "So," Charlie said, her sharp eyes darting to inventory tags as she trailed him, "tell me about all this."

Harry launched into an enthusiastic explanation, his voice carrying up into the racks. "Every item has a place. Every order gets logged. It's a machine, just like me."

"A machine that likes to stay well-oiled?" Charlie quipped, her voice tinged with dry humor.

Harry chortled. "Exactly."

At the back of the store, Harry pushed open the door to a small office. The walls were lined with filing cabinets, their labels peeling at the edges. A corkboard displayed faded military posters and a calendar marked with thick red X's. A worn wooden desk sat in the corner, its surface cluttered with paperwork, a chipped coffee mug, and framed photos.

Charlie gestured to one of the frames. "Cute kids."

Harry's expression softened. "You don't remember them? Those are my grandkids. Ellie and Max. They're the reason I'm counting the days." He tapped the edge of the calendar, where each crossed-off square seemed to carry a quiet sense of triumph.

Charlie folded her arms, studying the calendar. "Counting the days, huh?"

Harry sighed, the warmth in his voice fading. "Their dad, my son, he's not exactly reliable. A little too fond of the pipe. They need me, and I'm not wasting any more time here than I have to. When I retire, I'm taking them in. No more mess halls. No more deployments. Just family."

Charlie nodded slowly. "I've been hearing that a lot these days," she said softly.

"So, you said you're here for a fight?" Harry pulled a scuffed wooden chess set from beneath his desk, placing it on the table between them.

"You bet," Charlie replied, pulling a chair over and beginning to set up the pieces. Harry moved to the side.

"Tea?" He offered. "Black, no sugar, right?

Charlie smirked "Ah, what the hell. Maybe I'll treat myself. Half a sugar."

Harry chuckled. "Wow letting yourself go. Half a sugar, black tea, coming your way."

With tea and a formal handshake exchanged the game got underway.

Charlie moved her pieces with exaggerated caution, deliberately playing poorly to keep the game going. Harry brow was a cluster of cluttered furrows as he muttered to himself through every misplaced maneuver.

"You're not half-bad at this," Harry teased as he slid his knight into position.

"Just warming up," Charlie said with a faint smirk.

Charlie eyed the board, her queen poised just two moves away from checkmate. Harry hadn't seen it yet, his attention locked on a cluster of pawns that barely mattered. She could end the game right now. One decisive move, and it was over.

Instead, she shifted her queen backward, retreating it to a safe square. On the surface, it looked like a defensive maneuver, cautious and unsure. But in reality, it was deliberate. She was toying with him, stretching out the match.

Harry squinted at the board, oblivious to the mercy she'd just shown. "Huh, thought you had me for a second there," he said, moving a knight into a better position.

Charlie nodded, her expression neutral. "Guess you've got some fight left in you."

Harry beamed. "In more ways than one."

As the game dragged on, Charlie asked, "Mind topping me off?"

Harry stood, stretching. "Coming right up." His age showed as he moved, his steps slower, his posture slightly stooped. Charlie watched him carefully, waiting.

A while later, Harry returned with her tea but set his cup down quickly. "Hold the board, Agent Glass. Nature calls," he said with a chuckle, shuffling off toward the restroom.

The moment the door closed, Charlie sprang to her feet. She darted out of the office, weaving through the aisles of the store. Her shoulder banged a rack, such was her pace.

Her keen eyes scanned the rows of labeled drawers and shelves until she found what she was looking for, the racks holding the site keys.

Muttering as she went, her fingers moved quickly, rifling through the drawers in a whispered panic. "Armory, automotives, classified documents, communication center, information technology, facility access, maintenance and utility, medical supply, personnel…"

Personnel?

Under that sub heading she quickly found the drawers for office keys, then desk keys.

Each second felt heavier than the last as she pulled tags and flipped through labels, cross referencing the memorized codes for the selected desks.

As if trying to cheerlead her activities, the panicked whispers emerged. "Come on. Come on."

The faint sound of a toilet flushing jolted her. "Argh!" She hadn't found the exact match but decided she'd have to make do. Grabbing a handful of keys, she shoved them into her pocket. For good measure, she grabbed second helpings and sprinted back toward the office.

Hearing the toilet door unlock, Charlie made a split-second decision and darted towards the restroom. "Sorry, bit of an emergency," she called, as she barged past an exiting Harry.

Hearing her plea, he couldn't get out the way quick enough.

It took her a couple of minutes to compose herself and check her loot. The muffled "yes" she threw out didn't make it past the toilet door. She had her keys in hand.

It took another minute for her to regain her breath and another minute to regain her composure. No longer flushed, she pulled the lever on W.C. then stepped out and back towards the office.

"Sorry about that." Back in the office, Charlie sat down, pretending to study the chessboard. To her relief Harry looked none the wiser. She resumed the game, moving her pieces with a callous efficiency, wanting to end it.

After three moves, the deed was done.

Check mate.

"Rematch?" Harry asked, his tone hopeful as they finished.

Charlie hesitated. She had nothing better to do. And she liked his company. "Sure. Why not?"

They played into the night, chatting, and laughing. This time, every time Harry made a dumb move Charlie would such in air, to persuade him otherwise.

As the game progressed, she took in a lot of air.

Harry talked about his plans for retirement, his dreams of a quiet life, maybe some national guard work.

As they talked, Charlie warmed. He was a nice man. *Too nice for war.* She figured the national guard would suit him well.

But she couldn't dwell on that. The keys in her pocket were what mattered now.

All she had to do was figure out her next move.

CHAPTER 8

The only thing keeping her mind from wandering into her mental minefield was work.

Reemerging images of the rabid mob that killed Ross crowded her mind, yet thankfully, the distractions of the investigation held them at bay during her waking hours.

The following evening, Charlie used the pretext of a long-distance run to stake out her office. A series of jog-by glances had confirmed the offices were finally closed. With the guard schedules consigned to memory, the timings for her assault were well rehearsed. She defended her cavalier actions with the excuse that she had no one to confide in. Defendable evidence was thin on the ground, as were her reinforcements. She convinced herself this was the act that could break the case wide open.

On the last run past, she stopped to re-tie a tied lace before slipping back into the shadows. Charlie had felt asking for a copy of the key to the office front door would have raised suspicions, so the side window remained her only point of ingress. The tiredness in her limbs made the clamber up into the unit more difficult than before and did little to improve the quality of her landing back on the office floor.

Her scrambling boots left skid marks all up the wall. She made a mental note to wipe down the cladding on the building. An earlier trip to the water cooler had led to the window latch being opened to prepare for her arrival.

First port of call was the desk of the office nerd, Cartwright. With stolen keys working their dark magic, she was soon rifling through every unlocked drawer. Folders in a line, matching manifests, invoices that matched up, a half-written letter to his mum, asking about the local church. He was squeaky clean.

Right there and then she closed the book on Cartwright.

It was a similar story with Barrie. His desk was cleaner than a nun's habit. Nothing out of place. Charlie chastised herself. She should have guess that. Everything on Barrie's desk had been aligned perfectly. Even his matching pens sat bolt upright in their holder.

Barrie was a clean freak.

Barrie was another red herring.

She sighed. That left only one suspect.

Sanchez.

After sliding her flashlight between her teeth, she crawled across to Sanchez' desk on her hands and knees. It was a long shot that any incriminating evidence would be found in the desks, but she figured any books in the office stood a chance of being explained away. Any books held in their own housing units or personal storage spaces would yell. *Guilty as charged!*

The desk opened after the second key matched the lock. The flashlight glinted off the chrome frame on a small photograph sitting proudly on the desk. A Latino family grinned back lovingly to the camera. A beautiful wife and two young girls took center frame. The idyllic scene seemed to Charlie a million miles from the mendacity of Afghanistan. She hoped for good news.

Evidence that Sanchez was a good man.

Sanchez chewed tobacco, and the stains from the remnants of this pagan ritual contaminated the corners of his top drawer. Other than that, the drawer was clean.

As was the next.

A box file marked obsolete was pulled from the bottom of the bottom drawer. The container held notes relating to the Commander's Emergency Response Program. Charlie knew the fund paid for reconstruction. The dates were recent, so there was little chance that it deserved to be held in a box file marked obsolete.

Large bills for petrol to fuel the air conditioning generators were hand registered, even though most of the units looked as if they hadn't even been connected. The office equipment didn't have the sophistication to scan invoices and receipts and link them through a financial e-portal. All transactions looked to have been made manually. *Perfect for hiding cash.*

After cross-referencing a host of invoices and receipts, Charlie suspected Sanchez was under-paying, and overcharging local agents on the cash transaction deals. There was also a strong suspicion he was taking kickbacks from the winning bidders to ensure their award.

There was no evidence, yet, that the money was going his way, but the low bidders never seemed to win the contracts. The high bidders were the ones with the most deals. Suspect entries on security, water, and gasoline supplies were all pulled into question. As the Project Purchasing Officer, Sanchez bought supplies from local Afghan contractors as part of the Commander's Emergency Response Program.

The evidence suggested he could be siphoning money from funds allotted to purchase the mission critical items and services, unobtainable through conventional military channels.

Charlie needed proof, not suggestions. For her, the issues simply couldn't stop there.

She slumped to the linoleum and pondered her next moves. She dug deeper. In order, each drawer was pulled out completely and its contents emptied onto the desk for yet another inspection. When she tried to replace the third drawer, it jammed.

To her amazement, she found a padded envelope had been duct-taped to the underside of the drawer. Excitedly, she coaxed a black moleskin notebook from its hiding place.

Knew it.

Rampaging through the pages, she discovered details of transactions for funds, intended to support counterterrorism operations. That the entries were made in pencil, and in code, strengthened the case for the prosecution.

The names were in code and the monies were listed as charity donations, but the intent seemed obvious. Falsified receipts were being submitted to financial officials. She pulled off a blank single sheet of paper, from a nearby pad, to avoid any pressure bleed through onto the pad itself.

On the separated sheet, she noted the details of one of the formal documents hidden by Sanchez. The bill of goods reference, date, initiator, authorization sign off and value were all listed. Working her way through the dated entries in the logbook, she found the same date, the bill of goods reference in reverse, and two different coded initials for the initiator and authorizer.

It didn't surprise her that the values were mismatched. Hiding the notebook in the office made perfect sense.

Spot checks and barrack inspections were becoming more prevalent, so the best place to hide evidence would be at the source, almost hidden in plain sight.

If she hadn't broken the law, the book would likely never have been found. It made sense that the books were close by. They needed that detail daily and likely couldn't risk carrying the evidence around with them.

Across at the central filing cabinets, she found the fake replacement document. The values in the fake document were $15,000 dollars less than those tracked by in the moleskin handbook.

Money orders under various names were detailed and coded at a value of $995, just low enough to avoid flagging protocols. It was clear they were stealing money and sending it home in dribs and drabs.

But the sums of cash still unaccounted for back in DC were much higher. The evidence was vague, and the bulk of the monies being stolen remained untraced.

Every shred of evidence was rehoused in exactly the same location and all traces of her presence were eradicated.

It made her wonder just how much everyone in the office knew. In an hour's cursory examination, she had found more red flags than at the Moscow May-Day parade.

Staggered by the revelation, she retook her set on the linoleum and leaned her back against the wall.

Barrie and Cartwright were eliminated from the investigations, but Sanchez was her primary suspect. He was in it up to his swiveling eyes, but he was not the target.

There had to be others.

Charlie knew hooking a sardine wouldn't be enough.

She needed bigger fish, and for a bigger fish, she needed bigger bait.

CHAPTER 9

Charlie had called in sick to avoid direct contact with her suspects, but after three days, she still had no plan.

Her reports up the chain of command had been kept to a minimum. Sizemore, her boss back in the US, would only get involved if he could sniff glory. It wasn't caution that stayed her hand; it was contempt. She had no need or respect for the shallow glory hunter. Distant reconnaissance of the office and the Sanchez' personal quarters had only added delays and increased frustration. Realizing that progress could only be gained through interactions, today she ventured back into the office.

She breezed back into the office, keen to reconnect with everyone after her feigned bout of illness. After yet another morning of stale mates and no mates, she changed track, pivoting her interactions around a more personal agenda.

Having angled her chair to provide her with a view of the all-important water cooler, so sat in wait. Like a lioness stalking the watering hole, the moment Sanchez circled the cooler, Charlie struck.

"Hi Emilio How goes the day?"

"Morning, Charlie," Sanchez replied. His fatigues looked freshly pressed. "How's the world treating you today?"

"Same as always," Charlie kept her tone neutral, but she couldn't ignore his unwavering cheerfulness. "And you?"

"Living the dream," Sanchez said with a grin. "Not long to go." He tilted his cup under the spout, letting it fill slowly. "You holding up, okay? I know this place can… chew people up."

Charlie turned slightly to look at him. His expression seemed genuine, like he actually cared. "I'm fine."

"Glad to hear it," Sanchez said, leaning against the counter. His voice dropped a little, conspiratorial. He turned his back on the crew and leaned in with a whisper. "Listen, I've been thinking. If you're still poking around trying to make sense of all the… discrepancies, you might want to take a look at the supply chain logs. Start with the shipments that came in two months ago."

Charlie's eyebrow arched. "Why two months ago?"

"Let's just say the numbers didn't quite add up back then. They said it was an accounting error. Maybe it was. Maybe not." He shrugged, sipping his water like he hadn't just handed her a lead.

Charlie studied him carefully. His tone was light, but his words carried weight. Was he genuinely trying to help? Or was this some kind of misdirection?

It was in her nature to select option B.

"That's… good to know," Charlie said. She didn't elaborate and tried not to give her feelings away.

Sanchez nodded, his grin unwavering. "Check the requisitions too. Compare what's listed versus what actually arrived. Sometimes things… go missing in translation. You'd be surprised what that tells you."

She took another sip of water, watching him from the corner of her eye. It was either an earnest gesture or a calculated move, and Charlie wasn't sure which.

"I appreciate the tip," she said finally, her voice measured.

"Hey, anything to make your job easier," Sanchez said. He straightened, tossing his empty cup into the bin. "If you've got any questions, you know where to find me."

"I'll keep that in mind," Charlie said.

She pondered

Why is he so willing to help?

Was he trying to earn her trust?

Or was it something else entirely?

He'd handed her something useful, but she couldn't shake the feeling that he was playing a longer game.

As Sanchez walked away, his easygoing demeanor never faltered. The others in the office glanced at her, their expressions a mix of curiosity and mistrust.

The glaring stares Sanchez received from his co-workers gave her hope, that her suspicions could have been ill founded. New questions flashed.

Was he being set up to take the fall?

Could someone have planted the evidence?

It might just have been possible for someone to tape the details to the underside of the drawer from under the unit.

Charlie turned back to the water station, gripping her cup tighter than necessary.

Sanchez had given her a lead, but trusting him outright was a risk she wasn't ready to take. Still, she couldn't deny the flicker of appreciation for his support. Genuine or not, it had been a long time since anyone here had shown her any kindness.

For now, she decided follow his lead, but she'd keep her guard up.

Sanchez was a friend… or a foe.

Time would tell.

Tap. Tap. Tap.

The forming awkward silence was broken when an attractive thirty-something man with a weather-worn face peered around the corner. "Morning, everyone." The collective sigh that bounced around the office was both verbal and visual. The rugged stranger barged on, unperturbed. "Come on, everyone, why the long faces?"

The wall of silence fell heavily.

Sanchez didn't lose stride, grabbing his cap from his desk and sliding it into position as he moved for the door.

"Excuse me." He said.

"Don't leave on my account." Said the stranger.

Charlie guess that's exactly what Sanchez was doing.

One man appears, one man disappears. She thought.

His appearance seemed to annoy everyone. The fact he annoyed everyone made Charlie straighten up and listen in. The stranger bounced on in. "Just popping in to see if you have any scoops for me. Any gossip?"

"Come on, I can make you famous. I am on your side. Any more condolence packages? Any high value detainees or pending VIPs?"

Charlie loved the interaction. It seemed the new intruder was even less popular. She extended a hand. "Hello. I'm Charlie. And you are?"

"Noah. Associated Press. Embedded since '03."

Charlie offered him her hand, and subtly mocked his overtly masculine bout of ethos. "Federal Bureau of Investigation. Embedded since last month."

Charlie used the time to inspect the new arrival, up close and personal. He grinned in recognition of her efforts to bring him back into the fold of mere mortals.

Although clearly a Westerner, he was dressed in full Taliban regalia. His crimson beard was as patchy as his introduction. Gray, shell-shocked eyes, and fire-damaged complexion made him look fearless, yet futureless. Whether chasing a story or running from his past, it looked like life was about to catch up on Noah. Charlie took a chance on her fellow outcast. "Step into my office. I can fill you in." As she led him into the back room, Charlie felt the collective exacerbation taint the atmosphere.

For greater effect, she closed the office door behind her.

Once inside, Charlie ushered Noah into the only seat available. It lilted with his weight. "I'd offer you a stiff drink, but you look like that would be against your religion." Charlie pointed to Noah's traditional Shalwar Kameez. Dressed like a local, his knee-length, cotton smock was buttoned to the chest. Matching trousers flopped loosely over his scuffed combat boots. "You couldn't go the whole way with the footwear?"

"You can't wear sandals when you go around standing on everyone's toes."

"So, all this is for effect?"

Noah countered. "People are more likely to talk to, and less likely to shoot at, someone dressed like this."

Charlie conceded. "You have a point. So, mister journalist, what have you got to report?"

"I am the one meant to be asking the questions."

"Says who? I only said that, to get a rise out of the deadheads out there." Charlie kept her volume high enough that anyone listening at the door would hear. "I am new here. I have stories, but I need context and trust. What have you got?"

It was Noah's turn to yield. "What would you like to know?"

"Let's start with Noah. Noah What?"

He didn't yield far. "Just Noah."

Charlie attempted humor. "Better that than being Unjust Noah." Her quip fell short, so she pressed on. "What are you doing here, Just Noah?"

"I'm the photojournalist."

"I thought you were a writer?"

"You can't make a living off either profession, on their own. I freelance with photos and features. I've done articles for Life Magazine, the New Yorker, and National Geographic."

More ethos. "Have I seen any of your work?"

"I don't know. Have you read anything highbrow and informative?"

Charlie's cheek twitched. "Does the National Enquirer count?"

Noah laughed. "It's probably got more truth in it than most newspapers in the US right now."

"That bad, eh?"

"You don't want to know."

"I do."

Noah challenged her. "How badly do you want to know?"

"Try me."

"Can you handle yourself?"

Charlie threw his question back. "I have my moments."

"Ha. I like you."

Charlie didn't fall for his flattery. "If the crowd next door is your test market, you'd like anyone."

"Touché. For one so feisty, you seem ill-suited to paperwork."

"It's not my favorite thing. That's for sure. I'm going out of my mind. It's like a prison sentence."

"Why'd you accept it then?"

"Good question."

"I know it is. That's why I'm waiting for an answer."

"Comes with the territory, I guess."

"You can't be superwoman every day."

"I can't be superwoman, any day."

"Oh, I doubt that." Noah pondered. "Do you fancy a trip out into the wicked world? I can show you around."

Charlie fought to suppress her excitement. "And in return?"

"In return, you tell me why an FBI agent is holed up in the back room of a trailer near Kandahar airfield."

"That's confidential."

"Okay, let me start with something a little more public. What have you heard of a Western businessman being killed in town?"

"Wow. You are a straight to the point guy."

"I know no other way. Well?"

"I can hand on heart say that I have heard nothing of a businessman being killed in town."

"I heard some idiot drove into the heart of the Kandahar slums and got himself ambushed."

Charlie continued the dumb act.

"Are you sure you know nothing about that? They say he had a Western woman with him."

Charlie shrugged. "Wish I could help you."

Noah wasn't buying it. "Come on, what do you know? The world went crazy for a day. Security across town was amped. I thought we were past all that."

"Evidently not. What do you think happened?"

Noah smirked, knowing that the tables were being turned on him. His tone seemed deliberately inflammatory. "Some idiots fresh into town drove into a Taliban holdout and got what they deserved."

Charlie's lips quirked up. "Well, if that actually happened, why haven't we seen news reports on it?"

"Because of people like you covering it up."

"You couldn't be further from the truth."

"Enlighten me."

"You seem more enlightened than most already."

Noah pressed. "I've seen a grainy cell phone video. It happened."

Charlie deflected. "How did you get that?"

"Haven't you heard? I'm enlightened."

Charlie flinched under the verbal jousting, so Noah took another charge. "Come on, you know more than you're letting on. The city was peaceful. Even today, most of the town is safe for Westerners."

"Most."

"Come on. Help me understand why they were there?"

Charlie raised her shield. "Maybe if I saw the evidence, I could comment."

Noah made his move. "I could take you back out there. Maybe that would jog your memory."

Charlie's poker face quivered. "My memory? I hope you're not suggesting I was anywhere near this alleged incident."

Noah chuckled at her attempted bluff. He clapped his hands in celebration of his mini victory.

"Do you have a travel pass?"

"I do, but all transport has been blocked to me."

"I can sort that." Noah pointed beyond the walls. "Do you want to get out there?"

Charlie leaned back, uncertain of the answer. "Do I? Is it safe?"

"A bit gun shy after your incident?"

Charlie gave an amused look. "I have no idea what you're talking about."

Noah opened up. "Look, it's only dangerous in the no-go zone. And you won't make that mistake again."

Charlie closed him down. "Put your rod and reel away."

"Pardon?"

"Stop fishing."

Noah threw up his hands. "Come on, you said it yourself. You're bored out of your mind in here."

Charlie knew he was right, but the truth was terrifying. She was afraid to leave the camp.

Noah tried a new exit strategy. "Will you be missed?"

"Are you kidding me? Never. If I got hit by an IED, they'd complain about the noise."

Noah's laugh seemed genuine. "Do you have a gun?"

Charlie shook her head. "Do I need one?"

"It would be better. If I got you one, could you use it?"

Charlie tipped her head. "I'm FBI, not Peace Corps."

"What's the last thing you shot?"

Charlie grinned. "A condescending journalist."

Noah's scoffing was loud enough to have irked everyone in the next room. "Taking potshots at journalists. You'll fit right in."

The pair shared a snicker. Noah pointed out into the office. "You couldn't get me a water, could you?"

Charlie threw a sideways glance. "What's wrong with your legs?"

"They are attached to the rest of my body, which is hated by everyone next door. The last time I helped myself, they threatened to kick me off site for stealing government property."

"Wow, they must really hate you. In that case, I'd love to get you water." Charlie went next door and pulled a couple of cups of water. Everyone stared. Nobody liked what they saw, except Noah. Back inside the back-office, Charlie recommenced a different cross-examination. "Why would I need a gun if it's safe?"

"It's better to be safe than sorry, but there hasn't been an incident outside the slums for weeks. Come on, I go about my business day in and day out. No trouble at all."

"Why are you so keen to get me out there?"

"Why are you so afraid?"

Charlie hated the assumption and its accuracy. "Where would we go?"

Noah bumped the table. "There you go. I'll show you the town and its people."

Charlie didn't say no, leaving Noah to seal the deal. "So, tomorrow, 0800 hours? Just inside the front gate."

"What should I wear?"

"Now, who's inviting sexist comments?"

"You know what I mean?"

"Leggings and a t-shirt. I'll have a smock and headscarf for you."

Noah was already heading for the door. With one hand on the door handle and a finger to his lips, he urged caution. "Let's keep this between us girls."

A quick dip of her head signalled Charlie's agreement.

"Can I get your number?" Noah asked.

Uncertainty twisted Charlie's face, forcing Noah to explain. "In case there are any changes in plan."

After some deliberation, Charlie gestured for Noah to hand over his phone, an early generation Nokia. "Wow. Quite the museum piece." She set the ground rules. "Emergencies only, right?"

Noah held up his hands and retreated playfully. "Okay. I get it. Don't bring that BlackBerry with you tomorrow. It cried out US Agency. It's a museum-piece-only kind of place."

Charlie nodded her understanding. When Noah glided out through the doorway, he mockingly shouted back across an office filled with resentment and mistrust. "That's remarkably interesting, Special Agent. I will make sure the story runs tomorrow!"

Charlie didn't offer a response or hang around to look for reactions. Instead, she pulled the door closed to conceal her emotions.

She slumped back into her chair and considered. Noah could be leading her into another ambush, but he could also be the key to solving the investigation. She needed to find out more on every front. Fear and excitement coursed through her veins, pushing open the valves in her heart.

Tomorrow she would be back out over the wire.

CHAPTER 10

The gritty clouds tainting the morning skyline couldn't cloak Charlie's early bird optimism. She had been up for hours. Today she was bunking off. Being prepared always was her thing, but today, she had overdone it. Her father's advice, whilst never bursting with love, always steered her. *When in doubt, arrive early. When not in doubt, arrive early.*

Half an hour before their allocated meeting time, Charlie tried to stay cool in the morning shade. Listing from side to side, she hummed a tone-deaf tune and awaited her guide. The terrorizing horror show that surrounded Ross' death gnawed her insides, but she couldn't hide away forever. She pushed hard to exorcise the demons of the lynch mob injustice. She whittled her fears down to worried apprehension. It was the best she could hope for.

Deep breaths. You got this.

Outside, everyday life crept from its slumber, albeit a safe distance away from the security cordon set out by razor wire and blast walls. In the distance, a bright and early storekeeper did his best to encourage the purchase of nets and traps, whilst sitting on a pile of coiled rope. He had no takers.

A donkey stubbornly straddled a concrete culvert. Both animal and handler looked on the verge of giving up before the day had even begun. Jaundiced brick archways with steel shutter doors showed the location of shops, long closed down. Shaded awnings hung low over a group of males, lounging and leering. Nearby, smoke billowed from a steel drum. Only when they grinned between themselves did Charlie draw breath.

Terrorists don't smile.

The few women out on the street all wore burkas as they bustled forward to beat the early market rush. The barbed wire and security services held the locals away from the perimeter. Fear and resentment crept across the no-man's-land between society and security. It wasn't just Charlie's blonde hair, improvised headscarf and lashings of sun cream that set her apart from the sparse and doleful crowd. Afghanistan seemed even more on edge than Iraq. Less trusting. Less friendly.

Am I just tainted by the attack on Ross? She hoped terror wouldn't strike twice.

Suddenly, a white pickup truck with a blue canvas cover ripped around the corner, sending the locals scurrying for cover. Doorways were filled, and the street emptied. Everyone except the guards scrambled to high alert. Charlie called their attention and pointed.

"White truck! Twelve O'clock." Still, the truck came. Still, the guards stood. Barging on through the traffic, the truck scattered the crowd. "He's on a hostile approach!"

The panic in her voice seemed to amuse the Canadian policeman supervising the local guards, who themselves looked totally disinterested in the proceedings. "Do something!" Charlie moved to the fore, ready to grab a cop's gun. The laid-back Canadian, sensing that things may get out of control, twitched his untrimmed mustache, and set her hand on her shoulder. "Relax. That's Noah."

Charlie stayed her jittering hands. Dust blew and grit flew when he slung the pickup around, with inches and seconds to spare. The grin on his face seemed wider than the berth given to the truck by the locals. He could not have looked more pleased with himself. Against all protocols and common logic, he barged from the truck, rucksack in hand.

The local guards bundled forward like kids chasing an ice cream truck. He dished out gifts, like some out of season Santa Claus. Random DVDs, packets of Haribo sweets, and cartons of Marlboro red cigarettes ranked amongst this season's most popular gifts. Charlie was mad and made a point of showing it. She stamped her way forward and met her guide, more than halfway.

"Are you crazy? Things like that could get you killed."

"What, the Marlboros? They insist on the reds."

When the gift giving ceased, the mutual backslapping followed. Noah seemed quite the welcome distraction for the local security. Charlie was in no mood to let up. "You may think that grin's infectious, but I'm not catching it!"

"Come on, I just saved you half an hour of your precious time. Why hang around here when I could be showing you my city?"

"Your city? Wow. Did you buy it, or were you elected mayor?"

"That's not how it works. Around here you buy elections, not cities."

"Capitalism and democracy in all their tormented brilliance. So where are we going?"

"Come on. Jump in. I'll show you."

Charlie followed orders. The pickup's interior was overstocked with garbage. Charlie hauled the discarded cigarette packets, empty Coke cans, and depleted water bottles off the passenger seat into the footwell. "Don't tidy up on my account."

"Yeah, sorry about that. I am between cleaners." He offered.

"When did the last one leave? During Watergate?"

"Very good. If you can negotiate the garbage, hop into the back. I've laid out some coveralls for you."

"Are they clean?"

"They were until I threw them in the back."

Charlie twisted a grin out of the corner of her mouth as she squashed her way into the backseat. Noah cranked the engine and bumped his way back out into a recovering traffic flow. Fond adieus were bid to the French-Canadian policeman at the front gate, as they eased out into the big bad world.

The weaving between lanes started early in the journey. Charlie yelped when the pickup jolted to the side as she was halfway through, pulling on a large cotton thawb of midnight blue cotton. Her elbow cracked the window. "Easy!" Noah didn't seem to slow or care. Her attempt to put on the matching headdress was abandoned after one dismal effort.

With the aid of the cracked rearview mirror, Noah offered tips on how to set the angle and wrap the Afghan headdress. He soon gave up too. "Close enough. It's not fashion, it's protection."

"From what?"

"Have you not seen it out there?"

Charlie took it all in, as her guide gave her the lay of the land. "So, this is Kandahar, the second largest city in Afghanistan. It has a little over a quarter of a million inhabitants. Dates back to Alexander the Great. It's a major trading center for wool, cotton, silk, grains, fresh and dried fruit, even tobacco. It's a deeply conservative town, and one of the ideological heartlands of the Taliban."

Charlie bowed politely, as if what she was being told was news to her. "There's a reason you're packing heat." Noah's head gestured towards the glove compartment. Curious, Charlie moved forward and flipped the catch. A Beretta pistol slid off the pile of maps, tumbling from the stuffed compartment.

"Jesus! Careful!"

"Me, be careful? I'm not the one jamming a loaded gun into a glove box."

"How do you know it's loaded?"

"The weight."

Noah was impressed. "You are a strange one. Why are you here?"

"Same reason you are, to get to the truth. So where are we headed?"

"Why don't you show me where the abduction took place?"

"Wow, literally, right out the gate. I'm sorry. I've no idea. And if I did, I wouldn't want to go anywhere near such a place."

"How do you know where *such a place* is?" quizzed Noah.

"You said yourself it was in the no-go area. Just this time around, can we stay in the safe zones?"

Noah sighed and temporarily ceased the interrogation. "For now." A welcome silence filled the cabin. The truck slowed as the crowd thickened. Charlie leaned away from the world outside. Winding their way through the crowd, closer inspections were exchanged through the pickup window. A two-year-old, being led by a four-year-old, being led by a six-year-old, wandered into the road, forcing Noah to screech the brakes. Their colorful dresses stood out in beautiful contrast to their drab black trousers and misplaced smiles. Tall, dark, and far from handsome, a bearded man, straight from a Taliban recruiting poster, yelled at the girls to get out of his way.

He seemed annoyed by the miniscule delay in his journey, brought about by the girl's day out. The street scene was pure theater. Charlie made a snap decision. She twisted in her seat, reached back, and picked up Noah's camera from its place of prominence on the back seat. "Canon EOS. Great camera, even if the lenses are a little noisy."

"Not now. That's the ultrasonic version."

"I thought you said this gig doesn't pay?"

"Nothing gets past you, Agent Glass."

With the traffic opening up, the pickup was pushed hard down the road. "The same could be said about you, Just Noah."

Charlie clicked the camera on and gestured for permission to take some snaps. "Do you mind?"

Noah seemed to mind. "Looks like I have no choice."

Charlie took the response as a yes, and set to work, snapping away at the street scene. The lens seemed oversized for the work, making it impossible for Charlie to frame each shot. "Your zoom's almost too powerful for these street scenes. "How do you do it?"

"Skill, judgment, oh, and a range of lenses. You've just got the wrong one," joked Noah.

Charlie fidgeted around the camera's knobs, buttons. "This is more complicated than I can remember."

Noah was enjoying Charlie's struggle. "Oh, come on, that thing is idiot proof."

"Maybe I am an idiot. Maybe I have low blood sugar. I missed breakfast. Can we stop and grab something?"

"Sure. The streets are filled with great grub. How does Bolani sound to you?"

"To me? It sounds foreign. What is it?"

"It's a handful of heart attack, but it's fantastic."

"Bolani it is!"

A couple of streets later, Noah maneuvered the pickup near a section of street food vendors. He snatched the door handle. Charlie held her position. "Are you not coming?"

"Maybe next time. It's all still a bit much for me."

Noah seemed disappointed by her lack of gumption. "Okay. Keep the doors locked and your head down." Nodding, she jumped out and headed across to the street vendor. Charlie dropped the locks on each door.

With so much life milling around her, the second half of Noah's instructions was more difficult to comply with. Charlie couldn't keep her eyes off the surroundings. Across the sidewalk, a small boy plastered in flour, flattened dough pizza-style, while his brother coated each base with potatoes, onions, and spices. Their father sweated over a hot oil fryer jumping with deep fried bakes. Trade was brisk. Within a few minutes, Noah returned with the food, loosely wrapped in an old newspaper. She had forgotten the doors were locked, so when Noah lifted the door handle, the resistance almost made him drop his food.

Charlie shouted through the window and flicked the switch. "Sorry!"

Noah jumped in. "You take instructions well, either that or you're scared."

Charlie scoffed. "I *am* scared. Have you seen this food?" She presented the open package of bubbling fat to her traveling companion.

"Try it, you'll love it."

Much to Noah's amusement and enjoyment, after a couple of minutes, Charlie abandoned all efforts to endure the fast food. Noah devoured both food parcels, wiped the fat from his coated hands, and set the pickup back in motion. "For an FBI Agent, I didn't think you'd be so timid."

Charlie was back, snapping away with the camera, never lifting her eye from the viewfinder. "You'd be surprised." As the pickup jostled forward, the shutter on the camera worked overtime. The next street corner was infested with disenfranchised locals of fighting age.

Charlie zoomed in. "Slow down! Slow down! Look at those guys. I hope they're hiding their weapons, as poorly as they are hiding their feelings. What's their story? Ex-Taliban?"

"Likely. Demobilized fighters, waiting for the nod from God. Local militia-in-waiting. They will probably be waiting to get a gig protecting poppy fields, guarding an opium factory, or chaperoning a heroin shipment."

Charlie mused. "We've all gotta work."

A wagon laden with fabrics and textiles blocked her view, causing Charlie to lift her head from the camera. The open backed truck was packed with clothes, burst mattresses, and cushions of all shapes and shades.

Glorious and garish colors flooded the scene. A stream of tuk-tuks weaved through the crowd. Bright yellow with faded red roofs, each one was draped in beads, banners, and brightly colored adornments.

Alongside, a bearded driver jammed his Tuk-Tuk around the nearby truck. He revved the vehicle forward to outpace and drown out the large, colorful woman in the back, shouting directions and gesticulating as if his life depended on it. The driver sped on, eyes front, looking afraid of what he may find in his rearview mirror.

All around, white minivans blasted through the dusty smog, which clogged the city's vehicular arteries. A solitary archway leading to and from nowhere of interest stood silently, like an unwanted giant, lost in the crowd.

Noah pulled the pickup to the roadside, near a large traffic circular with an off-white tower in the middle. The main square seemed to be the place where all roads met, and all traffic collided.

"Why are we stopping here?" she asked.

"It's easier than driving around. All of Kandahar comes here. You see it all. Enjoy."

The pair settled in for a front-row seat. Handcarts and legwork were being put to good use as traders moved themselves into position for the day ahead. Pickup trucks found drop-off points for all manner of goods. A wheel-less barrow acted as the storefront for a smiling boy selling pristine pomegranates. The lack of trade did little to dull the youth's zest for life. Humanity flowed in waves as time drifted.

"They seem a resilient bunch," said Charlie admiringly.

"I'd say more resourceful than resilient. Around here, when life gives them lemons, they throw them at the fruit seller and steal his apples."

"Radical."

"In so many ways," Noah continued.

"The cleaners steal all kinds of crap from the army base and sell it on to stall holders, who peddle it in broad daylight. The garbage collectors wade through the waste to recover all kinds of crap, some of it useless, some of it dangerous."

"Such as?"

"You name it. Last year up at Bagram, they were selling stolen computer drives crammed with classified details of enemy targets, names of corrupt Afghans, and details of our troop movements and capabilities. Out in broad daylight for anyone to buy."

"That's not a true story?"

Noah shrugged. "Sadly, it is. Around here, the crazier the story, the more likely it is to be true."

"It must be tough to gauge things then."

Noah agreed. "True. The clothes don't help. All of them look as if they're wearing a disguise. Even down to faces masked with beards. Look at that one." He pointed across the road to a tall, broad woman whose face was totally covered by a burka. "You don't know if she's got Spandex or Semtex under those robes. That could be a man or a woman."

Charlie felt he was overreacting. "Have you spent much time with women?"

"Have you spent much time with terrorists?"

"More than you would think."

"I could say the same. All I am saying is, be careful. Everyone is not what they seem out here."

Charlie picked out the parts of the conversation she appreciated and stored them for future use. "Understood."

Noah broke the growing silence between the two voyeurs. "What brings you here?"

Charlie didn't like questions like that. "A C130 transport plane."

Noah screwed his face. "You know what I mean."

"I am here to do a job. Get in, get it done, get out."

"So, you're not falling in love with Afghanistan?" he asked.

"Not so far. This is as much as I've seen."

"You really don't get off base much."

Charlie shook her head. "Not at all."

"So, you just stay in at nights, washing your hair."

"No. I practice my languages."

"They have classes for that." Scoffed Noah.

"No. I listen in to local chatter on a scanner radio."

"Where did you get that?"

Charlie remembered her old friend, Harry Benning. The quartermaster and tapped her nose. "Confidential sources."

"Wow, do you think I could get in on that action."

"Possibly."

Noah's eyes lit up. "Really?"

Charlie laughed. "Don't be ridiculous."

Noah joined in the laughter. "Ha like most women, you're too good to be true."

Charlie chuckled. "And like most men you're gullible."

"Isn't that illegal?"

"What?"

"The radio."

She grinned. "Only if you get caught."

"Learned anything?"

"Only that the troopers over here swear more than they do in Iraq. And that is going some."

"Seriously. Have you found anything out?"

"Nothing of interest, really. My Pashto is dreadful. With the dialect and the speed they talk, it's tough to understand. Apart from the occasional English words and phrases, I am pretty much lost."

Noah scoffed. "That last part just about sums up my life."

"I've jotted a few words down, but nothing jumps out."

"Well, if I help you find your missing dollars, I'll want permission to write about it."

"What do you mean?"

"Come on, I know why you're here. Everybody does. The only difference is that I'm glad you're here. Everyone else hates the idea."

"Including me."

"You're not serious. People like you love this kind of crap."

"People like me?"

"Adventurers. We love it."

"Then it's people like us, not people like me."

"You may have a point. So, come on, now we've agreed we're in the same camp, tell me about the gig." Charlie stalled, prompting another prompt. "Come on. I can't help you if you don't help me."

"Off the record?"

"Around here there is no record."

"Tell me about it." After the pregnant pause went full term, Noah moved things forward. "You're after the missing bribe money."

"What bribe money?" Charlie stuttered.

Noah almost choked on his own guffaw. "Oh, come on. This place is awash with it. Some official, some not so. Some of it stolen, some of it given away. All of it poorly traced. You're federal, not military, and you're no Langley goon, I hope."

Charlie let her lips curve upward at the accusation, trying to throw uncertainty into the mix, even though she knew Noah was on the money.

"Listen, the rumor mill is putting out some story about a couple of mystery soldiers who have the whole thing wrapped up. All the angles covered."

Charlie nibbled at the bait. "Do you know who they are?"

"Oh, you'd love that, wouldn't you? I give you the names. Just in the door, and bang. The case is cracked wide open. You gain the credit and I'm left with nothing. I can't do that."

"Can't or won't."

Noah didn't flinch. "Both. I don't know who they are. No one does, but even if I did, I wouldn't trust you with the intel. I don't know you."

Charlie sympathized. She had suspected, but didn't want to share the details, for that same reason. As she stalled, Noah forced the issue. "Come on. What can you tell me?"

"After you? After all, this is your town."

In the intervening phase of deliberation, an old man clinging to the haunches of a hunched donkey sidled past. It would have been comical if the old beast hadn't looked in such a bad way. At a hole in the traffic, the old pair stalled. They both looked glad for the rest. The old man looked too weary to kick the donkey back into first gear.

Instead, he waited until his old mount had plucked up the energy to put one hoof in front of the other. Times were hard, but for others, they were harder. Noah eventually yielded, as if desperate to take their mind off the inhumanity staggering past. "Billions have been spent on sustainment; salaries, ammunition, equipment maintenance, information technology, and clothing."

Charlie wasn't impressed. "Everybody knows that. It's on CNN every week."

"What they haven't made public yet is just how much crap we are wasting on transport, infrastructure projects, operations, and training. We're giving it away. That's worse than having it stolen."

Charlie screwed her face. "Is it?"

"Yeah, because at least we won't look idiots to our enemies. They take our handouts and turn them against us at the first opportunity. When this is all said and done, we will have given them hundreds of thousands of rifles and pistols. They will get thousands of fighting vehicles and Humvees. The government gets drones, helicopters, and planes by the score, yet they still harbor terrorists and turn a blind eye to the thefts, so they can make money on the bribes and protection. It's a joke. A sick joke, but nobody is laughing."

Charlie was hooked. "So, where does it all end up?"

"In the hands of insurgents, Taliban holdouts, and across the borders into Iran and Pakistan. Afghan security forces have looted and embezzled for years. Our Government Accountability Office has estimated just under half the US military aid to Afghanistan has been stolen or misappropriated. That runs into the hundreds of millions of dollars since this whole shit show started. Sure, there have been token-gesture prosecutions, but it's always the low-level grunt that gets cuffed. The big guys go free, here, and back home."

All the time Noah was ranting, Charlie sat, head down, fidgeting with the camera. Suddenly, she stopped and looked up. "This time it will be different."

"Oh really? And why is that? Because you're here to make a difference? How many times have I heard that before?"

Charlie stood her ground. "You haven't heard it from me."

"And what makes you think you'll make any difference?"

Charlie was riled. “Well, for a start, I can name the crooked administrator.”

“Bullshit.”

“Not at all. They won’t come as a surprise to you to learn their names.”

Noah scoffed with skepticism. “And why is that?”

Charlie twisted the camera to present the viewer.

“Because I found photographs of him on your camera.”

CHAPTER 11

Noah slammed the pickup to a halt across a busy sidewalk, scattering livestock and livelihoods along the way. "I don't know whether to slap you or pat you on the back."

"Well, here's the clue. One of those moves will leave you with a broken arm."

"How's that possible?"

"Do you think I was desperate for fried food, or scared to leave the pickup?"

"You rifled through my memory card? Wow! You're a piece of work. Talk about an invasion of privacy."

"Oh, come on, let's cut past the fake outrage. You'd do worse to get a story."

"You don't know me."

"And that's why I did a little investigation. It's my job too, you know?"

Noah seemed as impressed as he was annoyed. "So, which ones are they? I followed everyone."

Charlie was coy. "First, answers. Why do you have photographs of the camp personnel in your camera?"

"I was doing a little investigation, too. Remember, it's my job."

Charlie shrugged her concession of the point before Noah continued. "Which ones are they, and how do you know?"

"All in good time. I am not interested in them, anyway. They are minnows. I need to get to the big fish."

"How can you be sure you have the right guys?"

"I am sure. You just need to trust me."

"Trust someone who goes through my images?"

"I've done worse."

Noah squinted and stared deep into her eyes, before bobbling out a non-committal grunt. "What do you need?"

"They get the same time off every week. I checked the logbook at the guardhouse earlier." Noah threw her a questioning glance. Charlie smiled back. "What? I was bored. Every day is a workday. Anyway, they leave the site an hour before dark every third Friday night. They arrive back in just before eleven hundred hours each week."

"Who?"

"Need another clue? I checked the rota. They have been doing it for months. They're embedded for sure."

"Not a great clue."

"Okay. This may help." Charlie flipped through the camera, scanned the memory stick, and centered a zoomed image on the display.

When she held the screen in Noah's line of sight, he thumped the wheel. "Sanchez. I knew it!"

Charlie scoffed. "Actually, you didn't."

"Ha, you have me there. You know what I mean. At least they were on my suspects list."

"Along with half the camp, judging from your camera's memory card."

Noah raised his defenses. "I knew it had to come from that office. That's why I followed them all. Many times. He gave nothing away. He takes differing routes, eats at different stalls. Meets no one. Just military tourists, sharing cups of tea and the odd hookah pipe."

"Different places, but the same face." Charlie pulled out her partner's camera and clicked through the photos. "Scroll left, notice anything?"

Noah followed the instructions, then threw out a blank look. "And?"

"Look in the background."

Noah blustered. "You got me."

"It's the same tea seller."

The camera was snatched from her grasp. "No way? Let me see that."

Charlie found it impossible not to look and feel smug. "Every time. The devil is in the detail."

Noah didn't seem used to being bested, especially by a woman. "What next?"

"Next, we follow them, the next time they leave camp."

"And we see where they lead us?"

"It's not where, it's who. We're after the big fish, remember?"

Over on the street's corner, an all-male crowd had slowly gathered. "What's that?" asked Charlie. Unsure, Noah shook his head and opened the van window. The snarling and jeering from a dogfight infected the air. "Is that?" Noah's shake of the head switched to a nod. Charlie was disgusted. "I can think of another name for these people, and it isn't resilient. Come on, let's get out of here. I've seen all I need to see today."

As the pickup window closed, the dog fight intensified. Charlie was incensed. "Get me away from here before I get myself involved in another riot."

CHAPTER 12

Two Fridays later, Charlie and Noah sat together in a faded blue 1960s Citroen van. Battered around the edges, the little van fitted the street scene perfectly.

The pair rode low in their seats, peering back in the door mirrors, for signs of suspicious life. Fifty yards back up the road, everyday life tried its best to seem normal, despite the circumstances. Tensions in the van were mounting as they anticipated the departure of their two suspects.

"Will this make it?" Charlie tapped the bashed dashboard.

"It's lasted this long."

"It doesn't scream, *high-speed chase*."

"True, but it whispers, *won't stand out from the crowd*."

Charlie conceded. "I guess you're more used to undercover work than me."

"You're catching on fast. That was good work uncovering the guys."

"Not really. It was basic police work."

"With a little extra curricular support activity."

"Maybe. It just seems to me that no one really wanted to get to the truth before now."

"Before you."

"I don't think anyone was looking seriously before. There were too many other priorities. Anyone willing to scratch beneath the surface would have found the evidence."

"Well, you're certainly a surface scratcher."

Before Charlie could catch Noah's pitch, she noticed movement behind her. "There!" In response, the pair slid lower in their seats.

The Sanchez ambled out, head held high, casual clothes. Little was said, as if they knew exactly where they were going. Charlie slid over her black burka before reaching for the door. Noah stayed her hand. "Hang on. Walk behind me. Carry this." Noah handed over a bulging plastic bag.

"What's in it?"

"Old washing, but it sits well. Walk stooped, they all do it."

Charlie's screwed-up face showed she was irked by the chauvinistic generalization. Noah pointed out his defense. "Look!"

To her great annoyance, when she scanned the populous present, the generalization seemed to hold true. Charlie understood the protocols, even if every cell in her body disagreed with them. "Let's get going." The door handles were pulled.

Under a cloud of silent observation, the separated pair entered through the crowd. Charlie waddled, five steps behind Noah, across the street from their targets. Keeping a distance, she kept her hidden eyes on the suspects. Noah moved forward, under the concealment of a change of outfit and a tight headdress. The main streets were preferred. The suspects moved with ease, as if they had nothing to hide. A quick dart across a busy junction almost caught Charlie off guard.

She moved toward Noah. As she crossed the street, an old man on a bicycle, at the end of his rope, clung to the rigging on a speeding canvas-covered truck.

Two vastly different worlds almost collided. With all positions regained, the pursuit adopted a more manageable pace. Paths deviated around a baby blue truck that stood out in stark contrast to the drab surroundings. As they gave the truck a wide berth, a faded red tractor and trailer hauling muddy soil rattled past.

Dirt flew.

Charlie waved to grab Noah's attention when the Sanchez suddenly darted sideways up a shaded alley. Noah jumped across the street to play catch up. Charlie followed in his quickened footsteps. Under a line of homemade flags, fluttering in the wind, Charlie bundled past a woman of indeterminate age, sheltering from the realities of her existence. A shrouded grandmother with a wide girth was given a wider berth as the pair rounded into the alley.

Charlie almost ran into the back of Noah when he stopped and hopped into a storefront.

Crumpled and disturbed, Charlie found the reason for the stoppage. Across the alley, Sanchez was stopping to take tea not ten yards away.

Charlie pushed Noah into the shop and out of sight. As Noah regained his bearings, Charlie exploited her vantage point behind the veil. The men were well placed, with a view of all four corners of the small dirt square that housed a brisk fruit and veg market. A small café was open for business and reaping the benefits of the renewed freedoms brought since the fall of the Taliban.

The rising optimism in the square bled through into the bright orange canvases covering every stand. Row after row of carrot salesmen sat chipping their goods into a bowl. Everyone sold the same thing to the same people. Each salesman seemed engaged in outshouting the others, to little effect.

They'll go home hoarse before they go home rich.

In the bedlam, the two sedentary suspects fidgeted. No words were exchanged. The longer they sat, the more they squirmed. Noah had repositioned himself behind a spinnable display, selling cheap plastic sunglasses. An overly keen salesman threatened to give the game away until Noah quietly ushered him away with the aid of a paper bribe. The pair went shopping for sunglasses together. "What do you think?"

"I can get close with the burka. I'm going in."

Noah grabbed her arm. "No! Wait!"

Charlie pulled on defiantly. Afraid of creating a scene, Noah let go. Emboldened by the presence of other women, out and about, she pushed on, up close and impersonal.

A kebab seller flapping smoke and flies with a well-thumbed newspaper provided the perfect distraction, as she positioned herself at a plastic table and chairs next to her prey.

The suspect didn't seem to suspect.

She held her shaky ground

The owners of nearby over-stocked stalls kept up a roaring trade that helped distract from Charlie's presence.

Charlie kept guard.

Nearby, a blackened bowl of rice and mystery meats sizzled under the watchful, smoky eyes of the young agitator, stirring the pot. A lazy-eyed man stabbed at roasting nuts with a large, curved knife, warding off customers with every flash of his blade.

Charlie ordered coffee to avoid the difficulties of eating with a face covering.

Looking around she spied Noah cowering in the corner of a newsagents, looking at faded post cards and plastic toys. The latest episode in her investigations looked to be giving Noah and episode all of his own.

When the tarry cup arrived, she paid cash and thanked the man.

Her language and her currency were both local.

Her smile was lost behind the veil.

Lifting the little cup to take her first sip, her heart ran cold.

Approaching front and center was her newfound friend from the stores, the quartermaster, Harry Benning.

CHAPTER 13

Charlie sat in panicked concealment behind the folds of her burka.

She partially lifted her fabric mask and took a sip of her coffee, the strong bitterness grounding her nerves. The clink of teacups and muted chatter of locals provided a steady hum of background noise, but her focus was elsewhere.

She had edged her chair to the table nearest to Sanchez. He sat alone, a man out of place but hiding it well. He stirred his coffee, craned his gaze, and glanced at his phone, many times. Charlie noted the tension in his shoulders,

He's waiting for someone.

Charlie's gaze flicked to the other patrons. Men in traditional Afghan attire smoked and laughed, paying her no mind. A woman in a brightly colored hijab haggled over the price of bread at a nearby stall.

The quartermaster looked out of place in his ill-fitting local garb, his pale face already slick with sweat. Charlie's anger was drowned out by her wailing disappointment.

What the hell is he doing here?

Harry's gaze darted around before he made a beeline for Sanchez's table. He slid into the seat across from him, leaning forward as if to make himself smaller. Sanchez's eyes widened briefly, then narrowed into a glare.

"What the hell are you doing here?" Sanchez's voice was low, but Charlie caught the edge in his tone.

Clearly this isn't who Sanchez was waiting to see or wanting to see.

Harry fidgeted, his hands clasped tightly on the table. "I had to come and see you."

"For God's sake, not here." Sanchez's voice dropped further, his lips barely moving.

Charlie leaned in so far, she almost fell over. Her chair took a nudging.

Too mad to notice. Harry's eyes flicked around nervously. "I can't talk to you inside. You know that."

"It's worse out here," Sanchez hissed. He leaned forward, fueled with frustration. "Jesus, Harry, think for once."

"Look around," Harry said, his voice trembling but insistent. "No one here speaks English. We're safe."

Charlie lowered her gaze and took another sip of her coffee. The ceramic cup was warm in her hand, the small gesture helping her maintain her cover. Her pulse quickened as she listened, her ears straining to catch every word.

"They'll never know," Harry added, almost pleading.

Sanchez's chair scraped against the ground as he shifted closer to Harry.

Unbeknownst to him, he had just edged closer to his eavesdropper. Charlie stopped leaning but kept listening.

"What the hell is this?" barked Sanchez.

"I don't like it," Harry interrupted, his voice cracking.

Sanchez's eyes narrowed. "What?"

Harry hesitated, then leaned closer. "Her."

"Who?" Sanchez's voice cut through the murmurs of the café.

"Glass." Harry's face twisted. "She's been snooping."

Sanchez leaned back, scoffing. "She's a nobody. Snooping is what they do."

"She's more than that," Harry insisted, his voice barely above a whisper.

Sanchez rolled his eyes. "She's an airhead wannabe. Thinks every man will faint in her presence. Typical dumb blonde."

Charlie's grip on her cup tightened, but she forced herself to remain still. The insult stung, but she dismissed the anger out of hand, out of practicality.

Let him think that, she thought, her mind racing.

It will give me the edge.

"I think we need to pull the plug," Harry said, his tone shaky.

Sanchez's smirk vanished, replaced by a glare. "I'll pull your plug. Man up. She's got nothing. I sent her on a wild goose chase. Silly bitch will be lost for weeks. By that time, she'll be sent home."

Harry shook his head. "I'm not so sure."

"Look, we both agreed," Sanchez said, his voice firm. "We need this. You run the authorizations, I do the rest. It's a few scribbled signatures from you. I'm doing all the work."

Harry shot back, making his rising voice easy to hear. "I'm taking the risk," "It will come back to haunt me."

"It's on us both," Sanchez countered, his tone sharp but lowered. "Look, we're nearly there."

"We've done enough," Harry said, his voice trembling.

Sanchez blazed. "My ass we have. We're one last score away from-"

"That's when the bank robbers get caught," Harry interrupted.

Sanchez leaned forward in agitation. "Jesus, take a look around. This isn't Hollywood. This is Afghanistan. This isn't the movies. Christ, man up."

Harry's shoulders slumped, his face pale. "Please," he said softly.

Sanchez's voice was a low growl. "Shut it."

Harry opened his mouth to protest, but Sanchez cut him off. "We can't get out. If we pull out, they'll come for us."

"Who?" Harry's voice cracked.

Sanchez's expression hardened. "You know who. The Pillars."

Charlie took a double take. *The Pillars?*

Terror flashed Harry across his face. "I didn't sign up for this."

"It doesn't matter what you signed up for," Sanchez said coldly. "The person who loaned you the pen gets to write the rules."

Harry blinked, his confusion evident. "What does that mean?"

"It means you're in it to the end," Sanchez said, his voice steely. "Or they will end you."

Harry's head dropped into his hands. "Oh, Jesus."

"You knew the score," Sanchez said, leaning back. His voice softened, almost reassuring. "Look, hang in there. We're nearly done."

Harry's lips quivered as he nodded slowly, looking more like a defeated man than a collaborator.

Charlie took another sip, the bitter tang or caffeine doing little to remove the bitter, taste of deceit.

With his agitation on the rise, it was Sanchez who pulled down the wall of silence.

Harry couldn't help himself. "Where is he?"

"Relax. This place is a zoo. It'll be the traffic."

"He's never late. I smell a rat."

"I smell panic. Get hold of yourself."

When the waiter arrived with the falafels, fake grins were thrown in all directions.

Sanchez couldn't wait for the waiter to leave. "Look, we have three more drops. Then, we'll be done and rich."

"I know, but-"

Across the open café trudged the tea seller, an urn strapped to his back, fluffy beard stuck to his chin. Low brow, high energy mid-twenties. A click of the fingers brought the tea boy to heel.

The ceremony began with practiced ease. Charlie lifted her veil slightly, sipped her coffee, and listened hard for a conversation that never materialized.

Out of the corner of her shroud, she noticed the tea seller set a small cloth underneath the tea urn. After the teas were dispensed and the monies exchanged, the seller busied himself in the quest for a new customer.

The cloth remained in situ.

After a few glances to the edges of the market, Sanchez lifted the cloth, mopped his brow, then slid it into his breast pocket.

Cool customer.

Across at the store, Noah jittered. His gesticulations seemed destined to give the game away. When a nearby seller confronted Noah, Charlie thought the game was up. She signaled for him to leave.

He didn't.

Instead, he pointed behind her.

Charlie's silent alarm bells rang at the sight of an approaching Afghan policeman. Charlie slowly turned her shoulder to a position where she could view the scene from a slightly offset angle. The officer walked with purpose, yet each stride brought more menace. A poor facsimile of the genuine article, his ragged uniform seemed at odds with his mirrored sunglasses. Onlookers looked away as he parted the crowd. Charlie leaned closer when everyone sloped away. Harry noticed the policemen first. "Oh, God."

Sanchez hung tough. "If he stops, let me do the talking. It's routine. There aren't a lot of Westerners out in the streets–"

Bang! Bang!

The policeman's service pistol called out twice. To Charlie's horror, Harry slumped without drawing breath. Sanchez dived to the floor, staggering to his feet.

Bang! Bang!

Two more shots. Sanchez stumbled sideways, writhing, and fumbling for a weapon. Instinctively, Charlie jumped for cover. Shrieks, screams, and smoke filled the air as the policeman moved in for the kill.

Bang!

Bang!

Single shots were sent into each flailing head before the policeman calmly holstered his weapon and marched from the square.

Blood, guts, and brains coated the scene. Panicked onlookers fled the scene faster than the assassin. Screeching, women yanked away gawking children. The policeman never broke sweat, as cool as any killer.

"Hey!" Fearlessly, Noah shouted and ran after the assassin.

Now under threat, the policeman broke into a sprint. Amid the terror, the foot race grew legs. Handgun on display, Noah chased after the killer, intent on justice.

Bang!

A callous, aimless shot snapped from the assassin's gun, sending everyone, including Noah, skidding to the floor. The assassin gathered pace as Noah rose and rejoined the pursuit.

As the crowds fled, Charlie held her ground. The cocktail of violence left her shaken. With faltering purpose, she forced herself to make a move. Under the pretense of trying to save the already departed souls, she ransacked the corpses.

Charlie knew the score.

Precise bullet strikes.

Head and heart shots.

A professional hit.

The car screeching off into the distance could barely be heard over the rabid cries of the crowd. Through the fog of fear, Charlie worked on. With great care, she callously stripped the bleeding corpses, irrespective of immediate interest or value.

Pockets were plundered and clues were captured.

Noah scrambled back around the corner, exacerbated and empty-handed. His shaking head spoke volumes. "They're gone. Come on. We need to get out of here." His pleas went unheeded.

Charlie lifted everything that could be used in evidence. I.D.s, the tea seller's cloth, and the hidden pistol were all pocketed. As the scattered crowd slowly circled, Charlie threw the bloody finds into her plastic bag. When the onlookers grew in number and curiosity, Noah became insistent. "We go. Now!" He grasped Charlie by the wrist, almost yanking her arm from its socket. "Now!"

Charlie yielded. "Who are we running from?"

"Everyone. We can't be here."

The pair ripped through the shredded fabric of the square, heads down, without looking back. Corner after corner were taken at speed. It took a good few twists and turns before Noah let go. The pair ran on, cannoning off walls and everything and everyone in their paths.

An old lady dressed head to toe in black vented her spleen after being knocked sideways by the rampaging couple. Apologies were not provided. They were too panicked to offer translations and too afraid to speak English. Onwards they fled, never looking back, never drawing breath.

Their pace eventually slowed a hundred yards into their flight. Noah took the lead as Charlie slowed back into a position of subservience. As soon as they could draw breath, their disbelief turned to debate. Charlie raged. "I thought you said it was safe!"

"That's not about this town. That's about money. There's no way that was random."

"Don't you think I can't work that out? That was a hit."

Noah gestured for them to lower their voices and their speed. In defiance of her pumping adrenaline, Charlie leveled out her pace and her voice. "The double tap. I have seen those tactics before. That was a stone-cold hit."

Noah shook. "Who would do that?"

Charlie didn't break her slowing stride. "Find out the why, then we will find out the who."

"So why?"

"Could be a host of reasons. My favorites would be that either they were getting greedy, or their partners were cleaning house."

"Cutting ties?"

"They knew a lot." She offered.

"Maybe they were owed a lot of money and their partners thought a hail of bullets would be a cheaper way to make payment."

"I don't know."

Lost for a reason, the pair tramped on, desperate to make sense of the world, desperate to distance themselves from recent events.

Out front, Noah led the way. Just when Charlie felt the need to offer up some suggested redirections, the old Citroen van fell into view. For once, she was glad to have kept her mouth shut. The pair bundled themselves into the back of the tiny old van. Noah was stunned. Reaching through under the front seat, he retrieved a half empty, half bottle of whiskey. The lid was twisted off. Ever the gentleman, Charlie was offered a first swig. Her new partner didn't stand on ceremony. After guzzling the greatest part of the remaining whisky, Noah coughed and sputtered his way to a question. "What the hell just happened?"

"You saw more than me. I was under a table. It was a targeted hit for sure."

Noah tousled his hair in turmoil. "Who were they?"

"Crooked police, getting in on the action? They could be double crossers or vigilantes, hell bent on removing infidels. There could be any number of explanations."

"One thing's for sure, they were not legit. They drove off in a battered old jeep."

"Understood."

Noah seemed on the verge of collapse, so she placed a hand on his arm. "You did well. Thanks for getting me out of there."

"Don't thank me. I was just desperate to get out. I've never seen a murder before."

"Your first is always your worst." The words flew from her mouth, without thought.

"Is that true?"

Charlie reconsidered. "Actually no. For me, they still hit hard. Especially when it's that up close."

Noah didn't seem to want to dwell on the deaths. He raced past the moment. "What will we do next?"

"We have time. Let's check the takings."

Charlie's pockets were emptied onto the wooden flip-down table. She separated the items into selected locations. Commentary and interruption were prevalent.

First on the table was the illicit sidearm. Charlie sniffed the muzzle. "Hasn't been fired recently."

There were two sets of assorted keys and another small key with no markings. A well-worn, poorly folded map of the region was the next item to be tabled. Next to be pulled out were the blood-soaked photos of Harry, surrounded by a proud and loving family.

The photos were shared.

They made tough viewing.

The tiny pocketbook that was produced next had most of its pages congealed in body matter. The men's wallets were equally stained and constrained. She found two lighters and a cigar cutter.

A half-smoked, liberally loaded joint was produced, much to Noah's delight.

"I'll maybe snag that later." Noah leaned back a little, concerned that one liner had backfired on him. "I'm not crazy."

Charlie made a big scene with a small prop. "Would your craziness stretch to this?" A small powdery packet of white powder flapped into view.

Noah became his very one on-person snatch squad. "Is that what I think it is?"

Charlie gave a resigned nod. "Looks like it. Only enough for personal use."

Noah was disgusted. "Personal misuse. This place really got to them. What do you make of it?"

Charlie had little clue. "Not much. They mentioned the Pillars, does that mean anything to you?"

"In what context?"

"In any context, have you heard of the Pillars?"

Noah caught up. "I've heard of them. Heroin smugglers. Low rent."

"Really? Do you think this was just them trying to score?"

Noah had his doubts. "Nah, why the hit?"

"So, what about these Pillars?"

Noah took his time with the explanation. "They emerged not long after the start of the war. Cash and drugs through the opium roads into Pakistan and Iran."

"Do you think these guys were involved in that?"

Noah sounded open to the suggestion. "Possibly. It all goes out through a neighboring town, Sangin. A lawless place all about heroin."

"Didn't we clean that up?"

Noah smirked. "My, you are new. They just got better at hiding it. With the threat of death from the Taliban gone, smuggling is rife."

"So, it's bigger than money."

Noah wasn't convinced. "It's possible, but it's a stretch. The likely explanation is that they were users who got in too deep."

"So, you shoot them in broad daylight?"

"It's one way of getting everyone else to pay up. Set an example."

Charlie felt her bottom lip numbing, a true sign of post traumatic shock setting in. Somehow, biting her lip wasn't an option. "First Ross, now these two. Notice the theme?"

Noah stalled.

"Westerners."

"It should be no surprise to you we're in the firing line. Look at what we've done around here."

"So, we're all targets?" she asked.

"We're all targets."

"These two are different, surely."

"Because?"

"They were criminals."

"So, they were asking for it?"

"Well, they were stealing money to fund their drug smuggling activities."

Noah bobbled his head, so Charlie continued. "Come on. It's a great plan. You hide the cash you're stealing and make a hefty profit in the bargain."

"Doesn't justify murder, though. Like I say. We're all targets."

Charlie thumbed through the blood-soaked pages of the notebook. "So, who can we take this to?"

"And say what? You were tailing suspects, watched them die, did nothing, stripped them, and left them to the locals? I realize you couldn't have done anything, but the fact you stripped them doesn't look good. And besides, who do you call? You said yourself your bosses are useless. Even then, the evidence is flimsy."

"There were witnesses."

"No one saw anything. In war, everyone keeps their head down, even when the bombs aren't flying."

Charlie gripped the book with both hands and stared at the stained cover. "I'll run through this tonight, do a bit more digging, and we can see about it in the morning."

"That's too late. The time to come clean is now. Digging around dead people's property is past the point of no return."

Charlie's mind was made up. "We still don't know how far through the organization these crimes have leached. Besides, we have nothing to hide and nothing to offer. I say we go on." Noah didn't argue.

She used a rag to wipe her prints off every item in order. The wallets were the last items to be polished off before they were cast down into the gutter, for some unsuspecting local to find.

Noah squinted. "They let you think that. So, we're doing this?"

Charlie dangled a set of keys in front of her. "Let's get back. I have a spot of ransacking to do before these are reported missing."

"You should have time. They are in civvies and have no IDs, and the investigators are Afghan police."

Charlie pulled a deep breath. "So, we go after the cash and the drugs. Wherever that leads."

Noah stalled. "I can only go so far. I am press, not FBI."

"Understood. I am taking this as far as I can. We talk to no one. Keep it out of the press, for now. Deal?"

Noah had no hesitation. "Deal. Oh, one last thing." He lifted his camera and snapped a host of photographs of Charlie. "What are you doing?"

"I'm a journalist. I need a face to name if all this goes south."

"And they said chivalry is dead. Print anything against my wishes and I'll be the one doing the shooting."

Noah laughed.

Charlie didn't.

"Ok, but you have to play your part too." Cautioned Noah.

"In what way?"

"No formal reports. We need to let this play out. If you send in a formal report, you acknowledge you were there."

"So, I wait for the formal identification."

"We both do. This is a hell of a story. We just need to play it out."

As Charlie bobbled her head in agreement, she looked down.

Not for the first time, she had blood on her hands.

CHAPTER 14

Behind the security of her housing unit's locked door, Charlie set to work.

The scrubbed notebook made no sense to Charlie. Its bloody leaves held a plethora of unintelligible clues and codes. Try as she might, she found no solace or inspiration from the intricately penciled entries. It had been a couple of hours since she had dropped the wallets in the blind spot outside the guardhouse. No findings had been made on any front since then.

She needed a breakthrough. She needed a break. A swig of her favorite quartermaster's Special Brew cleared her mind and her nasal passages. After two more mouthfuls and a couple of stretches, the investigations recommenced. This time investigations were completed as she paced inside the safety and seclusion of her own room.

Over the next few hours, Charlie scribbled key phrases, prominent words, and codes on large pieces of paper. Those notes were then taped to the steel walls. Distancing herself from the detail, she stepped back and stared. Scribbles morphed into scrolls.

Every new angle of attack seemed more obtuse than the last.

Nothing chimed, nothing rhymed.

The painfully slow internet connection dropped with such frequency that every follow up line of digital inquiry was closed down or stalled before it had even begun. Staring at the far-from-blank walls eventually gave her square eyes. She took a break from her studies. The remaining artifacts snatched from the bodies were set out across the bed. When she spied the tea seller's cloth, a new line of inquiry was opened.

Isolated from the rest of the booklet, the numbers on the cloth stood alone. Thin nib, permanent marker, bled into the cotton fabric: *609021- P1.25.*

The entries made difficult reading, despite her keen interest in ancient cyphers and rudimentary FBI code breaking training. She understood the stand-alone nature of the code would likely hold the key to the cypher. In sequence, she reviewed the alpha-numerical code.

Backwards, forwards, she scanned for patterns. Letters were switched for numbers and vice versa. Something sparked when she split the hyphenated text.

The number could be a date in reverse.

She scribbled in reverse. The patterns confirmed *609021* to be *12th September 2006.*

This only worked using UK style date and month formatting, but given the Afghan's history with the UK, she guessed this would be how the locals would write the date. It was a shoe-horned theory, but nothing else seemed to fit. She assumed the second section of the text was a time or a location. There weren't enough details for it to be a map reference, so a timing reference was more likely.

The timings were less contrived. Standard issue am and pm entries threw her mind. She had programmed on the twenty-four-hour clock. *P1* could mean 1pm. The *.25* suffix could equate to a twenty-five past or even one quarter past the hour. She stood back, her head spun at high revs. She had forced out a clue, a code.

Quarter past one in the afternoon of the 12th September 2006.

Conscious that there was every possibility she had contrived that clue to produce a credible outcome, Charlie gave it only a limited chance of success. On its own, an engineered date was of little use. She needed more. Inspired by her potential code breakthroughs, she returned to the pocketbook.

The names gleaned from the various entries seemed genuine, including Gasim, Feisal, Sherif.

The list of suspects was long, unrecognized, and vague.

One name stood out, Feisal.

It had been circled twice.

Eventually, patterns emerged. The Roman numerals described the value or weight of the transactions. M equaled a kilo or a thousand dollars. Then the hammer fell. There was a dash above the L, turning the entry into fifty thousand.

Whilst the last entry mentioned fifty thousand dollars, the previous entries totaled nearly five million dollars. *Incredible.*

Charlie's eyes watered at the magnitude of the mendacity. It looked like millions of dollars were being stolen and various routes were being taken to export the illicit gains. Hardest to follow were the locations.

Taking on board more brew and offloading her frustrations on the camp bed pillow focused her mind. The GPS co-ordinates made no sense. She remembered the previous heavy handed code manipulations. When the GPS co-ordinate coding was reversed, Charlie realized the *E 205 46N 22 4 23* entry actually translated into *32 4'22"N64°50'2"E.*

She went on a painfully slow virtual journey before the lethargic internet search yielded answers. Pulling up a geo-map on her laptop, the GPS co-ordinates finally pointed to a small compound west of a nearby town. She tapped the screen in confirmation. "Sangin."

When the pixelated location eventually scrolled across the screen, Charlie yelped in delight. She stood and punched the air, pleased with the outcome, proud of her work. Special Brew was endured in celebration.

Knowing the location was significant, but understanding the elements around how the information was disguised proved to be even more important. The trick of reversing the wording seemed central to their codification. She applied the same logic to the final code. *JRTPOM.*

As with most codes, she ran through the protocols, numbering the letters, reversing the digits. The hours of training on code breaking and security profiling were proving worthless. Every attempt failed. Every keystroke built her frustration. She thumped the board down on the desk, forcing it to jump to the side. Prompted by the shift, she changed lanes. One move to the right yielded nothing. Two moves to the right made no sense. One move to the left on the qwerty keyboard and the letters jumped from the screen. Hidden in the gobbledygook, *JRTPOM* had morphed into *HEROIN.*

Charlie matched the final entries from the book with the tea seller's textile.

609021 / p1.25/ _D / JRTPOM / E "2 '05 46N "22 '4 23 /

She leaned the table lamp in close, pulled out a clean sheet of paper, and etched out the broken codes.

On the twelfth of September, this year, at a quarter past one in the afternoon, 50 thousand dollars would be needed to buy heroin at the location, 32 4'22"N64°50'2"E near Sangin. Feisal could be the man.

She slapped the bunk mattress for a job well done. After reality truly set in, she told herself, *a job half done.* She knew the information would be worthless unless acted upon.

With so much at stake and zero time to think, Charlie fought hard to ground herself. She found solace in solitude, but only one person truly tempered her recklessness. Her father, Pop. Her BlackBerry was retrieved from the bottom of her kit bag. Most of the time it had lain, out of sight, out of mind, and out of battery.

Generally, her phone remained switched off. No one ever called. No colleagues, no friends, no family. Only her father knew the number, and he was under strict instructions to never call when she was on an operation.

Those that did call only ever tried to sell her something she didn't need. Her emails buzzed with junk most of the time. When official communications came through, they were typically low priority and behind the times.

Again, the green *on* switch didn't work, sending her in search of her charging cable. After it was retrieved and reconnected, she impatiently tapped away at the buttons until eventually power arrived.

Halfway through texting, she stalled and drew a breath.

The only thing certain about the road ahead was the inherent danger. Texting wouldn't do the trick.

She needed to hear his calming, safe voice. With a deep intake of breath, she flicked to the only phone number in the recent calls and pressed the green button. As always, the phone rang for an eternity.

Smiling at the prospect of speaking to her father, she waited with bated breath.

As soon as the line clicked on, she butted in.

"Hey, Pop."

CHAPTER 15

"My dear Charlotte. How are you doing, my girl?"

"Very good, very good."

"How's Kuwait?"

She had always added a little curvature to her home truths, but on this operation, the bend had become crooked to the point of breaking. Pop was better off not knowing, and she was better off knowing he didn't know. "It's hot and dusty." At least the weather wasn't a lie.

"Anything like Iraq?"

She said what he wanted to hear. "It's safer."

"And what is it you're doing again?"

"I told you. Tracking cash."

"Stolen cash?"

"No, nothing like that. It's admin. The Fed ships it over and we make sure the numbers add up. We don't do the protection. We have troops do that. It's basically the same boring research I do back home, without the donuts and aircon."

"But it's money, not artifacts?"

"Yeah, more paper trails than treasure maps."

"I like how that sounds."

"For you or for me?"

"For both of us." He laughed, although Charlie knew he wasn't joking. In Charlie's world, there were two kinds of people, those that evade conflict and those that enjoy it. Her father sat at the opposite end of that spectrum from her. He often said she got her feisty nature from the mother she never met. Confused by the difference between a sociopath and psychopath, she knew she had a boot in at least one of those camps. Her father stood as far away from those conditions as possible. "Are you sure it's safe?"

"As safe as Deanwood."

Pop recognized the reference to one of the most dangerous wards in DC. He didn't seem to enjoy her evasive response. "You know what I mean."

"Trust me. I am nowhere near the fighting. The only things I need to worry about are paper cuts."

"Are you making any friends?"

"I'm here to work."

"Do you have any nice colleagues at least?"

"Not really. They all view my involvement as an intrusion. They are all pretty defensive."

"Are they playing nice?"

"Actually, I am heading off to meet a guy soon."

"A mystery man? Not a stranger?"

Charlie snatched at an answer. "No. A colleague, named Feisal."

"Like the Prince in Lawrence of Arabia?"

Charlie had no clue what her father was babbling on about. "Yeah, something like that. He's certainly a character."

"What does he do?"

"He's a nomad. A trader. I'm off to see if he's selling anything interesting."

"You're becoming quite the nomad yourself."

"We can't all live in one house and have one job our whole life."

Pop sounded a little hurt by Charlie's swipe. "I can't see why not. Just tell me you're safe and sound."

"Don't worry, Pop. I am as safe as always and I am as sound as I will ever be. What have you been up to?"

Her father let out an almighty sign of disappointment. "New intake of students. Every one of them is less interested and dimmer than the last. What do they teach them at high school these days?"

"It can't be an easy start when they have to enter school through a metal detector."

"Don't you do that?"

"Yeah, but at least they issue me with a gun."

"You're not helping my nerves."

"Sorry, Pop. If it makes you feel any better, I wasn't given a gun with me on this tour."

"I guess it means you're in a safer position."

"Exactly. That's a good place to leave it, don't you think?"

"Over and done? Just like that? How's Rostam?"

Charlie knew Pop's question was one part interest in her dog and one part eagerness to elongate the conversation. "Oh, he's fine. One of my neighbors is looking after him."

"Glad to hear it. I don't want him to be neglected like you neglect your old Pop." The laugh he threw down the line only failed to take the tip off the barb.

"You know how it is over here, Pop. Limited telecoms, so the grunts get first pick on the bandwidth. Busy schedule. Gotta get up early."

"I understand, girl. I am just happy to have heard your voice. You know, I worry."

"You worry enough for both of us. That way, I don't need to."

"Thanks for the call. Love you."

"Love you too, Pop."

"Stay saf–"

Click.

She had killed the call before Pop's final sign off. She was glad to hear his voice, but gladder he didn't hear the truth. The prospect of the adventures to come set her nerves on edge. A simple tour of duty to find missing dollars had uncovered potential multi-million-dollar thefts and an international drug smuggling ring.

To Charlie, caution was a character flaw found in the weak and principled. The decision to plunge in headfirst was hers and hers alone. She knew her mission. She was going after the money, chasing down heroin, and hunting a man named Feisal. Given the nature of the criminality, she knew she couldn't go through normal channels. The very same channels that would be sectioning the funds release were the same ones responsible for the thefts.

Charlie admired the location of the rendezvous point, next to a canal linked with the infamous Helmand River. Good connectivity, easy access, covered egress. Her fingers twitched at the prospect of adventure. There were no doubts and only one option. She was stepping into the fray.

All she needed now was to get her hands on fifty thousand dollars.

She had a good idea where to find it.

Stealing it would be a different thing altogether.

CHAPTER 16

Charlie dismissed the ethical arguments around stealing stolen money. To her, referencing the *greater good* quelled her qualms. She deduced the cash would already have been squirreled away. It was too late in the game. Sanchez's meticulously planned thefts would not have been executed at the last minute. The drop date was too close. The clock had been ticking since the first deadly gunshots hit their mark. She knew the deaths would be traced back to camp. Time and cash were in short supply.

The ante needed to be raised. Under cover of the enveloping night, Sanchez's housing unit was the first to be searched. On the days she spent tracking Sanchez around the base, she had found no purpose or rhythm to his routines.

Retracing his steps and recalling their habits yielded nothing of interest, other than a casually captured mental map of the compound's security cameras.

Hastily configured and haphazardly deployed, the system's numerous blind spots were easy to detect. The good news was that the field of vision had been set up to capture external threats, leaving the internal surveillance levels at substandard levels. The cameras, like the regime's fiscal governance, had been designed to keep an eye on only the locals.

In line with the initial parlance, locals were the only ones who couldn't be trusted. After a few successful bouts of subtle camera dodging, Charlie arrived at her targeted waypoint. A darkened blind spot close to Sanchez' unit. As hoped, there were no caution tapes, no cordoning mechanisms. He obviously hadn't yet been reported missing. That fact disturbed an already suspicious Charlie.

Perhaps the only person who'd miss him would have been Sanchez.

Maybe it's a trap.

Charlie had allocated fifteen minutes of her time to check for would-be assailants. She doubled that allocation to be certain. After nothing had moved, Charlie headed out, knowing her standing there any longer would itself draw attention.

The blood-soaked keys captured after the double murder had been washed down with the periodically available boiling water in Charlie's housing unit.

Over at the unit, those keys were set to work. After a process of elimination that took too long and made way too much noise, Charlie found the right key. It slid in and turned with ease. Once inside, her gloved hands left nothing untouched or out of place.

Every conceivable hiding spot was eventually ruled out from her lines of investigation. Nothing incriminating was discovered. Charlie kicked herself, for wasting valuable time.

Sanchez was the leader.

Harry was the patsy. It was far more likely he would be the one left holding incriminating contraband.

Every care was taken on her exit.

Having slid past the compound cameras, and skirted any personal contact, Charlie finally arrived in the shadows outside

Harry's housing unit. After checking the coast was clear, another stolen key was put to no-good use. After one last scan, she slid inside. A gloved hand switched on the lamp, sitting on a small table.

The dimly lit, sparsely furnished unit took no time to search. The last unused key did not fit the lock on the drawer of the bedside table. Dejected by the lack of progress, she slumped onto the bunk. With no other potential leads in sight, she pulled her utility knife and jammed the big blade into the lock mechanism on the table drawer.

With rising frustrations, she jabbed and twisted the knife with heightened ferocity. When she leveraged hard, the knife slipped and dropped on the floor. It was only then that she realized the room layout was different from standard protocols. Excited by the discovery, she yanked the bunk to one side. Underneath, below a rug, she found a long personal locker, cut into the floor of the housing unit. A small padlock held the locker shut. None of the keys worked.

Annoyed, she yanked at the padlock. That didn't work or help. The padlock was small but industrial. She sat back on the bed, down but not out. She stared in disbelief at the makeshift safe below, marveling at the audacity and ingenuity. The angle grinder used to cut a home in the container floor must have reverberated throughout the entire container complex, yet no one noticed. She remembered Noah's words. *In war everyone keeps their head down.*

It made perfect sense; no random unit search would throw up this devious hiding spot. It was only fumbling luck that helped her discover it. The underside of every surface was checked for a small key taped up, out of sight. Nothing turned up. Even more time was wasted, looking for the non-existent angle grinder. She uncovered a packet of Gauloises cigarettes.

Once a secret smoker, always a secret smoker.

As she fumbled around at the back of the bedside drawer, a set of matches flipped into view. Charlie gave the box a rattle, then pulled out a few matches. Charlie's face lit up at the sight of the matches. Extra-long, high quality, strike-anywhere cigar matches. Safety matches would have been useless, but with these strike-anywhere match heads, she stood a chance.

She remembered her chemistry lessons and explosives training. Besides phosphorus sulfide, these matches likely contained the potassium chlorate that supplies oxygen to make the match burn brighter. Her idea was crazy, but it stood an outside chance of success. She pulled a page from the calendar on the wall.

Poignantly the dates marked until the return, stateside were being checked off. She bowed her head, knowing there would be no more check marks added. She picked a month from a bygone time to avoid problems in the future.

The page was set flat on the side table. One by one, the chemicals on the top of each match were scraped off with her utility knife. Match tip after match tip fell onto the glossy page until around ten matches were lopped. The handle of the knife carefully pulverized the chemicals into a homogeneous fine powder. The magazine page was then creased to form a chute. The end of a bare match was then whittled to a fine point. That match was then used to scrape the fiery talc down the creased paper on into the keyhole in the padlock.

The improvised gunpowder was then packed in tightly, like an old musket barrel. Once jammed to the hilt, the whittled match head was spiked carefully into the keyhole. The last remaining match lit the protruding matchstick before Charlie stepped back. The wooden fuse took an eternity to burn, and much to Charlie's annoyance, threatened to extinguish itself along the way. Eventually, the flame reached its mark.

Bang!

The explosion flared through the padlock, popping the actuator, and freeing the shackle. The smoke damaged padlock, and Charlie's jaw, fell open.

It worked!

No worries were wasted on the noise of the micro-explosion. If people chose to ignore an angle grinder, then that small crack wouldn't register on an interest scale. She grappled with the padlock shackle and yanked up the door. Inside the locker, two long galvanized cases filled the homemade vault. Rabid fumbling of the case latches brought success. Amazed, but unsurprised, she sat back on the bunk. Dejection had turned to elation. The unit contained sealed plastic bags tied with green tags marked *Bank of Jordan.*

"Yes!" Charlie yelled louder than any angle grinder.

Money. Lots of it.

A quick cash count set the level of funds to be around the fifty-thousand-dollar mark. She had found the stash.

The locker was closed, the rug replaced, and the room swept clean. With meticulous care, all signs of disturbance and intrusion were eliminated. To avoid questions surrounding the smoky padlock, it was pocketed for future disposal. One last scan of the room cleared the runway for her departure. With no sounds of life outside, Charlie pulled the housing unit door ajar. Coast clear, she coolly exited the unit, steel case in hand. Even in the cold night air, her hands sweated within her glove as the leather grappled with the handle of the case.

Back under the protection of the night, she worked her way to the sanctuary of her unit. She hoped the other camp residents, like the cameras, were looking elsewhere. Her heart thumped in time to her quickening steps. Fighting the desperate urge to run, her thoughts outpaced her measured steps. She had no clue what she would say if the MPs caught her out and about, but she convinced herself that no lines had been crossed.

Gathering evidence would be the excuse.

There would be no looking back and no turning back.

Armed with the funds, a rendezvous with drug traffickers out in the Taliban heartland awaited.

CHAPTER 17

Charlie's blood pressure, along with the morning sun, was on the rise. A round of covering emails had been sent off in order of importance. Firstly, she provided her father with a brief, friendly email, heavy with optimism and light on facts.

Rostam's keeper, her neighbor Gabrielle was offered messages of gratitude, support, and an offer to pay for any damages or injuries caused by his over-boisterous antics. Her boss, Joey Sizemore, got the last email. Light on content, heavy on smoke, the note gave nothing away. She added a read receipt to the email, ever hopeful that she would be back in circulation before he'd even checked it. Bases covered; she had turned herself to the day ahead.

Charlie stood dressed in traditional, masculine Afghan attire, watching Noah reverse the old Citroen van up to the side of her housing unit.

"How did you get this in?" she asked.

Noah rubbed his thumb and fingers together. "They know me?"

"Like that, is it?"

"It's risk and reward. I offer a little reward. They take a little risk."

"I hope you're right. Park over there." It wasn't a request.

"Yessir." Intrigued, Noah pulled the van around to a section behind an open-sided garage. Charlie's hand signals helped him hit her mark. Charlie swung her kit bag around off her shoulder. Noah was in a boisterous mood. He smirked. "Taking me behind the bike sheds?"

Charlie's face held no schoolgirl smirk. "You better hope not. The only time I took boys behind the bike sheds was to kick their asses."

"My god you're serious?"

Charlie held a poker face. "Why joke about something like that?"

As Noah twisted his face in disbelief, Charlie set him straight. "I'm just kidding."

"Phew, I was going to say-"

"Every boy I beat up, I did in plain sight."

It was clear Noah couldn't see where the blurred line between truth and fiction lay. Charlie liked it that way. "What do you suppose we do with this?" She opened the kitbag.

Noah glared in amazement, before fear sent his head swiveling in all directions. "Where did you get this?"

"Call it the repatriation of funds. Seizure of illicit earnings."

"So, this is coming with us?"

"All the way."

Noah seemed to center himself. "Okay. Love the contents. Hate the bag. I've got something for you." Noah threw her a superior look, before ushering her round and into the back of the van. The back door was pulled. "Here." Out of eyeshot, he pulled a small camelback rucksack of faded tan and green. "This one is more discreet, and it's the right size."

"For what?"

"In here." With the spare wheel removed, the rucksack fitted the space under the bed of the truck perfectly. "Made to measure."

Charlie was impressed and suspicious. "You've done this before?"

"Ha. Maybe. Whiskey and cigarettes to bribe sources and guards are my limit." Charlie was then offered the rucksack. "Take a look inside."

She obliged. "It's empty."

"Look again. In the base."

Charlie turned the rucksack upside down. A discreetly placed pocket was covered by a crude Velcro strip. From inside the pocket, Charlie pulled a small handgun. "Ever ready."

Noah pushed the gun gently to the side. "Easy there, Tex."

Noah explained. "Colt Mustang."

"Pocket lite, thirty-eight Cal? Not quite standard issue for a member of the press."

"Well suited for underhand outings. Just keep it out of sight."

"So, it's our insurance policy."

"Over and above your money."

"Bribe then shoot?"

"Could say that. But it's an improvement. When I set out this morning, I thought our option was shoot, then shoot."

Charlie enjoyed getting tooled up. "Comms?"

"Check the Velcro pocket in the padding."

Charlie did so and pulled out a chunky Nokia phone sealed in a poly bag. "This is like a Swiss army rucksack."

Noah seemed genuinely concerned about her welfare. "I'm just trying to keep you out of harm's way. It's dangerous out there."

Charlie had heard it all before. "I know, and I appreciate the support."

"So, your BlackBerry?"

"Back at base, as advised."

"Yeah, you won't get a signal out there, anyway. The Nokia will see you right in the places that have signal around Afghanistan. On the shoulder strap, there's a business card for a company and contact that doesn't exist. The number on the ID card is real, but the international dialing code is wrong. Ignore it. It's an Afghan number. Just call it without the code."

Charlie was uncertain. "When I call the number, who answers?"

Noah lifted his chin in mini triumph. "Me, of course."

"So, it's a last resort kind of deal?"

He laughed. "Yeah, and you never know. I may pick up."

After making sure there were no onlookers, the cash was transferred.

"How much is in there?"

"Fifty grand."

Noah was astonished. "What?"

"Not quite enough to start a war, but enough for a drugs trade."

"Are you kidding me? Fifty-K is enough to start a war around here. Especially between two tribes. Come on, where did you find it?"

Charlie remained coy. "Let's just say it's a gift from my rich uncle. Uncle Sam."

Noah shook his head in admiration. "So, you're going through with this."

"As far as I can. The funny thing is, the bank notes were labeled as currency from the Bank of Jordan."

Noah subtly pulled a wad of banknotes from the rucksack. "Yeah, they do that to throw people off the scent, but the money still stinks."

The wad of cash was slipped inside Noah's tunic, much to Charlie's obvious surprise.

"Insurance. Around here it's easier to spend your way out of trouble than shoot your way out. Remember, the dollar is mightier than the sword."

"Do people still have swords?" Charlie wondered.

"They do where you're going." He offered.

"And these people we're going to meet, are they affiliated?"

"Affiliated?"

"Are they sanctioned by us?"

"Us?"

"The coalition."

"You're kidding, aren't you? It's the other way around. They let us operate as long as we don't interfere."

"More like we're sanctioned by them." After the pair climbed into the van and set off, Noah moved the conversation forward. "So, how did you wangle time away?"

"I just emailed my boss. Told him the investigation has taken a turn toward the mountains."

"Not a complete lie."

"I sent my weekly update saying I'm moving into an area without cellphone coverage, uncontactable for the time being."

"And they are okay with that? You, traveling alone."

"I told them I was heading up into the mountains with a couple of guys from the agency. They would look after me."

"Not that you need looking after."

"No, but it's a good ass cover for my boss if I get into trouble. As long as his ass is covered, he's not interested."

Noah got on board. "Plus, it can never be corroborated, because the agency never gives out operatives details."

Charlie tapped her temple playfully. "It also shows that they know I'm here, so I won't be trampling all over their operations."

"But you could be."

"What?"

"Trampling over their operations."

"Unlikely. There's only you so far."

"But I could be CIA."

Charlie chortled. "You? Doubt it."

"Why not?"

"Well, for a start, look at your dumbass sunglasses."

"What about them?"

"Cheap plastic crap from the local market."

"And?"

"No one in the CIA would be seen dead wearing those things. That's how you spot them."

"So, if you're wearing designer glasses, you're definitely CIA?"

"No. If you're wearing crappy plastic glasses, you're definitely not."

Noah gave it some thought. "You could be on to something. Latest edition RayBans?"

"Or Oakley wraparounds?"

"Yes! The ones with the multi-colored mirror lenses."

"You got it."

"Remind me to go buy some good glasses to confuse the hell out of people." A moment was shared. Noah still had questions. "And the guys in the office?"

"They will be glad of the break. I told them I had been called in for a full team review of another army office."

"Which one?"

"That's the great thing about being an investigator. Everyone believes you when you say *sorry, but that's confidential.*"

Noah slapped his thigh. "True that! I hear it all the time. So, what's the script?"

Charlie faltered. "I'll explain more once we're out of town. You know the destination. Sangin. Let's just get past the guards and we can chat."

Noah seemed edgier than his words suggested. "Okay. Just stay relaxed. The Canadian police aren't on duty yet, so these local guys will be fine. They check for bombs coming in, not cash going out. Don't smile too hard. Avoid eye contact. Pretend to be asleep. They will probably want to chat with you for hours. They don't get sights like you around here very often, and when they do, they admire the view."

Noah pushed a threadbare cushion across to Charlie's side of the van. "Here, try this. Get your head down."

"So, that's why the early start?"

Noah grinned. "Of course. Crime never sleeps, but authorities do." As they slid past the tall inner blast wall, the first local three policemen beamed and threw out the most pitiful of untrained, sleep-deprived salutes. At the main gate, open salutes turned to open palms. Financial grease was applied to expedite the swift opening of the compound barriers. Charlie's averted eyes rolled as they passed through the final barrier.

Charlie threw her head to the opening dawn. In the rearview mirror, she noticed the guards counting their recent blessings. On the ride out of town, the city streets narrowed, bringing the emerging population into closer focus. The goats feeding on a rubbish pile looked in better shape than their handler. Two teenagers pulled a wheelbarrow filled to the brim with rubble. The load was shared, one handle each. Open fires crackled into life, lighting the route. A rusted three-wheel moped loaded with orange plastic drums tied together sat idly, like a spike-less porcupine. It seemed incongruous to Charlie that anyone would ever need that many orange containers. Some way up the road, kids on a street corner sold illicit fuel in the same orange container. Suddenly, the reasons became apparent.

Rounding a corner, their van slowed after instruction from a British Army soldier. Rifle at the ready, the squaddie was taking no chances, and likely no prisoners. A temporary, early morning checkpoint had been set up to guard the crew of Western contractors fixing the connections on a power line. Five guards protected the crew of two.

"Seems a bit pointless. Any sniper could pick those guys off from a couple of hundred yards."

"Bit of a sniper expert?" asked Noah.

"More of a bucket truck expert." Charlie chuckled inwardly, remembering her time on the Baghdad heist. The moment, like the checkpoint, passed. A pedestrian wearing an anorak of garish multicolored squares, popular in the west, twenty years prior, caught her eye line. The man stood proudly as a soldier searched him. Hands and head were held high. The man punched the air in defiance of the intrusion. After being pushed to the side, he walked on, undefeated. Up ahead, two dirty-faced children jammed into the back of an old estate car stared back at a world they longed to leave behind. A burned-out bus at the roadside leaked black acrid smoke into the weeping dawn. The detritus of a town in turmoil and despair marred every turn of the way.

Clutter eventually turned into calmer countryside. Mile after mile of chilled desert stretched before them. High above, the crisp coating of fresh mountain frost glistened in the morning sun. Charlie had space to think. "Under my mattress, I have left a note explaining everything."

Noah turned to face her. "So, you're going all the way."

"With or without you."

"It's got to be without me. I have a price on my head with some of these men. I can get you close, but that's it. After that, you're on your own. We agreed that, yeah?"

Charlie shrugged. "I like it that way."

"So, you prefer solo efforts."

Charlie didn't like to face that face. "It's more like I am getting used to them."

"Where is your team in all of this?"

"Stuck in a wasteland between ignorance and arrogance."

Noah. "As the old adage goes, Military Intelligence is an oxymoron."

"With the emphasis on moron."

Noah took some time to form his follow up. "There's another way to look at this. It's the true trait of a megalomaniac that they think only they can fix things."

Charlie was too sleepy and too much in agreement to argue. The moment drifted past. For breakfast, the couple ate up the miles. To stave off her hunger pains, Charlie raised the camera and started snapping. Permission was neither requested nor granted. Noah seemed too thoughtful to care. After a long period of reflection, Charlie opened up. "Take what you find to the press, not my bosses. They're blind, deaf, and dumb. Mostly dumb."

"It won't come to that."

Charlie continued. "Don't publish until you are certain I'm not coming back."

"You will be fine."

"I know, but like I told you after the murders, I'm going as far as I can."

"Okay, but remember, don't lose sight of your rucksack. That's your lifeline."

The pair rode on, maintaining a low profile, steering clear of crowded sections of road. Isolated villages with skylines littered with crippled citadels protected the roadways. Around halfway through the three-hour drive, the pair reached the bleak, lifeless town of Maiwand. Noah was in a reflective mood. "The British lost a major battle here."

"Really?"

"Yeah. A big one. They were routed."

Charlie was skeptical. "I never read about it."

"You wouldn't have. That was back in eighteen eighty."

Charlie threw out a look of disbelief.

"It's true. We've been fighting here for centuries. Nothing has changed. This is an unwinnable war."

"We're on top of this."

"That's what they said in eighteen eighty." Noah pulled his head back.

"So, where are we going, specifically?" enquired Noah.

"To meet a contact. A trafficker named Feisal."

The van swerved at the news. "Feisal? I should have brought a bigger gun."

"Is he a badass?"

"Worse than that. He's a mythical creature. No one has met him and lived to tell the tale."

"Well, Sanchez had lined up a drop with him in Sangin."

"I knew it would be Sangin, but Feisal? We're on a dangerous path."

Charlie sighed. "You're not making this any easier."

"But still not putting you off?"

Charlie remained resolute. "I've a job to do."

"Having a job to do is not the same as being able to do your job. Do you know what you're getting into."

"If I did, I wouldn't be here."

"What is that supposed to mean?"

"It means I'm going with or without you. I can handle myself."

Noah had his doubts. "So, what's the plan? Hello Mister Feisal. You're under arrest?"

"More like, hello Mister Feisal, take me to your leader."

"And why would he do that?"

"I can be persuasive," joked Charlie, but Noah seemed far from convinced. "You need to get up to speed on the local drug trade."

"You know the scoop?" asked Charlie.

Noah sighed and went on a roll. "When the mujahedeen were swarmed by the Taliban, their leader, Mohammud Omar, banned opium overnight, but that didn't last." Ever the journalist, he seemed clearly pleased to spout on about one of his many specialist subjects. "This year is one of the best harvests in decades. Everyone is back at it. A small farmer has a couple of acres. Big farmers have a couple of hundred."

"That much?"

"That's not the half of it. The small guys all have extended families. A small community can be fed and clothed from a tiny field. No other crop comes close. The big guys can have as many as three hundred workers supporting all their families.

"All out in the open?"

"As clear as a cloudless Afghan day." He gestured to the skies. "The farmers sell their opium to merchants, who trade the harvest to the heroin producers. The coalition has pledged over four billion dollars to eradicate the scourge, but they have no clue. A couple of years ago, Afghanistan produced seventy percent of the world's opium. Four thousand five hundred tons. Enough to make four hundred and fifty tons of heroin."

"So, with the Taliban gone, the poppies have returned?"

"They're not gone. They're the ones running the show. The warlords operating the protection rackets are mostly Taliban. The old ban only drove up prices. Those buds of death use half the water of wheat but give thirty times the profit. Opium is a better bet than foreign aid, and it gets cash into the heart of the economy. It's their oil. Everyone is in on it. Criminal, military, religious, political, business figures, it doesn't matter your background. They all have a piece of the pie."

"All roads lead to heroin. So, the soldiers were smuggling drugs."

Noah wasn't convinced. "Doubt it. They were probably funneling funds through the network."

"To get the cash out of the country?"

"Yeah, and maybe get a cut of the profits outside Afghanistan."

"Cash then wired to private accounts?"

Noah liked the hypothesis. "Likely they will devise ways of doing it themselves, but right now it's a third-party transaction."

"You make it sound so legit."

"When there is no rule of law, everything is legit."

Before Charlie could truly digest the commentary, Noah pulled his foot off the gas. "Hang on to that rucksack."

Charlie sat to attention. Up ahead, a checkpoint blocked the crossroads. Escape from the high banking on one side and the deep ditch on the other made a detour impossible. The old Citroen slowed. A temporary barrier lay ahead.

Over the crest of the slowly traversed incline, two white pickups lay angled across the road.

"God." Five heavily armed men with masked faces blocked the road. Bullet belts and automatic rifles were out on display. "What do we do?" asked Charlie.

"If we run, we'll get an RPG up our ass."

Charlie raged at her lack of preparedness. "My gun's in the back."

Noah set his hand across her forearm. "Easy there, Annie Oakley. We should be fine." He pulled a clump of notes from the pile requisitioned earlier. "It looks like a good, old-fashioned shake down. I think we're covered."

Charlie wasn't so sure. "And, if it isn't?" She didn't like developments. "Who are these guys?"

"We're about 20km from Sangin. This will be a handover point between licensed militias."

"Rebranded Taliban?"

Noah scoffed as they edged closer to the roadblock. "Loyalties shift more than these sands. Gone are the days of summary executions for anything resembling indulgence. But the public executioners have turned to public service. They are keen to be seen to help. On the pretext of searching for weapons, they shake down the locals. Although Sangin is the largest opium market in Afghanistan, the traffickers roam freely."

"So, we pay for safe passage?"

Noah shrugged. "It's the last few weeks of conflict season. It will soon be too cold to fight. These guys all go home for winter. That's why they'll be running these roadblocks."

"Stocking up for the cold months ahead?" asked Charlie.

"In one. This is about money. I hope."

"Hope?"

Noah's expression brightened as he checked the wad of cash newly pulled from his tunic. He pulled a pistol from under his seat and jammed it into the small of his back.

"They don't pull tricks like that back at the Washington Post."

Noah wasn't playing. "This isn't Washington. Get your headdress on."

Charlie obeyed without question or delay. As they neared the barrier, tensions and gun sights rose. Hard faces and crazed eyes stared into the cabin of the truck. "Whatever you do. Don't take off your headscarf, and don't get out." Noah slowed the truck to a crawl.

Four guards crowded into the driver's side of the van, allowing Charlie the chance to turn away. Through her headscarf, she kept watch. The youngest, freshest face on display squawked and gesticulated for the van to pull to a stop. The guard's bullet belt was wrapped diagonally across his chest like a bandit in a spaghetti western. Noah complied and rolled down the window.

"Hello, We were-"

Before he could offer dialogue, the van door was pulled open. Fear sparked in his eyes.

"Out! Out!"

He obeyed. It was no request. This was no routine stop.

Front and center, the diminutive leader in a gritty white headdress, struggled under the weight of his AK47. His eyes of charred umber raged with anger as he prodded the muzzle of his rifle into Noah's stomach. Cloaked with menace, the guards closed in, more heavily set, more heavily armed. As the rough interrogation commenced, two guards started a heavy-handed search of the back of the truck. Noah crumpled to the great delight of the outliers. The lead negotiator seemed less impressed; tempers flared when Noah bit back at the extortion. Charlie peered over the dash, petrified at the unfolding horrors. A sudden crack from a rifle butt sent Noah to the ground. Cash cascaded onto the desert floor. The guards called a temporary halt to the beating to retrieve the fluttering cash. Charlie glanced around to see the little leader turn the butt of his gun to his shoulder with a sneering grin. "No!" Against all logic and instruction, she barged the van door open. It was too late.

"Bang!"

The lead guard stood tall over Noah's dead body, smoking AK47 in hand. The first gang member to tackle her lost an eye socket, and the second gained a broken nose. Before she could inflict more damage, the guard arriving from the rear clubbed her neck. As she reeled and rocked on her knees, the guard set a choke hold and squeezed. She reached around, clawing at his eyes, but the bulk of the man made that move impossible. A choking blur descended. Just before she passed out, the leader called the execution to a halt. Charlie fell to the ground, gasping for air. Her nails dug into the dirt as she scrambled for an escape route. Powerless. To protect herself, she made one last desperate call for reinforcements. She pulled her head back and yelled at the top of her voice. "Feisal!"

In awe of the Western beauty or in fear of the name, the guards stepped back. Even the murderous ringleader stalled. Doubled up, Charlie doubled down. "Feisal! Feisal!"

Stunned and confused, the two guards locked and loaded their weapons. Through a vale of tears and confusion, Charlie spied the men scanning the horizon. The mere mention of Feisal's name terrorized them. They looked ready to shoot anything and anyone in sight. At the point where Charlie thought she had called in a Taliban strike, the little leader reached into his tunic. To Charlie's relief, a satellite phone slid into view. The fighter plugged in a number and turned away. Guns were trained, and triggers itched. Whispers turned to muttering, as the guard explained his current dilemma to the recipient of the call. Charlie knew she had rung a bell. Time would tell if it would be a death knell. The answer came swiftly. Panicked, the main guard dropped the call, then his rifle. He stepped over Noah's corpse and grappled Charlie to her feet. Fear had turned his tanned face to ash. The tone and veracity of his instructions told Charlie her gamble had worked. Looking down, her relief turned to despair. She had been too late to save her friend.

Pushers turned into ushers as Charlie was thrown back into the driver's seat of the van. A frantic bout of cash collection ensued.

When the lead guard emerged at the open van window, Charlie flinched. The recaptured cash was unceremoniously thrown back into the van. Charlie didn't stop to count it. The engine sparked, and the van skidded out onto the ragged road. Shaking with terror, she checked the rearview mirrors for stray bullets or parting shots. None came. Instead, she saw a fearful shuddering tribe arguing over the corpse of her dead friend. The van careened on, kicking up dust in its wake. Charlie rubbed her eyes. She was stranded. Her heart crashed through her chest. Ahead lay a rendezvous with a notorious killer, behind her a murderous gang.

Hauling the window down, she gulped for air. Afraid to look back, she gripped the wheel and set her sights on the distant horizon. She changed down a gear and floored the accelerator.

There was no turning back. There could be no holding back.

Afghanistan was living up to its lawless reputation.

Noah was dead.

She was on her own.

CHAPTER 18

Death lay in her wake. Tragic thoughts of Harry, Sanchez and Noah were thrown to four winds. They would haunt her later. Right now, she needed to focus. Too scared to look back, battling to escape the trauma of recent terrors, Charlie sped on.

After a traumatized half hour drive, doing nothing but stare at the horizon, Charlie spied Sangin's low level skyline crept into view.

To retain her anonymity for as long as possible, she pulled the van over, then set about throwing sandy grit over every window. The smudging windscreen wipers added yet more opacity to the windscreen. With the sun high overhead and a little porthole rubbed in the grit, her viewing position was secured. A restricted view was the price she was willing to pay for greater cover. She drove on, refusing to cast her mind back down the road, unable to entertain thoughts of the road ahead.

Pulling her headdress back in place bolstered her confidence. The rubble roadway fell victim to a squally shower passed through the edge of town. Pockets of mud splattered the streets as they became smattered with humanity. Through her smeared portal, the street life looked chaotic and colorless. Centuries-old traditions clashed with turn-of-the-century advances. A filthy urchin scratched an existence selling eggs. All his eggs were in one basket.

An old Soviet car crawled past with goats in the back and a wet boy on the roof rack. Charlie guessed it was practicalities, not popularity, that necessitated the respective seating positions. *Only the boy could hang on.*

Sand bagged pavements had been laid in preparation for the unpredictable rains. Stripped willow branches blanched under the emerging sun, helped prop up canopies of dampened grasses. The nearby shop owner seemed to have invested all his cash in steel shutters. Bicycle tires and tubes hung rotting in the sunlight. Charlie's printed map proved easy to follow, and progress through the small town was swift. On an open street corner.

A posse of youths talked and stalked. Their caps and tunics blended into their drab surroundings. *Future Taliban.*

Four turns later, the van veered into the shadow of a building. Up ahead lay the target compound. Charlie recognized the layout from the previously studied satellite imagery. She was forty minutes early for the deciphered rendezvous. Wooden poles protruded haphazardly from the sides of the building. The overhead sun threw disfigured shadows across the main wall. Sand colored concrete blocks formed the three-floor structure. Functional balconies stood watch over irregular elevations, each one sporting its very own rooftop areas.

Two sentries patrolled intermittently.

The main compound door stood well over eight feet tall and was protected by a canopy of dusty, rustic wood.

Two ground floor guards, sporting long beards, were too engrossed in a game of cards to notice Charlie's arrival. She cracked the van window open. Dogs barked inside a clay house next door to the compound. The rags over the doors gave the property an unloved air. Ripped and ragged fabrics that would have once offered shelter flapped pointlessly in the wind. Three undersized donkeys with barefoot riders and oversized loads helped partially obscured her view of the guards. The street life offered great cover, so Charlie tied her headscarf tight and moved in for a closer look.

An uneasy feeling choked the street. High walls and tall trees added to the air of claustrophobia. Telecom wires dangled loosely. Faded red plastic chairs lay buckled on a street corner, tempting the next soul brave or stupid enough to sit on them. Crowds filled the street perpendicular to the compound, yet the alley leading up to the building was deserted. Charlie vied for a viewing position amongst the everyday life. Less than fresh fish that looked to have arrived by hand cart baked in the growing heat. The copious quantities of fly spray being dispensed by the hirsute stall owner seemed to be warding off insects and customers in equal measure.

Fish soup fizzed and bubbled nearby. Through the steam from the soup, Charlie kept watch. The compound looked uninviting and uninteresting. Everyone passed by at pace. Nearby, three squawking geese followed the trail of bird feed thrown out by an old lady who waddled more than them. One wayward goose wandered into the alley, then quickly retreated, honking every webbed step of the way. *What does he know that I don't?*

The compound held more secrets, so further reconnaissance was decided upon. She had time to scope out the property before the drop time. Scouting the compound perimeter proved pointless. Blind alley after blind alley of high walls prevented the gathering of any form of useful intelligence. The high sun cast short shadows, making it impossible to gain cover. Overexposed and underwhelmed, she turned back toward the van's location. There seemed only one option. A full frontal, bold as brass, knock at the door. When she turned the corner on her way back to the van, a rifle butt sent her into the dirt.

Her world spun.

Blackness descended.

CHAPTER 19

A splitting headache brought Charlie back to half-life. Her double vision took time to singularize. Through her drowsy haze, she surveyed the scene and took inventory. The thumping at the back of her eyeballs forced her eyelids closed. It took three more attempts before she could overcome the throbbing pain. She looked again.

The back street grotto had never seen paint. An old metal bed frame lay on its side on an oily dirt floor. An old motorcycle minus a wheel sat next to its removed fuel tank. Open wall slits above head height brought in light and breeze but gave no views. She recognized the shape of the windows from her tour of the compound. Uncertain how long she had been out cold, she could tell she hadn't traveled far. Chickens cackled outside. All she could smell was oil. Her movement alerted the sleepy guard, a thirty-something man with receding hair, gnarled nose with a t-shirt as stained as his profession. Aghast, the man's fragile jawline quivered. His tinted, crooked teeth showed he was no stranger to a king-sized filter tip. He was up banging at the door and shouting as quick as his scabby sandals could carry him. The door couldn't open fast enough for his liking. He skittered off in a panic before the door was bolted behind him.

After a few minutes, the bolt slammed back open. The wooden door swung open with a horror-movie creak.

A man in a pitch-black headdress with a silver pinstripe eased into the room. Medium build, and traditionally dressed, his wraparound Oakley glasses were pulled off slowly and deliberately. Haunting dark eyes stared right through Charlie, yet she refused to cower. *All for effect*, she told herself. When the new arrival moved in and stared at close range, Charlie went on the offensive. "I like your sunglasses. A nice concession to capitalism." Her captor held his ground and his tongue, so Charlie took a gamble. "I speak with Feisal, and him alone!" She hoped she had sounded tough enough.

Wave after wave of creases on the black man's forehead rippled as if he was deciding upon a response. She stared at his featured face. Sun damage splattered cheeks sat on either side of a bulbous ruddy nose. His eyebrows had never been trimmed in his life. A tight cut mustache seemed at odds with his renegade eyebrows. Crimson-rimmed eyeballs gave the impression he had not slept for a decade. Wooden beads strung around a neck infested with small warts and skin tags.

"Why are you sneaking around my property?"

Decent English. She knew that concocting some story centered on her innocence would never be believed. Yet again, dishonesty remained her best policy. "I can only speak with Feisal."

The jailer bit hard. "Where is Sanchez?"

"Gone. We took him out."

"Dangerous. We look after our own."

Charlie even noted elements of an English accent. "Not when they steal from both sides. He needed taking care of."

The man seemed to like the concept of Sanchez being dead. "So, you are here to take his place?"

"To trade."

He gestured for the guard to supply water from an aluminum jug. She glugged a few mouthfuls and threw the remainder of the water over her head. It felt good, and it bought her time to think. "I work for the same organization as Sanchez."

"Sanchez is freelance."

Charlie bluffed on. "If you think that is true, you're not the man I need to speak to. I need to talk to Feisal."

"If you don't know who I am, you are not the woman I need to speak to."

"So, you are Feisal?"

A bobbling head was the only sign given that her assumption was correct. Charlie pushed hard. "Sanchez works for us. So do you."

"I work for no one."

Bluffing all the way, Charlie kept it vague. "We all have bosses. You and I work for the same people."

"Nice accent, East Coast America?"

"Nice accent, East London, England?"

The man now suspected of being Feisal leered. "I have not always lived there."

Charlie was impressed. "I could say the same thing. You speak very good English, Feisal. Where did you learn?"

The man wouldn't be drawn, but he did answer to the name. "University. I overstayed my welcome."

"So, this is payback?"

"No. This is just pay." Feisal altered course. "How does a pretty girl from a good upbringing end up in a hellhole like this?"

"Who says I had a good upbringing?"

"You do; every time you open your mouth. We are not all animals up here. Nor are we stupid. Answer the question."

"It's a long story that starts with falling for the wrong guy. I grew to love him. He loved his dope. Dope developed into opium, and I followed on."

"Show me your veins."

Charlie balked. "We smoke."

"Where is he now?"

"Being chased by a dragon."

"And you, here, now?"

"We got into debt."

"And working your debt off?"

Now Charlie bobbled her head. "They sent me to search out a name, your name, Feisal."

Feisal wasn't convinced. "You look too healthy."

"I am trying to get clean."

"How do I know you're not CIA?"

"No one goes alone in this part of the world. If I was CIA, they would have sent in the troops the minute your guy slugged me. Cheap move, by the way."

Feisal stomped from side to side, annoyed that he was not in total control. He pulled his phone. "Don't use that. They have new tracking systems linked to satellite surveillance. I think they are listening in. I needed to get rid of my phone. They scan this area frequently. Listen, there is only me. If I was CIA, I'd want you to use that phone, so they could trace me. That's why I am saying, don't use it."

Feisal growled and prowled. "What is your name?"

"My name is not important."

"You know mine; you have me at a disadvantage."

Charlie pointed towards the guard. "Not from where I am standing." She pushed home her point. "I have the money to prove my worth and my credibility." She took a chance. "Besides, Feisal is not your real name."

Her captor stopped in his tracks and bobbled his head. "We have many faces and many names."

Noticing his moment of smugness, Charlie made her play. "You have nothing to lose and everything to gain."

"Why is that?" he asked.

She took a swing. "There is a massive shipment due to come out of the country. I have been sent to check the route and make sure it's protectable."

"It's my route. It's protectable. Do not doubt me."

"Don't shoot the messenger! I am only doing my job."

"I have protected shipments for years. Don't doubt me."

"I don't, but others do. Particularly when there are five million dollars at stake."

The number made an impact. "How much?"

"You heard. We caught Sanchez stockpiling for his own gains. We killed him. Now we have all this money we need to shift. Five million dollars. You are our best bet, but we need to confirm it's safe."

"Are you here to score or here to sell?"

Charlie threw him her greatest glowing gaze. "Both."

Feisal was hooked. "I could help with both."

Charlie made it up along the way. "I need to check the route."

"Not possible."

She ignored the repost. "Then we send a squad through with the money shipment."

"What do I get?"

"Twenty percent. One million dollars. If I go missing, you will suffer the same fate as Sanchez ."

"Do not threaten me."

"It isn't a threat. I am just laying out the ground rules. I track the route, ensure its protectable, work out what we need, then make arrangements. All you need to do is get me through the chain and we will bring the cash."

"How much again? And when?"

"Four million dollars through in two months' time. Once that arrives safely, we will drop off the million dollars to you within five days."

Feisal's greed was transparent. "Where?"

"At a place and time to suit you."

"Cash?"

"US dollars, in one-hundred-dollar bills."

Charlie could tell the dollar signs were already skewing Feisal's vision, but the deal was not done yet. "I have the cash to pay for my passage. We want no credit against any shipments. I am the package this time."

"So, you are buying passage, not product?"

"If needs be, yes." She closed with flattery. "We hear you run the best and safest caravans; we just need to see it as well."

As he slithered, Charlie threw out the final offer. "I don't need to see the route. I can go parts of the way blindfolded. It's not the route I want to see, it's the level of protection." She needed to give something and that way she would still reach her end goal. Creepy Feisal rubbed the back of his hand across Charlie's face. "The road is no world for a pretty thing like you."

Charlie held her stare, kept her cool, and passed the test. "Try me."

Feisal chortled.

"You have nothing to lose. Fifty thousand dollars today and one million in a month's time."

His chortling stopped. "You could be a journalist sent to trap me."

"I don't know any journalist brave or dumb enough to follow this story." Her thoughts flashed to Noah. "At least none living."

"Where is the cash?"

Intrigued by the prospect of hunting down the money and drug route, self-preservation remained her priority. She needed time and the chance to grab her gun.

"If I tell you that, you could just kill me. I can show you."

A Glock emerged from the small of Feisal's back. "If you don't tell me, I will kill you. Here and now."

Charlie held her hands up in an exaggerated surrender. "You wouldn't."

"Try me."

"Kill me and you lose your chance at the payout. We need to trust each other."

"I will trust you when you tell me where the cash is."

Charlie yielded; intent on fighting another day. "Back of my van. Spare wheel."

The Glock disappeared, as did the guard. Feisal called after him. "Auosh!"

The guard halted on command. Feisal followed the guard from the room, slammed the heavy wooden door shut and jammed the bolt across into its bracket. It was impossible for Charlie to hear the muffled instructions being given, but for now, she was just relieved to be free from the interrogation and the immediate threat to life.

She fought hard to regain ground, for she realized the very same threat to life could return in no time.

CHAPTER 20

The ugly guard had no problem throwing a hood over Charlie's head. He looked like a man used to following callous orders. Feisal acted like a man used to giving them.

The handcuffs were non-negotiable.

As Charlie stood, she made a meal of being disorientated, forcing the guard to hold her up. If left on their own, she would pounce. As they moved outside, the blazing sunlight baked through the hood into her hair. Breaths were hard to come by. She made a big point of struggling to the point where the guard sounded concerned. Feisal remained close by, pushing him on. There would be no escape any time soon. Besides, to break free would be to break from the mission.

Confident that better opportunities would come in the future, Charlie stumbled on to meet her fate. After only twenty steps, she was halted. An opening vehicle door gave away its age by creaking badly. She was thrown inside to feel the painful impact of metallic flooring. With the door banged shut behind her, she used her boots to scope out the dimensions. There was no doubt she was back inside her old Citroen van.

To boost her confidence and quell her fears, she forced herself to believe that if they were going to kill her, it would have been easier to do it in the back of an old compound. Risking running into a patrol with a Western hostage seemed out of whack with a murder. Thoughts of kidnap and ransom were dispelled quickly, for the same reasons. The van barreled on up the rough roads, telling Charlie they were staying locally. Heat from the sun beat in through the cab. For the time of day, she guessed they were heading south. With each turn, the sun shone in through the windows on each side of the bus. Tracking the direction proved easy. Six or seven turns of ninety degrees had them turning south again.

The roads remained ragged.

They were simply driving around town to make her disorientated. They had gotten nowhere. She knew her location. When they turned east, she realized they were heading toward the scene of Noah's murder. She counted, in batches of sixty, to track the time and lose her fears. After twenty-five batches of sixty seconds, the van slowed and turned north. The road elevated and deteriorated as they bumbled up into the mountains. The thinning air made breathing a chore. Her hot yoga sessions were set to good use. Her breathing eased despite the bangs and bashes to her diaphragm.

Charlie reset her mental clock after half an hour. Before that process was halfway through a repeat cycle, the van slowed to a crawl. The irate Pashto being shouted through the windshield let Charlie know Feisal was probably still on board. Twenty-nine counted seconds later, squealing brakes halted the van on a steep incline. The driver wasted no time in pushing open the van door and moving around the back. The split doors opened, and Charlie braced for an impact that did not come. Instead, a firm hand slipped under her arm and lifted her gently. Once on her feet, and out in the late afternoon air, Charlie stretched her back and pretended not to listen for footsteps. *Three sets, maybe four.*

No words were exchanged. She was led silently up a series of canyons, each one steeper and more circuitous than the last. It seemed every rock on the pathway had been set to either catch her heel or stub her toe. Twice she almost lost her step count. *Almost. Two hundred and forty- five. Two hundred and forty-six.*

She felt the lowering sun casting shadows, indicating that the walls of the canyons were tightening as well as steepening. She trudged on, counting every step of the way.

Every now and again, she feigned bouts of breathlessness. In the intervening stoppages, she heard the guard dragging on board lung loads of air. She was tiring him out. She upped the ante and the pace. Her plan was soon discovered.

Flailing, one guard grabbed her shoulders and yanked her back to a smoker's pace.

Like the canyon walls, fear was also closing in. The group suddenly halted, spread out, and waited. Before she could react, someone pulled off her hood. The sun cracked through her creased eyelids. Four men stood in a circle: guns drawn. Feisal stood close by, holding the dark hood. He gestured to the nearest guard to open the handcuffs. Charlie's skin ripped during the uncuffing process. She made a point of showing her annoyance to the heavy-handed guard. She never faltered or whimpered. He seemed to enjoy himself. Feisal pulled her from the dirt before ushering her to a waiting wooden table. "Please. Eat."

Central to the scene sat a massive, charred steel bowl sitting atop a disguised fire. A palaw dish of rice, spices, raisins, and carrots simmered under a sweet smoke. Rags around his head and, armed with a towel to fend off the flies, the chef's makeshift whites were now charcoal in color and texture. Hunger and a keenness to be accepted into the circle of trust drove Charlie to welcome the offerings. Hot tea was poured by what Charlie assumed was the chef's son.

Crammed in near the blackened bowl, the crew devoured the delicious dishes. Laughs were exchanged between the men. Sitting around making conversation, the table soon became gossip central. Charlie pretended not to understand a word. It wasn't much of an act. Her language skills were no match for the pace of the conversation, but she realized the men offered little in the way of threat; at least for the time being. Just what she was doing there was a mystery to her, as much as the men, but like her they were under orders to get the job done.

The site was surveyed as the men broke out the illegal alcohol. Feisal caught Charlie staring. "Afghan drink."

"Moonshine?"

"What is moonshine?"

"Illegal whisky."

"This is no whisky. This is Afghan drink, made from green raisins."

Charlie remembered certain locals chewing raisins on her trips through town. "Where is it made?"

"Right here. Come see."

Like a proud neighbor showing off his new extension, Feisal took her for a tour. Keen to ingratiate herself and genuinely curious, Charlie jumped at the offer.

The wooden hut looked like a force-six gale would scatter it to the four winds. The tattered turf roof added camouflage and structure threatening weight. Charred carpet, acting as a screen door, was pulled to the side. Charlie was the first to be ushered inside. Acrid sweet smoke clung to her nostrils and tingled her eyes. On one side of the shed sat two large, crudely fashioned pot stills. The copper had taken a hell of a beating over the years. The devices looked to have been transported from the era of Appalachian Prohibition. One still bubbled away contently. The other seemed in poor spirits. In a corner sat box after box of large plastic water bottles. In the other corner rested numerous large bags of green raisins. Feisal, keen to show off his home brew, pulled a bottle, and twisted off the lid. He couldn't help but flinch when he set his nose near the bottle top.

"As good as that?" enquired Charlie.

"Here. There's only one way to find out."

The cloudy off-white liquor resembled a musky Muscadet all the way from the Loire Valley. That's where the similarities ceased. On contact, the liquor slashed at the cracks in her weather-beaten lips. Her mouth imploded on impact. The backdraft from the fireball stripped her esophagus. Any attempts to seem unaffected by the burning spirit were abandoned when the resulting coughing fit threatened to burst her lungs. Somehow, Feisal's laughter drowned out her hacking.

"Wow. Back home, we'd call that white lightning. A local taxidermist used to make firewater like that. They shut him down when too many people lost their eyesight!"

Feisal lifted the bottle, made eye contact, and took his fill. A large mouthful was swigged, swirled, swallowed, and demonstrably enjoyed. Charlie snatched the bottle and repeated the process twice. The spirit still burned, but no cough came. Feisal's facial muscles released minuscule signs of admiration. Charlie seized her chance and stated the obvious to get the conversation rolling. "With Sharia law, is this not dangerous?"

"Of course. Sixty lashes, fines that are too big to pay, jail time, and even deportation for foreigners, everything is possible. But is it worse than trading opium?" Charlie couldn't argue. Feisal continued. "The penalties change by person, and by offense, but mostly they change depending upon who catches you. It all comes down to baksheesh."

It wasn't just the liquor that screwed up Charlie's face. She had never heard of baksheesh. Noticing her reaction, Feisal elaborated. "Baksheesh? An old Persian word for gratuity."

"You mean a bribe?"

"You Westerners would call it a bribe, but we understand it as a gratuity. We were making raisin liquor long before the Taliban arrived, and we will be here long after they have left."

"Be careful. That could be classed as blasphemy, by some."

"Meh!" Feisal had shown and heard enough. He grappled the carpet door to one side and exited. Worried that she'd upset him, Charlie followed on and out. She took a moment to steady herself, back under the piercing sunlight. Uncertain whether the sudden bout of nausea was caused by a recent crack to the head or the Afghan drink. She staggered on; Feisal wasn't hanging around. He led a short, forced march across to a rustic grove clinging onto the edge of a ravine. The thick, low-level trees offered great coverage from the air. Ominously, traces of chemical odors rose from the cavern below. Feisal continued the tour. "Do you know what is down there?" he asked Charlie. She shrugged, keeping sight of the gas canister. "Come, let me show you."

Charlie lifted her gaze. "Lead on." Feisal took the front, and with an armed guard holding up the rear, as they escorted her down a set of ragged worn steps, cut from the rocks. A lack of handrails made the descent more precarious than it needed to be.

Halfway down the rocky steps, Charlie stopped stone dead. In an alcove, at face height, lay explosives and a detonator. Her panic amused Feisal. "Ha. Do not worry. It is not wired. We keep it for protection against a surprise attack. Thieves may come when we are gone. This is what awaits them. A noisy, portable generator led them further on down into the ravine. Close by a tributary cascaded rivulets of clean mountain water. "Welcome to our factory." The sinister tone of his voice matched the shadowy activities underway.

The site was small, ten yards by twenty. Concrete pipes had been turned on their end, buried and sealed. A wooden bucket sat on the wall of the rustic reservoir. The charred gas canister sitting near the fire looked ready to blow. Blackened oil drums bubbled away on top of a massive pit fire. A mammoth baking tray was being used to boil a frothing gray glop.

Charlie guessed the score. "Opium?"

Feisal bobbled his head, as if unwilling to answer the obvious question.

Additional gas canisters helped the fire on its way. This chef wore no whites. Sweat and steam stung his eyes as the filthy factory belched out its product. Sealed sacks were slit open before the oily contents were pushed out into the oil drum. The deadly treacle blistered on impact. Acrid smoke billowed into a set of underground chimneys, charring the ground but avoiding the sky. "No smoke signals," observed Feisal. Two workers sat on either side of a crude see-saw contraption squeezing out water from the last deadly batch. Immediately adjacent, the next stage in the production line was running at full volume. A contraption utilizing a heavy wooden beam and car jack was pressing the last of the noxious juices from the boiled opium.

Blood red sap drying in the sun was being treated with a range of chemicals by a boy around ten years old. "What are the chemicals?"

A glint of mischief flashed in Feisal's eyes. "Ah, that is our secret. It's what sets our grade to be the purest in the region. If I tell you, I will have to kill you."

Charlie deflected with humor. "Remind me not to ask questions again."

"That is a good position to take in Afghanistan." With a great show, Feisal pulled some litmus paper from a nearby plastic container and checked the PH levels in the compound. "Seven is the magic number. We are nearly there. This is the last batch of your shipment."

"My shipment?"

"You wanted to check our routes. This is your starting point. Do you expect me to risk my teams without the reward of the heroin shipment?"

Charlie kicked back. "I paid for safe passage."

"And you shall have it. You go along with the next delivery."

Charlie wasn't keen to be sent through Afghanistan with a load of illegal drugs, but she was in no position to argue. "Who will travel with me?"

"That is not important right now. How do you plan to get back out?"

Charlie had no clue. She didn't even know where she was going. "That is not important right now."

Feisal snorted. He seemed to like her style. "Is this like some initiation for you?"

Charlie pushed back. "No. They are sending their best to protect their assets. You know these people."

Feisal didn't believe the story. "So, this is your choice?"

"It is my role, not my choice. These people do not take no for an answer."

Feisal bobbled in agreement. He moved the dialogue and the direction of interest. He pointed at the evil cooks, hard at work. "This factory supports over three hundred people."

"Whilst still leaving a healthy profit for you."

"Please. I never said I was a saint. We pay good wages for bad work."

"And you keep a clean supply."

"Exactly. We buy nothing but the best from the brokers in Sangin."

"Paying around eight hundred dollars a kilo?" Charlie had done her research.

"Something like that."

"And that will have a street value well over a hundred and fifty thousand dollars."

"We do not see that. We are all part of a machine. The bulk of the money goes to the organization."

"And we are very grateful for it," Charlie bluffed.

Feisal beamed. "Of course. You take the money, but you give protection and opportunity. You own the distribution channels."

"Opportunity, distribution channels. You make it sound all very organized."

"It is. That's why we can guarantee your safety down the line."

"Your location is impressive. They will never find you here."

"They are not looking. The US is not interested in closing our operations. If we are trading drugs, we are not waging Jihad. Ninety percent of Europe's heroin comes from Afghan. Virtually none of it hits US streets. That's another reason they leave us alone."

"So, why the armed guard?"

"Rivals. Competitors. It is a perilous trade. That's why we conducted our business far from prying eyes."

"Isn't there space for more than one operator?"

Feisal shook his head. "No. Rivals stoke competition that drives up the price the farmers want. We cannot have that. We own the route from start to finish."

"All the Pillars?" she asked, hoping to get more insight.

"All seven Pillars," confirmed Feisal. Charlie would have wanted more answers, but all she got was one question. "So, what do you think?"

She would have called in an air strike right there and then, given the opportunity. Her words mismatched her aspirations. "Very impressive. I can't wait to see the next stage."

"You won't have long to wait. Let's share some tea while the men prepare the shipment. You go tonight."

Charlie's brain pounded with conflicting thoughts. She was getting out, but was she heading out of the heroin cauldron and into the fire?

CHAPTER 21

Despite her vehement protestations, the handcuffs were reapplied before she was pushed up into the back of the old Citroen van. The only concession gained was that they were not set as tightly around her wrists. Still, the constraints contorted her shoulders into a position that would be unbearably painful after a few hours. A more substantial hood was pulled in place. Before the wool was pulled over her eyes, Charlie scanned the back of the van's interior. To her great relief, three feet away sat her rucksack, and hopefully, her gun. To add to the secrecy, her new tour guide also covered his face, this time with a tightly wound headdress. All requests for support had gone unheeded. Quieting soft words from Feisal did little to settle her nerves, but it was good that he remained part of the journey. Hood or no hood, she could monitor him. Her heart thumped through her chest. Every step took her further into the spider's web. She needed to get to the phone before it ran out of coverage if it hadn't already done so. *Would it still have battery?*

With dark images over future terrors polluting her thoughts, she reluctantly turned to the past. Noah's horrific slaughter flashed before her. The callous young assassin. The single shot. The loss. The blame.

He was there because of me.

Am I to blame?

He knew what he was getting into.

That's no excuse.

It was all she had.

The photographs of Sanchez' family flickered into her mind's eye like some macabre, slow-mo, home move reel.

Could I have stopped it?

Those poor kids.

She cursed Sanchez, the clear leader. The obvious instigator. The loner. The antagonist. She wondered what came first, the temptation of the greed.

Money makes people do crazy things.

A massive pothole thumped her back to reality.

Then again, so does duty.

She held on.

In a land with no rules, she made her own. If her punishments for not gaining the right clearances were due, so be it. This thing was bigger than her career. *Too much at stake* was the phrase she used to convince herself that the mission needed to change. It was no longer tracking stolen money. It was now to destroy this thing called *The Pillars. The Seven Pillars,* as Feisal described them.

She was off the reservation, a renegade in hostile territory. There would be no turning back. The mission had been realigned, in the presence of clear facts and present danger. She would travel the route as far as she could make it, learn the stages, and bring the ringleaders to justice, any way she could. She had a few days of coverage before questions would be asked back at base. It could be weeks before her boss back in the States even noticed. She had the clearance, but the window was closing in.

Over time, her thoughts drifted back to poor Noah.

Why?

Could I have done anything differently?

What could we have achieved together?

He was a good man.

She sparked. *Quit your pointless pondering!*

Her survival instincts kick in, forcing her to focus on the work at hand. Recent history was just that, history. She needed to, and forced herself to, move on.

After what felt like four hours of travelling, the journey was taking its toll. The sounds of lax checkpoints coming and going had peppered the daylong journey. Every stop seemed less rigorous than the last. The good-natured shouts being exchanged by the checkpoint guards made Charlie think the security checks were designed for other, less well-connected sections of the community.

Fear dissipated, yet the pain increased along the way. The toughest challenge had been bearing the bangs and bumps of the roadway. Her joints had stiffened in protest at the cramped conditions. That image of her nearby rucksack sustained her for the duration of the blind, jarring journey.

After a long windy decline, the van slowed. When the gears crunched downwards for a right-handed turn, Charlie braced herself. The ride along the basin floor was as short as it was convoluted. Charlie counted less than six minutes before the squeaking brakes brought the van to a lurching stop. The journey's end arrived just before the end of her patience, but it was a close-run race. The van doors clunked open. Charlie felt the suspension take the weight of one man. A gruff hand clawed at her mask, then yanked it off without ceremony. Feisal sat opposite. "How are you feeling?"

"Get these cuffs off me."

The split-second after her captor complied, Charlie clawed her face. The heat and sweat from the hood had been unbearable. "This ends now. No more."

Feisal swithered. "You do not know where we are. There will be no need for the mask."

"Or the handcuffs!"

"No handcuffs. Come."

Feisal pulled a staggering Charlie back out into the real world. She kneaded and stretched every sinew of her body. The air felt fresh. The night had already drawn to a chilly close. She had totally underestimated the length of the journey. "What time is it?"

Feisal wasn't dumb. "That is not important. You have been traveling for some time. Let us leave it there." Having spent hours with her head in a hood, her eyes quickly acclimatized to the dark. Details were drawn as she was escorted in front of the idling van.

A regional town. Mud buildings. Scattered vegetation. No signage. Little to go on.

Feisal pulled her forward and eased her up into the front cab. Her bout outside in the cool night had taken its toll. Her chilled hands cupped the ineffective heater outlet. All the while, she kept her eyes peeled for movement. Across at an angle, fifty dark yards away, two women with steel basins on their heads carried garbage down into a tip bordering a nearby river. "They are out late," she commented.

"They need to be. They have our shipment." In the moonlight, the outlines of the women clambered across the trash down into the reeds. "I said this was a family affair."

Charlie's tensions rose sky high. She had some idea of the next destination, but to ask would have shown her to be out of the loop.

She guessed. *Kabul.*

CHAPTER 22

Outside in the courtyard, things were heating up. Feisal led Charlie to a waiting truck. As they approached, she was startled when a young man of fighting age eased out from the back of the vehicle.

Feisal initiated the introduction. "This is Gasim. He will be your escort."

The young warrior strode into the compound with the confidence of someone who had been through many battles. His wiry frame, wrapped in a dusty, faded keffiyeh, exuded an unsettling sense of assurance that belied his age. The fabric concealed much of his head and neck but did little to hide the sharp angles of his youthful, sun-hardened face.

He looked too young to have lived a full life, yet tough enough to have taken one.

His coal-black, piercing eyes scanned Charlie with a precision that defied his years, lingering long enough to send a silent message: don't mess with me. His features were lean, almost gaunt, with a nose that bore the tell-tale crook of fights lost and won.

A leather ammunition vest clung to his chest, its pockets bulging with small, unidentifiable items. Around his narrow waist, a belt held a sheathed, curved dagger, its hilt adorned with intricate tribal designs. The sleeves of his faded tunic were pushed up, exposing sinewy forearms marked with pale scars.

Although he had scars, Charlie guessed he was a harmer, not a self-harmer.

An AK-47 dangled casually over one shoulder.

The scout's wild, brindle eyes ensnared Charlie. His uncut mane had been scattered by the four winds. Over-cured skin, tarnished by the elements, clung to his wiry frame. His large, gap-toothed grimace expressed suspicion.

Keen to get and stay on his good side, Charlie extended a hand. "Tsenga yee?"

Gasim held back. Feisal explained, "He knows very little Pashto, and he will not shake a woman's hand. He is Tajik, an outsider. His name is Gasim, which means 'searcher' in his language."

Charlie smiled and bowed in respect. Gasim matched the gesture but not the expression.

Charlie stepped forward, her voice calm but deliberate. "Have you made this journey before?"

The young warrior's sharp eyes met hers, and his expression softened with a faint nod.

Charlie, filled with wishful thinking, took his answer as a 'yes.' She tilted her head slightly, studying him. "Will you take care of me?"

His cheeks flushed faintly beneath the grime and dust. For a moment, he hesitated, the tough exterior cracking just enough to reveal a flicker of vulnerability. Then he straightened his stance and touched his chest. "With my life," he said proudly in perfect Pashto.

Charlie allowed herself a small smile. "I hope it won't come to that," she said, her tone light but sincere.

The young guide said nothing, but his hand lingered over his heart for a moment longer before he nodded. The gesture spoke louder than words, a quiet promise, unspoken but deeply felt.

He seemed a man of few words who kept those thoughts to himself. She was glad he was on her side, but she wondered just how long that position would last.

When the conversation between the two men flowed in Tajik, Charlie pulled her thoughts to the mysterious Feisal. He was quite the enigma.

Multilingual. Multifaceted. Muti-faced?

"Okay. We go."

"One minute." In a move well-rehearsed in her mind, Charlie gathered the three bottles of water from the van. That gave her the excuse to grab her rucksack and stuff the bottles inside. She groped the base of the pack. To her relief, she felt the weight of the gun in the lining.

When she turned to open the compartment that held the spare tire, Feisal stepped in. "What are you doing?"

"We had a deal. You need to be paid."

Feisal sneered. "Payment was taken before we left."

Although far from surprised, Charlie raised her eyebrows.

The trio moved out at pace, Gasim at the lead. "Come on. They are loading the raft now."

"Raft?" asked Charlie.

"How else will you cross the Helmand River?"

Charlie choked on his words. Panicked breaths drew in a cold reality. *Westwards.*

That meant only one possible destination.

Iran.

CHAPTER 23

Down at the bank of the Helmand River, on the edge of a rancid garbage mound, the loading process was nearing completion. Although the junior of the operation, it was clear that Gasim ran the show.

Feisal walked amongst his people, handing out hot mint tea.

The moon shimmered off the water, lighting the litter cluttering the bank. Down below, repurposed wooden beams had been bound to a pontoon of inflated lorry tire inner tubes. The drugs were being hidden inside bags of seed and rice. Twelve poly-canvas drug bags were being tied between two guards, holding AK47s. As if to underline the gravity of the risk, an RPG and four shells had been set on top of the drug haul.

Hushed tones carried in on the chilled wind, as the men worked on with practiced efficiency.

Slightly removed from proceedings, Charlie sat on the riverbank, her confidence ebbing and flowing with every conflicting rumination.

Iran, a sworn enemy of her homeland, lay ahead. This would be no trip into the unknown. The threats had been well documented, the fanaticism well publicized. She would be on her own, thousands of miles from help that would never be sent.

Reporting on Sanchez and Harry would be a start, but going back and arresting Feisal as a local link in the chain would be met with a collective chorus of *meh.*

Few would care, and those that did wouldn't sanction a mission to search and destroy. She needed bigger fish. Feisal was no minnow, but the big fish lay downstream. For that, she had to widen the net. Then there was Feisal himself. If she pulled out now, he'd smell a rat. She wouldn't make it out alive. She had come too far, seen too much. No twisting of the narrative could bring her back through previous steps.

The angels and demons argued across her mind space.

Go back! Save yourself.

Go back and you die!

There would be no shame in calling off the search.

You signed up for this. Don't quit!

She fought the temptation to pull her talisman. This would be her decision and her decision alone.

She tried to find reason with a question. *What would Pop say?*

The answer came quickly. *"Get the hell out of Dodge as soon as possible."*

She didn't like the answer, but the alternative terrified her. Down below, the waters, like the moments, were passing too rapidly for Charlie's liking.

Unable to retreat, unwilling to go forward, she sat under a lead cloud of indecision, awaiting her fate.

That fate materialized in the form of Feisal. He appeared by her side and silently ushered her to the embarkation point.

Charlie stood, wiped off the dust, and followed on in a daze. In the end, it seemed Feisal had decided for her. She was too weary, and too lost to argue.

"You'll be heading downriver. Our competitors use brute force and motor vehicles. It's faster, but the losses are too high. Outlaws ambush road vehicles at will."

Charlie couldn't fathom how much he knew of Noah's killing. She didn't trust or even like him, but the very use of Feisal's name had saved her life. And for that, she would be eternally grateful. The man was an enigma to Charlie.

Locally, at least some good was coming from his wrongdoings. If not economic propensity, then employment and subsistence. Warlord, entrepreneur, guardian, gangster, protector, employer, enemy; every hat the man wore sat a little crookedly. When the time came to bring in the troops to close the smuggling routes, she didn't know how she would react to Feisal's arrest.

Those thoughts were for a later date. Right now, she had bigger players to hunt. Feisal produced a wad of cash, turned Charlie around, and stuffed it into her rucksack. She was grateful. "Thank you."

"Don't thank me. It's from the money you brought."

Charlie's gratitude was evident in her eyes. "Thank you, nonetheless."

"May your god go with you," said Feisal.

"And with you." She pulled the rucksack on tightly and prepared for the journey. Their handshake held more warmth than the night. Charlie needed closure on Noah's death. "Thank you for the safe passage, and for–"

She stopped in her tracks, noticing a red dot flickering across Feisal's chest, then lifted slowly onto his face.

"What's that?"

Feisal blinked. "What do you mean?"

It was at that split second, the sniper's bullet arrived.

CHAPTER 24

The bullet shattered his skull, then the silence.

Blood and body matter splattered into Charlie's eyes and gawping mouth. Temporarily blind and terrified, she collapsed to the ground. Spitting and coughing, she scrambled away from the direction of the bullet impact. Her mind raced.

There was no sound. A suppressor. A hit.

The men yelled in dismay and anger. They stood transfixed, waiting for the next round. Silence descended. The bush Charlie hid behind offered cover, but no ballistic protection. Spitting grime, she wiped Feisal's blood from her eyes.

Suddenly, a flare filled the night sky.

Bang! Bang! Bang!

Automatic weapons kicked in.

Bang! Bang! Bang!

Bullets flew in both directions. Charlie crawled across and dived into the garbage pile. Scattering rats and rubbish, she rolled down below the level of the banking.

Panic ensued.

Gasim scrambled the boat out into the water.

The front guard held his nerve, loading the RPG. His partner had lost his mind, letting rip with all he had in every direction. When the AK was spent, he picked up the spare and set himself back to work. Aimlessly blasting the night sky.

The bullets careered into the raft, bursting a tube, and splitting open the chest of the AK owner. When his partner sent the RPG into the window of the nearest building, a thunderous explosion ripped through the night air. Fizzing bullets ripped past in both directions.

Under cover of the enveloping detritus, Charlie scrambled headlong into the river.

Ice cold water clamped her lungs, dragging her underwater. Floundering in the icy undercurrent, she thrashed and splashed her way to the surface.

Gasping for air, she pulled her head up, unwilling to look back, she swam for the cover of the choppy rapids, ten yards away.

Back on dry land, the battle raged.

The icy Afghan waters roared through dark valley, swollen with snowmelt, its black waters churning and crashing against jagged rocks. Frozen, terrified, and exhausted, she hit her mark, with no breath to spare. Shivering fingers slithered over the smooth surface as she clambered behind the shelter of a protruding boulder.

Freezing up, she clung on.

Across the waterway, she slied Gasim making his watery escape, fearlessly piloting the raft under the steep nearside banking. His partner in crime reloaded the RPG and sent it landwards.

The landlocked cries and wails told Charlie the RPG had hit its mark. Risking a glance, and desperate to reset her grip, she clambered up onto the boulder.

Exposed, she saw the nearby building ablaze. Two dark figures darted to a new location, and recommenced firing.

Pros. Special ops.

Gasim and his partner returned fire then redirected the butts of their rifles into the river to act as oar. The paddled then fired, fired then paddled taking great care not to venture too far away from the shelter of the riverbank.

All around, the riverbank fizzled.

A scattering of automatic bullets landed close to her position, knocking her off balance and off the boulder.

With a gargled scream she crashed back into the frozen black water. Flailing and gasping through the troughs and peaks of the nearby rapids she twisted to gain any kind of viewpoint.

Scrambling to keep her head above water, she rolled with the river. Swimming as hard as she could, she eventually closed on the silhouette of the rubber raft.

Gasim and the other guard were obviously out of ammo, now they were only paddling.

In a crashing twist of fate, the sinking dingy hit a fast flowing section of the river. When the rubber hit the rapids, the raft careered forward. Charlie was playing catch up.

Again.

After a lung-bursting intake of breath, she battered and flailed, desperate to escape. She knew; her life depended upon it. Onward she swam, lungs bursting, ice forming at the edges of her soul. Every stroke depleted her energy reserves, every second in the water, dragged her body temperature nearer to zero. A hundred yards downriver, just as Charlie's resolve had dissolved, the raft swung back into view.

Desperate to not lose sight of the raft, she took the risk of shouting. "Gasim! Gasim!"

Nothing.

Her constricted lungs bellowed. "Gasim!" But her pitiful cries floundered on the crashing waves

Up ahead, salvation glinted in the moonlight. Spurred on by a wave of encouragement, Charlie doubled down her last efforts. Slowly and unsurely, she closed the gap. Ahead, she saw fleeting glimpses of the efforts being made to reposition the raft. This spurred her on.

Both parties converged as they cascaded through the raging rapids. The prospect of contact ebbed and flowed as the current drew them together, only to rip them agonizingly further apart. Even in the moonlight, she could see and feel the drag from a massive side chute rapid. With one last flail of her dying limbs, Charlie took a gamble and swam for the gap. The vortex effect from the channel catapulted her down and over the top of the fierce waterfall.

Tumbling in turbulence, her shoulder cracked a rock.

Gargling, she took on board the water.

Choking and spitting, she battled the menacing elements. The burble of the river drowned out the sound of distant gunfire and shouts echoing through the night.

Suddenly, dazing crack to the head split her sense, knocking her into a painful darkness. She drifted in and out of consciousness.

Drowning in anguish, blacking out, her last chance disappeared.

Out cold and numbed her senses her soul drifted on out under the rapids. The freezing water surged over her, pulling her under and then spitting her back up like a ragdoll.

The ice-cold water hauled her inexorably down into the darkness.

Down and down, she sank.

Chilled to the core and exhausted, the river pitched her over into a dead man's float.

Her dying words washed over her. *It's over.*

CHAPTER 25

Suddenly, a hand grabbed her hair, then her head. An arm around the throat pulled her up into the night air.

Gasping and puking, Charlie gulped cold air and freezing water.

Unable to support her weight, the arm pulled her close. Floating in the sanctuary of his arms, she let her angel carry her off.

With Charlie no better than an anchor, Gasim flailed and splashed his way across to the sanctuary of the raft, twenty yards away.

A turn in tide of fortune saw the raft crack a boulder and lurched to within reaching distance. The second guide was on hand, oar at the ready, reaching, shouting, encouraging.

Gasim clasped Charlie's hand forcing her to hold on, whilst the guard lashed a rope around the pair. It took all her effort just to be strapped in.

Through a chilly haze of semi-consciousness, Charlie saw the guard looming overhead, but she couldn't be sure.

Finally, with one last heave, the second guide stood and hauled away at the ropes, hoisting her onto the raft with a banshee howl. She flopped onto the deck, coughing and heaving, shivering, and chattering.

Dazed, she turned to find an exhausted Gasim being dragged out onto the raft. His arms shook from exertion, but his expression remained calm as he nodded toward her. Her chest heaved as she tried to speak, but the words caught in her throat.

"Thank you," she finally rasped.

The second man crouched beside her, rubbing her arms and hands to kickstart her blood flow.

She closed her eyes briefly, feeling the raft rock gently beneath her. The sound of the rushing river faded slightly, replaced by the murmurs of her rescuers.

But the relief was short-lived.

A sharp crack split the air. Charlie's eyes snapped open in time to see the second guide stiffen, his eyes wide in shock.

A black stain bloomed across his chest, stark against his drenched clothing. He swayed, his mouth opening as if to speak, but no sound came.

Gasim dived across, too late to save his friend.

Without a word or a heartbeat, the guide toppled forward, his body hitting the edge of the raft with a dull thud before slipping into the churning water.

The river swallowed him whole, leaving behind only a faint ripple.

Gasim grabbed her arm and pulled her down flat onto the raft as another gunshot echoed across the valley. The raft jolted violently as it slammed into fierce stretch of rapids. The current snarled and spun them sideways, the frothy waves crashing over the sides, drenching them. White water catapulted them upward, the entire vessel shuddering before plunging down the other side of the cascade. The roar of the river drowned out all else, masking their escape as the raft disappeared out of sight into the swirling darkness below.

The raft rocked beneath them as the river carried them forward, but Charlie's mind was fixated on the image of the guide's lifeless body disappearing into the water.

CHAPTER 26

The raft was beached an hour down river. Like its crew it ended its journey semi- submerged, and almost out of air.

With a little more air in his tank, Gasim hauled Charlie to the shore. Wheezing himself, he threw a blanket over her and punched fluids from her lungs.

Rubbing her hands, arms, and body in sequence, Gasim kick-started her circulation. She fought the fear of freezing by blowing on her hands. It made no difference.

What breath she had was stone cold.

Overcome with hypothermia and abject fear, she shivered uncontrollably.

As she rolled onto her side, Gasim picked her up and threw her over his shoulder in one sweeping motion. Helpless as a soggy rag doll, Charlie flopped and bounced as her savior ran for the darkness. Unable to comprehend the direction or distance, Charlie clung to what life she had left in her.

Seconds later, she was thumped into a sandy brush, and smothered by her blanket then coated in sand. The feeling of being buried alive seemed a blessed relief, she lay back and took it all in.

It was her burial.

On the edge of her field of vision, she saw Gasim return to the riverbank.

He returned minutes later with his second load. This time it was heroin. Without finding his breath, he turned and went again.

Charlie pushed back the against the cold and hauled herself up onto her staggering feet. Gasim eyes popped when he turned to find her joining the one-man human chain.

Charlie chattered. "I, I, I need to keep moving."

Gasim's grin caught the moonlight. She was unsure if he understood her words, but he appreciated his actions.

One by one the sacks were decanted. All the while the pair kept an eye out for pursuers. To Charlie's eventual relief it became apparent that they were not being followed.

As she wrestled with the last bag, Gasim motioned for her to send the raft on back into the river. As she turned to obey her orders Gasim disappeared into the bushes.

With her icy task competed she returned to the drug haul. Suddenly, the bushes rustled. She spun to find Gasim dragging a string of camels from the darkness.

With the lead camel tied to the biggest branch, Gasim set to work lifting the sacks. To Charlie's annoyance and shame, she was too weak to lift a sack, although god knows she tried. Seeing her struggle Gasim set his hand on her shoulder and set her down.

Feeling the burden lift from her weary shoulders, she slumped to the ground, too exhausted to sob.

One by one Gasim loaded the sacks of heroin onto the camels. The large poly sacks rustled and flexed as they found a position of balance on the beasts.

The beasts spat and bellowed in protest, reigniting worries that they could attract unwanted attention. Some swift whip work from Gasim silenced the camels.

With one last effort, her savior Gasim arrived in, and lifted Charlie back up over his shoulder. He staggered forward then hurled her up onto the back of a second camel. The beast bucked and reeled in protest, but Gasim held her on board.

Ropes were used to tie her down, but in a last defiant move, Charlie managed to straddle the camel and grip the saddle. Her hands were tied together at the wrists, leaving her free to grip the wooden pommel. She leaned forward and cowered in defiance of the deadly night's shade. She recovered her blanket and tied it around her neck. The pain and the fear subsided.

Only the cold now made her quake.

A fateful thought shattered the ice accumulating in Charlie's brain. *My rucksack.*

Shivering, she reached back and to her relief, she found the old rucksack still strapped to her back.

The phone.

Thank God it was in a plastic bag.

She rethought the reaction.

Don't thank God. Thank Noah.

Gasim cracked his leather whip and roused his camel. Now unable to control her mount, Charlie was in for a bumpy ride. Her head jerked with every step until camel and rider settled into a steady gait. The pace picked up; the long strides created a rhythm.

Somewhere between a canter and a gallop, the ungainly pair raced across the hard country, avoiding every bush that offered cover. Sure-footed, even in the dark, the camels loped on with Gasim leading the way.

Charlie knew her truth, that she had drifted long and far before Gasim had saved her. No stroke of luck, nor the Lord Almighty Himself, had intervened.

Gasim was the man to thank.

He had been true to his word.

The night wind sliced her flesh. The blanket flapped impotently, like the cape of a homeless superhero. Her wrists were taking a beating from the ropes, but the pain was a welcome distraction from the bone-deep cold.

A few miles later, Gasim led her down into the ravine.

The tall, heavy grasses offered ample cover and some shelter. At the bottom of the gulch, Gasim brought the camel to a halt and began campsite preparations. He pulled Charlie off the back of the camel, his wiry hands supporting her as her legs buckled, dropping her belly into the sand.

Without breaking stride, he collected dry grass and kindling from the edge of the ravine. Within a minute, sparks leapt from a flint stone into the dried tinder.

The moment jumped from a spark to flame.

A small fire sputtered, crackling and sparking, wrapping warmth around Charlie like a bear hug. Gasim yanked Charlie's small rucksack off her back. She reluctantly let it go and crawled across to the fire pit. Too cold to strip off her damp clothes she felt the heat burn and tingle in her face and hands. The sudden warmth coursed through her veins, the painful pins and needles reminding her she was still alive, contrary to all her expectations and beliefs.

The cold night air swept in, prickling Charlie's neck hairs. She drew out her talisman and fixed her chattering teeth, biting down aggressively against the chill.

Gasim moved with deliberation, building a shelter from an arrangement of fabric and branches angled in a teepee. Charlie watched him, her fatigue mingling with a growing admiration.

"Wait!" Charlie's voice sliced through the quiet as she rolled towards her rucksack. Her thawing tugged at the zipper. The look on Gasim's face changed when she pulled out what appeared to be a bottle of water.

She beamed in the fire glow. "Afghan water."

He grabbed the bottle, when he took a long, slow drink, he coughed and spluttered his face twisting in ecstasy.

Holding back a chattering snort, Charlie grabbed the bottle and took her fill. The spirit kicked like an angry mule, but its afterburn warmed her chilled core. She allowed the mule to kick her again and again until the fire inside her began to echo the fire outside.

In the silent moments that followed, images of recent murders filled her mind.

The cold gnawed at Charlie's bones. Her body shook uncontrollably as she crouched lower to the ground. She didn't realize how bad it had gotten until Gasim quietly shifted next to her, enveloping her with his body. The heat radiating from him was a welcome relief against the bitter wind that had numbed her fingers.

She wanted to thank him, to say something, anything. But he knew no English. There was no way she could convey her gratitude. His steady presence was all that kept her from fully succumbing to the cold.

As she pressed into him, her thoughts spiraled toward Feisal. The memory of his assassination hit hard. She could still picture his splintered head.

Her gut twisted. She had wanted to tell Gasim she was sorry for his loss. But who had done it?

The CIA? A rival gang? Someone from his own tribe?

She had no clue.

Charlie's shivering intensified, her teeth chattering so violently that she feared they would crack. She tightened her grip around Gasim. She clung to him, allowing his warmth to pull her back from the edge of the cold's merciless hold.

Her thoughts led on to excruciating frustration and confusion. There she stood, putting her life on the line for something as disgusting as money and something as dirty as drugs.

Before those thoughts turned into fears, she was rescued by a chattering sleep.

CHAPTER 27

A subconscious threat jarred Charlie awake.

Up close, a menacing shadow blocked the low dawn sun.

Gasim loomed over her, his expression unreadable, his presence imposing. His clothing, damp from the night, carried the scent of stale sweat and camel dust, an earthy mix that filled the air around her. His matted black hair and his beard gave him a wild, almost primal look. HE thrust a tin plate under Charlie's nose without a word. The unmistakable smell of fresh bread pulled her fully awake.

Charlie accepted the plate gratefully, her voice croaking out a quiet, "Tashakor."

Gasim gave a faint nod before stepping back. Charlie buried her face in the sweet flatbread, savoring its deliciously warm taste. She ate with vigor, each bite a comfort against the previous day's horrors. A good night's sleep had steadied her nerves, and the fire had thawed her blood. The bread was a welcome addition, though her fate remained as uncertain as ever.

Her eyes darted to her rucksack, lying nearby beside the smoldering remains of the fire. It had been set carefully to dry, and Charlie realized Gasim must have tended to it during the night.

Gasim returned with a steaming tin mug of tea. He extended it toward Charlie, his weathered face betraying no emotion. She accepted it with as warm a smile as she could muster.

He looked to have aged ten years in a day. Charlie guessed he had kept watch all night, fearless and unwavering.

They spent the day lying low in the tall grasses. Gasim worked methodically, dividing his time between keeping watch and tending to the fire.

Charlie offering to help, but Gasim dismissed her with a brief wave of his hand. Dialogue between them was scarce, limited to small gestures and the occasional glance, such was the gulf in language. She wished she could convey her gratitude, but even then, she knew even if he spoke English, she would not have the words.

She spent the remaining daylight hours confirming she still had the money, her phone, and her hidden gun. In a quieter moment, she checked the weapon's mechanism. It felt far from reliable, but she worked the pieces gently. The subtle creak of the metal sliding into place brought her a measure of comfort.

Charlie's mind churned with conflicting thoughts. Recent murders, betrayals, and the chaos of the mission loomed large. She had ventured far from her original objectives, and every step forward seemed to blur the line between duty and survival.

Now she was trapped in a web of violence with the only way out forward.

As the sun dipped low, Gasim began preparing for their next move. He worked quickly and efficiently, securing the camels, and packing their sparse supplies. Charlie mirrored his urgency, securing her rucksack and ensuring her pistol was concealed but accessible.

As the stars emerged, they set off through the tall grasses, moving westward. Gasim led the way, his camel surefooted even in the darkness. Charlie's camel followed, her body swaying with the animal's steady stride.

The terrain shifted as the night wore on, the grasses giving way to barren wasteland. Charlie's muscles ached from the relentless ride, but she pushed the discomfort aside.

At least she was moving.

Many hours later, just before dawn, they reached a narrow ravine sheltered by jagged rock faces. Gasim guided the camels into the concealment of the rocky alcove, pulling them to a halt.

Gasim dismounted and began setting up camp with practiced efficiency. Charlie followed his lead, helping where she could. She offered water to the camels and applied a soothing salve to their sore hides. Gasim watched her silently, his expression inscrutable, before returning to his tasks.

At what appeared to be a preset location, Gasim pulled the short caravan to a halt. Under the backdrop of a cliff, Gasim set a fire, in an alcove that had already been used for that purpose, many times before. Even the materials lay nearby buried under a canvas shroud.

Charlie was warming up. "This your usual haunt? Nice place."

Gasim smiled, oblivious to what had just been said. The two nomads rested near their campfire in silence, the quiet crackle of flames the only sound between them.

Gasim checked his watch twice before on the third attempt he rose.

"What is it? Charlie asked nervously.

Gasim ignored the question he didn't understand. Back under the buried tarpaulin he pulled a satellite phone.

Charlie swiveled her gaze. "What?"

He punched in a memorized number and barked one unrecognized word before the unit was switched off and rehoused.

The process took seconds.

The wait lasted an eternity.

Charlie filled the time edging slowly towards her pistol.

As she slipped her hand inside her rucksack, Gasim stood and pointed.

Down the track, trees were jostled, and branches whipped as the outline of a horse and rider crashed through a pathway in the undergrowth.

A black rider on his gray horse emerged through the dust, hard pressed for space and time. Gasim broke ranks first, waving at the approaching horseman. Charlie followed on, hidden gun at the ready.

Under the flickering firelight, the dark rider dismounted at pace and enveloped Gasim in a bear hug.

The pair seemed as relieved as they were pleased.

The rider rattled off his update in rapid, rabid Tajik. By his intonations and gesticulations, there was trouble ahead. When the new arrival spotted Charlie in the shadows, his words ceased, but his jaw kept moving.

Charlie moved forward, patting her chest. "Charlie. Charlie." That's when the new arrival's jaw stopped moving altogether.

Gasim proudly introduced the rider as a friend. "Sherif."

Dressed in black, the sinister nature of Sherif's attire did not match his youthful face, and keen expression. His sweeping black keffiyeh, sat around his neck.

In the soft morning light of the Afghan mountains, his hair stood out. His thick, wavy, and untamed, fell just past his ears. In the breeze, it danced to its own tune.

Fine lines crossed his forehead, and the faintest trace of a scar cut across one cheek, adding texture to a face already shaped by the elements. His complexion had a natural resilience to it, the kind earned by time spent in harsh, open landscapes, weathered but strong.

He was slim built but wiry.

Close up, Charlie could see he could handle himself, and others if needs be.

Gasim seemed intent on explaining the finer details, but Sherif cut him short.

Everything he now cared about stood a yard away. He stared like he had never seen beauty like it in his life. For the first time in ages, Charlie almost blushed.

To her relief, Sherif found his voice, introducing himself in Farsi. Charlie pretended to not understand, so the new arrival broke out his best English. "My name is Sherif."

"I heard that. Pleased to meet you."

Charlie realized he had been testing her with his Farsi.

And she had passed.

Keen to give updates, Gasim eased Serif to the side. The gesture seemed over dramatic given the fact she spoke very little Tajik. Irrespective, the men confided in each other with hush tones.

The shock on Sherif's face told Charlie he had just learned of Feisal's assassination. Disbelief soon turned to anger.

Questioning looks were thrown Charlie's way, as the two men provided a recent history lesson. It didn't take long for the arguments to gain heat. Their mistrust and anger seemed laced with worry and uncertainty. Charlie moved further out of earshot, but closer to her concealed handgun. She pulled the rucksack nearer when Sherif turned and marched toward her. When he leaned into Charlie's personal space, the campfire sent flickering shadows across his brooding face.

"What do you want in Iran?"

"I am checking the passage for the Pillars. We will bring out millions of dollars soon. I need to know the route is secure."

"I know nothing of this."

"It is above your pay grade."

"What is pay grade?"

"It is not your job to know about this. It is my job. We agreed all this with Feisal."

"His name does not matter now. He is dead. I decide who travels."

"I have an agree-"

"You must go back. It is too dangerous."

"Yeah. Dangerous for you if you turn me back."

Sherif became incensed. "This is no place for a woman. Police are on the border and demand taxes and bribes. If you do not pay, you die."

"Is there another way?" asked Charlie.

He shook his head. "The bandits cover the mountain passes. The police cover the roads. You cannot pass."

Charlie's went nuclear. "This is not your decision to make. Take me through or face the consequences."

Charlie knew this was not the point-of-no-return. "We go on!" She pointed ahead.

Sherif threw up his hands.

Charlie didn't know if this was in defiance or surrender.

CHAPTER 28

The tension of the canyon broke when Sherif whirled abruptly and raised a finger to signal me to stop. Charlie's gaze was immediately drawn to the movement. "Did you see that?" His voice was low, but sharp enough to cut through the taut desert air.

Carol's eyes narrowed as she straightened. The evening was a swirl of deep blacks and grays, illuminated only by the distant flicker of their campfire. Her voice was steady, but she was on edge. "What is it?"

Sherif kept his eyes on the jagged horizon, scowling as he tightened his jaw. "A light. Down below."

Without hesitation, Sherif reached for his saddlebag and pulled out a sleek pair of night vision goggles.

Charlie instantly identified the model: *AN/PVS, U.S. military, state-of-the-art.*

Sherif activated the goggles with a quick tap, and a faint mechanical hum filled the air around them. "There!" Urgency tinged his hiss as he pointed down toward the canyon floor, his body pressed against the rock. "Men on mules. Armed."

He conveyed this revelation to Gasim in clipped foreign tones.

Charlie leaned in. "How many?"

Sherif refocused the goggles, squinting. "Three, maybe four. Hard to count." The edge in his tone thickened the air around them.

Charlie's stomach twisted, but she timidly suggested, "Coincidence?" She didn't believe it even as she spoke.

Sherif didn't respond right away; his silence was telling. Then his tone shifted to grim certainty. "They're tracking us."

Charlie ducked behind a boulder three feet away, her shoulders pressed against the cool, sharp stone. It felt as if the very air around her was heavy with the potential for failure. She inhaled deeply, attempting to steady her breathing and brace for the worst.

Sherif's voice interrupted her thoughts. "Don't worry. They can't see us. They don't have the technology."

Gasim's voice was tight. "How long do we have?" His hand hovered over his holster, fingers twitching.

Without hesitation, Sherif ran back to his horse, drawing a sidearm as he moved briskly and decisively. "We're going nowhere," he said, his voice steely.

Charlie's jaw tightened, and her words spilled forth rapidly, sharply. "We can outrun them."

Sherif pivoted to face her, locking eyes. "They could call in our position?"

Charlie retorted, her mind racing. "They don't know we're here–"

"They know the path," Sherif interrupted, his voice hard. "They're either going to cut us down while we sleep or have waiting reinforcements on the other side."

Charlie pressed her lips together. "They could be friendly." The words felt thin, taut as a thread stretched too far.

Sherif's gaze didn't waver. "We will see whether they come in peace. If not…" His words trailed off, suggesting there was more left unsaid.

Gasim ran toward the fire, his hand reaching to extinguish it. Sherif's crisp command halted him. "No."

The three of them set to work, constructing a grim illusion. Frayed sleeves and loose fabric fluttered in the wind. Makeshift forms lay like bodies at rest, blurring the space near the fire. The ruse appeared unnervingly convincing under the strobing illumination.

Charlie watched Sherif tend the fire, embers swirling into darkness like little messengers. The gesture seemed to challenge, a statement that they wouldn't hide.

She clutched the polymer handle of her gun, the cool surface. Anxiety simmered beneath her skin, but she suppressed it and remained composed.

Sherif's voice softened when he met Charlie's gaze. "If they bring peace, we will be peaceful. If they bring death…" He paused, letting the weight of his words hang in the air. "We'll bring death."

Charlie nodded, her throat parched. She positioned herself behind a cluster of boulders, her gun drawn. The firelight was deceptive, so she concentrated on the dim spaces beyond, steering clear of panic's fog.

The night and the intruders closed in. Each sound was magnified, the occasional crackle of the fire, the whisper of the wind through the canyon. It was too quiet, the kind of silence that pressed down on her ears and made her want to strain to hear something, anything.

Then she heard it. A rustling sound, subtle but distinct. Her breath hitched. "This is it," she thought, muscles tensed like a coiled spring.

She faintly registered the shuffle of footsteps and the soft thud of men dismounting. "They come," she whispered, her eyes fixed on the shadows moving toward the fire, slow, deliberate. She gripped her gun tighter, the cold metal steadying her as her mantra replayed in her mind: "Please let them come in peace."

The men approached deliberately, their shadows stretching grotesquely in the firelight. Their stealthy advance churned Charlie's stomach. This wasn't a friendly visit.

The lead man waved his hand imperceptibly. Then, gunfire erupted, ripping through the night like a storm, savage, unbroken. "Boom!" The fake bodies near the fire erupted in a burst of shredded clothing and loose pillow filling.

Charlie jerked but remained still, holding her ground. The leader stepped forward, barking orders in Pashto, laughter low and raucous. There was a swagger in his confidence, a palpable contempt.

When he bent over to inspect their alleged kills, a shot rang out. Sherif's bullet found its mark, and the man collapsed in an instant, his cruel laughter stifled.

Chaos erupted. Sherif and Gasim pulled the trigger, firing accurate shots. Bullets flew indiscriminately, hitting their targets. One of the assailants stumbled into the flames, screams piercing the cacophony as the fire engulfed him.

Charlie sat there, gun raised but unused. Her fingers shook slightly, but she forced herself to steady. When the shooting stopped, an eerie silence fell over the canyon. The acrid smell of gunpowder mingled with the metallic taste of blood and the smoky char from the blaze.

Charlie walked gingerly over the scene, her eyes scanning the bodies lying lifeless on the ground. The sight turned her stomach, but she kept her expression neutral.

The silence was broken by Sherif's voice. "It was us or them." Firmness resonated in his tone, but weariness was etched on his face from the night's events.

Before she could respond, she was suddenly distracted by a rustling in the trees behind them. Adrenaline surged as Gasim yelled, "Charlie!"

Bang!

A gunshot rang out, and Gasim's body convulsed violently. He pitched forward, collapsing into Charlie's arms. His blood covered her hands, hot and slick, as he slumped against her.

Instinctively, Charlie spun around and fired into the darkness. Sherif emptied his magazine, and her ears rang. The last assailant lurched out of the shadows, crumpling into a heap just a few paces from the fire.

Gasim's breathing was shallow, his voice a faint murmur in his native language. Charlie placed her palm on his wound, moving frantically as her voice cracked. "What's he saying?"

Sherif knelt beside her, his face grim. "He says he swore to protect you with his life."

Gasim's body went limp as his last breath escaped him like a whisper on the wind. Charlie blinked at him, tears filling her eyes.

Her chest shook with a sobbing grief. The blood on her hands felt heavy beyond measure, a guilt she would bear for eternity.

CHAPTER 29

Later that morning, it took another two butt-blistering hours before the waypoint was reached. By that stage, tiredness had overtaken pain. Charlie's limbs ached and her head thumped. She hacked up to clear her throat.

Sherif tried his hand at humor. "You are already acting like an Iranian!"

Charlie didn't have the conviction of the energy to respond.

The fact he could raise even a grin seemed alien to her.

A sandy squall blasted the final few miles, adding abrasion to injury. Only when Sherif jumped down from his mount, did Charlie realize they were stopping.

The point of alighting seemed innocuous until the big reveal.

The battered and beaten Toyota pickup had been well disguised, jammed in between the cracks in a cliff face. It only became visible when the larger bushy offcuts were dragged to the side. Whilst the truck was being uncovered, the beasts recovered. Charlie fed them copious helpings from the stash of grain and water hidden behind the pickup. It took all their remaining strength to rehydrate. Charlie stood in awe as frothy sweat poured from the magnificent animals. As the truck edged out into the open, the fate of these creatures became Charlie's primary concern. "What do we do with them?"

"We leave them here."

Charlie protested. "They will die."

"We are not the animals you think we are. Here, help me."

Sherif pulled out blankets and covers from the rear of the truck bed. The three animals were watered once more, before being led down into the canyon. They were then bedded down in the shade. Each animal received a full nosebag of grain, and yet more water, before Sherif clapped each one of them goodbye. Charlie hugged each one. "We can't leave them here for long."

"You worry too much. We have a man to look after them."

"When will he get here?"

"He is here already. You just cannot see him. He will collect them after we leave. He does not want to be near the drugs."

Charlie looked round sharply, but nothing stirred. "How do I know you are telling the truth?"

"He is the one who brought the goats. Go round the back. You will see. Bring them back."

Charlie squinted at the preposterous proposal. "And what will you be doing?"

"Loading the shipment on the tuck."

Suitably chastised, and inherently curious, Charlie hauled her tired bones off round behind the large outcrop. Half expecting an ambush, she edged her way forward, annoyed that she had left her gun behind in the rucksack. Suspicions mounted as the canyon narrowed and the brush closed in. Afraid, with no means to defend herself, she slowed to a hesitant halt. Just as she turned to return to her handgun, the barely perceptible bleat from a solitary goat carried in on the breeze. She turned her head and listened in. *There it was again.*

Encouraged and relieved, she pushed on. In a craggy corner, under the shade of an olive tree, lay four sleeping goats tied to a metal spike. They jumped, bleated, and bounded for attention when they saw their new best friend. Mayhem ensued as Charlie wrangled the butting, bucking mass of hooves and horns.

When a chuckling Sherif entered the open-air corral, some order was installed. With two goats each, the pair were dragged and buffeted all the way back to the truck.

The responsibility for feeding and watering them landed on Charlie. She didn't mind the work, considering the only other employment available seemed to be a drug handler.

She watched from afar as Sherif continued his work. For once, she didn't mind the country's chauvinistic employment laws. The woven poly bags were slit, releasing the deadly cargo. Hidden catches on the pickup were unclipped, allowing the side panels to flip off the fake wheel arches. The poly packets of drugs were then crammed tightly inside before the panels were reattached. Excrement from the camel was then thrown into the back and washed into the edges of the panels, covering all mismatched paneling. The goats were then thrown in as a last act of concealment. Sherif was at the heart of all the dirty work.

"The police dogs attack the goats. That is why we are never stopped." He bounced his weight on the tailgate. "We have strengthened the suspension to stop the back from sitting too low with the extra hidden weight."

"Got it." Charlie liked simplicity of the deceit.

It made sense, unlike everything else at that moment in time. As Sherif loaded the rest of the supplies, Charlie checked her rucksack to make sure she hadn't lost her bribe money, handgun, or phone. The old phone given to her by Noah was pulled from its secret compartment. Although it had been switched off, it had long lost its charge. Being old school, its jack didn't match the charger in the truck. *Typical.*

Taking stock did little to ease her mind. With Gasim gone, the only route ahead was forward. She had lost her main sponsor, the warlord Feisal. Right now, she hoped, more danger lay behind her. She had to move on and face the consequences. When thoughts moved to planning how to get out of Iran, the future too looked bleak. There was no embassy. She could be captured and arrested as a spy.

Her defense was non-existent. She could say she was kidnapped whilst working for the FBI. That almost rang true. Quite how the Iranians differentiated between the CIA and the FBI seemed a moot point. She was an American woman without ID, smuggling drugs into Iran.

It was critical that she did everything possible to keep up appearances, so she appreciated Sherif bringing over a battleship gray burka. "From one of your lady friends?" she asked.

He didn't rise to the bait. "Jump in. We go."

She made sure the goats were not at the end of their tethers and then climbed inside. The cabin stank. The stench of the dirt caked around the door was disgusting. "Wow. Nice place you got here. Is all this part of the planning?"

Sherif stared coldly. "There is a nine-millimeter hidden in your door."

She checked to make sure he wasn't bluffing. Her clothing was switched, as Sherif set the truck in motion, across the scrubland. She searched in the rearview mirror for the mystery man who would look after the animals. Dust obscured her view before any positive sightings could be made. She took Sherif at his word, after all, the goats were in great shape. Quite how they would look after a run in with some police dogs was anyone's business. That was a problem for the future, for now she was just pleased to have traded a busted saddle for a bench seat. The hardened suspensions took the load. It didn't take long for her weary body to slide down into the rhythm of the journey.

When the scrub turned to rutted sand, the road ahead bent into view, coaxing Charlie to consider what may lie ahead. It would be difficult to track and fight her enemies in Iran. *Difficult, but not impossible.* Sherif was a useful cog, but she needed to find the man who ran the entire machine.

After glugging down a bottle of warm but clean water, Charlie's throat cleared. "Who will we see?"

"In Tehran?"

Charlie sucked in air, pleased that she had confirmed the long assumed the destination.

"He may not want to see you. If he does, you will not be introduced. I will show you the setup and you will be sent back."

Charlie pointed toward the recent ambush. "Back there?"

"Back by another route."

"You have more than one route."

Sherif threw out a look that made Charlie realize she had asked a dumb question.

She calculated the cost of failure. Millions of US dollars were being stolen to fund drug running and, no doubt, terrorism. She mulled over the positives. She had bribery cash, a great local contact, good cover, and free rein to act unimpeded by the US bureaucracy. It was unlikely that her phone would work, even if it was charged. But she could steal a phone or buy a burner in a market stall. Telecoms would not be a problem.

The truck eventually leveled out after bumping down onto a gravel road. The jolted change of direction allowed Sherif the chance to switch subjects. "It's best that you pull your burka close."

Charlie followed the guidelines without question. The inference of the trouble ahead refocused her thoughts on escape from Iran. She could pass as French in most circumstances. It would be better than being American, but not by much. The skeleton of a plan formed. She would follow this to the end. Once clued up and clear, she would contact a sympathetic embassy. They would contact her peers back in the US. They would get her out.

Iran lay ahead. She faced two murderous regimes on either side of her authority. Although the dawn sun was rising on a beautifully cloudless morning, things could not have looked darker.

Her breath quickened at the realization.

The point of no return had been passed some time ago.

It was impossible to turn back.

CHAPTER 30

The first gas station sign appeared an hour into the forecasted twenty-hour drive. A quick roadside stop to pick up fresh cooled water, hot flatbreads, boiled eggs, and pickles was the only concession. Before they hit the road, Charlie hit the washroom. Away from prying eyes, she washed herself down in a filthy sink. The contents from a police-issued first aid kit, supplied by Sherif, were set to good use, sterilizing, and covering her wounds. *Superficial.*

Somehow, under the stress of recent events, her old battle scars throbbed. Lastly, she filled the sink to the murky brim, then submerged her head. She slowed her heart rate and held her breath. A sudden irrational fear of being attacked forced her to yank her head back out of the sink. She splashed and swiveled, fearful of her surroundings. The restroom door remained locked from her side. The process wasn't repeated. Paranoia was setting in.

Charlie spied the sodden waif staring back at her, through the busted mirror above the sink. Drenched and pitiful. She didn't like the view. After giving herself a long, hard look. A long hard telling-to followed. Sherif banging on the door gave her the shake she needed. The remains of the first aid kit made their way inside her rucksack. The phone, gun, and drinks were all accounted for. Three deep breaths later, she slid back out the door.

Across at the pump, the engine revved. Sherif's face told her that such delays were not to be repeated. Not one to be rushed; she made a point of checking the goats. All her presence seemed to do was unsettle them. The passenger door was pushed upon in an attempt to hurry her along. Charlie got the message.

By the time Sherif skidded the pickup across and up on the gravel road, his temperature dial was approaching red.

The pickup eased on up the highway, through the sporadic traffic. Progress was measured and relentless as the old pickup ate up the miles. More formal, larger road signage told them they were approaching the edges of civilization. Three miles later, the gravel turned to tarmac, and the road widened. When the rubber hit the road, the pair turned to each other and enforced grins.

Their look was laced with shared unspoken encouragement.

Progress.

A mile or so up the road, Sherif's face flinched at the rearview mirror.

Charlie noticed him staring behind. "What is it?"

"Maybe nothing." He checked the speedometer. Without touching his brakes, he rode the clutch until friction and wind resistance dropped their speed from just over to just under the limit. Sherif held his nerve and his line. "Easy."

When Charlie moved to look behind her, Sherif cut her off. "Don't do that. Eyes dead ahead."

She complied, only breaking her glare with the process of pulling on her burka. The patrol car eased up within fifty yards of the pickup. Agonizingly, it slowed to a matching speed.

Charlie fidgeted, unable to check the view. "What are they doing?"

Sherif's voice faltered. "Scoping us out."

"What will we do?"

"What can we do? We can't outrun them."

Charlie sounded fatalistic. "Or out-gun them."

The pair were low on options. Sherif was spending so long looking in the rearview mirror, it was Charlie who raised the alarm. "Look out!"

Sherif jumped on the brakes. Rubber squealed and burned. Directly in front, a second police car straddled the center of the road. To add to the drama, the police lights were activated on the blocking patrol car.

Charlie stuttered. "Shit."

"It's okay. We have money." Drawing closer, he began to change his view. "I haven't seen these men before."

The policemen were armed and one of them had already drawn.

"Pull the studs on the door."

"Seriously?"

"Do it!"

Charlie pulled the studs and the Uzi 9mm mentioned earlier.

"If they ask you out, do not go. If they insist, point it, pull the trigger, and hold on."

Charlie held on, doubting she would be able to carry out the final stage of her orders. Petrified that the rucksack would be taken, she opened the bag and pulled out a wad of cash.

As they approached, Sherif wound down his window. "You keep your window up. Pretend it's broken."

The patrol car arrived in from the rear and halted ten yards behind them. Its flashing lights were sent into overdrive, causing Sherif to look away from his rearview mirror. Four policemen approached, two on either side. The pair twitched at the sight of a police dog dragging its handler ahead of the pack. Five yards out, Sherif's own Uzi made an appearance. Flashbacks of Noah's murder strengthened Charlie's grip on her weapon. She understood Iran wasn't Afghanistan, but shakedowns and drugs were the same the world over. Both Uzis were cocked simultaneously.

The look they shared this time around was far removed from, 'so far so good'.

As they encroached the five-yard line, Sherif breathed out. "They have old uniforms."

Charlie was lost. "And?"

"It's an amateur shakedown."

"How can you tell?"

"Police in new uniforms don't hustle people."

Bloody memories of Noah's brutal murder flooded her mind's eye. "My friend was killed by the fake police. I had to mention Feisal to save myself."

Sherif forced out his best smile and whispered.

"It is not the same in Iran. Mention Feisal and we die."

Charlie's burka hid her sweating brow, and the brass talisman clamped between her grinding teeth. The lead policemen banged the pistol butt against the driver's door. A routine police check disintegrated into a sham early in the rag-tag process. The policeman twisted his nineteen seventies porn star mustache up at the filthy stench emanating from the inside of the cab. He couldn't wait to walk around to the back of the truck. Deep breaths were taken. “Stay cool,” Sherif whispered.

The police dog went into meltdown, trying to attack the four hapless goats. Its bite looked worse than its bark. Given the confusion being wrought by the dog, the handler retired to a quiet location. Tensions rose.

A few cursory glances haphazardly thrown in all the wrong places ensured the drugs remained undiscovered. Phase two of the shakedown involved a direct request for taxes from the lead policemen. When Sherif offered two hundred US dollars, the policeman’s mustache twitched again. The interrogation started in Farsi. “Why so much money? Why US money?”

Sherif was reeling at his mistake. “My brother is an interpreter. He has access to US money.”

That seemed to make things worse. “Get out of the car.”

“Why?”

The policeman’s voice rose in pitch and volume. “Get out.” In response, the two closest guards closed in. Charlie froze, unsure of her next moves. Her nerves tingled under the pressure. Under her dress, the safety on the switch was eased on, then off. “Ready when you are.” She whispered to her comrade-in-arms. “Wait for it. When they pull your door handle, we go.”

Suddenly, the fourth policeman appeared from the rear car, waving his arms. His colleagues in crime stepped back from the bloody brink. The policeman rushed across to the ringleader, holding a cell phone aloft. He snatched it, clearly annoyed.

The leader’s level of annoyance only seemed to increase as the cell phone conversation progressed. Protest moved to capitulation when the leader folded under the weight of the telephone call. When the call was dropped, all hell broke loose. Angry instructions were spat at his scurrying crew. The two hundred-dollar bills made their way into the leader's breast pocket. He turned and stared into the pickup. Wild angry stares. Like a petulant kid who hadn't had it his way, he thumped the roof of the pickup. The intimidation subsided, as the shakedown was called off by the man on the other end of the line. The policemen retreated to the safety of their patrol cars without explanation. Charlie was lost. "What the hell is happening?"

Sherif already had the engine lit. "Who cares?"

They sped forward, kicking up gravel and setting off the goats in the back. They rode on, stupefied by the positive turn in events. Sherif checked his rearview mirror. "I don't know what that was."

"What do you mean?"

"Did you understand any of that?"

Charlie shook her head. "The man handing over the phone said the call came from the Phoenician. Who's that?"

Sherif seemed confused. "No one really knows."

"An ally? A competitor?"

Sherif wasn't helping. "Both. Neither." He seemed almost afraid to discuss the name.

Charlie snatched at straws. "If they were rivals, they would just have killed us."

Sherif was calming down and closing down. "Possibly."

Charlie opened her window to breathe. "I need a drink."

"There is water in the back."

"Not that kind of drink!"

She pulled the plastic water bottle from her rucksack and chewed down a few mouthfuls of local firewater. Sherif joined her in spirit.

Charlie jittered in the aftermath of the recent ambush. She couldn't comprehend events. Only one thing was certain.

The Phoenician had just saved their lives.

CHAPTER 31

Iran's beauty amazed and confused, in equal measures. The stunningly diverse topography was awash with humanity. The long journey had been broken up with gas station stops where the passengers and their vehicle took on fuel. Attempts to lever information from Sherif failed at every juncture. Losing Gasim was cutting deep, but Charlie guessed the code of silence ran deeper than grief. All questions about the run in with the shakedown police were ignored. Requests for information relating to the mystery Phoenician were immediately shot to pieces.

Her first sighting of Tehran was taken at a distance. The snow-capped mountains acted as the perfect backdrop to the city's medium rise towers of concrete and glass. "Wow. It reminds me of Salt Lake City. I doubt the religions could be any more different."

"What do you mean?"

Charlie hadn't the energy. "Forget it. All I am just saying is it's very pretty."

After a cautionary detour, the truck entered the sprawling outskirts of the city, from the foothills. The language differed, but the advertising hoardings lining the sides of the three-lane highway looked positively Western. A large telecom observation tower dominated a skyline filled with contracting architecture from a host of decades. Well ordered, clean, lush, heavily wooded, Tehran was nothing like its reputation. Compared with Afghanistan, Iran seemed almost sedate. Compared to Iraq, it was a veritable Zen garden. The traffic was ordered, the roads well maintained, the people apparently unconcerned for their safety. The reality jarred with Charlie's incorrect preconceptions. Hijabs and burkas looked to be enforced, but the demonic oppression reported by the Western media seemed light years from the reality spilling out before her.

The nation's green, red, and white flags flew everywhere. Yellow taxis filled the streets. A bizarre motorbike with built-in shade sped past, close enough to almost knock off the truck's wing mirror. The wide thoroughfares were lined with row after row of poplar trees, placed with pinpoint perfection. The gargantuan chimney from a nearby cement factory seemed the only blot on the beautiful landscape. Habits were forming. "Does everyone smoke around here?"

Her traveling companion shrugged. "Everyone. Iranians have addictive personalities. That is why they have the highest rate of heroin abuse in the world."

Charlie wanted to ask whether Sherif felt at all responsible for that particularly grim statistic, but instead she opened up another line of questioning. "You said *they* have the highest rate. Are you not Iranian?" Another wall of silence fell on her questioning.

They drove on. Charlie was all eyes. Sherif was no tongue.

Out the window, a short row of carpet shops stood waiting for customers. On a street corner, a bubbling pipe was being passed between friends sitting on the stone circle protecting a tree. Massive posters showing imams and their latest slogans offered guidance to the masses. On many streets, hundreds of motorcycles were crammed across the sidewalks, impairing the sightlines of those driving by, and impeding the pathways for those walking by. Closed shops with graffiti on the shutters told an all too familiar tale. White buildings lined the broad streets, acting as arteries into the city. A multitude of small white cars bustled around the busy streets like bleached ants marching to orders. From the high vantage point of the raised road, it became clear to Charlie that huge chunks of the city had been overgrown by the spread of slums. After spiraling off the highway's circular off ramp, they slid deeper into the shady underbelly of the city. Concrete and mud were the building materials of choice, further away from the main routes. In the seedier sections of the city, traffic clogged the narrowing back streets. One-way systems became no-way systems. Horns blared and tempers flared. The stifling fumes from the congestion clogged Charlie's lungs. Opening the window only made things worse. Sherif offered his doleful thoughts on the sights and sounds surrounding them. "Welcome to the city of the Shahs. The rich live in Bala-ye shahr, the upper city, but the poor live in Paeen-e shahr, the lower city."

Charlie took a look at the poverty all around. "I take it we're headed into Paeen-e shahr."

Sherif gestured to the chaos outside. "One in five live in slums in Tehran. There are 12 million people and four million vehicles. Thousands die each year from traffic pollution alone."

Charlie wafted the fumes around the cabin and closed the air vents. "That explains a lot. Maybe that's why the smoke."

"After the Shah was deposed in the revolution, Ayatollah Khomeini claimed all land to be the property of Allah. Everyone was free to develop everywhere. What you see is the result."

"Madness and mess."

"Yes, but it is your sanctions that have destroyed this land."

Charlie got defensive. "Not our sanctions. The UN's sanctions."

"Wake up. There is a reason the UN is in New York City."

Charlie tried to pivot away from a clearly unwinnable argument. "Doesn't the World Bank invest heavily to help with the housing problems?"

Sherif chortled. "None of it gets through. Their investment keeps us all in a job."

"You call this a career?"

"It pays better than being a terrorist, but not as much as being a politician."

Charlie almost understood. "And it helps take you away from all of this."

Outside, half-clothed kids splashed up and down inside an open drain. They kicked filthy water over each other, giggling all the way. Their friends, standing up on terra firma, ran the gauntlet as the city's old busses blasted past with only inches to spare. An old man sat on an open-sided cart made from blanched wood. Its rickety, flimsy cartwheels were on their last legs. Gray dust fell from his unkempt hair onto his once black jacket. It seemed combs and razors were in short supply back home. Markets ran wild under the watchful eye of highly visible policing. Tehran seemed an extraordinary amalgam of chaos and contradictions: freedoms coexisted alongside suffocating controls. The darker edge brought proceedings into a sharper focus for Charlie. "Where are we headed?"

"Our safe house."

"Where is that?"

"You will see."

As if prompted by the dialogue, Sherif reached across and pulled a phone from the truck's glove compartment. Charlie could have helped retrieve it, but for some reason, he made it a solo affair. The need for secrecy aside, Charlie could tell, events were taking their toll on her driver. He pressed the phone on, tapped in a number and waited. The one-way dialogue was transmitted in Farsi. Still, Charlie pretended not to understand as she translated the message as: *Ten minutes. Get ready. I have a passenger.*

After the call was killed, she continued to work over the witness for the prosecution, asking questions she had already translated the answers to.

"When will we get there?"

"Soon."

"Do they know I am coming?"

"What is with all the questions?"

Convincing Sherif further that she spoke no Farsi had been the goal, but Charlie didn't like how the conversation was tilting. With the short-term mission accomplished, she sat forward, to track the directional changes, and waited for the future to arrive. It didn't take long.

Five minutes later, the truck pulled a sharp U-turn. Fifty yards later, a turn was made into a very narrow side street. Two immediate left turns led to a long, narrow alley. All the while, the rear mirror got as much viewing time as the windshield, as Sherif checked for unwanted company. He seemed satisfied his tail was clean. From there one more right turn had them pulling in alongside a trail of static Tuk-Tuks. Drivers of various ages and keenness stood by awaiting their next rides. In all directions, tall walls closed in around their position. The industrial compounds and warehouses set a dismal scene.

Bunting made from makeshift materials hung low between two buildings. Filthy kids wearing hand-me-downs in desperate need of pick-me-ups sat dolefully on a busted curb. A sister teaching her smaller brother rhymes became suspicious of Charlie's presence and pushed him indoors. Charlie mused that when that pair grew older, those roles would be reversed. The car slowed to a squealing halt. Even the pickup was feeling the heat. The engine idled. The aircon worked overtime.

Nearby a back street tanner was hard at work bleaching leathers. Small hides were out on show, glistening as they dried off in the sunlight. Bottle after bottle of industrial bleach lay in a row around the top of a set of small walled wells. The tanner's white beard matched his pale complexion.

His happy grin was wrapped in fuzzy facial hair that had given up half-way on its journey up to his balding head. His threadbare clothes bore all the hole marks of a lifetime spent in or around acidic compounds. Two packets of cigarettes bulged from the ripped breast pocket of his home washed, stonewashed denim top. He stood, stretched, and coughed all over his dusty little alcove. Charlie stared, amazed and curious, at the one-man health hazard. In different circumstances, she would have loved to have gone over and helped out. When the man set back to work, Charlie realized she had to follow suit. After a couple more minutes of waiting, her impatience bled through. "What are we waiting for?"

"Him." Sherif pointed to a balding, overweight man in an undersized, sweat-stained tee shirt. He waddled across and collapsed into an old wooden chair. Only the chair looked under pressure. The man scratched his bristled chops, belching as he fidgeted with a set of prayer beads.

"Are we looking at the same guy?" asked Charlie.

"Look at his hands. If he is moving the beads to the left, we move on. If he is moving them to the right, the passage is safe."

"They're going right. Are we in business?"

"We are."

Sherif revved the engine, checked his mirror, and then eased the truck across the street. The round man slowly rose, tottered over, and opened the gate. In a slow and measured maneuver, the truck slipped inside the compound. It took longer for the day watchman to re-close the wooden gate. The large bolt was proving difficult to ease into its latch. The small courtyard's tall walls had seen cleaner days. An old scooter, painted in the colors of the national flag, sat in the corner. Chief amongst its numerous traffic scars were a busted fairing and a missing front light. The precariously attached silver blanket with tassels seemed an odd addition. Shipping boxes in various states of disrepair lay split and stacked along one edge of the compound. Diagonally opposite, a battered skip hid beneath an overflowing pile of rubbish. The trash pile smelled higher than the surrounding walls. The massive junkyard dog, snarling on its chain, looked eager to be released for a spot of guard duty. Everything about the site yelled, tip.

When the warehouseman saw Charlie, he pulled his chins to his chest and glared. Speechless, and doubtful, he led the truck in under a roller shutter door. His handgun protruded out of the back of his baggy pants. Charlie suspected her appearance had something to do with the two men not sharing any greetings. She held back, in the knowledge introductions would not be coming her way. Once through into the building, the charade became obvious. Inside, she discovered a well-ordered, clean warehouse. Racked to the ceiling, well-lit with blacked-out, barred windows, the building's aura felt professional. More barred windows than bar coding, but professional, nonetheless.

A forklift truck in good working order lay on charge outside a crisp new portable cabin, opposite the entrance. Beside the makeshift office sat a Toyota pickup, jacked up in mid repair. Charlie spotted the telltale signs of deception. The SUV wasn't being repaired; it was being prepared. The panels underneath the truck were undergoing the augmentation necessary to conceal drug shipments. Other than the running repairs, the internals looked every bit as polished as anything she had seen before. Even the warehouseman's demeanor professionalized once indoors. He seemed to gain a few inches and lose a few pounds.

What he hadn't lost was his attitude.

He took charge of the goats, pulling them off the back of the truck and dragging them out to the section of the compound housing the over-filled garbage cans. The guard dog went further out of control upon first sight of his new prey. Down every link in the drug supply chain, her contacts seemed less welcoming, and more dangerous. The dog was no exception. The goats made themselves at home as the dog spun himself dizzily around his steel tether. Chomping away at the garbage, it seemed as if the goats had seen and heard it all before. The same wasn't true for Charlie.

She surveyed the scene as she was led inside, rucksack in hand. Closer inspections uncovered a dizzying cocktail of weaponry and contraband. Military equipment, including handguns, rifles, night sights, flares, and communications gear, sat in aligned rows. The Russian lettering on the wooden crates nearby made identification impossible. The next section looked straight from a prohibition era gangster movie. Case upon case of Scotch whisky sat beside pallet loads of cigarettes. Shrink-wrapped boxes containing pharmaceuticals were set in a separate section of racking.

A small canning line had been shut down in mid production run. Charlie doubted the cans would ever hold the pistachio nuts the labels suggested. And if they did, they would likely be laced with something a little stronger.

The warehouseman's sideways glances were poisoned with suspicion. He paced on ahead before firing his opening shots of Farsi.

"Can we talk?"

Sherif shrugged. "She can't understand."

I understand well enough. Thought Charlie.

"Who is she?" asked the warehouseman.

"She is with the organization. She is here to see the Police Chief."

Charlie picked up on the title, *Police Chief.*

"Does he know she is here?"

Sherif acted as an interpreter. "It's okay. She is one of us."

Charlie feigned a lack of comprehension. She circled and gawked ignorantly before wandering off to the edge of her hearing capabilities. All the while, she took verbal and visual inventory. The Farsi argument continued at pace, backed by the fallacy, the woman was stupid.

"What do you want to do with her?" asked the warehouseman.

"She bought safe passage from Feisal."

"Feisal is dead. The Police Chief will say who gets safe passage."

The warehouseman shouted a question at Charlie. "How do you know, Feisal?"

She didn't even look up.

"See I told you."

"Stupid bitch. Who comes to Iran unable to speak Farsi? Maybe we can screw some sense into her?"

The men grunted like the pigs they were.

Sherif pressed her case. "I tell you she is blessed too."

"Blessed."

"We were caught by the police in the mountains. They took a call from the Phoenician, and we were freed. It's a sign."

"A sign she is trouble."

"How can helping us escape be trouble?"

"She could work for the Phoenician."

Sherif dismissed the idea. "I have seen enough to know she is one of us."

Charlie was confused by the emergence of the Phoenician. She was starting to convince herself that she had a recollection of hearing the name on the radio scanner back during her time as an airwave surfer, back in camp. She shook her head, confused by a distant memory from another world. Before the warehouseman could spread more poison, she went in again, in English. "I have safe passage. Who is in charge?"

Sherif acted up, not wanting to lose face with his gang member. "We ask the questions."

"You are not in charge." She played the ace card, knowing it had recently been dealt by Sherif.

"Feisal said I would be set in contact with Police Chief."

The fat man rounded on her. "What proof do you have?"

"Gasim told me." Replied Sherif.

"And where is he?"

"Dead."

"What? How?"

Charlie was on a charge. "Look, get your boss on the line, get him down here, now."

The men hesitated, so she doubled down. "Do it now, or face consequences."

The warehouseman got and hated the message. Charlie hid her relief when translating Sherif's decision. "Get him on the line. See what he wants to do. We will break up the truck."

The warehouseman sighed his reluctant agreement. "Here, let me help you." Before she could refuse, or come up with an excuse to keep it, the warehouseman had taken her rucksack. His chivalry seemed out of character, but to hold on to it in a panic would have raised suspicions. She felt exposed without her gun but needed to go along with it for the moment.

Sherif methodically led the strip down process. First off, the general trash was removed from the vehicle. She gained comfort when noticing her rucksack on the floor outside the Portakabin.

The drugs were next on the menu. One by one the compartments were cracked open, and the contents carefully exhumed. A digital scale and hand-written log were used to record individual bag weights. Charlie tried to sneak a peek at the logbook, but Sherif subtly twisted it out of Charlie's sightline. Uncertain if the move was deliberate. Operating in silence, the information noted was not shared.

With all drugs removed and all signs of criminal life obscured, the process of reassembling the vehicle commenced. A raised voice broke out from the cabin. Sherif moved off into the office before the job was finished. "Wait here." It wasn't a request. Charlie completed the work at hand, all the time spying through the office window. The warehouseman was remonstrating down the phone. Sherif looked lost for words. By the looks of the warehouseman's reactions, the person on the other end of the phone was not. When the warehouseman pulled the phone away from his ear and stared at the handset, Charlie sensed the other caller had just hung up. Concerned looks were shared inside the cabin, forcing Charlie to ease back towards her rucksack.

She couldn't get there quick enough.

She didn't get there quick enough.

The warehouseman packed heat. "Change of plan."

"What the hell do you think-"

Sherif kept cool. "It's just until we figure out what to do. We can't trust you."

Charlie bowed up. "We have a code."

"We have no code. We have bosses."

"So do I, and they will not be happy."

Sherif held up his palms. "I am sorry. We will work this out."

The warehouseman pushed her to turn around. She complied. The gun prodded the small of her back, pushing her forward. Under protest, she argued and bit back as she was pushed toward a separate room. All the time, she delayed her incarceration to scan the scene around. She stopped short of displaying panic for fear of breaking cover. A threat was sent to buy time. "You will hang in the street if you do not take me to Police Chief right now."

If the men were afraid, they did not show it. The scanning process went into overload. At the end of the warehouse lay a small workshop area. The paraphernalia of a chop shop lay all around. A workbench with a vise stood against the end wall two feet from the door she was about to be pushed through. Angle grinder, welder, drill and bits, nuts and bolts, tins of spray paint.

Hand tools in an open stacked toolbox were too far out of reach to be useful. Left of the door sat a large wire basket half full of wastepaper and oily rags next to a hand wash station with a mirror. Ten feet away, scrapped metal sat in an ordered fashion beside new sheet panels and an acetylene blowtorch.

The storeroom looked to have been converted into a bedsit for the warehouseman. The room stank of body odor and oil. The bed hadn't been made in days or washed in months. The detritus of a middle-aged man who had given up on life lay contaminated the room.

Charlie didn't break character. "Nice place you have here. Get a lot of girls round, do you?" A final shove in the back sent her fully into the windowless six by six cell. The key was pulled from inside the door and used to turn the lock from the outside. Hearing the key being removed from the lock didn't help the situation.

"This won't' stand!"

She shouted to no avail and watched as the men walked off in silence. She interpreted the sounds as the men jumping in the truck, exiting the building, then shutting up shop. The roller shutter door came down with a rattling clatter, leaving the building in eerie silence.

Pacing in a circle, her thoughts ricocheted around the small square room. She slowed, too tired to focus, too scared to face reality. She slumped in the bed exhausted, unable to escape her future, yet unwilling to face it. She took a moment just to lie down and think. Overpowered by fatigue. Her spiraling mind relented and allowed her to close her eyes and dream of five minutes of sleep.

The thoughts guarding her consciousness were soon overpowered.

Her head bowed, just for a moment.

She thumped the bed, angry at her lack of judgment. Worry arrived early, and it took all her fortitude and discipline to drive that invader from her mind. She understood a clear difference between fear and worry.

Fear motivates. Worry paralyzes.

Stay fearful. Stop worrying.

Start thinking!

Her recovering mind went into overdrive. The man on the call had been apoplectic. She hadn't convinced the foot soldiers, and with such poor arguments, it seemed doubtful she would convince the higher ranks. Only worse outcomes would likely return. She needed out. The emergence of the Phoenician further crowded the suspect list, but quite how, or even if, he fitted in, would be a subject for another day.

The room was scanned in detail, but nothing of use fell into view. She lowered herself and sat on the edge of the rickety, filthy bed. It squealed and creaked under her weight. She rocked back and forward, working out that if the men took the truck, they would be gone for some time. With nothing of use on show, inside the room, she scanned the world outside her room, through the eight-inch square vent in the door. A hard boot smashed against the vent improved the viewing. There was no access to any instruments of escape. Deflated by the lack of options, she retook her place on the bed before retracing her movements and replaying her memories.

Flushed with an idea, she thumped the cell wall with her right fist. It reverberated. In a fit of excitement, she took the small table beside the bed and cracked one of its legs against the wall. It cracked the plaster. Two more smacks and the scrappy brick construction fell into view.

Her heart sank. She had literally hit a brick wall. She sat back down on the bed, then battled off her negativity in order to retrace her steps. The answer had been staring her in the face. *The mirror.*

She pulled the filthy case from the pillow. It took a deal of courage to take a bite of the rancid cloth and rip open the fabric. She then wrapped a strip from the tattered remnant tightly around her left fist. Jumping across to the door, she pushed her clothed hand round the right side of the doorframe. Her outstretched hand reached the external wall mirror. Bracing for impact, she turned her palm to the ceiling, took a deep breath, and smacked the mirror. It shattered on impact, slicing through the cloth and sending shards into her palm. She gripped the splinters hard, pushing them further into her flesh. A yelp of defiance rose from within as the smashed glass was pulled back inside her room. She set the biggest fragment to one side, then set about pulling the glass smithereens from her hand. The blood was already soaking through the filthy fabric.

She had averted bleeding to death, but blood poisoning remained a distinct possibility. The thought made her scowl. She chewed and sucked at the wound, spitting out splinters and blood. With no clean fabric around, the wound was left to leach. The mirror was then spat upon, cleaned, and pushed back out the hole in the door. The cracked mirror was then tilted to provide a view of the left side of the door. Her next yelp was laced with excitement, not pain. She angled her viewing to count the bricks from the ground up and in from the edge of the door. Her target lay at a height of eight bricks and six bricks in from the doorframe.

Back inside the cell, she hammered away more plaster until enough brickwork was exposed to measure the brickwork pattern. Working against the clock, she smeared her injured hand on the wall. A bloody *X* marked the spot.

She lurched over and kicked the rickety old bed frame. Its loose bolts rattled under the strain. It didn't take much shaking for the bolts to loosen further. Within a minute, a section of the angled edge of the bed frame had been freed from the rest of the bed. The bed sheets were wrapped around one end of the steel section for better purchase. A pillow was deployed as a buffer. Set up like a battering ram, the metal frame was cracked into the wall. The impact of the attack jarred her shoulder into spasm. A chunk of plaster falling from the wall was the reward for her pain. Turning down her pain receptors, she rammed the metal back into the brickwork. Time after time, brick chippings and mortar flew. Progress was painfully slow and noisy, but with the warehouse empty, she cared less about the noise. So much so that grunting outbursts were deployed to add impact to the ramming motion. Her rhythm was only interrupted to track the pitiful progress.

When a point of purchase was achieved, the most buckled edging on the metal was used to saw along the mortar line. Blistering pain pulsed through her hands, but after about thirty minutes, she tasted success. The metal broke through the cavity in the mortar. Using the frame as a lever, she eventually loosened the brick. With an almighty crash, a gap was forced in the brickwork, big enough for her to slip her hand through. Her heart spun when she managed to find her target, the angle grinder on the bench. When she flipped the switch, the power tool whizzed into life.

Enthused by the prospect of escape, she turned the angle grinder upside down in her hand. The blade whirred inches away from her exposed wrists. Visions of dying from shredded wrists were pushed to the back of her mind, and she dug the spinning wheel into the brickwork. Dust flew as the grinder splintered into the brick and mortar. The stench of hot steel and decaying brick clogged her nasal passages. Although designed for metal, the barbaric action of the grinder made short work of the flimsy brickwork. Two minutes later, the halved brick fell away. As it dropped, the grinder followed through, its hot blade slicing a chunk from her forearm.

Punching the wall in anger seemed to help. The grinder was then dragged into the cell. With only a few inches of cable to spare, the power tool was pulled across to the door. Eye closed, with both hands on the job, the grinder was pushed hard into the hinge. Progress against the harder metal was slow. The grinding wheel was gaining heat and losing efficacy and size.

She stopped to check for progress and listen out for intrusions. With little progress and no interruptions, she pushed on, determined to keep the pressure up. Either the hinge or the grinder would give up, but she would not. Sparks flew as the hinge deteriorated under the shearing power of the grinding wheel.

Losing one hinge was enough; when it split, she pushed the metal frame into the gap to wedge open the corner of the door. Using her weight for purchase, she yanked an angled at the corner of the door, big enough for her to escape through. With the door waggling on its one hinge, she crawled through into the warehouse space. Adrenaline pushed her on. Escape lay nearby. She bolted for the entrance.

"Damn it!" Her unbandaged hand thumped the door frame. All exits were locked from the outside and all the windows were barred. *Another idea.*

She retraced her steps, unplugged the grinder, and ran for the main shutter door. The mechanism was protected, so it could only be opened from the outside. Worse still, there were no power outlets or extension leads available to set up the grinder for action. In frustration, the grinder was thrown across the warehouse floor. It spun, bumped, and slid across to the truck currently undergoing its makeover.

An idea cracked Charlie's strained face.

She raced across to the truck and let down the jack. In double quick time, she had unwound the screw sufficiently that the vehicle lapsed onto its side. After a few twists, the jack was freed.

The tallest window with the widest spacing between bars was targeted. The jack was jammed half-way up between the two central bars. With as much energy as she could muster, the process of opening the jack commenced. Easy at first, the action grew more difficult as the pressure increased on the bars. Using a spanner to help pull the jack around slowed the process but increased the purchase.

Inch by inch, the gap between the bars slowly widened. The blood from her weeping hand coated the spanner, making it more difficult to keep a grip. Her spanner suddenly slipped, smashing her hand through the blackened window. Glass smashed out into the courtyard floor, setting the guard dog on high alert, and the goats into meltdown. The barking and bleating added to her panic. Not for the first time, her hand broke glass. Thankfully, the additional damage was minimal. The sun crashed in through the window, offering light and hope.

She turned to drink. After running over to the cache of whisky, a box was ripped open, and a bottle retrieved. Her DNA coated the scene as the cut was washed down with the amber firewater. She took a great swig to fend off the pain. It was more than a little nip. Her hand was bandaged with the cleanest rag available after both items had been smothered in more spirit.

Petrified she would be discovered; her efforts grew more frantic. She reset the spanner and resumed her escape bid. A metal pole was then added to the end of the spanner, offering yet more purchase. After another couple of turns, she tried her luck. It took three more turns before she managed to fit through the gap. With her head and shoulders out the window, she scanned the compound.

The scooter stood in the corner, asking to be stolen.

The dog was another story.

She turned and ran to the office to try to find the keys to the scooter. The crappy lock on the cabin door was no match for the heel of her combat boot. Inside, on the table, she spied her rucksack.

The gun was gone, but the phone remained. She pulled it from its compartment. *Dead.*

Realizing getting outside wouldn't be good enough, she plundered the office. At the back of a set of drawers, one of the jacks from a clump of assorted chargers fitted her phone. She afforded herself a three-minute charge. Enough for a last emergency call. In the interim, a short-term plan formulated.

Get prepared and make an impact.

Escape was imminent. Her long-term survival would be worried about later. Pace took precedence over thought. A small wad of local currency was confiscated, along with any keys she could find. Four sets of filthy overalls hung up behind the door.

The smallest size was found, then pulled on. The drugs were hauled across to the oily rags and wastepaper. The cleanest rag was sized up as headgear. It looked ridiculous. On further investigation, a flat topped, khaki pakol, woolen cap was found and tried on for size. The broad cord at its base held it in place. Her look was checked in the remnants of the smashed wall mirror. Her blonde bob protruded from the edges of her cap. A smattering of grease from a nearby can dampened and darkened her locks. Her high cheekbones were more difficult to disguise, as were her Nordic sea-blue eyes. The sun damage helped.

Passible. She hoped.

A couple of cases of whisky were set nearby to act as an accelerant. The acetylene torch was then lit, dropped on the ground, and kicked into position right beside the wastepaper and oily rags. The fire caught instantly, spewing flames up and across the wall. The bags of drugs were the last thing to be thrown on the fire. Deadly drug fumes danced in the raging flames. Petrified of asphyxiation, Charlie ran for the gap in the barred window, grabbing her phone and rucksack on the way past. On exit, she pulled an overcoat from the coat rack inside the doorway.

The popping and crackling of the spreading fire accompanied her exit. At the end of its tether, the dog yelped and snarled, desperate to attack. The goats joined each other in a crazed and fearful dance. Every combination of key was attempted, until finally, one of the keys fitted the scooter lock. It started as easily as the raging fire behind her. The bolt on the compound gate was then pulled before the goats were released and the scooter was kicked into motion. The goats made it out of the compound first.

Last to be freed was the dog. Concerns for its survival outweighed her fear of being attacked. As soon as the spike was pulled from the ground, the dog snarled and ran for the exit. His anger toward incarceration outweighed any misplaced loyalties.

Twenty seconds later, the scooter slipped out and across the busy street. She pulled into the first lane across the street. Once clear, she drew breath and eased the throttle. Just as the waves of relief started to wash over her, she turned the tide. After confirming the escape had gone unnoticed, she yanked the scooter around in a one-eighty-degree turn.

She had nowhere to go and nothing to lose. Fleeing made no sense.

Time was taken for her to regroup into an army of one.

The scooter pitched to the side as she dismounted.

The plan was never to flee.

The fire was a trap.

CHAPTER 32

With the winter winds sliding down from the mountains, everyone out that morning was wrapped up tightly against the elements. *Great cover.* Hungry and thirsty, Charlie held her ground. Across from the warehouse, sitting in a crumpled heap, smothered by her newly stolen jacket, she shivered and stared across the road. The scooter sat close by. An old tin bowl, lifted from a side street table, accessorized her attire. The disheveled posture of a beggar was struck to complete the look. The world walked by in droves. They didn't give her a single Rial or a second look. She preferred it that way. Her warped sense of humor arrived just in time when she realized she had only been in the drugs game a few days and already she was homeless and begging in the streets.

The pang of pain from her cut hand brought her back to reality. A handkerchief from the inside of the jacket was used to stem the bitter slice on her hand made by the broken mirror. She hadn't really noticed it until now. She assumed the pumping blood and adrenaline must have exacerbated the flow from the wound. Worried about infection, she sucked the cut before biting down hard to close the edges. As she clamped her jaws and sucked the blood, everyday life gathered pace around her. The handkerchief was wrapped as tightly as her pain threshold permitted. The rag turned red.

An old woman not content with supporting a massive poly sack on her head stumbled past, carrying a wooden basket filled with clothes over her right shoulder. The padded hijab helped; her age didn't. Nearby, two women acted as bookends on a concrete street bench. At either end of the spectrum, the mother and daughter lived in their own worlds. Both wore colorful ornate shawls. The youngster found herself in her phone. The older lady seemed lost in a delightful book.

A trash truck noisily pulled up, blocking her view of the warehouse. Both truck and trash man clattered on up the sidewalk. The bin wrangler seemed to be throwing as much trash into the street as into the truck. He was chattering and cluttering in equal measures. No one seemed to listen of care. He bashed on regardless of efficacy or hygiene. The irony seemed lost on everyone around.

The street theater was laced with black comedy, yet no one raised a snicker.

Charlie craned her gaze past the moving health violation. Across the street, Charlie's home cooking had just come to the boil. The popping sounds inside the warehouse were only noticeable if you listened out for them. Acrid smoke loomed over the compound wall. An otherworldly bang shook the street and everyone in it. Paces quickened. Only when the flames and fumes started to billow and taint the clear blue sky did people stop and stare. As more people arrived to watch the fire, Charlie wondered for their safety. When the crowd grew to the point of trampling, she wondered about her own safety.

The wail of a distant fire engine caught her attention. Thankfully, it took an eternity to arrive. Even after it swung into view, the busy streets and the obstinate driving styles of the locals hindered its progress at every slowing turn. Loud bangs cracked open the sky as flashing flames licked over the compound wall.

Charlie's eyes crinkled in quiet amusement.

She had put on quite the show. As the fire crew set to work tackling the blaze, jeers lifted into the afternoon sky. It was as if the local knew exactly what had been going on behind closed doors.

With neither the crowd nor the fire under control, Charlie shuffled off to gain a new vantage point. A thunderous explosion within the building pushed the crowd back, giving her the opportunity to grab a curbside view. The heat from the fire warmed the faces and the hearts of the locals. They seemed pleased that the fire was taking hold. It was now obvious. They had known what was going on inside the building.

When the two blaring police cars finally showed up, the dynamic changed. The cars moved to the side immediately, as did the crowd. Heads bowed. Looks were averted. Onlookers sloped off. Curiosity turned to fear in a matter of seconds. Four police officers piled out of the first white-with-a-green-stripe patrol car. They were dressed for business. A cordon of intimidation formed swiftly, forcing the crowd further from the brink. The second car had two police in the front and one in the back. Intriguingly, the men remained inside for some time, surveying the scene and the crowd.

A sinister aura cloaked the vehicle, so Charlie slid around for a closer look. It was difficult to catch a clear view as the high sun cast reflections across the angled car windows. She moved closer still. Inside, the outline of the man in the back seemed animated. Wild gesticulations showed the full force of his anger. The berated men in the front held their gazes dead ahead. There was no talking back or looking back. Drawn like a moth to an angry flame, Charlie edged closer. Uncertain if it was her intuition or her training, she realized something wasn't right with the second police car. When the policeman in the passenger seat rolled down his window to call over his colleague, Charlie moved closer still.

She spun in horror when the policemen cast his gaze in her direction. Fearful of discovery, she jumped back into the crowd and dipped below head level. Without looking back, she barged her way through the crowds, head down, elbows in. Ten yards into her flight, she checked for trouble. No one followed. Danger had been delayed, at least.

Still, she ran on, panicked by the moment. Her scooter was hurriedly retrieved, pulled into position, and sparked into life.

After shoving through the milling crowd, she pulled the scooter over to gain an angled view of the second police car. Her engine revved for an early departure. When the policemen inside had finished receiving an update from their colleague, the car window slid closed. When the suspect police car's lights switched on, Charlie jumped to attention. *This is it.*

When it barged out into the traffic, Charlie followed suits, causing a blaring row between her fellow road users.

Head down, she charged into a position where she could follow her new target at a discreet distance. Without its siren, the patrol car's pace matched the traffic, making tracking much easier. To lose sight of the car would spell disaster, so she erred on the side of discovery. Thankfully, the parties inside seemed much more distracted and animated by events to check their surroundings. Still, she rode on, eagle eyed and determined to follow her quest through to a conclusion. Uncertainties and fear were cast aside in favor of hope and determination. Focusing hard, she gawked at the policeman sitting up front in the patrol car. She confirmed her initial sighting.

As bold as the brass on his shiny buttons, there sat her ex-traveling partner, Sherif.

CHAPTER 33

The rusty little scooter was a fine machine. It ran hot, in pursuit of the truth. Narrow streets gradually widened. Twisty lanes straightened into streets. Manic throngs transitioned into ordered pedestrians. An easing of the congestion occurred as they moved into the more affluent sections of the city. The openings in the traffic increased her exposure, making it more dangerous to stay close. She pulled her scarf across her face and pulled her pakol down tightly. The tracking was easier, as the vehicle could be seen from further away.

Charlie rode hard to strike a balance between losing her target and becoming one herself. Three young men suddenly sped past, joined at the hip, on one moped. The lead rider, the only one with sunglasses, clung to the handlebars, the other two clung on to each other, enduring every bump and hump in the roadway. They were the perfect cover. Staying the course, she kept the youths between her and the patrol car. The gentrification of the roadways continued as gravel turned to asphalt. As they neared the more historic sections of the city, ornate cobbled sections became the pavement of choice.

The men on the motorbike shuddered at the latest developments. When the front rider spied Charlie in his rear mirrors, he shouted to his traveling companions. Their gesticulations deteriorated into unwanted attention. She bobbed, weaved, and ignored, much to the annoyance of the young men. She held her pakol down in protest at the voyeurs. Eventually, they gave up their childish ways. Two junctions ahead, they turned left and were never seen or heard from again. Relieved, Charlie eased back into a more comfortable pursuit position.

The motorcade moved from slums to riches. The streets broadened to make way for more trees. Advertisements replaced graffiti. Murals of Muslim fighters disappeared in favor of billboards of clerics. Impressive mosques grew in stature and number. Charlie recognized the incredible turquoise tiled twin towers as the Mamzadeh Saleh mosque. All she could afford was a glance. Two hundred yards up the road, panic set in. Distracted by the surroundings, Charlie hadn't noticed the orange flashing traffic lights on the gantry overhead. The traffic slowed in an orderly fashion at a pedestrian crossing. The police patrol car made it through before the rest of the traffic stopped, stranding Charlie on the wrong side of the law. They sped off, grounding her in a sea of traffic. Like a boorish commuter, she pushed her way to the starting grid. The waiting was painful. She immediately regretted leaving such a gap.

She thumped the handlebars in annoyance at her stupidity. As soon as the offending pedestrians, two elderly ladies out shopping, sidled past, Charlie revved her engine and zipped out at the head of the rush.

There was no patrol car in sight. She ripped the scooter open, only slowing slightly at each junction. Desperation gripped her throttle as she slammed her way through the traffic. Terrified, she had just lost her only true lead; she zigzagged furiously between the jammed traffic. Suddenly, at right angles, down the third cross street, she spied a patrol car making great progress in the distance. Unable to turn in time, she took her life in her handlebars and barged straight across into the oncoming traffic. Horns and tops blew as she bashed her way back across the roadway. Forced to bump the sides of cars, she nearly fell under the wheels of a truck after being shunted by a minivan full of irate locals. She kicked on, throwing a boot against the front wing of a yellow taxi for stability and protection. Bile and insults flew at her from every direction.

Near misses and screeches abounded. The traffic snarled to an angry stop. Fenders bent. Tempers flared. She clattered on through the gaps in the traffic, denting doors, and mangling mirrors along the way. When a man stepped from his pickup to remonstrate, she booted the driver's door, pinning him to his truck. She kicked on, fearful of getting trapped, knowing if she slowed, there could be a lynching. She needed to keep moving, and the sidewalk was her only exit. Jamming the bike perpendicularly to the direction of travel, she pushed her way through to the roadside.

Pedestrians had turned into bystanders by the time Charlie landed on the sidewalk. Panic ensued as she yanked the scooter in and out of the fleeing masses. Thankfully, there were no have-a-go-heroes willing to step in. Everyone stepped or jumped aside. Shrieks and shouts rang out over the scooter's wailing engine. Altered by the noise behind them, the crowd parted in fear of the incoming chaos. Her pace quickened. She convinced herself she could still see the unlit lamps and signs from the top of a police car. It turned sharply right. She followed at speed.

With the main road blocked by panic, the side road was virtually traffic free, allowing her the chance to ride hard and close the gap on the patrol car way up ahead. Questions over whether it was even the correct police car were immediately objected to and thrown out of court. Belief turned to relief when she was eventually able to catch up and confirm the outline of the passengers.

The frigid air bit through Charlie's clothing, chilling the sweat clinging to her body. The enemy lay ahead. That was enough to drag her forward. She squirmed under the realization the trouble she was in was of her own making. A boring desk job had spiraled into a deadly, illegal invasion of a foreign power. Things were spiraling, but she couldn't tell if they were spiraling down or out of control.

Ahead, the patrol car slowed, forcing Charlie to ease back into the curb. The congestion made it easy to stay hidden. Emboldened by that fact, she moved in close. Suddenly, the brakes pumped, and the car slewed to an abrupt stop. Charlie nearly rear-ended the car in front as it took evasive action. Fully uniformed, Sherif jumped from the car, ran around, and pulled the rear door. The Police Chief clambered out, minus his cap, enveloped in a large sheepskin coat. His three-man entourage led the procession. The crew exuded presence and arrogance.

Traffic was halted in order to allow them to cross the street. The Police Chief displayed a superiority complex that seemed far from complex. He looked like he owned the place. Self-importance was built into every stride. Charlie flung her scooter across and up against a wall. Her jacket was yanked off, then thrown over her slumped shoulders. Every effort was made to look like a homeless bum as she shuffled on behind. When the targets rounded the corner, the mystery deepened. Charlie was bemused to find an incredible Arabic arch in the shape of an inverted dome. Tiles of stars and suns cast colorful motifs around brightly colored signage. Pristine intricate pavements of inlay created a crowded roadway that led down and into a dungeon of delights. Ahead lay Tehran's famed Grand Bazaar. She screwed her face. This was no shopping trip.

The men didn't browse as they barged through the busy entrance. Marching onwards, they shunted shoppers congregating inside the entrance. People jammed every space of the walkway, but things didn't stay that way for long. Tourists admiring the interior were brushed aside to make way for the Police Chief, as he stomped past with disdain.

Charlie took it all in. The steel-structured roof could have done with a lick of rust proof paint. The sand-colored rooms overhead seemed to have been jammed into the space as an afterthought. Some of the tiny square windows still held glass. Mostly boarded up, channels of rickety glazing allowed some light in at the apex of the roof space. Leather goods spilled out into the thoroughfare. Multicolored footwear and handbags vied for a prime spot-on various stall. Litter lay everywhere. The small army of street sweepers looked close to desertion.

A steel wheeled handcart carrying various cardboard boxes was being unloaded by a man, educating a boy who should have been at school. Spices of all shapes, colors and prices covered massive sections of the second section they entered. Polysacks filled with unseen, unsold delights were piled high in the next corner. Carpets and rugs were jammed to the rooftops. Dusty and dim, the domed lighting tried its best.

A brightly tiled shop with flashing neon lights sold a pick and mix of pickles and fixings. The nearby fruit seller's goods were laid out in a chromatically aligned display. Motor scooters with canopies were pushed through the dull indoors. The place was as much hassle as it was hustle. In another life, Charlie would have loved the place.

Ahead, the men stopped abruptly, then circled to hear exactly what the Police Chief was saying. At her current angle and distance, the main man spun into clear view. He seemed an odd creature, receding hairline, protruding teeth, gaunt hollow features, and wire-rimmed glasses.

Shallow, gritty eyes threw out an unsympathetic gaze as he chastised one of his crew. His tightly trimmed beard jutted out, giving him the look of a Shakespearean villain.

Charlie glanced as she pretended to be interested in the shop next door. A beleaguered salesman with an olive complexion and a turned down persona sat amongst his trinkets. With all the enthusiasm of a condemned man waiting for death to carry him off, the stallholder gazed out with pale, sad eyes. With multiple layers of clothing and a wooly hat, he had wrapped up early for the night. His jagged edged plates and wretched baubles were under appreciated and overstocked. The tainted pewter was as jaded and lackluster as the stall owner. He seemed resigned to a life selling yesterday's goods to people from yesteryear. When Charlie moved off to follow the Police Chief, the owner seemed relieved to have avoided the disappointment of another failed sales pitch.

In the next alleyway, a butcher with salt and pepper flaring hair rolled up his bloody sleeves, then threw out his latest delicacy, camel hooves, and shins. All manner of death stared out from his window. The shop's open-door policy seemed designed to allow the flies easy access. It allowed Charlie the chance to stare, not at the butchery, but at the reflection in the shop window.

The entourage had slowed and were loitering near a set of weathered wooden doors. For the wood to be so weathered, Charlie deduced this must be one of the original sections of the old marketplace. The ornate rusting adornments complimented and supported two large doors sitting inside a domed archway. Another small half-door had been cut into one section. A single light did little more than to cast shadows from the archway. Outside, an old man sat on duty. Gnarled knuckles gripped the brass tipped cane jammed under his fragile chin. His face and his wooly hat were equally fuzzy.

Jersey, jacket, overcoat, and blanket. The man was going nowhere warm and nowhere fast.

When he saw the Police Chief, he tried to straighten, waited for the nod, and then tapped the rod on the door. When the door didn't open after five seconds, the tap became a rap.

Before the men moved, Sherif turned to scan the scene. Charlie lowered her gaze from the window. Concerns she had been spotted crept across her consciousness, but the dread was short-lived. The men turned for the door as one. Timing her walk-by to perfection; she lifted her gaze through the doorway to see the Police Chief come under fire from a barrage of salutes from his sycophantic men-in-waiting. Charlie sped on, memorizing all she could of the mystery men. Above her, the light from a disguised CCTV caught her eye. *Quite the façade.*

It occurred to her the bazaar was a suitable place to be shipping from and delivering into. The sheer volume of produce and people would make it easy to stay hidden.

She liked their plan, whatever it was.

She drew up her own one-point-plan. Get behind that door.

Counting her steps back to the main entrance, she tracked the twists in orientation. Once outside, she ventured round the outer edge of the bazaar.

Recounting her steps and orientated, she traced the corresponding location in the back of the warehouse. There were only two or three options in the narrow back alley, but they were difficult to find amongst the shadowy confines. The unit selected was cloaked in a similar wooden shroud, but there were no windows and no doors built into the cedar cladding.

Across the narrow alley, an emergency exit clung to a newer building. Charlie liked the staircase as an option, but hated the thought of having to jump across the alley once she reached the top. With no other obvious option, she slid across the narrow alley.

With no one in sight, she leapt into action. After clambering up onto the edge of a rusted open skip, she drew breath and focused. Like a gymnast on a balance beam, she hurtled forward, gathering pace with every measured stride. At the skip edge, she threw herself forward. Her flailing arm reached through the bottom rung of the dangling fire escape ladder. Her torso shouldered the impact, buckling her body. Her flailing legs crashed against the wall, helping to reduce the momentum. The ladder's rust loosened her grip, cracking open the cut made by the broken mirror. Blood leached out as she reached out, yet she held on. Like a crazed circus performer, she swung her body up onto the next rungs on the ladder.

Clambering up to the next level, at the first opportunity, she jumped off the ladder and slid up into a blind spot. She waited for any sight or sound of trouble. *Nothing sinister.*

After regathering her breath, she climbed up two further stories of the fire escape and up onto the roof.

The alleyway was much wider at the top than it looked on the ground.

The gap in her mind seemed wider.

There were louvers allowing air into the warehouse. That would be her point of ingress. If she had the wrong warehouse, she could work her way into the adjoining units from there. If she made it across to the other side, she couldn't be certain what the strength of the old roof would be. There were lines of rivets straddling the framework on the corrugated roof. That would be her landing strip. The stanchions underneath the far roof would likely be strong enough. *Likely?*

Looking down would only bring visions of terrible consequences. Before making the mad dash, she planned her run, filling her head with facts and a plan, rather than fear and doubt. She looked across.

She stepped out a run of fifteen steps along the roof, turned and stared at her takeoff point. Nothing else mattered. Head down, she made her move. Stride after stride, faster, faster. Never faltering, she sped for the launch point. With a yelp, she hit her mark and flung herself across the chasm. She flailed at the sky, never losing sight of her landing spot.

With inches to spare, she hot her mark. The roof held firm. Her legs did not. She crumpled forward, cracking open her knee and thumping her head. Flesh ripped from her right ear. She took a minute to recover. The magnificent Tehran skyline was scanned, not for its beauty, but for its beasts. No unwelcome attention, no overzealous guards, no snooping locals. She took long breaths.

When doubts edged their way into her psyche, the minute was cut short. The roof had been sturdy enough that it made little noise. *Safe. For now.*

Her knuckles rapped on the steel beam as she kick-started the journey along the line of rivets. She paced on down the line of the frame over to the louvered ventilation. Once there, she sat with her back to the units.

An array of fans clanked and spun in the unit behind her head. She pulled a leaf from the louver and glanced inwards. Three large fans equally spaced out. The cabling was checked. She bumped the frame. Separate power feeds. Down below remained a mystery, as the fans blocked the view and drowned the sounds. Charlie's eyes followed the cabling from the fans round and through onto the pillar housing the louvers. She reached round and gripped the nearest cable. It held firm. She grappled with one of the many staples holding the cabling in place.

Her close-cropped nails were useless at gaining purchase on the staple, but she persevered, pulling, twisting, picking, and levering.

Annoyed with the lack of impact, she pounded the frame. It was pointless. She needed more purchase. After slumping to the floor, she untied her boot and pulled out the lace completely. With renewed focus, she threaded the end of the lace in through the gap between the cable and the wall. Unable to see around the corner, the process was attempted by feel, using the slightly dislodged staple as a point of reference. Frustrations rose as the lace missed its mark repeatedly. Eventually, the lace end found the small cavity.

Excitedly, Charlie grasped the end and pulled the lace tight. With the ends lined up together, Charlie wrapped the lace around her good hand and yanked it as hard as she could. The staples popped in sequence, sending her flailing backward. The laces rasped her hand; she neither cared nor noticed. The cable had been freed. Reaching in with both hands, she yanked and hauled the cable from its housing. A rigorous bout of back and forth eventually loosened the cable housing.

Spurred on by the movement, Charlie took a moment, refilled her lungs, reset her stance, and re-gripped the cabling.

After only a few more yanks, the cable wiring burst from its tether. The fan slowed to a silent stop. The live cable was carefully pulled to one side. Charlie took great care not to zap herself in the process. The remaining covering louvers were then pulled in sequence to gain access to the large fan. With the two fans still working away alongside, Charlie moved on, hopeful that her actions hadn't been seen or heard. She climbed out onto the fan. Its housing was sturdy. Its fins were flimsy. Through a space in the fins, she studied the scene below. She caught sight of a balding man dressed in a dark lab coat tending to a massive green clunking machine.

She tightened her grip on reality when the police uniforms showed up on deck. *Yes!*

She had hit the spot.

She held her higher ground, stretching her gaze into the four corners of her field of visions.

After a few moments, she tipped her head back in recoil. There he was. The Police Chief.

The men who greeted him wore lab coats. The clanking and whirring down below covered any noise she could make. Under the veil of the industrial noise, she pulled the flimsy fan fins to one side. Her hand took yet more punishment as she lowered herself down in through the roof. Her dangling boot reached out toward the metal stanchion holding up the roof. Her unlaced boot trembled as her legs extended in search of a safe platform. Once a more secure footing was gained, she took yet one more leap of faith. Two more acrobatic exertions carried her to the safety of a main pillar.

Clambering down the metallic buttress, the machine below looked and sounded increasingly like a printing press. When she looked over the ledge, blood splattered from her hand, dripping crimson ink blotches onto the floor, twenty feet below. Voices crept up from below, enticing her further into the web. High above the lights, in the shadows of the roof, she worked her way toward the voices.

Her heart skipped.

The Police Chief walked right under her position. Fully animated, he argued with two members of staff, who busied themselves with any task that looked to be helpful. A pile of white papers, crumpled for disposal, lay directly below in a large waste bin.

Down below, the remonstrating Police Chief seemed to be complaining about the paper wastage, for some bizarre reason.

Suddenly, the Police Chief's cell phone interrupted the rhythm of the printing press. His animation turned to agitation when he read the screen on his phone. He ordered the machine to be switched off. Two men ran to compete for the one-man job. As the men cantered toward the off switch, Charlie climbed across the stanchion to eavesdrop on the call. She arrived above her target just as the press whirred to a halt. The Police Chief took a breath then took the call. Charlie yelled inwardly. She couldn't hear him. The Police Chief leaned on the bin of shredded crumpled papers, as if bracing himself for the onslaught coming down the phone. Charlie needed to get closer. Lost for words, she switched on her phone, and prayed it had been set on silent. As soon as it buzzed on, she checked its status. No bars of service, but her bout of battery charging back at the garage had done its trick. *So far, no good.* She clicked through the limited options until the voice recorder app flipped into view. Her sliced hand was then held on a line she hoped would be behind the Police Chief. The first drops squeezed from her wound, fell silently, missing the bin by some distance. She reached out further and squeezed harder.

Her next handful of blood splattered around the unit. Down below, all hell broke out over the phone. The superior Police Chief looked to have lost his status. Charlie guessed the big boss was on the phone. She slid across another two feet. Keeping a grip, the bloodletting continued. The ruby drops narrowly missed the Police chief's shaking head but hit their mark. The voice recorder was swiftly activated. After taking careful aim, the phone dropped six inches further back from her last wet run. The crash landing was as silent as it was accurate.

The Police Chief only flinched in response to the dialogue.

Quite how far the phone had fallen into the paper pile remained a mystery, but for now, all that could be done had been done. Charlie moved back to the building's edge and found a position lying on a plinth over a buttress. She set about repairing the self-inflicted damage to her wound. Her talisman was pulled off and wrapped tightly around the cloth now protecting her hand. She closed her eyes and waited for her moment. Too far away to decipher any of the dialogue, she hoped her bloody eavesdropping had paid off.

After around a minute, a yelp of annoyance told Charlie the Police Chief's call had ended. The nearby table was kicked hard. The crew was called in and orders were issued with pace and volume. Obedience turned to blind panic as the entourage rampaged around the unit. The Police Chief had been tipped off or told off. They were in full flight.

The hasty dismantling commenced immediately. Key parts from the press were pulled from the opened carcass, then set into old fruit boxes. Across in a nearby open office area, all manner of documentation was being sent to the shredder. The Police Chief grew impatient and hoarse as the workers failed to meet his timescales and expectations. Threats were now being handed out alongside promises of reprisals. The men couldn't work faster. Once confident that the men were now up to speed, the Police Chief fled the scene. The biggest of his bodyguards acted as pathfinder. Sherif was left to pick up the pieces or cut down the incompetents. Well above the high drama, Charlie waited impatiently for silence.

She ran out of patience before they had run out of things to do.

The piles of fruit boxes were set onto pallet trucks and pulled out of sight. The street sounds wafted in from the market when the front door opened. *Daylight robbery.* Charlie surmised. The sound of an inner shutter door being pulled down arrived long after the voices disappeared. The lights were killed just after the extractor fans were silenced.

The roller shutter eventually clanked shut.

Only the shafts of daylight creeping in through the fans and louvers lit the unit. Charlie had to wait a few more agonizing moments before her eyes acclimatized to the low light levels. The second she could see sufficiently, she climbed across, then lowered herself off the stanchion. Gangling over her chosen landing target, she took a deep breath, then let go. She crumpled, boots-first, onto a stack of fruit boxes. A calamitous clatter rattled around the workshop. The pain in her ankles was short-lived. She needed to move fast, fearing she could have alerted the old sentry outside.

The bin that housed her phone was checked. "Argh!" The bin got the boot. *Nothing.*

Remembering that the frantic crew tipped it over to get all the paper out, she checked the dispensing angle. Four feet away, under the shadow of a pallet, lay the phone. She punched the air, then punched herself. The phone was dead. She hadn't given it enough charge at the warehouse stakeout. How long its death roll had lasted was unknown. *Not so smart after all.*

She needed to move on.

The unit had been stripped, barring the remains of what she confirmed was printing equipment. Wires had been pulled. The electrics looked and smelled as if they had been recently fried.

The shredder was the latest model. Two-way shearing. They had learned their lessons from the US Embassy siege where the single-slit shredded paper was meticulously hand inspected and pieced back together. Painstaking work, spurred on by hatred.

The printing press had no badge, no serial number of registration plates. The electronics looked US in origin. Green ink tainted the concrete floor. She guessed the equipment included an embosser, a foil printing, and serial number generator, but they were nowhere to be found. An old poster proclaiming the glory of the republic was pulled from the wall and turned. The unprinted side was then lifted onto the exit roller of the press. The transfer was blurred, but conclusive. The image became seared into her mind. She had seen enough. *Time to go.*

A cleanup crew would likely be on their way to strip and ship the kit. After finding an old rag, she wiped her wound and moved on to the exit. The CCTV display showed a sea of shoppers.

Thankfully, it looked like the old guard had finally retired. She decommissioned the CCTV system to prevent her exit from being recorded. The latch on the door was pulled, and she walked out confidently.

Head down, with purpose, she barged out into the bustling mayhem of the bazaar. Her pace quickened amongst the throng as the magnitude of the criminality washed over her.

She had no shelter, no allies, and only one lead.

The face on the ink transfer was Benjamin Franklin.

They were counterfeiting thousands of hundred-dollar bills.

CHAPTER 34

Although she had no clue about her destination or even direction, Charlie's pace quickened. She needed time to think and needed to be as far away from the print shop as possible. Once back out of the Grand Bazaar entrance, her steps lengthened. A rare squall had done nothing to dampen the city's enthusiasm for horn blaring and yelling. The cars and the people were in fine voice. As the throng thinned to a crowd, she extended her perimeter, taking a circuitous route back to her bike.

Just when she felt clear from the danger, a beat-up white van crept into the edge of her peripheral vision. It prowled the wet streets, keeping pace with her stride, but holding up the traffic.

Defiance formed in the face of fear. *Amateurs.*

She scanned the line of motorcycles and mopeds mounted on the already crowded sidewalks. In turn, each bike was checked for loose items. Five bikes into the search, a rickety mirror was yanked from its housing. She knelt to tie her lace and positioned the mirror in the flat of her palm. She couldn't outrun the van, and besides, it could all be paranoia. The men in the van could be her only lead.

She slowed, turned, and stared through the traffic. She spied two men clad in black. She liked her odds. The van pulled to the side, allowing her time to turn and walk away. She picked the spot they would strike. The space in the parked cars was twenty yards away. She gripped the hidden mirror stalk. Her heart raced.

Charlie faced two choices. Fight or flight.

She chose the former.

Listening to the van splashing through the puddles helped her judge its speed and ETA. The mirror stalk jutted out too far, and the sweaty palms couldn't grip it properly. Her confidence was starting to fade with every step. The truck slowed. The side door noisily opening was her signal.

She braced herself. *Showtime.*

Scuffing boots charged from behind. In a flash, the mirror stalk burst the first attacker's neck. Blood gushed as he faltered. *Three of them.* The second attempted a chokehold, but a kick to the knee and a punch loosened his grip on reality.

As she turned to dispatch the last man, a stun gun sent her world into excruciating darkness.

CHAPTER 35

Charlie woke up with her greasy forehead on the metal desk. A thumping headache kept it there.

The cold metallic surface soothed her splitting brow. Long after she had awoken, her head remained bloodied and bowed. She felt her handcuffs had been attached to a rod attached to the immovable desk.

She eased her head up, giving no clues that she was fully awake. The process took five minutes, but eventually she had the handcuffs at the far reaches of her sight. Things weren't adding up. Encouragingly, her hand wound had been tended to and covered. That didn't seem like the work of criminals or terrorists. The cuffs were standard US Government Issue.

Through her clearing vision, she scanned the room. It was empty, but she wasn't alone. The mirror to her left side filled way too much space on the wall. The walls were lined with gray acoustic panels. Her heart swelled with partial relief. The room was the standard setup for an interrogation cell. This was no terrorist splinter cell.

She set her own tone, translating her exclamations into pitch perfect French.

"Okay guys, I am awake. Get me out of these."

Silence. She waited for the low-level grunt, who was probably monitoring her on the other side of the glass, to run and fetch his boss. After five minutes, she went again. "I am a French Citizen. I demand to be released. I must speak with my embassy immediately." Her words counted for nothing. The silence only brought her headache into razor sharp focus. She set her head back down on the table and waited. Time drifted as the after-effects of the stun gun circled through her system.

When she woke, sometime later, a man was sitting on a newly arrived chair. He never spoke. Instead, he lifted a camera and snapped her face. The snap was over before she could react. When the man left, he limped up and tapped on the cell door three times. Charlie chased him out the door with more angry French. "Did I give you that? You are weak."

An unseen guard let him out and closed the door. Charlie's words escorted him down the corridor. "What do they call it, poor field craft?"

The shouting hadn't helped. She set her head back on the desk. She didn't have to wait long before the boredom brought on another French outburst. "Release me or you'll be the ones in cuffs."

Nothing.

The cuffs took another rattling. "Get ready to be wearing these for years."

Still nothing.

After another long delay, the steel door creaked open. She kept her head down and listed for the entrants.

"Hello, Charlotte. You are a long way from Afghanistan."

She lifted her head to find the scowling face of O'Hara, the CIA agent who had interviewed her about Ross' murder, back in Afghanistan.

CHAPTER 36

Looming large, O'Hara leaned in close. His interrogation techniques hadn't changed. "What the hell are you doing here?"

Charlie wasn't biting. "I could ask the same thing."

"You could if you weren't the one in cuffs." O'Hara wasn't playing. He made a big show of rolling up his freshly ironed white cotton shirtsleeves. His khaki combats remained, but the rimless sunglasses were gone.

"You look a little red in the face. Too long in the sun or too long interrogating uncooperative witnesses?"

"Now is not the time to be a wiseass."

Charlie rattled her wrists. "No, now is the time to get these off me."

"I don't think so. Not yet."

She leaned over as far as her cuffs would allow. "Took three of you and a stun gun to take me down. No wonder you're scared to release me. Worried that I'll kick your ass? What if I promised to go easy on you?"

"How did you get here?"

"Planes, trains, and automobiles. Oh, and the odd pony trek."

"Being a wise ass won't save you. You've really screwed things up. You're done."

"Don't threaten me. I am a goddamn US agent. I should be the one asking the questions. Under what authority are you holding me?"

"Under the authority of the jurisdiction of our latest operation. Codename, Operation Screw You."

Charlie snarled back. "What are you doing in Iran?"

Her interviewer asked, "Oh, and you're here on vacation?"

"You got it in one. I was walking around the bazaar, and I was jumped. When I woke, my passport had been stolen along with my wallet."

"So, the authorities will have a record of you entering the country?"

Charlie was enjoying the back and forth. "Sure. Give them a call. I'm sure they'd be delighted to hear from you. Be sure to give them the address to pick me up from."

"What were you doing at the print shop?"

"The same as you."

"Oh, I doubt that." O'Hara had spoken out of turn. He looked at the mirror and fingered his ear.

Charlie was beside herself. "Is that an earpiece? Wow, you're being told what to say." She turned to face the mirror. "I want to speak to the organ grinder, not the idiot who feeds the monkey." She went in search of more dialogue. "Come on, get these off."

A voice entered O'Hara's earpiece. He appeared to follow instructions. The cuffs were released. Charlie rubbed her wrists and wailed at the wall. "Why don't you come out from behind your hiding spot?"

Nothing. She turned to O'Hara. "The Iranians. You're helping them print money?"

"I am not at liberty to divulge that."

"What are you able to divulge?"

"Nothing other than you're getting too close."

Charlie threw up her hands in mock surrender. "Don't tell me it's below your pay grade? That's what all you desk jockeys say."

O'Hara shrugged. "No. It's above your comprehension."

"Wow, God bless America. With guys like you, it's more like God help America. Sizemore. Get him on the phone now."

"Who?"

It was Charlie's turn to quit games. "You know. Sizemore, my boss. Get him on the phone or face the full force of the Bureau."

"You need to tell us what your involvement is with the printing operation first."

"I don't need to tell you anything. Why don't you do me a solid and tell me why you sucker punched me with a zapper, instead of just pulling me in on the quiet."

"What's the fun in that?" O'Hara conceded. "We were going to, but you didn't make that possible. I have a guy nursing ten stitches that will testify to that."

"Only ten? I must be getting weak in my old age."

O'Hara touched his ear, tutted under his breath, and left the room. Charlie had no clue if it was fear or relief driving her forceful character; but she liked it all the same. She lowered her head when the urge to smirk threatened to crack her face. She knew she was still under surveillance.

A few moments later, O'Hara returned. The joy she felt at being unshackled never showed. She felt the questions looming. "If you share, I share. If you play dumb, I play dumber."

O'Hara moved in for a quid pro quo. "What are you doing here?"

"What is it you said about *below my level of comprehension*? You're getting nothing until you get me out of here. I will file a full report through the correct channels. Front page will concentrate on how I was treated."

Before their mating rituals could become any staler, the steel door was rapped from the outside. O'Hara took the delivery of a cloth bag from the limping agent. He pulled it across and onto the desk. "Here."

Charlie looked inside to find women's clothes and a wash bag. O'Hara had kept the door open. "Get showered up. Second door along on the left."

Charlie couldn't get out fast enough. She took no chances with any backchat. She bounded into the small shower area and locked the door behind her. The shower was yanked on to drown the tears of relief that had been damning up over the last terror filled days. Once inside, she sat on the floor, knees under her chin. She shivered when realizing not all the congealed blood swirling down the drain was hers. The back of her head tapped and stained the white tiles. The water temperature was jacked up to just-below-scalding. Her blood flowed. She spent a long time in the shower. De-greasing the hair took a lot longer than clearing her mind.

She needed to get her story straight. In most parts, the truth would suffice. She mentally noted the wins that would justify her going so far off the reservation. She had identified the thieves. Closed off their channels of distribution. Traced and smashed the channels for an entire international drug network. The murders along the way were reportable, not attributable. She had everything to show and nothing to hide. She could be accused of being reckless, nothing more. Her thoughts slid back to the departed, not all of them dear. Feisal the drug lord. Noah, the victim of circumstance, whose only crime was to search for the truth. Gasim, a brave player in a deadly game. Her own people, Harry, and Sanchez were probably decent people corrupted by greed. They just lost their way in the fog of war. She had seen it too often before. All of them, in their own way, victims.

She shivered at the thought of how her life may have turned out if things had been different.

Once outside, towel dried and dressed, she checked her reflection. She'd looked worse. She'd felt worse. The first agent with the limp awaited her exit from the shower room. With no words, he ushered her back to another room.

"You should see someone about that leg. It looks sore." Charlie felt the agent's hatred burn through her damp bob. She slapped her thigh. "This khaki's a little tight."

"We didn't want to give you anything baggy. You're not allowed a belt."

"For my protection or yours?"

Her witticism went unappreciated as the agent led Charlie into a room with desk space and a single bed. Windows didn't exist in this new, sinister world.

"What's this?"

"Home sweet home."

"It's freezing. At least it's warm in Guantanamo."

The agent sat her down and held out his hand. "Show me your hand. It looks bad."

"It's not as bad as it looks. The band aid has come free in the shower, that's all," she lied.

A first aid kit had been laid out on the desk. "Let me see to this. It could go bad."

Charlie realized he was right. She pushed her hand into the basin of warm water set up by the agent. "This is good of you. Does this mean we're friends?" The agent sent a scrubbing brush into her wound, causing her to jump. "Sorry about that, my friend."

"Have you done this before?"

"On a battlefield."

"How did that work out?"

"He died."

Charlie saw the pain in the junior's eyes. "I'm sorry."

The agent carried on with so little emotion, it was obvious he was keeping it all in. Antiseptic cream was then smothered on the cleaned wound.

He pulled a needle. "No anesthetic. Sorry."

Charlie tried to appear unflinching. "No. It will be fine."

The agent seemed to relish pulling the needle and thread through her skin. Charlie immediately regretted her bravado but didn't let it show. The agent was taking great delight with his fleshy needlepoint. After the bandaging Charlie threw him a nod of appreciation, she received a nod of admiration in return. A fistful of painkillers was her only concession.

After a knock at the door, the captor exchange was completed. The junior agent offered his goodbyes as O'Hara returned carrying a small leather attaché.

"So, what now?" she asked.

"Now you go home."

"Kabul?"

O'Hara's lips lifted slightly. "Washington."

Charlie almost collapsed with relief. She held her head in her hands to stop the shaking.

"Here." The agent handed her a new driver's license and passport.

"Swiss? I can't speak Swiss-Deutsch."

"No one can. That's the idea. You're going out as a student from Geneva. Your French will carry you through."

"Wow, you guys don't mess around."

"Not when we have liabilities threatening our mission."

O'Hara threw Charlie her phone. "You travel light."

"You charged it?"

"Only to see what you were up to."

"And?"

"You don't have many friends."

"I'm sure you know the feeling."

O'Hara's tone dripped with derision. "No emails, no calls, no texts, no contact, no service. Pretty pointless, really."

"It's more of a good luck charm."

"Well, your luck just ran out. Your plane leaves in the morning."

"And what if I said no?"

"We'd insist."

"And what if I insisted?"

"We'd cuff you and send you to Gitmo."

"A US citizen? You're bluffing."

"Then maybe we hand you over to the Revolutionary Guard."

Charlie bit back hard. "And have them hang me from the highest crane? How bad would that look?"

"You're a liability, Glass. You need to be gone. One way or another."

Charlie sighed in muffled acceptance of her enforced deportation.

"Atta girl." A smirking O'Hara rose for the door. "Come through, we've set a bed for you."

Charlie shuffled on behind, desperate to take up the offer. Next door, an identical cell had been kitted out with a camp bed covered in harsh fabrics. Charlie didn't mind one bit. Exhausted, she slumped onto the rough blanket.

"You'll be escorted all the way. Just in case you get other ideas." As O'Hara moved outside, he tapped the lock on the door. "Sweet dreams."

"Do I get a chance to appeal?"

She never received a reply. It was then she realized the room's light switch was operated from the outside. She slammed her head into the hard pillow and let the firm mattress take the strain.

Despite the circumstances, she fought sleep. Fought reality.

There were so many unanswered questions for her to retreat from the field.

There were many loose ends for her to go quietly into that dark night.

Despite her best efforts, that's exactly what she did.

CHAPTER 37

The next morning, Charlie was up with the desert lark, but had been left caged until noon. Three hours before her scheduled departure, she was sitting in the back of a beat-up sedan. Sweating underneath a burka and cuffed to the car door handle wasn't her idea of traveling in style.

"This isn't necessary."

O'Hara was warming up to the prospect of her removal. "No, but it's fun."

"When I get out of this, remind me to kick your ass."

O'Hara sneered behind gritted teeth. Outside, smatterings of Farsi graffiti lay beside roughly scrolled English translations. The theme of the evil etchings was a hatred of all things Western; all things USA, to be precise. A beautifully crafted mural of the Iranian flag proudly adorned a half brick wall. High security fencing seemed popular. A painting of the Ayatollah Khomeini threw flowers across a wall topped off with huge metal spikes. Tall cedar trees lined gardens that led to a large brick building with columns either side. Charlie recognized the metal fenced building they just drove past. The irony hit hard.

"Are you kidding me? Our old Embassy?"

"The den of espionage itself. Nice cover. They have no idea we're located next door."

"How do you get away with it? What's your cover?"

O'Hara hesitated on the wrong side of cooperation, so Charlie nudged him. "Come on, I'm leaving. We're on the same side."

Still nothing.

"If you tell me, I promise I won't track you down when you're back stateside."

The pair shared their first snickers. After some consideration, O'Hara opened up. "We're a Panamanian import and export business."

"Shipping what?"

"Sensitive equipment."

"The kind the US doesn't allow people to ship?"

"Exactly. We outlawed a vast number of items as part of our efforts to prevent Iran from developing nuclear weapons. Some of them are vital, others don't work. Guess which ones we ship?"

"They're not stupid."

"You'd be surprised. It's more sophisticated than that. We let slip sensitive documents detailing intricate guidance systems that will never work. We offer the components through black markets at extortionate prices."

"You're not doing this to make money?"

"Hell no, but the risks taken are so high, any legitimate criminal would charge the earth. We're doing this to find the channels, to track the equipment."

"And?"

O'Hara shook his head. "It's a process. The counterfeiting helps."

"How?"

His head shook again, but for different reasons. He had said too much already. He changed the subject by pointing out the window. "You'll like these. They are my favorite."

Protest posters corrupted walls infested with pop-culture terrorism symbols. *Death to USA* murals, with guns representing the stars and blood depicting the stripes dripped from the walls. A gaunt faced statue of liberty stood tall, draped in a bloody shroud.

The talented but tainted artistry seemed lost on the locals as they ambled past, oblivious to the propaganda. Everyday life bustled past. A young man in an oversized, out-of-date Nike jacket walking with a stack of brightly colored balloons. In a trance, it seemed uncertain if he was selling them or looking to buy more so he could be carried far away.

Charlie had been given the flight plans; Tehran to Istanbul, then home to the US. She was headed under escort to the airport. *An ignominious exit.*

She was not born before the hostage crisis of 1979, but it had been ingrained in her training and history lessons. However ignominious the departure seemed, it possessed a great deal more dignity and a lot less danger than those souls trapped under Carter's presidency. She told herself to get a grip. She tightened her throbbing hand and thought of home.

The rest of the journey was spent in quiet resignation. She was leaving with so many unanswered questions ringing in her ears.

Mission unaccomplished.

When she arrived at the curbside drop off, her cuff was unlocked. "That was totally uncalled for, and it's going in my report." Charlie hated how that sounded. Her trusted rucksack and untrustworthy phone had been returned. Otherwise, she was traveling light.

The agent smirked. "I'd shake your hand but, protocols."

"I'd smack your mouth, but protocols."

"Good luck, Agent. I genuinely mean that."

"Likewise." Charlie's genuine smile seemed to take them both by surprise.

"I'll be with you every step of the way. One step behind you until you board." He handed her the plane ticket.

Charlie leered. "How can I forget?"

Inside, the airport looked surprisingly modernized; even Westernized. Most of the passengers and staff were Middle Eastern. Flying business class allowed her to jump to the lead of the security queues. Chaos surrounded the process. Queuing seemed an alien concept to everyone involved, even the staff. Prying eyes landed on the Western beauty traveling alone. The guards pulled her into the check-in process as a priority, leaving O'Hara in her wake.

She smiled at the guards but grinned at the agent.

He looked unimpressed and set to work, barging his way through the crowd. An exceptionally large woman with an even larger family blocked his progress.

Charlie had bigger issues than an irate American. Ahead, the police presence darkened and closed in, like a gathering storm. Black uniforms and dark eyes loomed large as she neared the check-in. Scowls were the facial impression of choice. The guards seemed to mistrust everyone. The check-in agents beamed, but the looming vultures set all the early birds on edge.

Charlie didn't fidget or flinch. Thoughts of present circumstances and future consequences were replaced by echoes of her past. The tradecraft kicked in. She took deep breaths and pulled happy thoughts to the front of her mind. Her first flight from Washington D.C. to Paris sprung to mind. She mentally listed her favorite restaurants in Paris, in order. Attempts to repeat the process for DC were cut short. She only really liked one place, an old grill house over on 15th Street. Memories of eating their legendary pastrami sandwich distracted her from the troubles ahead. By the time she handed over her well-traveled Swiss passport, she was more hungry than scared.

Charlie never lost smiling eye contact with the young check in operator. The twenty-something girl was pretty, yet doleful. She looked desperate to switch places with Charlie and get the hell out of Iran. Despite its recent production date, the passport looked well thumbed; the multiple fake stamps made her seem well traveled. The photograph was unsurprisingly current. The check in operator thumbed through the passport with agonizing detail. Heavy energy arrived on the scene in the shape of a lecherous old guard. Keen to get a closer look at both passenger and passport, he leered in close. His gray mustache twitched. Irked by the older man's intrusion, the young check in operator slapped Charlie's passport open on the desk, thumped the inky stamp into a blank page and handed it back in double quick time. She had seen enough. The grumbling, gruff old man clearly hadn't. Charlie was grateful for the old letch. His lascivious presence had inadvertently sped up the process. With only carry on, she sped between the lines.

Once through, Charlie skipped to the nearest travel themed store. A universal phone charger was purchased, along with some water. Across the terminal walkway lay her next stop, the ladies' toilet.

She clashed gazes with O'Hara just before she entered. Not that it mattered to her. There was no way he would be barging in anytime soon. The power point for the floor cleaner lay in the back of the service cupboard. It wasn't difficult to find. The waiting dragged. The *on* button was hit continually until eventually a power signal blinked into being. Checking there was no one close by, she lowered the phone's volume, held the unit to her ear, and pressed play. To her relief, the voice recorder crackled into life. Her heart raced. The unit had picked up every word the Police Chief uttered. Unsurprisingly, the other caller had remained out of the mic-shot. This would be a one-sided investigation. After running through the recording, she stalled.

Stunned and amazed, she was left with only one conclusion.

She was not going home.

CHAPTER 38

Charlie was grateful to O'Hara for one thing. His search of her phone had been limited to call records, texts, and contacts. The voice recording had gone unnoticed, and unaltered. She reset the recording and went again from the start, to make sure she'd captured everything. Only the Police Chief's voice could be heard. Disappointingly, no introductions were made. The people on either side of the phone seemed to know each other and understood the value of anonymity.

Sections were paused and repeated as she struggled with the translation. The pace of the dialogue told Charlie the two participants were two things; native Farsi speakers and panicked.

The biggest difficulty was she only had one side of the story.

"I know it's late. There's a problem" / ------

"A fire." / ------

"The warehouse." / ------

"We lost everything." / ------

"I know. I am sorry. It's just-" / ------

"Some woman." / ------

"American." / ------

"Maybe. She-"/ ------

"Sherif brought her. He said Feisal gave her passage." / -----
-

"Understand. I will handle him." / ------

"Gone. She disappeared after the fire." / ------

"I have no idea." / ------

"They must know we've been double dealing." / ------

"We are right to run." / ------

"I know I am just sayi–"/ ------

"The money? It's safe. Last shipment is on its way." / ------

"Do not threaten me. I have friends on both sides." / ------

"Last of the drugs fly out tomorrow." / ------

"The kit? Stripped and shipped before dawn."/ ------

"Yes. I said I would handle it. Tonight." / ------

"The gala at Golestan Palace." / ------

"I said I would do it. I will." / ------

But–"/ ------

Screamed Farsi expletives marked the period after the call ending. Charlie couldn't tell who was on the other end of the line.

Who was running the show?

Where was the money going?

What airport were they using?

She was disturbed by the Police Chief's phrase, *connections on both sides*. It made it impossible for her to trust anyone. Could O'Hara be one of the co-conspirators? *Possibly. Maybe even probably.*

Why else was he so keen to get her stateside?

She relished the prospect of making it a solo effort. The mission took a massive change in direction. The flight was leaving without her.

She was headed to the only solid clue given on the call.

The gala at the Golestan Palace.

CHAPTER 39

O'Hara marched up beside Charlie the second she sauntered out of the restroom. He looked straight past her, but his words didn't miss. "What the hell are you playing at?"

Charlie touched her stomach. "Iranian cuisine. Back off. You look like an amateur."

The agent retreated to a discreet distance, suitably chastised. With phase one complete, Charlie plotted her retreat. Negotiating security would be her next threat and her only real opportunity. She bundled her way forward and waved her business class ticket. After being ushered from a distance to the head of the security line, Charlie took full advantage of the preferential treatment. The rucksack was thrown onto the scanner belt, alongside her combat boots. Whilst waiting for her belongings, she peered at the x-ray display.

She was intrigued by the patterns and set about calculating the chances of anyone ever catching anything through the process. Suddenly, a mind-blowing schematic eased across the display monitor. She squinted and cricked her neck. Her rucksack looked strangely electrical. To her trained eye, it looked like a small device had been embedded into the extra wide strap. Worried by what she had discovered, and petrified that others would follow suit, she distracted the guards. She stepped back onto the foot of a nearby small girl, around six years old.

The whimpering tears that followed were the perfect cover.

The guards looked away. The mother was understanding and considerate. The screaming kid was unforgiving and accusatory. Charlie looked oblivious.

She clawed the pack off the conveyor belt and pushed on through the crowd. Behind her it looked like both the little girl and O'Hara were bleating, for totally different reasons. Charlie grappled the rucksack straps. The device inside felt like a tracker; the kind used to monitor criminals. Her dislike for the CIA was morphing into disgust. At a nearby security line, an overzealous guard berated a middle-aged woman for taking too long. Her chastising husband joined in the condemnation. Leaning across, Charlie stole nail clippers from a collection of confiscated items. A *Welcome to Tehran* cap made it into her rucksack. Before O'Hara could play catch up, she was off and running. All angles and exits, people, faces, items, and places were visually scoured. When she passed a cleaner's cart, she lifted a dangling Hi-Viz vest. Industrial cleaning fluid was lifted. At a corner spot, out of sight from the security cameras, the fluid was spilled across the floor. The slippage caused a melee.

She barged on through the crowd as cries of angst and turmoil congested the walkway behind her. She ran straight to her gate and pushed into the boarding queue. As her fellow passengers pushed their way through to the plane, she let them slide past. All the while, she waited for her tail to be reconnected. Worried that an abandoned bag would raise greater alarm, she used the stolen nail clippers to cut the fabric from her rucksack. The device was pulled. *A tracker, for sure.*

She pulled the pack close and waited for a new arrival.

After ten minutes, O'Hara showed up, floundering his way past the loitering passengers. Panting, he craned his gaze through the crowd, apparently petrified that he had screwed up again. The split second she made sure she had been spotted, Charlie passed through the ticket check and moved down the covered walkway. Once out of sight, she slipped the tracker inside the first handbag she could find. The old lady was oblivious. Charlie hoped when the CIA raid to retrieve the tracker fell, the old lady would survive the onslaught. The Hi-Viz jacket was pulled on, along with the tourist cap. Officiously, she pushed down the gangway, requesting free passage. The High-Viz worked. The passengers obliged. At the entrance to the plane, she grabbed a folded kid's stroller, threw it over her left shoulder and headed down and out the side stairs. When the stairs changed orientation, she changed shoulders. All the while, the stroller covered her face from the angle of the terminal building. Back down amongst the baggage handlers, she moved off to the nearest empty baggage train. To make her flight look more legitimate, she dislocated the train of baggage carts.

The tractor was electric, and it ran well. With her back to the terminal windows, she set off down the gate service areas. The ride across to the domestic arrivals was long, but necessary. They would have no questioning passport controls in that area. The big signs were easy to follow. Once outside the area, she found the team of handlers with the least number of cases still to be loaded. The team were casually throwing in the last of the luggage from a recently arrived flight. Charlie pulled the biggest case she could find and pulled it up onto the short conveyor. Checking the absence of an audience, she lay on the conveyor and followed her case through the hole in the wall. The journey was short, the odds of success long. Passing through the plastic flaps, she was delighted to find most of the passengers had already collected their cases. She spun off the conveyor and pretended to be checking the flaps on the entrance into the baggage hall. Strange looks were cast by the remaining weary travelers. The flap inspection seemed to work, as a ruse.

She turned away from the crowd and the cameras and walked on, hoping her arrival hadn't sparked interest. Across at the busiest baggage belt, a scrum had formed. People of all shapes and sizes were grappling for access to luggage of all shapes and sizes. Jousting for positions, no quarter was asked, and none given. Charlie profiled the crowd. After two or three false calls and locked cases, she searched for her next mark. A young woman, reasonably tall and athletic, in the mid-distance, caught her eye. Well turned out, she pulled a large, branded case from the conveyor belt. When she turned and waited for her next piece, Charlie moved in, all the while checking for security.

On closer inspection, she noted the combination locks on the case remained at *000*. She had found her next target. With the woman distracted by her search for a second bag, Charlie made her move. On the run, the case was lifted and pulled into the most congested section. Through a circuitous route lined by the most people cover, Charlie made her way to the disabled toilet. The case was hauled into an open cubicle. It didn't fit. She jammed herself back out and sought out a larger disabled cubicle. The wider layout allowed for the suitcase to be set on the tile floor. The unset combination locks opened easily at *000*.

Up against the clock, fearing discovery, at any stage, Charlie rapidly rifled the case. She selected the only item of clothing passible for a gala event at a palace. Thankfully, the profiling worked. The clothes fitted the function and her form. Raking through the toiletries, she did her best to make herself look half-way presentable. Dampened hair, a freshen up and lashings of deodorant delivered the look she couldn't confirm. She worked on. The case held no phone, but a side pocket did house a fistful of rials. Her own phone was useless, so she smashed the handset, bit the SIM card in two and stuffed the remains in the cistern, along with her rucksack. Only her fake Swiss passport and cash were retained. In a smaller bag, she found a stunning necklace. Too gaudy to be real, she tried it on. Her talisman was a giveaway, but there was no way it would be left behind. She yanked it off and threw it inside her sports bra. A silk headscarf, a fake designer purse, and oversized shades of equal dubiety closed out her look. Her very own stolen dressing-up box was delivering the goods.

She pulled a cleaning sign to block the door after her exit. She understood it would count for nothing if she didn't make it past security. Chin up, shoulders back, she bounded for the exit.

Tall heels heightened her gait, encouraging each and every guard to stare, male and female. Arrogance was bliss. Everyone held back in awe or fear of the beauty marching past imperiously.

Once outside, a startled young porter volunteered to act as her personal guide. Charlie cut him short, handed over some rials, and asked him to hail a cab. He bowed lightly and complied. The cab arrived in double quick time. The extra tip was most appreciated.

Once inside the cab, the destination was given as the Golestan Palace.

The driver raised his eyebrows, impressed.

Charlie raised her eyebrows, afraid.

CHAPTER 40

Upon the raised highway infrastructure, the views of the city were magnificent. Squalor lay a million miles away in parts of town the rich didn't need to look at, or even care about. The mountains in the background framed the vista perfectly. The lowering sun cast incredible shades and hues across the tips of the mountains to the northwest. Free from animals, beggars, and peddlers, the traffic moved more quickly around town. At the sixth junction, the taxi took its leave of the concrete overpass. Back down on the ground, these suburbs were filled with regal affluence, not religious influence. Back in the slums, they used walls to pen people in; here they were used to keep people out. There was no trash for the street cleaner to mismanage. Lush gardens flourished behind ornate gates. Outside the largest of the mansions, private security guards made themselves highly visible. Eastern European accents styled the architecture of the mansions adorning the streets. The boulevard held few cars. The immaculate sidewalks were bereft of pedestrians. It was the kind of place stray dogs never strayed. *How the other point zero, zero, one percent live.*

Deep in the heart of the gentrified section of town, the taxi slowed. Manicured trees took center stage in the tiny square. Mansions overlooked ornately designed, perfectly maintained havens. The oasis was light years away from the abject poverty of the slums, only a stoning's throw away. *Perfect cover.*

Dressed to the hilt in her white one-piece trouser suit, silk scarf fashioned into a hajib, high heels, and designed bag, Charlie looked a million rials. The night looked chilly, so Charlie paid extra for the rug lining the backseat of the taxi. The brightly colored shawl helped stave off the cold and the stares.

As the dusk closed in, it dawned on her; she had no place to stay, no shelter. The trees in a small park offered some cover but fears over being noticed as a loiterer set her into motion. When the call to prayer marked the onset of night, she marveled at the mystical sounds drifting up into the cloudless night sky. It was going to be a cold one. Discreetly set lamps lit the fading greenery perfectly. As the chilly winds cracked open the night sky, cold reality seeped into her bones. She needed the heat of battle to keep her alive. Those miserable nights camping in the Virginia hills were no preparation for the night to come. Memories of Virginia brought forward thoughts of Pop.

He'd be worried. He'd be annoyed. He'd be proud.

When the shivering worsened, she realized changes needed to be made. She wouldn't last the night. Regretted not layering up. Uncertain, she knew the answers could only be found inside the palace. She scanned the building. The CCTV cameras were her first challenge. High walls, a big steel gate, and security guards were added to her list of reasons why breaking and entering was no option. When throwing her head back in dismay, she caught the sight of a gray sedan sitting across the street. The car matched many parked nearby. *This one is different.* She glanced across to confirm her doubts. Three men sat in the car. No one ever sat in a darkened car for long. It looked more than suspicious. She gave the vehicle five minutes to make its move.

When it did nothing, she made moves of her own. Unable and unwilling to confront the occupants head-on, she stole away. With her back to the sedan, she walked and listened.

Her pulse raced when the car engine kindled to life. The vehicle's side lights became the most prominent features in the park. She was being followed. After breaking out into a full-blooded march, she made good time across the open square. As soon as she turned into the most heavily wooded area, she flipped off her heels and ran. Flat out, she kept to the shadows, leaping from tree to tree. Over her quickening breathing, she heard the car accelerating. At the last second, she darted behind the largest tree and circled the trunk, keeping it directly between her and the passing car. At the square's perimeter, the car rolled off into the night.

Like a prowling alley cat with many lives, she had lost another tail. It took a few moments for Charlie to catch her breath and gather her thoughts. Despite the appearance and disappearance of what she assumed was a carload of secret police, the plan hadn't changed. It couldn't change. There were no other options.

Across the grass square, tall trees bent in reverence before two magnificent main towers. The lighting from the fountain dominating the brick-blocked plaza cascaded over the intricate tiling that coated the entire palace. Semi-circular topped mahogany windows stood proudly within a façade featuring spiraled stone columns. Emerald lighting coated the inside of the domed archways. Suddenly, the gates opened to allow a jet-black Mercedes to glide inside. When they arrived at the entrance, the usual suspects made their presence known. Charlie's heartbeat jolted. Sherif was riding shotgun. Charlie wondered just how long it would be before he ran out of lives.

She skulked into the shadows. A throng of support staff rushed to assist the new arrivals. Charlie held her position and checked her points of potential access. The main gate lay open, tempting her closer. It took two guards to open the Mercedes door for the Police Chief. With great ceremony, he stepped out into the night, sending his groveling entourage into raptures. As he mounted the winding stone stairs, all eyes fell upon him and his overly flamboyant uniform. It was obvious that corruption lay at the top of the justice tree.

Two columns of fighting men straddled the main entrance. Ten men, on each side, standing proudly at attention, AK47s on display. Their bottle green uniforms with red epaulets were finished off with sashes of green, white, red, and gold. The uniformity spread to identically trimmed bears, shiny black boots, white spats, and gloves. The black and gold badges on their caps showed the squad in all their glory.

Her world darkened at the realization she stood in the presence of the unmistakably evil Islamic Revolutionary Guard.

She stared, bewitched by the spectacle playing out before her. The glitterati of Tehran sauntered past the stern-faced fanatics of the Islamic Revolutionary Guard. Neither segment of society noticed the other. Lost in their own worlds, true to their own beliefs. The military dress did not complement the cocktail dress. The cloaks, coats, and hats failed to conceal the opulent air surrounding the guests, as they funneled past the guard of honor, unaware of their surroundings or their surrounders. She had heard tales of the Guard's fanaticism. She knew if they discovered her identity, she wouldn't see the dawn. Tickets were presented with pride and checked with vigilance.

Charlie understood, a flashy outfit and a glittering grin would not be enough. She needed another way in.

Head down, she passed through the crowd, cowering under the line of heads surrounding her. It seemed every uniformed eye was burning a hole in every living soul. Sweat dripped down the small of her back as she made a dash for the dark side of the entrance. Skip-stepping across the cobbles, she hit the concealment behind a giant Azalea. Its wilting flowers proved the perfect camouflage against the colorful sideshow playing out in the front courtyard.

Round the back of the palace, a gated entrance had been commandeered to accept deliveries. Twitching in all directions, she studied the scene.

After three minutes, a truck arrived at the side gate. She counted and observed.

Forty seconds, no search of the rear. Paperwork check only.

When another van arrived on the scene, Charlie spied servers and porters scrambling around the cramped courtyard. With the delivery driver distracted by the unwanted attentions of an overly zealous guard, Charlie made her move. She slipped over, out of sight of the rearview mirrors and the inquisitive guard. She turned the handle on the rear door. Her thundering heart raced on ahead.

To her surprise, it opened. To her terror, she climbed inside.

She eased close the door and set her ear against the back door. *Silence.*

Her heart thumped through her ribcage. Up front, the driver's muffled voice bled through. His short blunt answer did the trick. When the van jolted forward, she almost lost her footing and her nerve. Only the fear of being seen exiting the van prevented her from fleeing back out into the night.

A red jacket from a server's uniform hung on the wall separating the cabin from the back of the van. It was the right color, but the wrong fit. She almost drowned in a sea of starched cotton. Uncertain if the uniform was spare or if it belonged to the driver, she needed to get moving. Kind shouts from outside and inside the van were the signals she needed. She braced herself in time for the van's departure. Having previously spied the lie of the land through the open gate, Charlie knew the journey would be short. She picked up a wooden crate filled with fresh lettuce, threw it over her shoulder, then clambered to the rear door. The split second the van halted, she pulled the lever and jumped out. Turning away from the driver's side, she gently closed the rear door and slid around the back of the van.

The driver's shuffling feet arrived only a moment after she had turned the corner. Hearing the van door opening behind her drove her forward. She bounded confidently onwards, keeping her head on the other side of the box from any potential viewers. A flash of inspiration came in the form of another red jacketed member of staff. *The jacket could work.* A huge white tablecloth was pulled into her ensemble to help her blend with the crisp uniforms of the waiting staff. Her white trousers were no match with the other black trousered uniforms, but the sheet helped the disguise. When anyone got close, she pivoted. With every turn, she eased herself ever closer to the event. Suddenly, an irate Farsi voice rasped her ears.

"Hey you!" She turned to stone.

"Wrong way. The kitchen is through there."

She held her hands up apologetically, changed course, and bundled herself off into what she hoped was the kitchen.

Success came in the form of an industrial kitchen filled to the brim with staff, all at various stages of panic. Charlie dumped the greens and pushed on through the crowd, head bowed. Getting into the kitchens was one thing; getting into the party was another. With an event so large, additional portable toilets had been installed for the waiting staff. Charlie saw her opportunity, raced across, and clambered inside the first one available. The smell was ungodly. She had to grimace and bear it. Her red overcoat was pulled. Her trouser suit was checked, as was her look.

A wave of panic landed on her. She began to question her ethnicity. She had been the only Western face she could recall seeing. She took an extra five minutes to convince herself that there had to be other Caucasian women on the invite list. It seemed the only way she stood a chance of fitting in. She filled her cupped hand with a splash of water from the plastic tap and took a sip. The next handful was sent across her face. A few squares of industrial toilet roll were used to mop her brow and damp down her sweat. As one last act of preparation, her hair was checked. She waited an eternity for the right kind of voices to arrive. Two men could be heard arriving outside the cubicle, but their gruff tones did not fit her profile. The unmistakable smell of hash and a volley of chortles explained the delay in their departure. Eventually, they left.

Soon after, two girls cackled ever closer. When the cubicle next door opened, Charlie bundled herself out of into the closest girl, a waitress. Apologies were thrown as Charlie indicated she was suffering from stomach cramps. Her faux embarrassment persuaded the waitress to help. Sympathy was immediately forthcoming.

The young waitress couldn't have been long out of home-school. Gaunt features exaggerated her big brown eyes. Charlie was pulled to the side and sat down. She requisitioned a wet cloth, along with a glass of water. Her brow was mopped gently. After five excruciatingly long minutes, Charlie motioned that she would like to return to the event. The waitress led the way. On route, Charlie asked for permission to stop at a sink, wash her hands, and take another drink of water. She didn't ask permission to slip a small fileting knife up her sleeve. Her bandaged hand did not match her glamorous persona, so both hands were placed behind her back before she bowed and allowed herself to be escorted onwards. The security guards were waved to the side as the waitress assisted in Charlie's apparent return to the big room.

The waitress pulled open the door and ushered her forward. Inside the anteroom, Charlie gave her a nod of thanks.

In return, she received a nod of sympathy.

The waitress took her leave as Charlie took stock of the magnificence before her. The room even outshone the event's illuminati and glitterati. Solid silver wallpaper adorned the walls. Each leaf shone with intricate inlays and detailed filigree. Crystal chandeliers dripped elegantly from the silver ceilings. Each wall housed a massive marble fireplace that supported a mirror that stretched up into the silvery heavens. Immaculate Persian rugs covered swathes of delicately inlaid oak flooring. Glasses and silverware gleamed from the reflections off the silver-topped, octagonal, mahogany table. Vases and urns of all shapes and large sizes lay strategically placed within discreet alcoves and prominent positions. Untouched velvet upholstery draped chaise-lounges and feature armchairs. The room caught her breath, but the people stopped the show.

The gathering was a bizarre cacophony of conjoined classes holding separate views and similar glasses. Seventy people or so milled under the watchful eye of the Revolutionary Guard. Submissive staff offered nourishment as the dismissive guests dished out admonishments. The class system was alive and well in the Islamic Republic of Iran.

The majority of the men attended in traditional attire. In one corner stood a collection of men in suits styled in the eighties. Satin grays, double-breasted, wide lapels, and wider ties were in vogue. Thin features and thick glasses gave each one of them a geeky persona. Regimented mustaches were also on parade.

A group of women with their faces partially covered wore traditional attire. Delicate hands beautified by henna tattoos held their veils in place. Charlie felt relieved there were Western women present. Only a few of them, but enough that she didn't stand out. For once in her life, she had guessed the dress code correctly. Her trouser suit merged perfectly with the mood. Her stolen gems glittered enough that she fitted in, but not so much that she stood out. Gazing at the opulence on parade, she found it hard to imagine or forget the millions of poverty-stricken souls living in slum conditions a world away on the other end of town.

This was a gala with, and for, the greater good of the republic. Islam seemed to have taken a back seat for the evening. Chilled water and alcohol-free champagne were freely available.

She kept her sun damaged head low as she mingled with the highbrows. All eye contact was shunned for fear of getting pulled into a conversation. Her feet kept moving to avoid being cornered.

Fitting in, she lifted a sample from a passing tray of Persian canapes. Fruit juices, nuts, stuffed olives, and sweet bakes tempted her senses. The opulence tainted her taste buds. Worried that she may be discovered, she leaned in again, but the less than attentive attendant never lifted her gaze. Like everyone else, she was too busy staring across the room.

A hush had descended.

Over at the top of a three-tier staircase stood the center of everyone's attention. Charlie, along with everyone else in the room, gazed in wonderment at the most beautiful woman imaginable. Her vulcanite hair fell softly around savagely high cheekbones. Crescent brows framed eyes of the deepest ochre. Red, molten lips matched her dress and complimented her nutmeg skin.

Elegant, cosmopolitan, beguiling. Charlie wasn't lost for adjectives.

The men in the room looked lost for words at the scarlet siren's arrival. Conversation levels and jaws dropped when the mystery woman glided down into the room.

Her velvet shawl matched a dress that clung to her tapered, athletic frame. A satin sash of midnight crimson partially obscured the cut away sides of the dress that revealed a toned and bronzed torso. Loopy, oversized earrings of rose gold matched her heavy necklace, and delicate bangles. Golden pumps peeked out from beneath the long dress as she floated amongst the throng. The wave of interest gained intensity with every step.

The crowd milled like sheep encircling a farmer rattling a bag of feed. The hangers-on hung on her every word. To Charlie, the vision looked polite, erudite, and perfectly placed; one rung below aloof. Even the omnipresent Revolutionary Guard surrendered in her presence.

There stood a woman of undeniable beauty and unquestionable influence.

Irrespective of who organized the event, Charlie knew one thing.

The vision of beauty standing before her ran the show.

CHAPTER 41

Charlie spun and darted for an alcove. *Did he see me?* She checked a nearby gold trimmed mirror. Its convex shape provided a three-sixty-degree view of the room. The Police Chief stood tall, beside him, lurked Sherif. Charlie used the vantage point to study her adversaries through the misshapen looking glass. The Police Chief looked an odd creature, a deformed mole with wire-rimmed glasses. The warped mirror didn't help his look.

To the side, Sherif received his orders. In double quick time, he waltzed around the room toward the beautiful woman. He waited his turn for an audience, much to the Police Chief's annoyance. Her all-in-black handlers were working overtime, maintaining the security cordon around their charge. Dignitaries lost their dignity attempting to gain access to the alluring goddess. Her power over the crowd transcended the allure of simple beauty. Sherif moved in close for a side glancing conversation with the most thuggish handler. His message was carried over and repeated in a similar manner beside the beauty.

She looked ahead, as the message was conveyed. One glance at Sherif and another at the Police Chief closed off her decision-making process. After whispering a response to her minder, she glided from the room, parting the sea of admiring faces before her. If her entrance looked grand, her exit was positively Palladian.

The go-betweens conveyed her messages across the room. The Police Chief brightened, apparently enthused by the developments. He slinked to a side entrance, for what Charlie assumed would be an out-of-sight rendezvous with the mystery woman. Charlie lifted a couple of drinks from a waitress' tray and slid across to the large, connected anteroom. She gripped the stems tightly. The non-alcoholic champagne could still hold some punch. She broke out into a skip. In every way, she played catch up. The mirrored hallways connecting the massive anterooms were as extravagant as the central drawing rooms. Tall claret shaded velvet curtains stretched to high ceilings furnished with bronzed etchings.

Voices.

She slowed at the corner and craned her hearing round into the long corridor. The accents were moving away at pace, so she took a chance at a peek. Sherif and the Police Chief were engrossed in a deep, muffled dialogue. They stalled outside an open side-door. Charlie jumped behind a statue, taking pride of place in a nearby alcove. In a heartbeat, the men were through the door. Two beats later, Charlie rejoined the hunt.

Slipping in through the door, she followed on, down an incredible corridor. The men's footsteps echoed around the granite echo chamber. She followed on surrounded by gold inlay, velvet, ancient tapestries, marble flooring, massive colonnades of dark granite. *All this for a corridor?*

In every way possible, she wondered what lay ahead.

She weaved in and out of the pillars, never losing sight of the deadly duo.

Twenty yards ahead, the Police Chief motioned for Sherif to yank at the cornice on a curved section of the hallway. Amazingly, the edging gave way. A secret door opened. The pair disappeared down a concealed back staircase.

If Charlie had blinked, she would have missed the turning.

Charlie's shoes clipped off the wooden floor, forcing her to kick them to the skirting. She ran on, barefoot, drinks in hand. Right now, they seemed her only weapon. She recalled the door opened quietly, so she had few qualms about opening it. After the latch clicked, she slid through.

She eased down the spiral stone steps, intent on discovering more. A cellar door lay at the bottom of the first curved flight. She set her ear to the wide gap around the old oak door's edge. A third of the way up, the door stand had rooted away, providing Charlie with a sliver of sightline. She slid her gaze through the crack and hung on every Farsi word creeping through the cloistered cellar.

The mystery woman seemed calm. "Be reasonable, Hosseini. What is this?"

She assumed Hosseini was the Police Chief. He spoke next. "The boss made a file. I delivered it tonight."

"What?"

"A file. The Republican Guard have orders to arrest you."

The woman held firm. "Why?"

"It doesn't matter. You will be dead before they get to you."

"I don't understand."

"Someone is closing the circle. They are sending hit squads."

"It's not me!" she protested.

"Well, the boss thinks it is. That's why everything and everybody needs to go."

"I'm going nowhere."

"They know someone was trading secrets and stealing the real cash."

"That wasn't me."

Hosseini, the Police Chief, snorted. "I know. It was me." A sniveling Sherif squawked sycophantically. Hosseini continued. "Right now, I am a suspect, but after the dossier has been shared, you are now the guilty one. I will be gone and our friends, the Iranians, will have their traitor."

The woman stepped into Charlie's field of view. Her mouth had lost its gloss. "You know who I am and what I represent."

"Look upon this as a favor, Roxanne. A bullet in the head will be better than falling into the hands of the Iranians, especially after they've just learned you have been double-crossing them."

As the woman called Roxanne turned, her two henchmen muscled their way into the scene. "You and everyone you hold dear will never survive if I am harmed. Every generation will be wiped from this planet. Your greed will destroy everything."

"I like my chances. I am just protecting my interests. I kill you. I make my boss and the Republic happy. Everybody wins. Except you, of course."

The look Roxanne threw at the sniffling Sherif could have turned him to stone. Charlie spun with indecision. The beguiling Roxanne was about to be murdered. Innocence or guilt played no part in her verdict. Any enemy of the Police Chief was a potential ally.

A staged gun battle was the last thing she needed. She saw redemption in the shape of a beauty. Fearful that further thought could damage her resolve, she made her move, stumbling headlong into the room; glasses raised to head height. "There you are, Roxanne."

Roxanne looked as shocked as anyone, as Charlie moved in close. The Police Chief lowered his previously unseen weapon. Sherif stalled, apparently unwilling to call Charlie out.

Suddenly, in the confusion, Roxanne's guards pulled their weapons. Fear filled the room.

Sweaty gun hands flinched and faltered.

Two guns against two guns. Everyone stalled. A standoff ensued.

The Police chief turned negotiator. "Look we can-"

Roxanne broke the stalemate. "Shoot him!"

The Police Chief leered. "You underestimate survival. You should know better. Faced with a choice between making money and surviving, everyone chooses the latter."

Roxanne's two guards coldly turned their guns. One pointed to Charlie, the other one turned coldly towards his boss. They said nothing. Their guns said enough.

If the betrayal cut Roxanne, it never drew blood. "You will die for this." She scanned the room. "You will all die for this."

Charlie gazed in amazement at Roxanne's steadfast resolve. Despite having a room full of guns pointed in her direction, she still owned the room. Charlie staggered back until she hit the cellar wall. Hosseini, the Police Chief cackled. "Well, some of us might die." Callously, he turned and pointed his gun directly at Sherif. "Isn't that right?"

"No-" Panicked, Sherif lunged at the double crosser, knocking the Police Chief sideways.

Bang! Bang!

In the melee, Roxanne snatched the nearest shooter's gun. Charlie smashed the glasses into the face of the second guard as he fumbled the decision to shoot. She rained down blows on the second guard, sending him backward.

Bang!

The Police Chief scrambled out from underneath Sherif's gargling body, just as the first guard's pistol discharged. Through the smoke, Charlie spied Roxanne choking out the first guard as they wrestled for ownership of the smoking gun. Both guard and gun dropped to the ground. When the Police Chief rose, gun in hand, Roxanne dropped to her knee, lifted the gun, and fired.

Bang! Bang!

The Police Chief staggered backward. The second guard crumpled under the beating as Charlie turned to see Roxanne lunging forward, crashing the butt of the gun into the dying man's eye. The pistol erupted again.

Bang! Bang! Bang

Her overkill looked and sounded demonic. Smoke billowed around the room. Charlie steadied herself against the wall, straightened and stared. Roxanne's eyes, face and dress were bloodshot. She edged the barrel of her gun in Charlie's direction and then sent out a sly, disarming grin. "You have some pair of balls."

"Takes one to know one."

When Sherif groaned, Roxanne broke off to help him. Charlie joined the triage team. The chest wound wept badly. Roxanne pulled his torso to the vertical. "Help me!"

Her efforts to breathe life into Sherif's lungs were hampered when gulps of blood frothed from his esophagus. His gullet choked and writhed. After one last desperate heave of panic, Sherif fell still. Silence descended. He was gone.

Roxanne relit her short fuse. Thumping the corpse with her fist. "They will have heard the gunshots. We need to move. Come on! Get the guns. Get the door." Charlie did as instructed. She had already fallen under her spell. "Where are we going?" She cried.

"Up."

Roxanne lifted her skirt and raced into and down the nearby corridor. Charlie stumbled after her in panic-filled pursuit. Roxanne stalled beside a wall mirror in an alcove, then tapped its frame. The structure clicked open to reveal a false door at the entrance to a tunnel. Charlie was totally lost. "How do you know about that?"

"Friends. We've operated here for years." She took a moment to wipe the blood from the mirror frame and gently clicked the doorway shut. A motion detector clicked light across Roxanne's face. "Come on."

Along a narrow tunnel, the pair fled through the underground network. "These are former escape routes built by the last shah. They're a secret to the public, but the Republican Guard knows of them. They will be covering the exit." At a bend in the tunnel, Roxanne threw a one-eighty and turned up a very narrow spiral staircase. Cobwebs told tales of the staircase's redundancy. The pair flapped and flailed their way through the webs on up the stairway. Distant shouts barreling down the tunnel behind them, causing Charlie to falter and slip. Painfully, she cracked her knee in the misstep. Roxanne spiraled on ahead, surefooted in her flight. Upwards she spun, step after step. At the top of the stairwell, a low steel door with four slider bolts was easily negotiated.

Roxanne handed Charlie her gun. "Watch the door. Anyone comes through. Send them to hell." Again, Charlie followed the instructions, leveling both handguns on the exit. Roxanne went in search of security. It arrived in the shape of a stone block from a section of wall under partial repair. She hauled the stone under the bottom of the door, jamming it firmly at an angle. Charlie was stunned at how cool her confederate remained under pressure. When Roxanne lifted her head, Charlie stood holding both guns in her direction. The moment of peril didn't last.

"Use it or lose it." She walked up to the blinking Charlie and snatched a gun.

Roxanne then turned and raced across the rooftop courtyard, under the cover of a high rooftop wall. In her stride, she ignored a fire escape down to ground level. Instead, she raced on toward the rear section of the roof. Mud bricks and collapsed plaster marked the section furthest away from the main entrance. She then lowered Charlie down one high section before clambering down herself. They ran across roofs leading to a darkened street corner. Rubble and roof sweepings covered half the thoroughfare. Trip hazards aplenty hindered their flight. Angry cats scampered. Towels and sheets hung up for drying flapped lazily across their path. Another building, another drop, but this time Charlie took the lead. Aerials and telecom cabling threatened to garrote them at every turn. They leapt over the crumbling walls being used to dry, bright clothes. Roxanne had the peace of mind to orchestrate a wardrobe adjustment. Headscarves and wraps were snagged. They ran on, jumping between buildings with tightly set rooftops stained by illicit fires and broken chimneys. Onwards and downwards, they raced, skidding on the rubbish discarded from the higher buildings. Two houses over, they eventually found a stairway that dropped them back down to earth.

The pair checked out and approved each other's look.

Charlie looked around, lost in every way. Even in the deadly circumstances and dismal lighting, Roxanne's beauty and poise shone. She set her hand on Charlie's shoulder. "We're not safe yet."

The night scene teemed with family diners, busy outdoor cafes, and late-night shoppers. The splattered blood and mud made venturing out in public throng impossible. Like a pair of escaped lab-rats the pair scurried down the first dark alley they could find. A line of skips and bins gave perfect cover. Keeping in the shadows, they walked the side streets of downtown Tehran.

When her shaking eventually ceased, Charlie ushered her seemingly unmoved traveling companion into a dimly lit corner. She had questions. "Who are you?"

"I could ask the same." Roxanne's guess sounded educated. "CIA?"

Charlie glanced around and took a chance. "I dare say we are in this together. I am FBI." The disclosure felt like a relief.

Roxanne didn't let up. "Why is the FBI sending agents into banned countries?"

"They didn't. The mission lines just got a little blurred."

"Blurred lines lead to crossed lanes."

"That led to head-on collisions. Like Sherif."

Roxanne shrugged the shoulders of her Amazonian frame. "With the Republican guard coming after you, people tend to panic."

"But not you?"

Roxanne beamed. "I am not people." She strode off before any further interrogation could take place. She stepped out in front of two boisterous youths, sharing stories and jokes.

The hilarity and mirth died when they saw Roxanne. Charlie held back and watched in awe as she snake-charmed the two youths into submission. After she gesticulated, both boys offered up their cell phones simultaneously. Roxanne took one handset, made a call, offered her thanks, and returned to Charlie's side. The boys staggered off in giggling disbelief at what had just happened.

"Does everybody just do as you ask?"

Roxanne remained confident without being arrogant. "Pretty much, up until they try to kill me." Charlie noted the distance in her eyes; Roxanne sounded deadly serious.

Two streets and ten minutes later, the pair waited in a tree-lined section near the city courthouse. Cases were not being heard at this time of night. The scene was as close to quiet as any part of the downtown. *A wise choice.*

The pair kept watch from the sidelines.

Blue lights and sirens from multiple police cars filled the streets. Army trucks rifled past. Charlie remained curious. "Are they all for us?"

"No, they are for me. The Revolutionary Guard want blood and our friend the Police Chief has made sure it's my blood they are after." Roxanne didn't seem moved. Events overtook the moment. "Over there." Charlie pointed out a pitch-black SUV creeping around the street corner. It slid to a halt twenty yards away. Roxanne held back. The driver exited the vehicle, opened the driver's door, rear doors, and tailgate. "What's he doing?" asked Charlie.

"Showing me he's on his own." All the doors were closed, giving Roxanne the signal, she must have requested. She tapped Charlie's gun hand. "Let's go. Keep that close." The short walk to the SUV took an eternity. Charlie craned and gawked in fear. Roxanne glided. With feet to go, the driver jumped from the vehicle and opened the rear door, chauffeur style. Roxanne slipped in as if en route to a movie premiere. Charlie clambered in like a criminal, leaving court under a swarm of paparazzi. The doors closed, allowing them to bask in the warm security of the SUV and its heaters. Roxanne threw out an address.

The driver was the only one to catch it. He looked straight ahead, discretion to the fore. The cold night had gnawed away at them, but fear had kept them up to temperature. The shivering started once the heaters went into full flow. As with all well chauffeured outings, blankets were provided. Recent events seemed to shock the pair into a thoughtful silence. It took a number of twisting, turning miles before their bodies and their conversation heated back up.

Charlie profiled the chauffeur. *"Middle Eastern. Twenty-five. Ex-special forces. Battle ready. Well built. Well turned out. Loyal."*

Roxanne caught her staring. "Do you like what you see?"

Charlie ignored the innuendo. "I like feeling safe. Where are we going?"

"I told you, home. We need to get out. We killed a Police Chief."

"We?"

"We're in this together, sister. You knew that the moment you staggered into the cellar." Roxanne threw out a cold sneer. "Why did you even bother?"

"With what?"

"Saving me. I'd have let you die."

"I guess we're different animals. I saw a woman in danger."

"I am always in danger. That's how I like it."

"So, you didn't need my help?"

"Not saying that. I'm just saying I wouldn't have helped you."

"Are you not the least bit grateful?"

"I had it covered."

"I bet you did."

Roxanne stretched her gaze outside. "You need to lose that Girl Guide attitude if you are going to survive in this world."

"This world?"

"The world of murderers, drug runners, and counterfeiters."

"I don't understand the counterfeiting. Who set it up?"

"The Phoenician."

Charlie sparked. "The Phoenician? I keep hearing that name. Why didn't I meet him?"

"Lady, you're staring at him."

"No!"

Roxanne's words held no evil. "Ah, but yes."

"How?"

"Easy. The difficult thing is the crispiness in the paper. Light sensitive watermarks, UV strips, color shifting eagle motifs, forbidden fonts. raised ink, reduced starch levels in the paper. Seventy-five percent of forgery is the paper, so we just smuggled ours through into the country."

"If it was caught, it would just be-"

"Industrial paper."

Roxanne let out a low hum of amusement. "Well done."

"But I don't get it. To what end?"

"The engraving plates were imperceptibly flawed. Only the US mint could tell the difference. Four color offset printing, embossing, foils, sequential serial numbers. All extremely complicated. That's why they brought in US mint experts and equipment. Pretty straight forward, really."

"Why give them money at all?"

"You can't guess?"

Charlie drew a blank. Roxanne filled things in.

"The CIA was running operations to destabilize Iran's nuclear program."

"What?"

"After the failure of Operation International Games."

"What was that?"

"A debacle. Look it up some time. Anyway, they needed to regain lost ground."

Charlie recalled the rumors. "Ah, the flawed operation against the Iranian Nuclear Program?"

Roxanne brightened at her knowledge. "Operation International-Screw-Up if you ask me. The money was to grab the attention of the nuclear scientists."

"That's a dumb idea. Those guys are fanatics. They couldn't be bought."

"The CIA weren't interested in buying them, they were only interested in finding and tracking them."

"How?"

"Radio frequency identification in bank notes. The latest European technology. They embedded tags into the fibers of banknotes. Wire transfers were tracked."

Charlie rocked. "Ingenious. The cash was used to track bad guys?"

Roxanne's shrugs had morphed into a full-sized grin.

"When the cash turns up through regulated channels, we're able to identify those that need special attention."

"Special attention?"

"You must have read reports of scientists falling prey to accidents, or key figures going missing."

"So, the operation was-"

"CIA sponsored counterintelligence, with the help from allies in a nearby country."

"I can guess which one."

"Then you're fully up to speed."

"Why tell me all this?"

"So that you keep your mouth shut."

"I don't get it."

"There are a number of people on your side that would be very willing to add your name to the list of those requiring special attention, if they felt you were a security risk."

"Now you're looking out for my best interests?"

"No. I am telling you to keep your mouth closed. For all our sakes. Any of this gets out-"

"And I get special attention."

"Exactly."

Worried that she may be being played, Charlie pushed back. "There's a safe house not far from here. You can drop me. If you set me down close by, I can make the final walk."

Roxanne scoffed. "That secret CIA safe house near your old embassy?"

Charlie glared, speechless, at the intelligence levels.

"You're not going there. You'll never get out."

"Why?"

"There are two sides to that coin. You must know it's corrupt, or you wouldn't be doing all this solo flying. You don't know the ones you can trust. Right?"

Despite having no clue, Charlie nodded.

"Well, the trustworthy guys will be after you, too."

"I don't get it."

Roxanne cupped her hands in before the heater outlet. "You got one of their own killed."

The hairs on the back of her head stood up. "The Police Chief?"

Roxanne raised her eyebrows. "Maybe you don't know who you can trust."

Charlie took another shot. "Sherif?"

Roxanne clapped her warming hands. "He was more of an unlicensed contractor."

Things started to make sense for Charlie. "That's why he saved me. That's why he had all the gear. IR glasses and US equipment."

"That's why the Police Chief had to kill him." A strange and thoughtful pause gave Charlie the chance to consider the latest findings.

"So, you're CIA?"

Roxanne gave no real answer. "I wouldn't go that far."

Before Charlie could press her case, the SUV glided to a halt near a grove of trees at the edge of high compound walls made from iron-oxide-colored bricks, topped with concrete edging and high steel spikes. The sliding metal gate gave the entire building a prison-chic look.

"Where is this?"

Roxanne indicated the brass plaque on the wall. "This is where you leave me."

Charlie read the signs. "The British Embassy?"

Roxanne chortled confidently. "You can just see the tops of their statues celebrating their long-lost empire. Proudly hidden away. I don't know if it's defiance or delusion."

"Maybe both."

"You could be right. Look at that plaque. Someone probably runs out twice a day to polish it before they run back inside for cover."

"Why here?"

"Tell them you're a walk in, a Swiss diplomat. That will send them into a spin and get you through the door. Once you're inside, your story can ring almost true. Say you were abducted in Afghanistan and trafficked here. Say you escaped. You will eventually get back in through the US channels. They'll never admit to a cell in Tehran, so keep that to yourself."

Charlie liked the plan. "Why don't you join me?"

A wry smile was returned. "I am afraid not. I have no friends inside that establishment. Don't worry. I can look after myself. And I suspect, so can you. Agent?"

"Charlie. Charlie Glass. And you are Roxanne."

The pair shook hands. "I have been called that, yes."

Roxanne pulled a silver case from a hidden compartment. She peeled out a white business card and offered it across. It showed an international number and the letter R. "If you ever need anything, call me. If I can, I will answer. There is no messaging service, so keep trying. All I ask is that you never mention, describe, or follow me. I never existed. We can agree on that?"

Charlie got the message. *Nothing more to say.*

She stared at the card, bowed her head briefly then exited the vehicle.

As she walked away, the rear electric window slid down. She turned to catch her final sight of Roxanne.

"You are either brave or foolish, Agent Charlie Glass."

"I can be both at times." Smiles were shared. "I owe you."

Roxanne offered her own parting words. "We owe each other. Just don't give me a reason to come after you."

Her beguiling smile disappeared long before the car window slid closed.

CHAPTER 42

Dubrovnik, Croatia. Six months later.

The sun blessed another day in the ancient walled city. Tourists baked in the heat, cracking off the well-worn cobbled streets. Wrap around glasses, floppy hat, and a recently purchased Hermes scarf topped off Charlie's summer dress look. She sipped a heavily iced Old-Fashioned cocktail. The whisky brought back memories of her warehouse breakout in Tehran. The crude stitching from the CIA Agent had left its mark on her hand, but the scar emerged as a proud reminder of work well done.

She felt in a reflective mood as she neared the end of her trip. She called for, and paid, her check, before checking her large purse. It felt comforting to be reunited with her BlackBerry. No new e-mails. No new messages. Like her handset, Charlie found herself fully charged and silent. The trip was running to plan.

Tradecraft encouraged her to check her sightlines. She rose with expanding lungs, pulled off her mirrored glasses, flipped them and checked behind her. Reflective shop windows were also checked as she moved on. The glances were more for sanity than vanity. Two back streets were followed before she clambered behind the ancient buildings built up into the old walls. Climbing onto a stone platform, she transitioned under a recently refurbished brick archway. Up another two flights of stairs, she entered a high landing with a solitary wooden door.

Placing her thumb over the spyhole, she rapped on the door and waited.

When the maid answered, Charlie lifted her silenced Glock.

The old lady almost fainted. Charlie pulled her finger to her lips. Whimpering, the hired help was coaxed back into a nearby store cupboard. The maid's expressions showed she had received the message, silent and clear. She stuttered on the spot, grateful to be alive.

Charlie brandished the Glock once more for bad measure, before sitting the maid down on the cupboard floor. Charlie snatched the key from the lock for extra security. It found its way into a plant pot nearby. Charlie had hoped her target would answer the door, but the maid had been silenced, and had thankfully remained unharmed.

A lone female voice carried in on the winds. Giggles whisked through the long, flowing white curtains that framed the open floor-to-ceiling concertina doors. She glanced through to find a blonde model falling out of a bright red bikini that shook more than her cocktail maker. Her light veil dress went with the flow. She slid up close, then eased across her sightline, gun in hand. The cocktail clattered off the marble floor. The girl still shook.

A man's voice sounded outside. "Everything okay?"

Charlie held the gun and her gaze. "Say yes."

The shocked model obeyed. "Ya."

She motioned her toward the front door. The model got her big break. She fled in terror, scarlet flip-flops flying out the door.

Out on the massive roof deck, a bleached linen sail flapped gently in a breeze. The sunken swimming pool looked inviting. Mediterranean chill music soothed the senses. Cocktail glasses and a bowl of green olives sat on the bedside table. A man lay across a gigantic daybed, partially hidden by its screens. He spoke. "Is everything alright, darling?"

His thinning mouse brown hair had been replaced by a bleached buzz cut, now toned, and tinted. Despite the alterations, Charlie had found her man. She rounded the bottom of the daybed, blocked the sun, and raised the barrel of the gun.

"I don't know. You tell me, darling."

Shocked into silence Charlie stared into the eyes of the dead analyst, Ross.

CHAPTER 43

Ross stalled, very much alive and in rude, defiant health. "I have guards. They will be here any minute."

"No, you don't. They get every third Sunday off."

"What have you done with Natasha?"

"The cocktail shaker? She's off and running. Not that you care, but your housekeeper is also fine. Besides, you should be more worried about your own wellbeing."

"What do you want from me?"

Charlie silently rattled the Glock. "I would have thought that obvious."

Ross squirmed, clearly buying time. "How did you find me?"

Charlie played along, proud of her work. "I didn't, really. In a way, Pop, my father, found you."

"He was watching your funeral. I took him along. Full military service and all the trimmings. You would have liked it."

Ross sneered. "I did. I was there."

Charlie shook her head. It was just the kind of move a narcissist would pull off. "It struck him as odd."

"What did?"

"Your name. John Hume Ross."

"It's not that rare a name."

"Perhaps. Many months ago, I mentioned Feisal to him. It never registered, but the John Hume Ross reference set his nomadic mind wandering off into the desert. He's a scholar. Military history."

Ross scoffed knowingly. "So, he got the reference? It's a stretch to bring you here."

Charlie motioned for them to move across to the al fresco dining table. She didn't like the glaring sun's angle. "When he told me the reference, I did my own digging. I recalled something you said to me when we met."

"Which was?"

"You said, *I want to lie forever in the shade, till I become a shade myself.*"

"And?"

"I found it strange thing for someone to say, until I found it, quoted in the great man's autobiography."

"The great man?"

Charlie flapped her hands. "Oh, come on. The game is up. Do I need to spell it out?"

"Apparently."

"OK. Gasim, Feisal, Sherif, they are all pseudonyms, all characters from his memoirs."

"Who's memoirs?"

"Lawrence of Arabia."

Nothing.

Charlie went again. "It struck me that you shared the same name as the great man himself."

"His name was Thomas Edward Lawrence."

"You seem well informed on the subject."

"What can I say? I am well read."

"Apparently. But when he tried to re-enlist in the Royal Air Force, he changed his name."

Ross refused to fill in his blank look. "Surprise me."

"Oh, we both know that's not possible. John Hume Ross, or whatever your name really is. I don't get it. How did you get past our CIA vetting?"

Ross's vanity started to break through. "Please. I speak 5 languages, have an IQ of one hundred and fifty-five and was never caught breaking any laws. That, matched with an expensive and thoroughly fictitious back story, made me an obvious choice to join the Central Incompetence Agency."

"So that's it? You're better, smarter, faster than the CIA?"

"I'm not saying that, although they have buried themselves in the shallow grave of public duty."

"Do you even know you're doing it?"

"Doing what?"

"Quoting Lawrence."

"My, you have been doing your research."

"I've had time. And that is where I found Lawrence's favorite quote. Proverbs, 9:1,"

Ross hated not being the smartest man in the room. "Wisdom has built her house; she has hewn her Seven Pillars."

"That's when I knew you ran the show."

Ross clapped mockingly. "Oh well done, but had you forgotten I died?"

"I hadn't forgotten, but I hadn't remembered seeing the hood being placed over your head. You stuffed me in the back of the SUV. I could see nothing. You didn't die. You switched in some patsy to take the fall."

Ross was folding. "Not some patsy. Someone who deserved to die."

"No one deserved to die in that way."

"That's a matter for debate."

"You set the whole thing up. Right down to dragging me in?"

"No. I heard you were coming. You came with a reputation. I do research too, you know. The noose was tightening. I needed to disappear. They don't hang dead men."

"And who better to have an FBI agent as your star witness."

"Now you're catching on."

"It always puzzled me why a timid little analyst came to visit me at the airport."

Ross sneered. "Not so timid after all."

Charlie waggled the Glock. "Not too analytical either, from where I'm sitting. What happened to the driver?"

"He was in on it; he fled and left the doors open."

Charlie banged the butt of the gun on the table. "I knew it. He was nowhere to be seen. There was no blood."

"Exactly. We had drugged the traitor and then dressed him to look like me. The ambush setup and switch were easy. We only used five people, but my god how the locals got on board. That thing got out of hand. We barely escaped with our lives. They hate us."

"And you wonder why."

"Don't give me that. I didn't exploit or persecute them under the banner of freedom."

"No, you just stole and murdered."

"I'd like to call it narcotic entrepreneurship."

"I am sure you would, but that's not how they'll see it in a US court of law. How did you cover it up so well?"

"Easy. We had two guys waiting below the bridge to recover the body. Swept away by a current."

"Who was he? The guy you killed."

"An interpreter, the lowest of the low."

"Someone just trying to get on."

"Yeah, by grassing up their enemies or reporting feuding families who had done nothing wrong." He sniggered. "We even got paid by the Taliban for his death; three for the price of one. We get paid, a traitor dies, and I have my escape route."

"So, when did you upgrade to counterfeiting?"

"I didn't. Uncle Sam did."

"They knew someone was bringing in drugs and stolen money, but they didn't know how, who or where. Idiots."

"We infiltrated their operation, channeled some of our stolen monies through their operation, and offered them channels into the local underworld. Then we joined forces and flooded the black market with counterfeit US dollars."

"And real dollars, presumably."

Ross guffawed. "You'd think. There's more to that story but seeing as the police will be here any minute, I'm gonna plead the fifth."

"The police aren't coming; your little Barbie won't save the day. What's her accent? Ukraine? She's probably here illegally, terrified of getting sent home. She'll be hiding out, hoping her sugar daddy makes it through another hour."

Ross flinched. "I still don't understand it. How did you find me?"

Charlie knew his scare tactic had failed, and that a new tack was being attempted. *Stalling.* She didn't mind. This moment had been planned in detail. She had all the time in the world. "When you died, your alias died. So, you just reinvented yourself, again, just like Lawrence. When his cover was blown in the Royal Air Force and the Army."

"And there you had me."

Charlie felt quite proud. "And there I had you. T.E. Shaw."

Ross moved to stand and walk about. Charlie tapped the table. "This is an interrogation, not a chat. Sit down."

"You won't kill me."

"True, but I will maim you. Sit!"

Ross's stalling continued from a sedentary position. "That explains the who, but not the where. How did you know I was here?"

Charlie found her answers increasingly boastful. "When I overheard you on the phone to the Police Chief killing the operat–"

"You were there?"

"Nearby, eavesdropping. When I overheard the Police Chief on the call to you, he told me the shipments were leaving that night. I checked the flight manifests for flights from the small local airports but found nothing. Then I figured you'd be shipping out from a regional, so I retraced my steps, back to the Afghan border. The chances are you'd be pulling in drugs and money directly from your bases in Helmand. Guess what I found?"

Ross waved away the question, so she continued.

"A flight out of Zahedan, chartered by a Jordanian shell company. Wadi Rum Airlines." Charlie beamed. "You just can't stop playing your games. The flight went through Turkey and on to Dubrovnik, Croatia. Did you get on in Turkey?"

A smirking Ross yielded. "Never travel with, or sample, your own goods."

Charlie gesticulated around the rooftop. "Looks like you're sampling your own goods with all this."

"How did you know I lived here?"

"Oh, that's easy. I knew you'd be the kind of guy who buys a boat once he gets rich."

"How did you know?

"Because you have a dick. Yachts, not motorboats. Every guy does that, even the ones that don't like sailing."

Ross reddened as Charlie continued. "I checked the Croatian boat yards for new registrations because guys like you wouldn't buy secondhand. Money talks. Guess who recently bought a shiny new sixty-five-foot wayfarer. You guessed it. T.E. Shaw. Bribery still works in these parts, so your address was easily come by, even though you did use a shell company to buy the thing."

Charlie couldn't tell if Ross' stare was one of admiration, stupefaction, or hatred. She continued. "I've been stalking you out for a couple of weeks. You don't get out much, do you? In fact, you don't get out at all. It must be tough living in this open prison."

"It's only temporary."

"Yeah, temporary until you go back into a jail cell."

"The one thing I don't get is why you? Why isn't the CIA here arresting me?"

"I wanted to give you a chance to come peacefully. Walk with me to the police station and hand yourself in."

"Bullshit. You didn't know if your hunch was right, so you took a chance of playing the Lone Ranger."

"I just wanted to make sure before I sent this one up the chain of command."

"Your boss, Sizemore, is an idiot."

Charlie wobbled her head. She couldn't argue. "So, you run The Pillars. All that was you?"

Ross smirked with pride.

Charlie kept at him. "Lawrence's Seven Pillars were the greatest cities across the Middle East. Does your network stretch that far?"

Ross couldn't resist. "No, the pillars were the operations holding up my house of crime. Kabul, Kandahar, the poppy fields at Sangin, the opium factories, the mountain passes, Tehran, and Zahedan airfield."

"You're quite proud of it."

He puffed his chest. "*The Pillars of Evil.* It has a nice ring to it."

"I think *Fort Leavenworth* has a nicer ring to it."

Ross cowered. "You have little proof."

"We both realize I have enough to send you to jail for the rest of your miserable life."

Ross held out. "It's gone. Our rivals cleared us out. They had the inside track. We had a rat in our camp. Our routes were tracked, our best people murdered."

Charlie remembered the first of the main smugglers to die. Shot through the head by a laser guided sniper bullet. "Feisal?"

Ross swithered. "Amongst others. Even if I wanted to, I couldn't start again. I'm done."

"Oh, just like that? You've stolen and killed all you need. Now we just leave you alone."

"This has to be a shakedown. I have millions, tens of millions with your name on it. That's why you're here. No one will ever find me."

"I did."

"You're not no one."

"I can't let you away. I am sworn–"

"These people mean nothing. Screw that. I never harmed anyone you knew."

"You killed a friend of mine, a journalist. On the road, outside Sangin."

Ross looked at her as if she had two heads. "Lady, you're crazy. Why would I do that?"

"You tell me."

"The only word journalists spell is *trouble*. Killing one only brings more. Think. I'd have nothing to do with any journalist hit."

For the first time in a long time, she had no answer.

A silent zephyr filled the void just before the bullet arrived.

CHAPTER 44

Crack!

The headshot snapped through Ross' chin. Blood, bones, and body matter flew in all directions.

Yelping, Charlie hit the tiles.

Crack!

The next shot splintered off the tabletop. Face to the floor, she scrambled in terror across to the sanctuary of the nearby wall.

She was trapped. Against the odds, under fire, she slowed her terrified mind. Constructive thoughts replaced fearful consequences. She checked the direction of the bullet and the impact radius. The blood splatter set the sniper's position just behind her left shoulder when she sat opposite Ross.

High-powered rifle.

Shot from close range.

Probably the city wall.

She stared across at Ross' obliterated head. There was nothing that could be done for him.

No other shots arrived, allowing Charlie space to breathe. *He's likely gunning and running.*

Snatching a garden cane from a nearby pot plant. With a look to the sky, she aligned the cane with the blood splatter patterns. From the angle of impact, she spied the likely location and height of the sniper. Charlie stared down the angle of the cane. She sniped back, guessing the shooter would have been on the rooftops, right behind where she had been sitting.

He wouldn't run in broad daylight.

He had a minute's start.

He'd likely still be up there.

She shielded her eyes and scanned the rooftops. The exit to the city sat on the north side. She set her eyes to work and her mind into overdrive.

He wouldn't leave the gun.

He also wouldn't carry it through the middle of town.

He'd likely take the weapon on a circuitous route.

A high-level departure made the most sense.

Between the busloads of tourists, she watched for something out of the ordinary. Lovers hand in hand. Pensioners in a pod. Bored kids sitting on a step, heads in hands. Suddenly, she caught a glimpse of a man walking in the gap between two buildings. *Walking too fast.*

Charlie focused and held her breath. *There he is!*

The distant power walker bustled through a guided tour. *Walking too fast. Carrying a holdall.* He wore the clothes of a tourist, but he walked with martial precision. His military gait was a dead giveaway. *A hoodie, in broad daylight, really?* Charlie had her man, and he was speeding for the exit.

There was no time to alert the authorities. The damage was done. She needed to do some damage of her own.

"Damn it!"

She had lost her discarded Glock. It had gone spinning into a corner when the sniper attacked. It took her a couple of panicked seconds before the gun was retrieved. After regaining her grip, she kicked off her heeled shoes, clambered over the railing and jumped across onto the steep angle of the wall.

In a flash, she was up on top of the city walls. Hurried thoughts ran through her mind. If he was running for a water exit, she could cut him off by running counterclockwise. It was unlikely he would risk the congested vagaries of the roadways out of the city. The cable car out of the old town would be too constricted. She jumped across onto the high rampart and hit the walkway, bare feet running. At speed, she barged past unsuspecting tourists. Haranguing those ahead helped clear the narrow walkway. On she ran, at full tilt, stone steps were taken four at a time. Corners were cut. The sight of a Glock quickened two young tourists' sidesteps.

She ran on and on. Efforts to scan for the sniper only slowed her down. This was no time for second guesses or second glances. She had made her decision. *Get to the harbor.*

If that was the wrong choice, she would have to live with it. Two sets of stone steps were climbed at speed. A gantry was crossed. An elderly couple pinned to the wall, awestruck by her appearance. "Sorry!"

Another set of steps lifted her up onto the highest rampart. Below, she had full sight of the cobbled walkway and its inhabitants. Screaming for everyone to make way gave her the time and space she needed to gather pace. When she hit the wall overlooking the harbor, her blistering feet skidded to a gritty halt. Wheezing, she took a breath and a view. She scanned the horizon. Heaving fresh air into her bleating lungs, she checked her status.

The roadways could be swarming, uncertain, and easily cordoned off. The logical assumption remained fixed in her mind. The sniper would take a boat across the bay then on to the airport, probably private jet. *That's what I'd do.* Breathing difficulties blurred her focus.

She steadied her gaze, shielded her eyes, and scanned. Suddenly, under the archway leading from the city, the man emerged. *Gotcha!*

She kept partial sightings of the suspect, weaving through the milling tourists. He looked slightly built, but totally guilty. The long bag he carried could easily hold a broken-down rifle.

With no time to lose, or think, she climbed to the top of the parapet and checked her landing zone. The angle of the high wall worried her. The height terrified her. She took a step back, afraid to move forward, determined to get her man. Spinning in the eye of the storm, she guessed she could make the water. *Miss this, you die.*

She spun and counted back ten steps. Ignoring the deadly consequences, she turned and ran full speed toward the end of the high harbor wall. Her feet hit a blistering pace as she timed the take-off with less than a foot to spare. Grappling thin air, she crossed the void to meet her fate, death, or the deep blue sea.

Eyes closed, flailing, she pulled in air.

Nearing the ground, she pulled her feet, arms, and chin in tight. Her back scraped the harbor wall as she cannonballed into the water.

Choking up salt, air burst from her heaving lungs as she scrambled for the surface. The chilly water froze her bending mind. Icy fingers gripped the Glock as she flailed and gulped her way to safety.

Floundering forward, she flapped her way to dry land, finally beaching herself on the nearby quayside steps. Drawing breath and onlookers, she held on.

Her Glock was stuffed down the front of her dress as she clambered up onto the stone quay. A group of highly bemused tourists looked on as she righted herself.

The tourists scattered like frightened sparrows as Charlie raced down the dock, too far gone to try to conceal herself.

At the quayside, she spied the assassin climbing down into a wooden motor yacht. With so much ground to cover, she threw caution to the wind. Her mind raced. She wasn't sure enough to shoot the suspect. If she called him out, he would likely run. She needed to bring him in. Head down, she raced past the smattering of tourists, who were slowing to stare at the soaking wet beauty racing past.

The target looked to be stowing his bag and casting off. She ran on, with hope and doubt. That was his only weapon. Turning the craft took time.

The reversing motion slowed his departure. The delay spurred Charlie on. Harder and faster, her feet thumped the cobbled quay.

With the craft positioned for exit, the assassin leaned across to the throttle. Too far gone to ask questions, too desperate to care about mistaken identities, Charlie leapt on board at full tilt.

Without warning, the target turned.

He snatched at his waistband, but before any weapon could be pulled, Charlie landed on the scene. Her shoulder cracked his neck. The pair crumpled and skidded across the deck. Under the sightline of the gunwale, a titanic struggle ensued.

Charlie won the race to recovery. She tried to execute a choke hold, but the wiry, fiery assassin wriggled free. As the craft puttered out to sea, the assassin broke free and rolled. Stunned and afraid, he pulled a pistol, but it was too late. Charlie's Glock barked twice.

Bang! Bang!

The one bullet that hit ripped through the assassin's heart. He slumped. Blood seeped.

Without looking back, Charlie crawled across to right the ship. She set the course for open water and eased the throttle. It seemed unlikely that the killing had gone unnoticed, but she needed time to think. Fighting every urge to open up the engine, she eased the craft out through the harbor's no wake zone.

She gradually spiraled her gaze like an awe-struck tourist. Miraculously, she found no worried onlookers, and heard no alarms. She stood and repeated the process. The coast looked clear. One last scan confirmed her status.

At her feet lay the assassin, face to the deck and dead to the world. A couple of beach towels were hastily thrown over the body. Blood leached through the toweling.

Only when she left the limits of the outer harbor did Charlie gun the throttle. Out of sight from the city walls, she bent her bearing away from shore. The bow of the craft was turned shoreward for extra privacy. The sniper's dead body was rolled onto its back. Charlie sat back on the deck, plunking her hand in the blood sloshing around the deck. She neither noticed nor cared. All she did was stare. The mystery man remained just that to her, a mystery.

Away from prying eyes, the body received a closer inspection. No ID, no wallet, no cards, a fistful of euros.

The pistol was pulled. Walther PPK. *Old School.*

The rifle in the holdall was studied. A broken down telescopic, US military. M24. *New School.*

Save for a map of the city, the rifle bag was empty. The craft bobbed on the tide as Charlie floundered for answers. She stared again at the dead man. A leering grin disfigured his young, bloody face.

She stared again. *No?*

Charlie tilted the assassin's face to the light. It was late in the day, but things were dawning. Unbelievably, she had seen the man before. The beard had gone, but there could be no doubt.

He was the young bandit who shot Noah dead at the roadblock.

She checked his hands. *Manicured. Never done a day's work in his life.*

He was no random Taliban thug. He was a hired assassin, a skilled killer, sent to execute.

The ambush must have been a setup. A Pillar's Set up? Ross had denied all knowledge.

It seemed incredible. Noah's murderer lay at her feet. This could only mean one thing. The murders must have been part of a bigger picture; a much darker, bigger picture.

Were the Serpent on a spree killing everyone linked with the Pillars?

With Feisal and Ross, they were taking out the competition. Noah needed to be silenced. She stared down in disgust at the dead assassin. A contract killer on the payroll of the Serpent. The revelations churned her stomach as much as the blackened blood oozing across the teak decking.

A slopping wave lifted the boat, forcing her to get a grip. She steadied herself. *Think! Think!*

After confirming her approaches were clear, Charlie set an offshore bearing and moved below deck. The latch had been locked. The keyring in the motor launch's ignition held another, smaller, key. She tried her luck. The chrome latch slid open. She was in. Half-way down the steps, she recoiled. Down in the bottom of the boat lay another body. It took courage to jump down and confirm her worst suspicions. The man was dead. Cause of death blunt force trauma to the temple. *Sucker punch.*

Charlie surveyed the scene. The old man's cold, dead eyes stared right through her. He looked kind. He must have been the pilot for the hotel's water shuttle. It seemed likely the assassin had killed the old man to protect his anonymity and guarantee his escape.

Any guilt she felt over her part in the assassin's death went out the porthole.

Sixty something, the dead man's uniform was more ornate than military. The logo on his white tunic seemed familiar. *The Dubrovnik Majestic Hotel.* She discovered the hotel when researching places to stay. It had been excluded from her enquiries early on due to the high pricing. It was the most luxurious hotel in Dubrovnik. It sat directly across the bay, in a direct line with the nearby airport.

Destructive thoughts became constructive. The uniformed jacket of the pilot was yanked off his corpse without ceremony. Attempts to keep the congealed blood off his scuffed whites were largely successful. Across the galley table, a white captain's cap with gold braiding was tucked under her arm. Back up on the deck, the uniform was set to the side to make way for a bout of body snatching.

All incriminating evidence was dragged down into the launch. Hearing the assassin's body clattering down the stairs gave her no sense of justice. The old pilot took another hit. As if to cover up the past, the latch was pulled and locked.

With the decks cleared, buckets of seawater were cast across the decking before a bearing was set toward the hotel. More seawater was deployed in a vain attempt to clean up the dead pilot's white jacket and cap. They were tried on for size.

Soaking wet, filthy, and oversized. Right at that moment, nothing fitted.

With the throttle opened to cruising speed, Charlie turned her face to the sun. The sea spray could not wash away her sins. She stared forward, knowing there would be more to come. The scope was pulled from the rifle and set as a nautical telescope. With so much unfinished, dirty business dead ahead, she opened the throttle even further. The tide and wind felt favorable as she blasted out over the white caps. With a clear sea ahead, she punched the throttle even harder. The waves cracked her back, but she didn't let off, full throttle through a stiffening crosswind. The Dubrovnik Majestic Hotel lay dead ahead.

Fifty yards out, she sniper-scoped the dock. A tall figure looked vague, but prominently positioned. She slowed and lowered the trim of the boat and the brim of her cap.

Twenty yards away, the man on the dock held firm. With the element of surprise on her side, she set preparations for whatever lay ahead. Nearing the hotel's dock, she prepared for a rocky landing. After dropping the throttle and pulling the engine into reverse, she cut the power and jumped. The man approached, offering help. Charlie kept her back turned, held her cap down, and averted her gaze until the last minute. Her heart banged like a taught drum. As the man closed in, Charlie swiveled and raised her gun sight.

Speechless, swaying and staring, stood Noah.

CHAPTER 45

Charlie held the gun and with it, the power. "Get in." She eased back, allowing space for Noah to jump on board. "Don't!" Charlie cut through his scheming thoughts. "Get in!" He yielded.

Charlie held the gun close and low. "Take the controls, get us out of here."

Her prisoner obeyed, turned, and shot her a look. "You don't seem surprised to see me."

Charlie took the moment. "I'm not."

Noah played it casually. "We learned from Ross' sham disappearance."

Charlie screwed up her face. "We?"

Noah repositioned for a better angle of conversation. "You haven't figured it out yet?"

Charlie dismissed the jibe with the rattle of her pistol. "Eyes front."

Noah lifted his hands from the wheel in mock surrender, just as a squall crashed across the bow. The launch tipped and dipped.

She knew Noah was testing the waters. "Hands on the wheel. Lay off the big waves too."

Noah seemed curious. "Where's my friend?"

Charlie tested the waters. "In the same place and condition as the pilot of this boat."

Noah moved ahead, dead slow. "So?"

"Your ambush stank the more I thought of it. The guard shouted, *Out,* when we approached. How did he know we were English?"

Noah rocked his head, half in agreement, half under the influence of the waves. "When did that occur to you?"

"On the way over here. When I recognized the gunman, I kept an eye on the dock from the boat, through the rifle's telescope. And there you were, as bold as tarnished brass."

Noah swayed as Charlie continued. "How did you track him down?"

"We didn't, we just followed you. When we found out who you were chasing him down, we brought in our baby-faced assassin."

"And the two guides killed in the Iranian mountains. His work?"

"I may have lent a hand."

Charlie pistol-whipped the grin off his face.

Noah stared coldly and dabbed the blood from his split lip. "It wasn't our fault. We were tracking you, and then that dumbass coward wandered straight into our guns. He brought it on himself."

Charlie didn't like the accusation. "Bullshit! It was a cold-blooded murder."

Noah pointed his head to below decks. "You'd know all about that."

"If I was to dignify that with a response, it would be made of lead." It was her turn to move things forward. "Did he kill Harry and Sanchez?"

Noah shrugged.

"So, when you pulled a gun and chased after him, you were just making sure he got away?"

Noah shrugged, but this time Charlie pulled back from pistol whipping him. "So, you set up the hits?"

"Not all of them. You helped. We just didn't know the targets. So, thanks for that. In a lot of ways, you're responsible for their deaths, too."

Charlie bit. "I was doing my job."

"As was I. They were scum."

"Scum? They were human beings. Sanchez had a family."

"Yet still he risked it all. Stealing from you and wrecking our drugs operations."

"So, if they were scum, what does that make you?"

"Scum, that was here first. They had no honor."

Charlie scoffed. "So, this is all about honor?"

"Wow. Climb down off your high horse. We did the world a favor. You are no different."

"Hardly!"

"You exploit war zones, and so do we. The only difference is we don't start the wars, we just make the most of them when they happen."

"And Feisal? Your murdering minion pulled the trigger that night, too?"

The shrugging ended. "Nah. That was me."

"I owed him."

"For what."

"Old Scores."

Charlie gripped the gun hard. "Why not take me out earlier?"

"You were delivering everything we couldn't do, finding the army thieves, uncovering the drug factory. You even killed that crooked agent, Sherif."

"Not me."

"Not what I heard."

A hard wave hit the broadside, rocking the boat. Noah eased a little too close as the pair settled their feet. Charlie's handgun rose once more.

With Noah back at an unsafe distance, another wave hit. Charlie switched gun hand. "So, the US sent over cash to help fund infrastructure development."

"Correct."

"Harry and Sanchez then started stealing the money."

"Correct again." Noah took over. "They started out shipping small amounts back home. When the thefts were more than the standard channels could cope with, they turned to the local smuggling operation."

Charlie kept up. "The Pillars?"

Noah drew in air. "When the Pillars took over the majority of the routes, I was charged with closing them down. And that's where you came in."

"I led you through the entire chain, and you followed on, breaking every link in the chain along the way. Feisal, Gasim, and others."

"My little friend down the stairs freed me up to come behind you, cleaning house."

"It's ironic." Offered Noah.

"What is?"

"Ross really was an analyst. He ran the numbers. He knew his time was up, he needed to disappear and what better way than to stage his own death and flee in a plane filled with drugs and dollars."

"So, when the Police Chief heard about the death, he knew something was up?"

"We all did."

"That wanna-be station chief, the one who pulled you in, in Tehran. What a clown."

Charlie couldn't deny the categorization. "O'Hara?"

"Who else? He runs around trying to start World War Three. Every panic button from Kabul to Tehran was thumped because of the way he ran around after Ross' death."

"What a cluster."

"The Iranians were in on it, moving the traceable cash to dead end locations. Worse still, they sent it to their enemies, knowing they would be attacked as a result. All hell would then rain down on people who were actually on our side. Evil genius."

"So, he got paid by the CIA, stole the laundered cash, and tipped off the Iranians for even more money."

"A ballsy play."

"Yes, but not his play. Remember, Ross was the mastermind. He orchestrated everything."

"But they underestimated the mighty Phoenician?"

Noah spoke with admiration. "No one has ever done that and lived."

"She is some woman."

"As are you. What's your plan?"

"I go straight back to Dubrovnik and confess to killing an already dead rogue CIA agent and an assassin. The locals will be fearful of using the phrase terrorist incident, so they will downgrade it to domestic violence, and sweep it under the rug."

"That only leaves me."

"You will be handed over and arrested."

"For what?"

"Let's start with aiding and abetting multiple murders."

The waves swelled and dashed against the bobbing boat. Charlie held on. The choppy waves buffeted harder.

Suddenly, Noah yanked the throttle and spun the steering wheel. As the boat wheeled and dipped, Charlie flailed, losing her balance. Noah jumped to the side, thumped his shoulder into her chest, and sent Charlie and her gun flying. In a flash, Noah dived for the weapon. Charlie staggered to her feet, out of breath and out of reach. Before she recovered, Noah rose two feet away, pistol in hand.

The tide had turned.

Noah's tone switched with the change in gun ownership.

"Amateur move. You're not as good as your reputation."

Charlie floundered. "I once shot a man before he had the true opportunity to show his character. Now you have your chance. It's not too late. I can hand you in."

"Really? That's your play? If I wasn't convinced before, I am certainly not convinced now."

Waves lolled the boat from side to side, forcing Noah to kill the throttle and idle the engine. "Sorry. You've had your chance. We're out of time and you're out of options."

Charlie held out her hand as Noah lifted the Glock.

"No, please!'

"Goodbye, Agent Glass. I'll see you in hell." Without a second though, Noah pulled the trigger.

Click! Click!

He re-cocked the gun and fired again.

Click! Click!

Charlie stood tall. "I told you. We're different."

She hauled the dead assassin's Walther PPK out of the waistband at the small of her back. "Remember, I know the weight of an empty gun."

Boiling with anger, Noah hurled the gun and lunged headlong toward Charlie. She pitched sideward in a wave of panic. When Noah landed, the PPK let out a muffled *crack*.

Noah thumped facedown into the deck.

Blood poured from beneath his crumpled torso.

This time, Noah was gone for good.

CHAPTER 46

Jittering, Charlie crabbed backward and surveyed the scene. This death would be more difficult to explain than Ross and the assassin. There would be gunshot residue on him and her. There was no faked death to confirm her story.

Uncertain of her next moves, she considered throwing the body overboard.

Someone on the coastline might have seen me.

They may still be watching.

She scanned the land but found no signs of life. Death lay all around.

Noah's phone suddenly vibrated. She crawled all over the seeping body.

It didn't take long to find the phone.

She lifted the handset and stared at the screen. It simply read, R. She clicked the call open.

"Is it done?"

"Hello, Roxanne?" Silence jammed the line for a few seconds.

"Where's Noah?"

"Gone."

"I thought highly of you, but even that now seems to have been an underestimation."

"Apparently so."

"I sent a good man."

"Like most men, he wasn't good enough."

"They never are. I sent a boy to do a woman's job."

Charlie threw Roxanne's old words back down the line. "You have some balls."

The gesture was returned. "Takes one to know one."

Charlie bristled with excitement. "Don't be hard on yourself. It must have been difficult keeping up with all your appearances, playing all the sides. What is it today? Working for the CIA, betraying the Iranians, killing off the Pillars, double-crossing the Serpent?

Roxanne would not be goaded. So, Charlie prodded. "I thought the Serpent didn't allow in women."

"Way off. That's the Legion. The Serpent is a more cunning beast. But I need to thank you. I couldn't have done it without you."

"It is a shame you're not here to say thank you in person." Charlie stared down at her PPK. "I have a little present for you."

Roxanne played along. "How charming. And why would I need a present?"

"To say thank you."

"For what?"

"You gave me safe passage from the police back in the mountains, remember?"

Roxanne snorted. "Sure. They were there to keep the lines open. We knew you were coming. We just wanted to make sure some loose-triggered bandits didn't kill you. The place is full of them."

"Always one step ahead, Roxanne?"

"Thanks to you."

"I didn't do it intentionally."

"No, but you'll get the credit back in D.C. Smashing the drugs ring and finding the thieves in Afghanistan."

"You should join us. We are not that different. You have the skill set."

"But not the mindset. What are you? Ex-Lebanese Armed Forces?"

Roxanne stayed silent, as if deciding on a response. "How did you know?"

"They called you the Phoenician. I took a guess that you were from Lebanon."

"I have lived many lives. That could have been one of them."

"I am sorry for ruining the life you had built."

Roxanne sounded in a philosophical mood. "It wasn't built. It was invented. Like all good inventions, it became obsolete. These things are inevitable."

Charlie was pushing it. "Are you close? Perhaps we can meet up."

"We may meet, but on my terms, in my time. Can you give assurances that your organization won't come after me?"

"Can you make assurances that I will stay safe?"

"You will be safe as long as you don't interfere. Arrangements change if the terms change."

"We have a deal, but I can't promise how long it will last." Offered Charlie.

"Neither can I. Just remember what I told you in Tehran."

Charlie remembered. "Don't give you a reason to come after me."

Roxanne's laugh sounded genuine. She offered closure. "So, we are even?"

"For now."

The line clicked dead, without ceremony or emotion. Charlie removed the SIM card and snapped it in two. The phone was smashed and dumped over the side. Any evidence bringing her involvement into the proceedings was wiped from the face of the earth. Her dark secrets would remain hidden in the recesses of her memory.

A huge breath, laced with trepidation, filled her lungs as she kindled the engine and steered the launch on a bearing back to Dubrovnik harbor.

She had some explaining to do.

CHAPTER 47

The Ritz Hotel, Paris. Three months later.

Charlie sat facing out from a voluptuous velvet booth. All the angles were covered. Across the table, her father, Pop, spun his head like an old owl. Hoots were plentiful as he marveled at the sights, sounds and smells.

Apparently amazed to be dining out during the daylight hours. Everything was being compared favorably to D.C. as Charlie drifted on a wave of mindless observation. She too surveyed the scene. *This is where it all began.* She mused. With old Pop's vocalized observations clattering around the booth, Charlie gazed uncertainly at the surroundings and the clientele. She wondered how these fickle fashionistas could giggle and titter with such frivolity. Half a world away, people died in a world where poverty and crime were sewn together by threads of desperation. Yet here they all sat, oblivious and impervious, sipping champagne and complaining about the minutia, like the temperature of the egg-plant jus.

Pop gawked. "My. Is this how you live your life."

"Hardly. This is a very rare occasion, as you well kno-"

"Good afternoon, Miss Glass. How lovely to see you again." Gustav, the lecherous Maitre d' slid in, offering a greasy hand. "I see you found your favorite booth."

Pop raised his eyebrows as Charlie did the introductions. "Hello Gustav. Please let me introduce my father."

"Everyone calls me Pop."

"I am not *everyone*. Good day, Mister Glass."

"Professor Glass." Pitched a proud Charlie.

"Profound apologies. A pleasure, Professor Glass."

"And Pop, this is Gustav. The Ritz' world famous front of house."

Gustav appeared to like the distinction, but not the description. "I cannot of course comment on the *world famous*, accolade. I will leave that to others."

Pop offered a hearty handshake. "It is a pleasure to meet you, Gustav."

"So, Miss Glass. A cocktail? The usual?"

Pop beamed. "The usual?"

Gustav's suggestion made quite the splash. "Vodka Martini, parched, Belvedere, straight up, two olives?"

Charlie threw up her hands and blushed. "Thank you."

Pleased with his work, Gustav twitched his whiskers. "And for you, Professor? Will you be joining your daughter in a libation?"

"Looks like it. Have you got any good bourbon?"

"Good Bourbon? An oxymoron? No? As you are in Paris, may I recommend a fine Armagnac?"

"Sure. Try anything once. I will let you decide."

"A wise choice." Gustav's leer slid into position. He bowed and exited booth left.

Light chit chat surrounding the décor, the day's events and Pop's travel schedule filled the interlude, until a sharply attired waitress brought the drinks. Charlie found it odd that Gustav hadn't brought then along with lashings of his descriptive pomp and ceremony.

Pop squeezed a grin out from under his large moustache. "How long have you been drinking vodka?"

"Ah, I'm all grown up, Pop."

"And how well you turned out. I am so proud of you."

Glasses were raised. "To you."

"No to you," replied Charlie.

Pop pulled in his puffy cheeks, as his battle to acquaint himself with the local spirit got underway.

"So, this last jaunt."

Charlie set her glass down with a cutlery-bumping thud. Her tone was clipped. "It wasn't a jaunt, Pop."

Pop raised an eyebrow, a chubby grin playing at the corners of his moustache. "Mission, then?"

Charlie scoffed, folding her arms across her chest. "I'm not James Bond."

Pop chuckled. "Well, what would you call it?"

Charlie opened her mouth, then hesitated. "An assignment?"

"Sounds like you're handing in homework. 'Here's my neatly typed report on infiltrating international crime syndicates, Professor.'"

Charlie rolled her eyes but couldn't stop the ghost of a smile. "It was far from that."

"I get it," He reached across the space between them, his hand resting briefly on her arm. "I appreciate that you confided in me… eventually."

Charlie looked away. "I couldn't tell you before. It would have…" Her voice trailed off.

"Compromised the assignment?" Pop asked, though his tone carried no judgment.

"Made you worry," Charlie corrected, the words coming out quieter than she intended.

Pop took a slow sip, letting the silence sit for a moment. "I wouldn't want that."

"Exactly."

Pop studied her for a moment. "But you're good? Back safe and sound?"

Charlie twitched. "I'm back safe."

Pop caught the distinction immediately. "But not sound?"

Charlie paused, her jaw tightening. "I have my moments."

Pop leaned forward. "You must be proud of what you achieved."

Charlie's memory sped to Gasim, and his fear filled final moments. "I lost a good friend out there."

Pop nodded solemnly. "The man, Gasim, right? Didn't you say he was a drug runner?"

Charlie downed the last of her drink. "It's never that simple, Pop."

"Yes, sorry." Pop shifted, keen to make amends. "But the thefts… you broke the gang."

Charlie nodded slowly. "The report went down well. My boss–"

"Sizemore?" Pop interjected.

"The very same. He stalled until I took it above his pay grade," Charlie said, her words carrying a faint edge of triumph.

Pop smirked. "That wouldn't have made you popular."

"Not with him," Charlie admitted. "But the higher-ups loved it. The FBI never misses a chance to brag. They sent in extra agents to the areas I flagged."

"And?" Pop prompted.

"Ten more arrests. Millions recovered," Charlie added without pride.

Pop added the missing emotion. "Well done, you," he said warmly.

Charlie shook her head. "It doesn't feel well done."

"Why?".

Charlie stared at the tablecloth. "No matter."

Pop wasn't letting it drop. "There's more, though."

"In what way?"

"The gang," Pop said. "You pulled their house down."

Charlie exhaled. "I guess I landed lucky. Or unlucky, depending on how you look at it."

"What do you mean?"

"I started by following the money, but pretty soon, that road got bloody. Real bloody."

Pop frowned. "Why didn't you turn back?"

"I couldn't. My contact was killed. I had no way back,"

"This Noah man?" Pop asked. "Didn't you say he faked his death?"

Charlie gave a short, bitter laugh. "To force me on. So that they could track me."

"Track you? Who?"

"Noah worked for a rival organization. They wanted to eliminate the opposition"

"The Serpent?" Pop asked.

"Well remembered," Charlie replied. "They realized they'd found someone dumb enough–"

"Brave enough," Pop corrected firmly.

Charlie shook her head. "Dumb enough, brave enough. It's gotten so I can't tell the difference."

"There is a difference, Charlotte."

"Maybe," Charlie said. "But I can't see it."

Pop leaned back. "So, this Noah faked his death to leave you stranded?"

"In one," Charlie said. "His crew, the Serpent, followed behind, cleaning up. Killing anyone and everyone in the supply chain."

Pop let out a low whistle. "Supply chain? Sounds almost civilized."

Charlie shrugged, more than a little perturbed by the cross examination. She was starting to regret her first attempts at bringing pop into her circle of trust.

It was as if he sensed her negativity. "You closed that down too, right?" he asked.

"Mostly," Charlie said, her tone even but guarded.

"Mostly? I hope there aren't any dangerous loose ends?"

Charlie pressed her lips into a thin line. "Don't think so. I got the leader of the Pillars drug ring."

Pop's voice dropped a notch. "But then the Serpent killed him because they followed you. Again."

Charlie winced at the truth laid bare. "Thanks for that reminder, yes."

Pop responded keen to give her that win. "But then you eliminated the assassin and that ringleader, Noah,"

"Something like that. We don't say 'eliminated.' It's more civilized to say, 'took off the streets.'"

Pop smirked. "Semantics."

Charlie chose not to elaborate further.

Pop stretched. "Well, I'm proud of you. I hope you know that."

Charlie tightened. "Not so proud that you'll ever mention it. I'm taking a risk just telling you. I broke laws, Pop. Went to places you don't come back from."

Pop's expression softened. "I understand. More than you know."

"I doubt that Pop."

"But surely the CIA will have your back."

Charlie let out a dry laugh. "What makes you think that? I wrecked their counterfeiting operation."

Pop frowned, visibly confused. "Yeah, I don't get that."

Charlie tilted her head, as though mentally retracing the steps. "The CIA in Tehran noticed cash coming in from illegal sources," she explained.

Pop leaned forward. "And?"

"And they knew large chunks of that cash were being 'confiscated' by the government, to pay for nuclear scientists-"

"And corrupt insiders," Pop concluded, nodding grimly.

"Exactly. And in order for the CIA to track and trace those people–"

"They made their own bank notes," Pop interrupted, catching on.

Charlie gave him a small, approving nod. "With means of tracking them, yes."

"So, they could, erm…" Pop faltered, searching for the right phrasing, "take the guilty parties off the streets?"

Charlie shrugged, her face unreadable. "Something like that. Or persuade them to reconsider their life choices."

"Turn them," Pop said simply.

"Maybe," Charlie replied, her voice carrying the faintest trace of a smile.

"So, what went wrong?" Pop asked, his brow furrowing.

"What always goes wrong, The local police chief got greedy, the authorities got vengeful, and so the CIA got the hell out of town."

Pop sat back, exhaling sharply. "So… are you in trouble?"

"No," Charlie said, her expression unreadable. "We've come to an agreement."

Pop didn't look convinced. "Safe and sound from them, at least?"

A shadow of a smile crossed Charlie's face as she thought of Roxanne. "Safe and sound from the CIA, at least."

In the following moments, Charlie's thoughts ran deep. A stiff martini couldn't remove the distaste lingering after another tough mission.

Her skin had hardened, as had her views. The world she lived in was not the world she grew up in. Paris was her home, yet she lived in another world.

She lived for another world. The mention of her dog, Rostam, brought her back into the room.

"Sorry. I was miles away."

Pop understood. "My ranting probably drove you there. I said, it looks like Rostam has settled in well."

"He has."

"And you? Have you settled back in?"

"As best as I can, Pop."

"So, you're staying in Paris?"

"We'll see."

"Ha. You're learning from me. That's what I always told you when I didn't have the heart to tell you, no. All I would say was, *we'll see*."

"We'll see." Charlie slid behind an oversized menu. "Let's agree on the starters, at least."

"Shared langoustines?

She gave him a knowing look. "That's a start."

"Mademoiselle, there is a call for you at the reception."

"Who is it?"

"They didn't say. The page just delivered the note."

"Can't you get them to take a message?"

Her father looked a little uneasy. He was old school. "Charlotte, if someone has gone to the trouble of tracking you down on your birthday, the least you can do is say thank you."

Pop was right. She was irked. Her napkin hit the crisp linen tablecloth. "Get them langoustines on the go, Pop, but don't start without me." Intrigued who could have tracked her down, she took her leave. She stood, straightened her little black dress, and pointed her pumps towards the reception. Everyone around her seemed lost in their own worlds. Clattering cutlery and chattering clientele accompanied her departure. Skipping down the long-mirrored corridor, she was hopeful that the call would be from someone or some organization offering to take her away from all this.

She loved her dad, but everything else was a boring walk in the park. She slid into the side of a conversation underway at the front desk; much to the annoyance of an old French lady wearing an angry-looking fox stole. Charlie's responding apology in perfect French went some ways to restoring cordial relations. The reception pointed to an old-fashioned telephone sitting out in the center of a carved oak table. The receiver sat patiently. When she picked it up, the line sounded open.

"Hello? This is Charlie. Hello?"

Immediately, the line clicked dead. Bemusement turned to concern as she marched back to her table. Uncertain of the motives or implications from the call out, her strides lengthened and quickened as she returned down the mirrored corridor. Back at the restaurant door, she slowed her heart rate.

Pop was fine.

Noticing her, he waved and beckoned her back to the table.

"Everything okay?" he asked.

"All good."

"What was that about?"

"Wrong number."

"Strange. How can it be a wrong number if they asked for you by name?"

Charlie pivoted. "It's just work. I told them to leave me alone on my day off."

"But if it's important, then-"

"It's not. Trust me."

Pop let the disruption settle before picking up the conversation. "Anyhow, what about this?"

Pop pulled up his half-moon spectacles and then started to read the label of an impressive-looking bottle of wine. "Just arrived."

"Who left it?"

"A charming young man. Waiter." Pop lifted his gaze and scanned the room. "I don't see him. What is it?"

Pop held the bottle at arm's length to set the label in focus. "Wow. I've read about this. It's a wine made by the Foreign Legion."

Charlie's blood chilled. "Let me see."

She lifted the dark bottle and studied its blood-red label. "Le Légion Etrangère, Réserve du Generale."

Charlie scanned the room. "Where's the guy that dropped this off?"

Pop noted the change in Charlie's expression. "I can't see him. Is something wrong?"

Remarkably, Gustav the Maitre d' was nowhere to be seen.

"What is it?"

Charlie sensed she was putting Pop on edge, so she lowered the drama and handed back the bottle. "It seems strange, that's all."

"It must be a gift from the management." Pop read the back of the label. "There's a phrase in French. *Tu n'abandonnes jamais les tiens, ni au combat, ni dans la vie*. What does that mean?"

"You never abandon your own, in combat or in life" She scanned the room with barely concealed terror, knowing all too well the meaning. The Serpent was close by, watching her every move.

"There's a card. The strangest thing, it's written in Arabic."

Charlie slid forward onto the edge of her seat, took the card, read it, and swallowed hard.

"What does it say?"

She took some time to answer. "I don't know. It's some strange dialect."

She lied. The message was clear.

We need to talk !

- *Rx*

AFTERWORD

The 2021 opium harvest marked the fifth year in a row, production achieved the historic highs of more than 6,000 tons. This volume had the potential to yield up to 320 tons of pure heroin, for distribution around the world.

According to the recent United Nations report, income from opiates in Afghanistan amounted to some $1.8-$2.7 billion in 2021. Taxes on opiates cultivation, production and trafficking represent a lucrative potential source of financing for non-state actors in the country. Far greater sums are accrued throughout the illicit drug supply chains outside Afghanistan.

- *United Nations Office on Drugs and Crime 2021*

NOTE OF THANKS

Thank you very much for taking the time to read my novel. I hope you loved reading it as much as I enjoyed writing it. If you loved the book, I'd be keen to hear your thoughts. Quality reviews are an author's lifeblood. They have the power to make or break careers. I'd be delighted if you would take a moment to leave a positive book review on your preferred book purchasing site.

To keep pace with Charlie's adventures, learn more about the issues uncovered, receive updates, advance viewings, offers, freebies, and much more, please visit:

jj-carson.com
https://twitter.com/jjcarsonbooks
https://www.facebook.com/jjcarsonauthor/
https://www.instagram.com/jjcarsonauthor/

In order to encourage you to follow Charlie, I have included overleaf an excerpt from her latest deadly adventure, Curse of the Catalan Atlas.

Thanks again for your keen interest and valued support.

All the very best,

J.J. Carson

CHARLIE GLASS THRILLERS

DISCLAIMER & COPYRIGHT

Pillars of Evil is a work of fiction. All incidents and dialogue, and all characters, are products of the author's imagination and are not to be construed as real. Where real-life locales, articles or incidents may appear, the situations, events, and dialogues concerning those entities are entirely fictional and are not intended to depict actual events or to change the entirely fictional nature of the work. In all other respects, any resemblance to actual persons, living or dead, events, items, or locales is entirely coincidental.

Book and Cover Design by JJ Carson

ISBN 978-1-7393956-4-3 Pillars of Evil - Paperback

ISBN 978-1-7393956-5-0 Pillars of Evil – Hardback

BISAC Codes

FIC050000 FICTION / Crime

FIC031010 FICTION / Thrillers / Crime

FIC022080 FICTION/Mystery & Detective/International Crime & Mystery

2nd Edition: March 2025

Printed in Great Britain
by Amazon

62761145R00221